TO TH
SURVIVORS

By

Philip G Henley

Published by Phenweb Publishing

Kindle ISBN 978-0-9575749-4-6
Paperback ISBN 979-8-7346388-7-3

All characters appearing in this work are fictitious. Any resemblance to real persons, living or dead is purely coincidental. This work is *fiction*, so none of this is real, but some of it is science. I have seen and read plenty of *end of the world* or *post apocalypse* fiction such as *I am Legend*, both of the BBC's *Survivor* series, *Jeremiah,* to name a few. I cannot forget what I have seen and read, but this is my take on the subject. Some of the navigation and geographical locations exist and some do not, but mostly they do, forgive me if the locations are not described accurately.

I have written another book, it doesn't matter that I live in Hampshire in the UK, and I'm married with two children and two dogs. I have no personal experience of the end of the world as we know it, but neither do you, nor does it matter what I have done before. I still have an imagination and can make things up. As I said its *Fiction.*

I have written this because I wanted to.

I might write something else.

Part One

The Black Death

The governments of Europe had no apparent response to the crisis because no one knew its cause or how it spread. In 1348, the plague spread so rapidly that before any physicians or government authorities had time to reflect upon its origins, about a third of the European population had already perished. In crowded cities, it was not uncommon for as much as fifty percent of the population to die. Europeans living in isolated areas suffered less, and monasteries and priests were especially hard hit since they cared for the Black Death's victims.

Judith M. Bennett and C. Warren Hollister (2006) - *Medieval Europe: A Short History*. New York: McGraw-Hill

The Fall of the Roman Empire

If the empire had been afflicted by any recent calamity, by a plague, a famine, or an unsuccessful war; if the Tiber had, or if the Nile had not, risen beyond its banks; if the earth had shaken, or if the temperate order of the seasons had been interrupted, the superstitious Pagans were convinced that the crimes and the impiety of the Christians, who were spared by the excessive lenity of the government had at length provoked the divine justice.

Edward Gibbon - *The Decline and Fall of the Roman Empire*

CHAPTER ONE

The Announcement, A-Day

The Chief Medical Officer, CMO, Professor Kieran Graves, sat at his desk. He was at the peak of respectability of his profession. His experience and research in his chosen field had not won him a Nobel Prize, but his reputation was well established across the medical sphere. His early surgical career had switched from oncology surgery, to genetics and biochemistry, and then he spent several years directly in cancer research. He had then moved into the politics of science, the research grants, government committees, and the climbing of that particular career slope. Now, he was the United Kingdom government's principal medical advisor. He was the professional leader on medical matters for public health in the United Kingdom. He was the UK's representative within the World Health Organisation, the WHO. He frequently contributed to media discussions on health. He was renowned for his terse questioning style. Whereas his highly detailed reports quickly summed up years of painstaking research and clinical trials, in straightforward recommendations and resultant potential cures. He was respected throughout the scientific community, and not just in medicine. Kieran Graves had been in post for only eight months. He had been a popular choice for the role, eliciting cross-party support, backed, unusually, by both the medical and mainstream media. He was a friend of the previous Secretary of State for Health, who was now, since the last election, on the opposition benches. He was developing a friendly relationship with the new Secretary of State at the Department for Health, Caroline McCoy. He was also more than a passing acquaintance of The Prime Minister, his wife, and two children, having spent two enjoyable weekends at Chequers. As he contemplated the report in front of him, all that history, all his career achievements, all that respect, counted for nothing.

The CMO's heart rate was high; he could feel perspiration building. He breathed deeply to try to control his emotions as he read the executive summary of the report in front of him. He inadvertently stroked his head, smoothing the almost non-existent hair that his wife had finally persuaded him to cut short, disguising his spreading bald patch. He wanted to smoke, even though he had given up ten years previously. He was fifty-two, trim and fit. He was scared witless by what he was reading. His main assistant, Howard Belman, was a civil service appointee. He stood to one side of his desk. Belman was not a medical man. He would not understand the technical details of the report, but he would understand the conclusion. Graves handed the report to him, without a word. There was silence in the room, except for the background hub of the London traffic, and the click of the air conditioning system. It appeared to be on the blink, again. Whilst the CMO's assistant started to read, Graves looked at the two professors sitting opposite; they had requested the urgent meeting.

His assistant mumbled, "What?" He then sat down heavily on the side of the desk, looking in disbelief at the CMO.

Professor Richard Hargreaves and Professor Diane Selkirk were key scientists working for Cancer Research, the charity, in between their academic careers at Oxford and Cambridge respectively. Both in their late forties they were genetic specialists, studying cell replication. They were hoping to expand on the advancements of genetic therapy to treat and potentially cure cancer, or at least some of the many variations that were commonly called cancers. Their joint report, which Howard Belman now placed back on the desk in front of the CMO, was the result of five months of work. The report was not what had been expected. The report scared them.

"Take me through it," the CMO requested, "just the highlights."

Professor Hargreaves replied, after swallowing a sip of

water. "We had a study group of fifteen spread across four locations, and the group was receiving standard treatment for Hodgkin's Lymphoma. They were trial patients for a new version of haematopoietic stem cell transplantation. Seven of the group were in the early age group, their ages are in the table at the start of the report, and the remaining eight were over fifty-five."

"Were?" Belman asked.

"Yes, were," explained Professor Selkirk. "Look, all these patients were seriously ill, that's why many of them volunteer in the first place. Standard treatments were not working, including an earlier attempt at cell therapy."

"But survival rates for Hodgkin's have been improving dramatically?" The CMO questioned the Professors, "98 or 99%, I thought I read recently."

"Yes, they have," said Hargreaves. "That's why we were interested in these patients. The normal treatments hadn't worked, so why was that? We hoped this international trial would tell us. It would also provide further advances in genetic cell therapy, but instead we have found," he paused, "this," he said, indicating the report.

"Go on," said the CMO.

Selkirk continued. "We took biopsies, and cell samples following the patient's deaths and analysed what their composition was, looking to see if the cell therapy had made any difference. When we completed the genetic mapping, we found the anomaly. We went back and checked because that anomaly should not have arisen, but there it was."

Hargreaves took up the explanation, "We checked back with test animals and cultures, then we remodelled on the computer simulations, but the results were the same."

"They hadn't died from Hodgkin's," interrupted the CMO.

"No," said Selkirk, "it's a virus, a genetic one."

"Why is that important?" Belman asked, feeling out of his depth, his scientific background was physics, not biology.

"Most viral infections are non-segmented. Using

Ribonucleic Acid, RNA, they mutate relatively quickly and, consequently, they kill themselves off by mutation of their genetic code," said Hargreaves. "Segmented viruses are Deoxyribonucleic Acid, DNA, and they are more stable; consequently, the host will, through evolution, learn to deal with them. You understand that DNA has a four letter coding, G, C, A, T for Guanine, Cytosine, Adenine, and Thymine, and that a table of sixty-four codes is normally used to describe the combinations." Belman nodded. Hargreaves continued, "DNA, in turn, is one of the three macromolecules used for life as we know it, producing the double helix you'll be familiar with. With RNA and Proteins, DNA is combined to give the overall genome for a particular organism; this gives us billions of potential combinations, but also commonality across life species, down to viruses and other extremely small cellular life forms. We clearly have more in common with other mammals than we do with plants, birds, reptiles, or insects. This virus is in a mammal specific gene, we think."

Belman continued to nod his way through the explanation, trying to keep up. "So what do we have here, what's gone wrong?"

"We don't know," said Selkirk, but before Belman could again interrupt she continued, "but we *do know* that we have a change." She tried to explain. "For example, we know that Ultra Violet light can damage thymine. That is not the case here, but an example. The anomaly in *this* case is a mutation. The gene group is impacted, but much worse than that, we have established it is viral in nature. It is segmented and triggering Lymphomas on a rapid and serious scale, and that is why we are here. We believe it's infectious, very infectious."

Belman's fear rose, "Are you two?"

"Not so far, as of this morning's tests that is. Yes, we have a test," Hargreaves said to the CMO. "It's a straightforward blood test scanning for a particular gene combination with the virus showing as active. The tests produce a simple yes or no, and it comes through in about an hour. We are trying to speed that up. The test doesn't mean you're immune though, just that you are clear, for now." If they had a test for immunity they might stand a chance of finding a cure, Professor Hargreaves thought.

"Spread?" Kieran Graves asked. The CMO was famous for his one-word questions.

"Nearly 100% of contacts; we think it will be close to 100%; the computer models are at 99.99% so minimal immunity. We don't know if we'll achieve that," Selkirk knew achieve was the wrong word, "but all the lab animals have succumbed, we…"

"How does it spread?" Howard Belman interrupted.

"The epidemiological model we have used is based principally on contact and respiratory ingestion. The virus has an airborne life of over three hours in a still room, and a contact life of seven hours on human skin," said Selkirk.

Hargreaves continued. "In the lab, we have seen infections establish with as little as ten individual cells, that gives a greater than 10% chance of full infection. As soon as there are fifty or more active cells, infection jumps to 85% or greater." Belman felt lost again.

"Symptoms?" The CMO asked.

"Lymphomas in the thyroid, pituitary, breast, it could be anywhere. The lungs, so respiratory, we don't truly know yet. The test subjects had tumours already. Which ones were the original disease, and which ones are the virus, we weren't able to tell."

"Remission or recovery?"

"None, that we have seen, but it's too early, the test subjects were all ill already. We needed healthy subjects to test and monitor." Professor Selkirk realised how odd that sounded. "We have some now, and that has demonstrated the viral nature of the anomaly. It has also started to tell us which tumours are likely to appear first. It's the thyroid, showing as neck swelling."

"Cure?" Again the CMO interrupted.

"None. We are trying, but nothing so far, nothing chemical anyway. Surgery may be possible, but the risk will be cross-contamination from blood and plasma," Professor Selkirk stopped, but was looking distraught.

"I thought viral diseases killed themselves off?" Belman

hoped.

"RNA yes, but this is DNA. It has reached stability and is now spreading."

"But surely it will kill itself off? Even the Plague died out." Belman was sweating now.

"It has nearly seven billion hosts to find first," said Hargreaves. Belman audibly gulped.

"Containment?" The CMO hoped for some good news.

"Too late," Hargreaves paused, this was the critical element. "The patients were spread across the country, and around the world. The trial was over a three month period, and that finished almost two months ago. We've had five months, if not longer, of potential spread. It's highly possible that the virus was live before that; it could have been spreading for years, just not triggering lymphomas. The test subjects were in regular hospitals during their treatment. Three died at their homes, four were in hospices, and the rest were in hospital wards. Our best assessment, probability less than 20%, is that we have half a million carriers already. The more realistic proposition, 80% probability, is that we have well over one million carriers or infections in the UK alone. That's assuming that only the fifteen in the UK are the originating hosts *and* that the new drug was the trigger that prompted the condition. We doubt that the test drug was the trigger, but we can't confirm that. If it was, then the virus is also in the States, Japan, Germany, Canada, and Sweden. One theory we have, in the research group, is that the virus has always been around, but just hidden in the deaths of patients. The ones who were ill with Hodgkin's who haven't responded to regular treatment. We have discreetly checked eighteen relatives of the original fifteen in our test group. They already have symptoms, and their blood tests are positive. We have taken biopsies on the tumours, where possible, that have appeared in nine of those eighteen. All the biopsies show the same genetic discrepancies. Because the relatives tested positive for the virus, it would appear that they have caught it from the test subject. That or they suffer from the same genetic cell mutation. That is unlikely, mainly because some were not blood relatives. We wanted to bring this to you as soon as we could, we..."

Graves held up a hand, "How long," he stumbled, "how long have we got?"

"These types of cancers usually terminate within three to six months, without treatment, but we don't know yet. The fifteen study patients went through early diagnosis and other treatment failures and took from four months to a year. Our estimate in the report is three months to fifteen months. It's so variable because it depends on which lymphomas materialise," said Selkirk.

"Survivors?"

"We don't know, very few, without a mutation or cure."

"God help us," said Belman.

"One other aspect," said Hargreaves, "it's not human specific. The rats and a couple of monkeys have it. The computer model implies all mammals, as the gene is common at least in mammals. We have a lot more tests to try but that's what the computer says."

The CMO said, "Extinction, mammal extinction?"

"Yes," said Hargreaves and Selkirk together.

"Have you spoken to your colleagues overseas?" Graves asked.

"Yes, the US confirmed our findings, and they are back checking their study groups. They had the biggest test set, with over one hundred subjects across the States. They are briefing the CDC," Professor Selkirk added. The Center for Disease Control and Prevention had primary responsibility in the USA for disease incidents.

Professor Hargreaves took up the narrative, "The chief scientist in the USA is Professor Callum. He's in Connecticut. He is trying to contact the Surgeon General this morning, Washington time. He has already reported that three of their scientists and researchers, including him, are infected; now they know what they are looking for. Canada will receive our messages when they wake up. Japan has them, but they probably won't see them till tomorrow. Sweden has not returned our calls, and Germany is waiting for us to have this meeting."

The CMO was concerned about the information being widespread, but there was nothing he could do. "WHO?" He asked, the WHO was the World Health Organisation.

"We have sent them the report. They partially funded the research. The team at Cancer Research, well they know that we have found something, but not what. The doctors of the new cases are also concerned, that's GPs, nurses, radiologists and their Consultant Oncologists across the country." GPs were General Practitioners the primary source of health care in the UK. "The normal reporting to the NHS, would have picked this up as hot spots of tumours and cancers in a few months." The NHS was the UK's National Health Service.

Kieran Graves realised he needed to get moving. "Howard, please draft a statement with the professors. It will need to be cleared, but get something ready. I need to talk to the Secretary of State and The Prime Minister."

The others left the office to work on the statement. Graves called the Permanent Secretary at the Department for Health. He demanded, to the consternation of the Permanent Secretary, a meeting with the Secretary of State immediately. That could not happen, as the Secretary was in Cabinet; of course, Graves realised, it was the regular meeting. He hung up and then called Downing Street. He said that he had an emergency, and he needed to talk to The Prime Minister and Secretary of State for Health immediately. Finally, an assistant to the Cabinet Office came on the line and got a flea in his ear. It was not uncommon for the CMO to advise The Prime Minister, just not for an emergency. Downing Street finally relented when the CMO insisted that the National Security Council and COBRA, the emergency planning committee, would need to be prepared. He was invited over.

CHAPTER TWO

Cabinet

The Prime Minister, James Greening had been elected ten months before. His honeymoon period with the electorate was already waning, not helped by the resignation of one of his key allies over a procurement scandal. He was half way through the Cabinet agenda, with little hope of completion before he had to leave for Parliament. He was going through a recurring argument with his colleagues on the latest approach to a new draft European Treaty. An aide had come through the Cabinet meeting room doors and spoken to the Cabinet Secretary, Sir Clive Grainger. Sir Clive had listened to the whispered comment from the aide, before interrupting the Secretary of State for Trade, Gerald Sanders, in mid-rant and telling The Prime Minister that the Chief Medical Officer and the Heads of the Security Service and the Secret Intelligence Service were also on their way for an extremely urgent briefing. The CMO had called for the meeting, explaining that there was a serious emergency impacting national security. There were concerned looks around the Cabinet table, with shakes of heads to whispered *do you know anything* comments. The Secretary of State for Health, Caroline McCoy, shook her head to the Prime Minister's direct question.

"You might as well all stay," the Prime Minister said, "now you all know something is up. We'll take a break whilst we wait for them to arrive." People got up and stretched their legs, no one dared to visit the bathroom, for fear of missing anything. Caroline McCoy insisted she did not know, when pressed further by the Home Secretary. First to arrive was the Head of the Security

Service, MI5, Hector Crossdean. He had a quick word with the Home Secretary, John Turner, before taking a seat. Crossdean was surprised, because he did not know anything either, and his aides had not been able to help. The CMO, and the Head of the Secret Intelligence Service, MI6, Alison Stuart, arrived together; although neither knew the other. They both were shown in. The CMO's aide and the two professors were kept outside in an anteroom.

The Prime Minster shook the CMO's hand with a, "Good to see you Kieran, what's so urgent?" The Prime Minister noted the CMO's ashen expression and palpable sense of urgency. "Please take a seat and tell us what the problem is."

The first explanation took fifteen minutes, then the second slightly longer, by which time the CMO's aide, Howard Belman, and Professors Selkirk and Hargreaves, had been called in to answer specific questions. No one had left. The Cabinet Room was unusually crowded. The Chief Press Officer, Tony Smith, had been called down. He was now working on a draft statement, dramatically changing the pessimistic tone of the original, until The Prime Minister stopped him. "We can't cover this up, Tony. The news is going to be worldwide soon, so no dressing up the truth. Try; 'we are devoting the necessary resources to finding a cure, and we are working, with our overseas allies, to ensure that we will be successful'. How's that?"

"Prime Minister," said Professor Selkirk nervously, "I don't think you understand. The medical community has been working on a cure for AIDs for over thirty years, and this is far more viral, and not limited to susceptible carrier groups. There is no time for *necessary resources*. This has to be the *only* priority. We may already be infected through tertiary and higher contacts, even if the cell blood test doesn't show up as positive." People looked at each other, almost coiling away from human contact.

The CMO took up the briefing. "I concur with Professor Selkirk. The likelihood is that we will *all* become infected; sooner rather than later. If we do not devote our *entire* efforts to finding a cure, then we all, the *entire* human race, may be extinct in less than two years."

"It must be a mistake, this can't be true," said Caroline

McCoy with agreement from the near silent Trade Secretary.

"I'm afraid the report is correct, Caroline," said the CMO. "According to the professors here, it has been confirmed with their US counterparts amongst others. As for our own risk, I'm sure the professors can carry out their test to check, but it's probably too late for effective quarantine action."

"I need to call the President," said The Prime Minister. He thought it best to wake him, and then his own staff could brief him. "Start contingency planning, no one leave, and no one call anybody. Tony," he said looking at the Press Officer, "rewrite it." The Prime Minister strode out, heading for his private office in Downing Street. His private secretary, who had not been in the Cabinet Room, chased after him. Other staff, seeing the speed of the Prime Minister's approach, got out of the way. Call the US President and yes, wake him up, he thought as he sat at his desk reeling from the news.

***

The USA's Chief Surgeon was an early riser and, therefore, had got the message from Professor Callum, who had been trying to contact him since late the previous night. The Chief Surgeon had listened on the phone to Professor Callum with a growing sense of understanding and dread. Professor Callum had been awake all night, trading information with his colleagues around the world, and then briefing the CDC. The conversation finished when Professor Callum said that he had tested himself, and he had contracted the virus. He would not be leaving the Research Laboratory building, where he sat, and had imposed strict quarantine on himself and one colleague. They were awaiting the arrival of a biohazard team from the CDC in Atlanta. The Chief Surgeon, a survivor of the previous administration, was now trying to get an urgent appointment with the President. He had put down his home phone for the fifth time, in frustration with the White House switchboard, when it immediately rang. It was the President's Chief of Staff. He was demanding the immediate attendance of the Chief Surgeon in front of the President. The Chief Surgeon guessed correctly that someone else had woken and told the President.

***

The Prime Minister had returned to the Cabinet Room, to a debate on quarantine between the Secretary of State for Defence and the Home Secretary. Tempers were flaring. The heads of MI5 and 6 were in a corner with one of the professors, Hargreaves he thought. Professor Selkirk, the CMO, and Caroline McCoy were together with the Chief Press Officer.

He called the meeting to order. "We probably have less than an hour before this is on 24 hour news, if it isn't already, and I'm late for Prime Minister's Questions." The Prime Minister answered questions every week in Parliament, usually a robust booing session with the opposition. He had a feeling this one would be remarkably different. "I'll announce it there. We can't sit on this. The President told me that he will announce the virus at eight, Washington time, on national television. He is speaking to his Chief Surgeon, his CMO, and his Security Council before and after that broadcast." The Prime Minister continued, "Professors please go over to COBRA with the National Security Council, and you Caroline, start working on what you need for a cure. As a separate activity, Defence and Intelligence, along with the Home Secretary, work on contingency planning. The rest of you better come with me to Parliament. I'll need to talk to Her Majesty on the way."

"What about infection?" Cried the Trade Secretary. "We can't just go off around town; we may all catch it!"

"A cure is our only hope. We will *all* catch it, unless we are completely isolated, like the Space Station or Antarctica, maybe some Amazonian tribes," said the CMO, but he trailed off. The scale was still dawning on him.

***

The Prime Minister entered the House of Commons chamber of the British Parliament, fifteen minutes late. He apologised for his nearly unprecedented lateness to the Speaker of the House of Commons as he passed him on the way to his seat. The Speaker, as usual, looked pompous and annoyed as he walked by him. He had phoned the Queen on the way, and had to wait whilst she left a meeting with the head of some visiting minor nation. The Queen had listened patiently. She then asked if he could send a briefing over later that day, but to tell the nation via Parliament as soon as possible. She had offered to go on national television and proffered any other help she could. He thought an address from her would be helpful. He agreed to update her later in the day. Her last words to him summed up her faith and approach, "I pray God will give you the strength you will need over the coming weeks."

He'd mumbled a "Thank you, Ma'am," before hanging up.

The Prime Minister took his seat in The Commons; the Government front bench was extremely short of senior ministers, both the Speaker and the Leader of the Opposition noted. What was going on?

"Questions to The Prime Minister," announced The Speaker.

"Eventually," and "nice of you to turn up," were some of the politer calls from the backbenchers, with the usual shouted cheers and jeers from the two sides of the primary legislative chamber.

The Prime Minister, waited for the din to subside, which it did slowly, as people saw his expression. "Mr. Speaker, Right Honourable and Honourable Members of Parliament…"

"This doesn't sound good," thought the Leader of The Opposition. It was supposed to be questions, not a statement. He had his permitted three questions ready and waiting. He was now sitting bolt upright, the smile from the backbencher comments disappearing from his face.

"I have grave news for this country and for the world." The House quietened, "I have been informed this morning of a major threat to the world's population, in the form of a serious virus…"

"Not another SARS fiasco," shouted a noted backbench troublemaker before being ssh'd by his own colleagues.

The Prime Minister gave him a withering look. "Mr. Speaker, I regret to inform the House, that this virus has, so far, a 100% mortality rate, and is highly contagious. It also has a relatively long incubation period; however, so far there is no successful treatment available. I must tell the House that I only became aware of the existence of the virus this morning, following a briefing by the Chief Medical Officer. Further details will be announced later today, but I ask the House's forgiveness in that I am unable to take questions at this stage. I shall arrange for the necessary reports to be placed in the Common's library immediately. I now ask that the Leader of the Opposition, the Leader of the House," who was traditionally the longest serving Member of Parliament, "and the Leaders of the other parties accompany me to a COBRA meeting, where I will provide further details." He opened his arms in a gesture to his political rivals; this was unprecedented. There was no movement, so The Prime Minister turned and walked back past the Speaker, ending his Question session with no questions. He was barely out the door behind the Speaker's chair, when uproar erupted behind him. He carried on walking. He wanted to get to COBRA as soon as possible. If the others wanted to stay and shout, that was their problem. He had an emergency. He needed a State of Emergency. His secretary had to fight to keep up as people began to spill out behind them into the corridor. His security detail guided him out to the official car, and then, a couple of minutes later, they were arriving at the COBRA entrance.

TV channels interrupted their coverage with news flashes, but all they had to go on was the Prime Minister from the Parliamentary TV feeds. CNN and Fox broke off their US breakfast coverage to flash the news, just as the White House called through requesting, no demanding, an 8:00 a.m., East Coast time, Presidential Address. The *Good Morning America* team broke off their coverage of gun crime in Southern States, to go back to their anchors, and report the UK news flash, and then the coming Presidential address, in less than fifteen minutes. Other channels announced, then speculated on what was going on. Some understood the British Prime Minister's statement, some did not, but the *virus* word was rushing around in ear pieces as researchers scrambled to line up experts, who could only provide ill-informed comment. A CNN reporter managed to get hold of someone at the CDC, to find out that several teams were dispatched around the country, including one in Connecticut at a research laboratory. They rushed to broadcast the lurid news whilst at the same time stealing a march on their competitors.

***

The President had not liked being awakened; he didn't particularly like the British Prime Minister either, who insisted on speaking to him. As he listened to the Prime Minister, he slowly understood the implications, if not the science. He also understood that he needed more scientific information, and then he would have to tell the nation. He thanked the Prime Minister, maybe he wasn't so bad after all. It was just his accent that grated. He had been woken just before six-thirty. By seven-thirty the Chief Surgeon had been in the Oval Office, and then a call had come through to Professor Callum, who had confirmed what the Prime Minister had told him. He set up the emergency national broadcast as soon as he finished with the British Prime Minister. He told his wife, and called the Leader of Congress and the Senate. He put on a black tie, eschewing make up. He walked into the White House press room at one minute to eight. He didn't want to do the broadcast from the Oval Office. He wanted to see the press eye-to-eye.

"My fellow Americans," he started, and then echoed, unbeknown to him, the British Prime Minister's words. "I have grave news for this country and the world…" he began. He didn't take questions from the stunned press, and finished with, "God bless us all and God bless America." He then turned and strode out, heading down to the basement, and the White House's Situation Room, where the National Security Council were gathering.

CHAPTER THREE

Mammal Briefing

The CMO, Kieran Graves, sat down the corridor from COBRA, in COBRD to be precise, according to the door nameplate. He would have to make the short walk in an hour or so when the Prime Minister would convene the latest session. With him was Professor Diane Selkirk, looking exhausted, as he knew he did. Professor Richard Hargreaves was in Oxford checking with his research team, but he was due back in London that evening. Two civil service analysts were present; he couldn't remember their names. His main interest was with the Chief Veterinary Officer, Doctor Elizabeth McQueen. Dr. McQueen had arrived a few minutes previously, with one of the analysts, Brian, he thought she called him. The two analysts were trying to load her presentation onto the COBR Presentation System, and Doctor McQueen probably would give The Prime Minister the same brief in an hour. An IT technician had been called and ordered to remove the security system blocking access to USB memory sticks. That had taken a directive from the Permanent Secretary to the Cabinet Office. The Technician had left mumbling about security and viruses. It was a much more serious virus that concerned the CMO.

Finally, Brian got the PowerPoint slides up onto a screen and nodded his readiness to Elizabeth McQueen. "Kieran," she started, "these are the latest projections for mammal species, based on adaptions of your human modelling and our initial results. We still have a lot of testing to do, but you insisted on numbers for today. I'm not happy…"

The CMO interrupted her. "Elizabeth, we know they are little more than guesstimates, but they are all we have. We will take it as read that you don't have confidence in the numbers at this stage. Please just give us your best effort." He tried not to get cross with her, but the COBRA meetings were turning into a bear pit of blame and accusation. Elizabeth, if she went in and briefed, had to be as clear and concise as possible.

"Sorry, Kieran, it's just…"

"I know, but let's see the figures. Go on."

"We modelled using TB, Foot and Mouth, Swine, and Bird Flu data. This first graph shows the potential impact on mice, rats and other rodents; we are seeing incubation periods in the lab of only five days, based on some of your test data and our own trials. The smaller rodents will be quicker it seems. We estimate three to six months maximum in the UK for all mice, voles, dormice, and so on. Rats might take longer to succumb, but not by much, except for isolated pockets on small islands; they may escape for a while. There will be a knock-on impact on birds, and other species in the food chain, mainly birds of prey as *their* prey die out." Elizabeth paused and sipped a glass of water; she could not believe she was saying these things. "Foxes and mink will spread the disease as they scavenge. Cattle, sheep, pigs should be slower, although pigs seem to develop the virus faster than the other two, based on current tests. It's too early to give accurate projections, but we think six to eight months. Factory farms, or high intensity farms and group collections may well be quicker on infection; but disease progress, we don't know."

"I'll have better projections in a week when we have more results, now we have a blood test for these groups, but the likelihood is that they are already infected. Given that we believe that the virus has already been live for five months or more, these projections might have to come forward. Vets are already reporting some serious infections. The DEFRA, inspection teams are quarantining sites, probably too late." DEFRA was the UK's Department for the Environment, Food and Rural Affairs. "The teams only have outbreaks of Foot and Mouth to go on, they don't know what they are doing, they're scared for themselves. They might well be spreading the virus as well." Kieran had not considered that either. Were their actions hindering the fight and not helping prevent the viruses' spread? Elizabeth continued, "My best projection, based on near 100% fatality rates, is seven months. Seven months before all livestock is gone; it might be out by two months either way."

Brian spoke. "The statistical probabilities have an error factor of…"

The CMO held up his hand. Brian stopped. "Please continue Elizabeth."

"Stored fresh meat stocks will rapidly decline, and of course it is possible that the meat is contaminated by the virus as well. We are testing with the Food Standards Agency, but we don't know, we just don't know." She stopped and sipped her water. "Other mammals, we presume, will follow the same pattern, deer, similar to sheep, goats, we don't know. Rabbit we have looked at Myxomatosis and its spread, they will be quick based on some lab work, that will in turn impact foxes and some birds of prey. Larger mammals will, we think, take longer. Zoo vets are testing, but they are being seconded away to help with the DEFRA work. Marine mammals, we don't have any data yet, otters and so on we think will succumb like water rats and voles. Our colleagues in the States are testing dolphins, but it's too early to say, same with whales."

"Cures?" The CMO asked, already suspecting the answer.

"Nothing yet, the colleges and research institutes are flat out, but we are losing staff to the human research, understandably." Elizabeth came to a stop tears in her eyes.

"Okay, let's take a break, and then we'll figure out what you will tell The Prime Minister."

"Me?" Elizabeth had not been expecting that.

"Yes, you; better from the horse's mouth, so to speak, and yes, it's a bad joke, sorry."

***

Prime Minister James Greening had listened to the Chief Veterinary Officer and the CMO explain the impact on mammals. They had now left, and the COBRA meeting was on a two-minute comfort break. He shook his head at the enormity of what was happening. What about Africa, South America, Asia? He struggled to understand what a world without lions, tigers, and elephants would be like. Even the rats had shocked him. He had known since the first briefing that it would be extremely bad, but maybe he had not truly comprehended the overall impact on the world. He looked at the rest of the agenda. Contingency planning for cultural objects, for sport, for… The list went on, as each aspect of human life was laid bare before him. He knew there would be some hard, no impossible, decisions to make in the next few months. The money situation had just imploded. He needed to see what the latest food and water plans were. He knew the experts needed time, but he also knew time was running out.

CHAPTER FOUR

Survivors

It was forty very long and tiring days after the announcement. Hector Crossdean, the Director General of MI5, was chairing the latest sub-committee on contingency planning on behalf of the Home Secretary, who was en-route to a bunker in the midlands. Hector would join him there after the meeting. Hector was sat in COBRD. There had been a full National Security Council Meeting in COBRA earlier that had implemented the Government dispersal plan. Now Hector had to plan for survivors with Professor Selkirk, Tony Smith, the Press Secretary and a Professor of Psychology from the University College of London, Andrew Jacobs. Jacobs had a sideline interest and part time media career, as an anthropologist discussing social impacts of historic and future policies. Two analysts had briefed the four-person team sitting in COBRD, for the last hour; now they had to decide on recommendations for The Prime Minister.

"Let's start with Scenario *One*," said Hector after a short coffee and bathroom break. The Scenarios were all based on a population of approximately sixty-five-million. Scenario *One* was the most optimistic forecast. The basic parameters had a cure being discovered within four months. No one in the room believed it. Scenario *One* had a probability based on mathematical modelling of less than 5%. "Fatalities?" Hector asked.

"Five to ten-million, minimum, probably more…" Diane Selkirk had become immune to the horror of the figures. They were just unbelievable numbers. "… A further twenty-million we would need to vaccinate, prior to infection, and the remainder we'd have to cure with a drug or using cell therapy. We will not have the people to do cell therapy for thirty-five to forty-million people. If we find a drug, we may be able to immunise the ten or twenty-million, but probably fewer. I need more information on drug production capabilities to give a more realistic number."

"Social impacts, Andrew?" Hector requested.

Andrew Jacobs was still getting used to the idea he was in a room in the Cabinet Office meeting with the Head of MI5. He had been introduced to the Prime Minister that morning. He followed the news of course, and he was honoured to be a part of the committee, but the sheer horror of what was being contemplated was difficult to comprehend. Now he was already flagged as a virus positive person, and yet still having to go through this plan. He felt hopeless and out of his depth, but they needed some advice on what would happen. "Societal breakdown, as we are already seeing. At least two years before capital assets have worth, after the cure. We should expect to have serious problems issuing the vaccination if that's what it is. Priorities for vaccination would have to be established, starting with the security staff, police, military, and so on."

"Not medical?" Tony Smith asked.

"No," Andrew continued, "the medical staff won't get a chance without security, look what is happening at pharmacies, hospitals and GP surgeries now."

"I agree," said Hector, "Scenarios *Two* and *Three* seem to be revisions of *One*, but with a delay on the cure. I don't propose to waste our time on the variations, the fatalities go up, but the survivor numbers are what for, *Three*?"

"Ten-million or so, 1801 census levels." Diane replied, "The numbers go down the longer the cure takes."

"Again, social impacts Andrew?"

"The longer it goes on the more survivor characteristics become dominant. The grief aspects will increase with a large degree of hopelessness. Ruthlessness will become apparent in those that do survive. My view though is that these numbers will be worse than the main scenarios describe. As Diane has said before, we have adverse impacts caused by the loss of medical staff, and then food and water issues. A drought or famine will have significant impacts as will any severe winter weather. The geographic spread will vary as will power and sewage. Recovery times will increase, before society functions."

"One of the analysts mentioned cannibalism earlier," Tony interrupted, "is that realistic?"

"I think not, there may be isolated cases, but not generally, clean water is, by far, more essential. One of the charts has typhoid, dysentery, and cholera projections. There will be enough food for a while, and of course as numbers go down food will increase per head of population. I need more information on food stocks and the mammal impact; well at least meat and milk production."

"Thank you Andrew, I think we've wasted enough of our time on the unlikely scenarios, and I'll add *Four* to *Six* in that mix as well." Scenario's *Four* to *Six* covered a vaccination, but no cure, so all infected would die, but new infections would cease, they were all time dependent and had probabilities of less than 10%. "Let's concentrate on the main projections Scenarios *Seven* to *Ten* are just timing variations as I see it, the outcome is the same." There was no disagreement. "I see we have a new probability of 95% on the original 99.99% fatality rate."

"Yes," said Professor Diane Selkirk, it was based on her original report with Professor Hargreaves.

"So 6,500 survivors," said Hector shaking his head.

"It will be less a year later," said Andrew.

"I agree," said Diane. "That number is based on survivors from the virus. It takes no account of other impacts like diseases, accidents, conflicts, and mostly famine and drought."

"Explain further, please Diane, for Tony's benefit. He missed the report last week."

"The survival percentages are based on the population demographic analysis, but these are flattened. In other words, 0.01% of the population should survive, irrespective of other factors such as age, health, sex, race, and location. This takes no account of the very old, the young, or other helpless groups. They will not survive, unless they are even luckier than surviving the virus, for the young and infirm that means finding a parent or carer that *also* survives. That is a possibility if the disease is purely about genetics, meaning we have a parent and child surviving, but we don't know, I hope we'll have time to find out. For the old, they simply won't get food or water or medical help for ailments." Diane paused for another sip of water. "The percentages from the 2011 census are just under 12% under 10 and under 5% over eighty. I estimate 20% of the 6,500 won't last a year. I've added in the number who will die of other things like heart attacks."

"We need to further reduce by conflict and suicide," said Andrew. They knew suicide was rapidly on the increase, but they thought this was amongst the sick, not potential survivors.

"Conflict, you mean these people will fight?" Tony asked.

"Yes, over resources, they might. Tribes did, Nations still do," Andrew commented.

"And suicide?" Crossdean added.

"Very difficult to know, the grief maybe unbearable, add in loneliness, despair and survivor guilt, we have very little to go on. Survivors of other disasters have reported suicidal feelings. It may just accelerate the death rate of those sick as they give up."

"All these scenarios are pretty much worthless then," said Hector. "My Service always said to plan for the worst and hope for the best. So what can we do to help the survivors?"

"Dispersed stores of food, fuel, water and medical supplies," said Andrew.

"But won't we need those soon, for the ill in the next few months?" Tony questioned.

"They won't help, apart from by allowing the living to bury the dead, and probably prolonging the disease. It will only make it harder for the eventual survivors. We have to help them, not the dying, and that includes me. I'm Red," said Andrew. There were sympathetic looks but no comments. "We have another problem for the survivors."

"What could be worse than what they are going to face?" Tony asked with a half laugh of resignation.

"The UK's population was last at these levels around 5,000 BC," Andrew explained. "The human beings of that time had one advantage, they were hunter gatherers; farming came later. They had a wealth of game to hunt for meat. Those inhabitants also had years of knowledge of how to live. Our survivors will have fishing, and hunting birds like duck and geese, chickens of course. They will have to live on vegetables and so on. Possible, but they will need protein to work the land and survive if they know how. Our current society barely knows where eggs come from, let alone how to harvest a field. They will have to fish, so we can expect some migration to the coast or near rivers, but they will have to know how to gut and clean fish and the same with chickens, ducks, and geese. Domesticated stocks will die trapped in their pens from lack of food, but we can expect some to survive. Mankind is going to have to learn basic survival skills; maybe we could get something on TV whilst it's still running. Lack of knowledge will kill more along with food and water poisoning, unless they cooperate and learn quickly," concluded Andrew.

"Scenarios *Eleven* and *Twelve*, might be as equally discredited as the others, but they show significantly lower numbers of survivors," Diane Selkirk added. "One of the analysts insists that the 0.01% rate is out by a factor of more than five, so only fifteen-hundred survivors."

"I saw that as well, but I can't believe that either, let's focus on the five to six thousand. So what can we do for them?" Hector asked again.

"Survivor dumps," said Andrew. "A collection of locations around the country with extensive stocks of food, fuel, medical supplies, and documents."

"I agree," said Diane. "It's not my area but…"

"You're on the committee Diane, not just for your genetics, but because we want you here. Your opinion is as valid as anyone else's. The same goes for the rest of you," Hector emphasised.

"Okay, if we divert resources to the Survivor plan, what

loses?" Tony questioned.

"We need a logistics expert to work it out properly. At the moment, we are trying to save all the population by dispersing food, fuel, and water and trying to save whole towns and cities. I'm afraid this effort will be wasted. Five thousand will not need much in comparison. If we provide two or three years supply, per dump, that should give them enough time to establish farms and then survive."

"How will we be able to prevent the food and medical supplies going off?" Hector asked.

"We need different expertise to figure that out, but if we can run power we can long term freeze medical supplies. There's a new process on maintaining vaccines and other drugs in sugar that is then encased in plastic, and this potentially gives indefinite shelf life. Food should last in tins, not sure about frozen. Surely the Government had plans for a *Nuclear Winter* and so on?" Andrew asked.

"Yes, we'll have to ask the Ministry of Defence for some of their plans, and their logistics men."

"One problem," Tony said.

"What is it Tony?" Hector asked.

"If this becomes public the dumps won't last, the ill, or soon to be ill, will use it all up. We have to arm the guards at the new fuel dumps now."

"Yes, I see your point." Hector pondered the issue. "Andrew, I'd like you to come up with lists of what's needed. We'll get some MoD expertise in to help, but think about everything they might need. If the MoD cause problems let me know." Andrew nodded and gulped at the responsibility. "Tony, I'll talk to you later about how we keep the places secure, but please, none of you talk about this, otherwise the survivors won't be surviving, with our help anyway. Diane, let's stop wasting the analysts time on the Scenarios, if your colleagues find a cure, or prevention, it will be fantastic. They need to go full out on that. Switch the analysts to giving us better numbers on survivors, human and mammal." With that Hector stood and rubbing his neck said, "Thank you for the meeting, we'll reconvene in two days-time, by video link."

CHAPTER FIVE

Medical Testing

Three months after A-Day, Craig Jennings was sweating heavily in his full body protection suit. He had been in it over an hour already as he carried out blood tests on patients in the makeshift hospital. It was converted from an army base, located just off the A1 in Durham. This particular ward held fifteen people, all with early stage lymphoma's, all deteriorating and none responding to the limited supplies of chemotherapy drugs, or the radiotherapy attempts. No one would allow cell replacement drugs to be used, just in case. The virus' trigger had not been the test cell gene therapy, according to the news last month. The worst cases were already suffering with unsightly swellings and respiratory problems. He had heard on the morning regional briefing that a hundred had died in Newcastle and one hundred and fifty in Sunderland. There were an estimated 10,000 new cases in the Northeast area alone. He had taken his mandatory blood test that morning and been passed as negative, no virus.

He finished his round of the beds. There was an improvised plastic sheet airlock before the door. All the windows had been sealed with plastic sheets making the room hot for patients who complained of dehydration. The nurse assigned to the ward had failed the blood test and was now confined in another ward. He promised to get some water sent in and some medical support. He exited the ward locking the door, and went straight outside. He could hear the diggers preparing the pits, which he had seen that morning. No one talked about it at the briefing. He walked the bloods to the lab that was set up in yet another barrack block. He deposited the tubed syringes into a hastily installed air cabinet. He nodded at the full bio-suited person taking the bloods from another ward and screening them. He could not see who it was in the suit. He went back out, and around to the kitchens. He explained the need for water to the gas masked army corporal who was preparing a meal.

"Where are the others?" Craig asked.

The corporal pointed towards where the diggers could be heard. In his gas masked muffled voice he said, "There are some water jerry cans around the side, you'll have to carry them yourself."

Craig thanked him and went and grabbed two 25-litre containers; he struggled with their weight and his suit, but managed to take them back to the ward. He unlocked the door and placed the containers inside the plastic airlock. One of the patients came forward, "Please distribute the water, I have to go and check another ward." The man mumbled a reply, his swollen neck slurring his speech. Craig turned and left, re-locking the door. He walked towards the HQ; he had other wards to take bloods from. The nurses assigned to the barracks were all going sick along with the doctors. There had not been enough bio suits to go round, so the doctors and nurses had insisted on working anyway. Now they were amongst the sick. Craig reached the HQ. He could hear shouting before he reached the door. Doctor Annette Carter had her suit helmet off. She was shouting at a fully bio-suited man. He was Lieutenant Colonel David Colleridge, not a medic, a Royal Logistics man. Mild-mannered, he had also lost his temper as he shouted back through his mask to Doctor Carter to put her mask back on. They stopped when they realised he was in the room.

"There's no more Chemo," said Dr. Carter, with tears in her eyes. Her grey hair was flattened against her temples by sweat and the suit helmet. She was in her fifties and had come out of retirement for the emergency. "These bastards have failed to deliver it."

"We have not failed," insisted the Colonel, "the delivery is late that's all. I have chased HQ and they have promised a batch soon."

"It will be too late," said Dr. Carter, "it's all too late." She sat down, the anger flowing out of her.

"Annette, you need to put your helmet on," Craig said quietly.

"It's too late," she said. She held up a small piece of paper gripped in her left hand. "I tested positive today."

"I'm sorry," said the Colonel.

"So am I," said Annette, placing her hand over the hand that the Colonel had put on her arm. "If I stay in the suit and isolated I'll help as long as I can," she said to Craig.

"We'll need it," Craig said.

Craig Jennings was already beginning to forget what life was like before the announcement day, A-Day as it was now called. He was a biogenetic researcher assigned to Professor Hargreaves' team researching Lymphomas. Now he was a blood taker and water carrier assigned to the camp a week after A-Day, in a terse phone call from the Professor himself. He'd helped to establish the facility, and then watched it slowly fill up as more and more wards opened. He estimated there were now nearly three hundred patients dying around the barracks. The Chemo drugs did not matter, they did not stop the disease; he knew that before they started. Still they tried. Technically he was part of the team looking for a cure. His research colleague from Professor Selkirk's team was Amy Weatherton, and she was dressed in the biohazard suit, in the Test Laboratory. Craig presumed it was her. He still could not actually tell, not without seeing her face through the mask. He would switch with her that afternoon, as she took her turn on the wards, collecting more blood samples. The ward he had just visited was not the worst. He had that to look forward to after he finished the discussion with the Colonel and Annette. Amy and Craig collected and analysed the blood, feeding the results into the computer that then sent them down to London, where the results were collated by a central team, led by the two professors. The professors had not been seen in public since a chaotic press conference, where everyone was wearing surgical masks, apart from the Professors. The conference, beamed live around the nation, had been abandoned as the Press wouldn't stay quiet long enough for the professors to answer a single question. The police had escorted them out. The Press had decided that the scientists were responsible. They might have been, Craig thought, but they were also the best hope for a cure. Still, better than in Germany and Sweden, where colleagues had been physically attacked and one of them shot.

"There's no medical support on Ward Two," he announced. There was no point saying anything else. "I've dropped in some water, but nothing else."

"I'll see to it," said Annette. "We need more clinical staff?" Annette looked at the Colonel.

"I'll ask," he said, but knowing there wouldn't be anymore.

"Have you been to Ward One yet?" Annette asked.

"I'm going now," said Craig.

"I'll come with you," she replied.

Annette placed her helmet back on and followed Craig out of the HQ. They turned right, their route to Ward One taking them closer to the diggers. They stopped and watched, but said nothing. There really was nothing to say as the digger seemed to finish one hole and immediately start on another. The drivers could be seen in their military nuclear, biological and chemical, NBC, suits with standard military issue gas masks. As far as Craig was aware, no one knew if the military suits and masks worked against the airborne version of the virus. The suits should be okay against touch, but no one knew for certain, and time was running out. They unlocked the ward door and pushed their way past the plastic. The duty nurse was monitoring one of the few electronic machines on the camp. Requisitioned from a medical supply company, the device was monitoring the thirteen-year-old boy patient; he also suffered from Asthma. His parents were in another ward. His breathing was terribly shallow, his heart rate erratic. It would not be long Craig thought. The nurse looked up. Two of the beds had sheets pulled up over the still shapes, former patients; the nurse said she was waiting for the mortuary team to collect them. The mortuary team were out with the diggers by the pits, or taking their first bodies into those pits. Craig went and took bloods from the live patients and noted the patient numbers for the victims under the sheet. By the time he was finished, the boy had succumbed. He noted the change on his sheet as the nurse disconnected the machine helped by Annette. They attached the machine to one of the other patients. The bleeps broke the near silence in the ward. There were three empty beds, plus the three bodies. There was now space in the ward for six more patients. Most of the others were unconscious or sedated.

"I found the morphine supply," said the nurse. "I should have asked the doctor, I know, but…"

"That's all right, June," Annette was beyond worrying about morphine records. "Do what you need to." The morphine would at least ease the patient's suffering.

Craig looked around; the Chemo IVs by two beds were empty, so he helped the nurse detach the IV feeds on the arms of the unconscious patients. They looked grey and weak. "Another couple of days," she said, "they'll all be gone."

"I know," said Craig. Craig took the bloods back towards the test lab. Annette went off towards Ward Two. They left Ward One unlocked; no one was going to be running away and infecting anyone from there. He passed two soldiers carrying black plastic bags towards Ward One. "There's three gone there," Craig said pointing. They nodded and held up the bags showing more than ten. They were prepared at least.

Back at the Lab, Amy had gone, if the shapeless suit had been Amy. He guessed she was starting her round of other wards. He loaded the blood tubes into the forced air closet and began to test the samples; he could predict their results. He worked steadily.

***

A shapeless suit walked into the lab an hour later. "Have you heard about Annette?" a young woman's voice asked. The suit was Amy.

"Yes," there was nothing he could say to change the inevitable outcome.

"There's an email from the Professors, asking about Ward One mortality rates, I thought I would wait for you before I replied."

"Three," Craig said, "the rest will be gone before the week's out, Ward Two maybe two weeks."

"There's no more coming in," Amy remarked.

"I doubt if there's anybody left in authority or medical services, to bring them in. People are staying at home, they're not even going out for food, in case they become infected."

"Another radio channel went off the air today, saying the staff were sick."

Craig did not reply; there was no point. Instead, he typed the response to the Professors, if it was still them, who knew? He sent the reply, copied as required to CDC, WHO, and around the world. He returned to the tests. The phone rang, jarring them both from their own thoughts. Craig clicked on speaker. It was better than trying to position the handset around the suit helmet.

"Craig?" It was Professor Hargreaves, he sounded exhausted.

"Yes, Professor," said Craig.

"Is Amy with you?"

"Yes," said Craig and Amy together.

"I want you both to stop with the samples. We have more than enough data. I, I mean, we, need you both in Cambridge at Professor Selkirk's lab checking the test results; we're sending a helicopter. It should be with you within the hour."

"Is Professor Selkirk there?" Amy asked.

"No, she is unwell, I'm sorry to say. Most of us are, I'm also positive," he paused, "that's why we need you in Cambridge. We are trying to get Professor Hanson from Sweden over to oversee, but that might take a while. In the meantime we need you both to conduct the research effort, please be ready to go, I'll call the Colonel to advise him." He hung up.

They looked at each other. Then Craig shut down the computer and switched off the centrifuge and freezer. He took the samples to the mini-incinerator. Amy carried over the latest samples. The incinerator burst into life at a switch of the ignition. "Pack?" Craig asked.

"Five minutes at most, I want to say goodbye though."

"I'll see you in the HQ tent, in ten."

They finished tidying and went to their separate accommodation areas. Typical army, Craig thought, separating the men and women. He packed what few things were not in his kit bag. He grabbed the spare bio-suit he had, although he only had one helmet. He collected his iPod and his one book. He walked to the HQ and could already see a helicopter approaching. He entered the HQ. Amy and the Colonel were both already there; Annette was walking towards them. Amy hugged the Colonel. A weird sight, with their suits and helmets on. The Colonel shook Craig's hand with a good luck and an unrealistic hope of seeing him again. A hug from Annette, tears again. Then Craig and Amy were walking toward the helicopter, a new experience for them both, Craig guessed. They were welcomed on board by a crewman in military NBC kit. They were shown to a seat, and strapped in. Then they were taking off and climbing. Craig looked down as they climbed. He could see the black plastic bags laid out in one of the pits. Two figures were unloading more bodies from a lorry. He looked away before the camp was hidden in the gathering gloom.

***

The flight lasted the best part of two hours before they touched down at the research laboratories, an offshoot of Cambridge University but a modern part of the campus. Despite the noise and vibration, Craig dozed in his seat opposite Amy. They couldn't talk over the noise and through the helmets. It was nearly dark as they landed at the Cambridge Research Facility.

CHAPTER SIX
COBRA

The Prime Minister was chairing his 60th Cobra meeting 140 days after he had made the announcement. He had tested positive for the virus two weeks before, and his wife and children the week before that. They were positive, despite the precautions they had taken as a family, and the extra precautions from the Government security team. It was highly likely his wife had developed the infection during the hospital visit she had made on the day before A-Day. The scientists now estimated the incubation at between two weeks and three months. He and his family were getting the best available medical help, but James Greening also realised it wouldn't work. The best, most optimistic, estimates said they might have a cure in eighteen months. If the research scientists survived long enough to find one and they were lucky, and. An analyst in the Cabinet Office had mapped out declining scenarios as the illness attacked the people who were trying to stop it. Another analyst assigned from the Department of Health had just shown the latest projection graphs, the upward trend of a hyperbolic curve was obvious to all. Death rates were increasing, although they were lagging behind the known infection rate. The reported infection rate was an underestimation. People were staying away from hospitals, and doctors, or worse the hospitals, and doctors were already losing staff, so they were not able to diagnose or record new infections.

Professor Hargreaves thanked the analyst for the projections, and the Prime Minister nodded, adding his thanks. After the analyst left the CMO, Professor Graves, Professor

Hargreaves, The Secretary of State for Health, Caroline McCoy, The Press Officer Tony Smith, and representatives from the Security Services and the MoD remained. The room's attendees, including the Prime Minister, had all now tested positive. The Head of MI6 was away to be with her dying husband. She was unlikely to return. The Head of MI5, Hector Crossdean was located in a separate bunker somewhere in the Midlands with the Home Secretary, John Turner, as an alternate Government location. They were linked by video and audio to the COBRA room. The Royal Family had gone first to Sandringham, and then Balmoral, which was sealed off. The Prime Minister had received a note from the Queen that morning, saying that her staff had shown signs of infection; they had not escaped.

The entire financial system had broken down almost immediately, as all long-term assets and loans, mortgages, and other investments were worthless or would never be repaid. If people wanted things, they had to barter for them. Food shortages were widespread and the army had to help to distribute stocks. Anti-looting laws were in place under the State of Emergency but, the Prime Minister doubted if they could be enforced. All military forces were deployed on body duties or transport.

The Prime Minister had exchanged a fruitless call with the US President, who had also spoken with the Chinese and Russian presidents. The Chinese were reluctant to say how grim things were there but, the Ambassador in Beijing had reported body fires in the streets. Russia was effectively closed, but half the British Embassy there were sick, so they had not escaped the virus. Japan had closed doors as well, to no effect. The USA was a mixture of cities in melt down and calmer accepting locations. The worldwide effort to find a cure was getting nowhere. There were whole countries where no reports had filtered out, maybe some small Islands had escaped, but not if they had any links to mainland areas, especially international links. Professor Callum, the lead researcher in the USA, was close to death, spending his last days in a CDC tent. His deputy was in a US Air Force bunker somewhere, being checked hourly, whilst he tried to make sense of test results. The Chief Surgeon had killed himself after shooting his wife, whilst a riot went on outside his house. The Prime Minister had not told the USA that he was positive. What good would it do? He had heard that even the ultrasurvivalist loners in the USA were under threat. The mammals they hunted, spread the disease just as effectively as humans did.

They went through the agenda items. Nuclear power station shutdown, police shut down, nuclear submarines return to base and shut down, although they were tempted to stay at sea until they needed to come in for food. That would not help the sailors' families. Despite the risks, the commanders had chosen to come ashore and face the consequences. The British Antarctic mission had returned, as had all British Troops overseas. The extra work force had been useful, but was now declining. The Home Secretary reported, via video link, that the police were at 70% strength and declining. Crime, after a brief spurt of looting, had almost stopped, if you ignored the murder suicides that no one had time to investigate; or, more likely, crime was not being reported.

Caroline McCoy reported that medical and clinical staff numbers were below 50% and falling fast. Everyone knew this would accelerate the death rates. There had been an initial surge in deaths, as one of the most controversial elements of the State of Emergency, came into effect. It was not publicised. No one wanted to talk about how hospitals, doctors, and other medical staff were implementing triage. All the other normal regular causes of death still happened, but treatment, which would have been provided, was not available. Life support machines were switched off, and the ICU staff redeployed. Lifesaving drugs for other diseases were no longer being produced. There were still painkillers in pharmacies, and some stocks, but no replenishment. Old people's homes suddenly had no medical cover, as clinical teams were ordered to medical centres to help with the virus.

Probably most upsetting to all in the COBRA room, and in authority, was the closure of neonatal units, premature births that were taken in and given a chance were instead allowed to die, to the great distress of the parents and the medical staff. Cardiac units and other surgery were switched to tumour removal. The tumours grew back. Blood supplies were short and frequently contaminated by the virus, if they were checked at all. Early diagnosis patients, that had surgery, frequently ended up with more lymphomas and blood cancer. As a result, surgery had effectively stopped. The regular A&E case load of accidents dropped dramatically. People did not travel far for fear of catching the virus, but there was far less mobility of the population, roads were nearly empty. Accidents were few and far between. People were learning quickly to depend only on themselves, and their main concerns were food and water.

"Research?" The Prime Minister asked. He looked twenty years older than he had when the CMO had entered the Cabinet Meeting Room on A-Day. He had also taken up the CMO's one-word questions. He got annoyed if answers took much longer.

"The latest batch of cell replacement therapy is only two days in, no change in the subject's condition," said the CMO. The Cambridge Research facility had fifty volunteers with early stages of the virus. They were being fed cocktails of cell replacement drugs in five different batches, one of which was a control group. Cancer progress of the groups appeared on the screen behind Professor Graves. He did not look at it; nothing had changed since the trials had started reporting.

"Lab rats and mice?"

"We've gone back using artificial insemination to try and get clean specimens. Rats are on a fifty-six day cycle, five weeks for maturity from birth, and another twenty-one days to the next breeding cycle. So far we have *no* clean samples, including using old sperm and eggs from over a year ago. We have what appear to be green, I mean clear embryos, and then clear offspring, but despite lab conditions they are showing as infected in two to three weeks. Even when the tests are green to start with, it doesn't mean they are immune. We've tried surgery, radiotherapy, chemotherapy, and cell therapy; nothing is working. I'm sorry, Prime Minister, we are struggling; the teams don't have time to do proper controlled elements."

"Anything more we can provide?" The Prime Minister always asked.

"Increased security, so that we don't lose samples again."

"How many incidents, John?" The Prime Minister asked The Home Secretary.

"Two incidents where they got in, and one where we stopped them." The Home Secretary was referring to attacks from

Animal Liberation Groups on two test facilities, where the Liberationists had violently attacked the building and released all the test animals. Three scientists had been killed and a further five seriously injured. In the third attack, the police had shot dead six attackers as they tried to get into the facility. They had made sure that it was publicised hoping to deter any further attacks. "We have provided some army personnel at other facilities, all now have armed guards."

"Anything else you need Kieran?"

Graves thought. Another thousand research scientists, who weren't ill and were fully trained. That *might* help and then they *might* start to make progress. The CMO said instead, "We have everything we need, Prime Minister." This included the weapons scientists from Aldermaston and Porton Down, every research chemist they could find in the country, and any teaching hospital medical staff that knew something about genetics. Research students all over the country supported these efforts. They volunteered to help, even as they were getting sick. The new checkers would help speed diagnosis. What they *actually* needed was someone who, or a lab animal that, was immune, or went into remission. The immunity may take years to find. Progress of the disease, once subjects tested positive, was varied, just like other cancers.

"Fatality rate?"

"Our best estimate…" The CMO corrected himself. There was no best estimate "Our latest estimate remains at 99.99%. There is a possibility that some cases may go into remission, or even recover, but we have no evidence of that."

"Just *hope*," Caroline McCoy added.

There wasn't much of that around either, the Prime Minister thought. "Timing?" The Prime Minister asked, even though he could see the projections himself.

"Faster than our initial thoughts, the models have now programmed in water, and food impacts; people will starve or drink contaminated water. The pits need to be carefully placed so as not to contaminate water tables and wells," said the CMO. There was a pause as the meeting absorbed the projections. Nobody asked about upsides or optimistic forecasts anymore. Every time optimistic projections had been presented to COBRA, the impact of the virus on modern society destroyed them. The previous week, one of the projections had shown a reduction in normal rates of serious illness diagnosis, especially diabetes. People were allegedly getting thinner due to the food shortages, or more likely they were staying away from doctors, and therefore, new cases were not being diagnosed. Long term, the projections showed this would reduce obesity and consequent diabetes. That moment of optimism was lost when the next projection had gone up on the presentation screen. The chart showed increased deaths of Type 1 diabetic patients due to lack of insulin drugs or access to them. Patients failed to attend hospital in time, if they got treated when they went. Heart attacks and strokes both added to the initial rise of death rates.

Two weeks before a report on drug addiction had shown how fast that group of victims would perish or be forced to kick the habit. The report from the police had also shown an increase in gang related violence as supplies of Heroin and Cocaine ceased. No money could buy the drugs, so several gun fights had broken out. Ambulance and police had refused to attend. The injured who turned up at the hospital were turned away by police, causing several more armed confrontations; even these incidents were now declining. Rapes were on the increase in some areas, but after an initial surge, they had also started to decline, or more likely were not reported. A confidential report from MI5 and the police showed an expected increase in rape in exchange for food or shelter. Food and water were the only currency that was universally accepted. The Prime Minister allowed the members of COBRA to absorb the gravity of the situation, before he continued the meeting by asking, "Infrastructure?"

The Home Secretary responded, "All commercial aviation has now ceased. There are some international flights, but that's mainly military returning home." The Transport Secretary should have reported, but he had gone to his constituency on A-Day plus five and refused to take up his office. The Prime Minister had threatened, up to and including, having him shot under the Emergency Powers Act that he had enabled on A-Day plus two. In the end, it was better he was away. His Minister of State, Susan Hamilton, had gone to Scotland. She was in a bunker there but, the Scottish Government were arguing jurisdiction and had cut off her communications. The Prime Minister had seriously contemplated bombing the Scottish Executive. The Chairman of the Joint Chiefs had dissuaded him from ordering such an attack by sending in the Special Air Service to establish communications with the beleaguered Minister. They hoped to get her onto the next COBRA meeting via radio or video link.

"Power and gas?" The Prime Minister broke from his contemplation.

"All nuclear is in controlled shut down; gas and the others are being run down, based on the number of staff reporting for work. We will be down to wind, solar, isolated geo-thermal, and some hydro, if we can keep the turbines running. The crews are working on ensuring all maintenance is complete, but if a turbine goes and there is no crew, then the fail-safes will kick in and shut down. Based on projections, we might have a crisis in about forty days, but it will depend on the weather. Gas will cause serious heating and cooking issues, especially if the winter is severe." The Home Secretary paused for breath. It would depend on the death rate of the support staff as well, the Prime Minister thought. "Water and sewage are a more pressing concern. We are expecting to have pumping station failures when the power goes off. The maintenance failures will increase as the staff numbers dwindle before that. Then we will have water shortages and have to provide bowsers. If there is anyone left to drive them?"

"How long on the water?"

"Maybe longer than the power, but it could be a week earlier." The Home Secretary suspected it would be faster, and therefore worse.

"We'll then start to have the potential for typhoid, dysentery and even cholera," Caroline McCoy added, before the CMO did. The CMO had discussed with her the impact of those diseases killing potential survivors of the virus. There was no point raising that today. Some of the Scenario projections showed far fewer survivors than 5,000, and she was beginning to believe it would be more accurate. How would the survivors, survive?

"Thank you, all of you. I know I've left these to last, so let's go through it, the prisons and the pits. Prisons first."

"Prime Minister," said the representative from the Police, "we've discussed this before, we can't see any alternative. If the prison officers continue to reduce at the current rate, we cannot support the prison population. I know we have already released all offenders serving less than five years, and many are already sick, but we have to do something about the high security ones." He paused. "They take the most officers to guard, and they pose the highest threat to the rest of society."

"You've seen the list, John?" The Prime Minister waived a paper at The Home Secretary.

"Yes, I hate the idea as well, but I can't see we have any choice," he replied.

"Changes?"

"Not since the last issue. You have to decide." John Turner didn't want to pressure his old friend, James Greening unnecessarily, but he also knew he had to. Time was running out.

"Objections?" The Prime Minister studied the faces around the table and across the video link; there were none, or none that had any better ideas. "Coverage?"

"It will not get reported, Prime Minister, the Emergency Powers will block it. The public won't care. Good riddance most will say." Tony Smith rushed out the words.

"Authorised," the Prime Minister said with a heavy heart. He signed the document in front of him, sentencing to death, by lethal injection of morphine and potassium chloride, 4,000 murderers and serious criminals. The list included some of the most notorious criminals in British history. There were over 7,000 life sentence prisoners, and a bar had been set based on the length of the prisoner's minimum term remaining and their behaviour behind bars. The day before, the US President had authorised the immediate execution of every prisoner on death row, and full life term inmates. The President had disclosed that on the phone earlier. There were thousands on his conscience, the Prime Minister thought. He shook his head. "Clear out, I mean release the others as well; I won't have people starving to death in cells. It's still no on the psychiatric hospitals, although I can't... well it's still no, for now, but Broadmoor and Rampton are with the prisons." Broadmoor, near Reading, and Rampton, near Nottingham, housed the UK's criminally insane prisoners. They were the ones who were considered a serious risk to the general public.

The CMO knew that Darwinism would operate at extreme levels; anyone with a disability or impairment would perish if they did not find a cure. If the survivors could not fend for themselves, they would die.

The Prime Minister jolted the CMO from his contemplation, "Are we ready to issue the proclamation yet?"

"Yes, Prime Minister," said The Home Secretary. "The BBC will transmit at seven p.m. They won't see the text before." The proclamation would tell the UK's population that all dead bodies should be taken to central pits for disposal. The army would run the pits, and when a pit was full, the army would burn, then bury the resultant bodies. There would be over 20,000 pits, each capable of a minimum of 2,000 bodies. Ten thousand larger pits would hold 5,000 and one hundred super pits would hold more than 100,000. Large city locations would hold over 250,000. The pit capacity would not be the issue, James Greening knew. They could always dig more holes, getting the bodies there would eventually be impossible.

"Potential reaction?" The Prime Minister was not expecting to be reassured.

"Probably, not as bad as it would have been a few weeks ago. The news of the pits in camps didn't leak out, and now people are too scared to riot or demonstrate," Tony Smith said. "What remains of the working press is publishing stories about small groups' plans to avoid the disease by hiding in secluded areas."

"How are they getting the stories, if the groups are hiding?" Professor Hargreaves asked.

"They are making them up, I suppose. They need to report something other than the death or illness of the latest former celebrity."

"How long can the BBC continue, or the internet for that matter?" The Prime Minister asked, with his longest question for weeks.

The Home Secretary replied, "The BBC are already cutting to emergency staff, maybe another three months before we only have the Emergency Radio broadcast system, ERS. The Internet will depend on power and network, or phone lines, but it will stop, due to lack of content and data centres before that."

"Military Discipline?" The Prime Minister had discussed this with the Secretary of State for Defence, prior to the meeting, but COBRA needed to know.

"Still holding, but it will drop. There will be detrimental behaviour by some groups or elements as the numbers decline," the Secretary of State replied. "We don't believe our NBC suits are protecting us, because infection rates are increasing. Once the officers and senior NCO's go, then some of their work will stop; another reason to get the main pits running as soon as possible."

"Tony, once the pits transmission is done, start working on announcements for the shut down of services. Let's get the ERS going so that people have a chance to tune radios to a.m. We need to warn them that the power and water will go soon."

"Prime Minister," Hector Crossdean raised his hand, which flashed out of the picture on the video conferencing link. "One thing more we need to consider."

"What is it Hector?"

"We are getting reports from some of these new religious cults that they are planning mass suicides."

"What?" The Home Secretary chipped in.

"But why? I mean… are these attempts serious, or just a few…" he struggled for the right words, "… misguided individuals?"

"Yes, Prime Minister they are serious and could impact thousands in the population. The danger is they'll indoctrinate some potential survivors. We've already stopped a so called reverend from brewing up a cyanide cocktail."

The Prime Minister looked around his colleagues, "The martial law orders. I want to see them at my next meeting. I have some treatment scheduled tomorrow. The Home Secretary will chair until I return, thank you everyone." The Prime Minister rose. God help me, God help us all, he thought.

CHAPTER SEVEN

The Farewells Commence

Craig Jennings noted his actions on day two hundred after the announcement as he changed the drip on Amy's IV feed. She was on test batch 26B a combination of cell replacement gene therapy, chemotherapy chemicals, and some radioactive isotopes. Researchers in Japan had said that the test drug appeared to cause some slowing of the disease in their test patients. Not that they had heard from that source for two weeks. Amy had tested positive three days after arriving back at the Cambridge Research Facility. They didn't know how Amy had caught the disease. A week later, Craig had ripped his bio-suit whilst trying to calm a test patient. So far he was still negative, but he had not bothered with the suits since, he didn't want to. Amy smiled up at him. She was still able to work, and the only swelling that was apparent was in her breasts, which had both gone up two-cup sizes. Amy had joked she had always wanted a boob job. They had become lovers only a day after arriving. They had been quartered in a former student halls, which had been biologically protected. Following a long work session, they had both returned together and gone through to the showers. They hadn't bothered to get dressed before grabbing a moment of human contact from each other.

Craig held Amy's hand. "Ready for the next scan?"

"If you're ready for your blood test?" They were virtually alone in the research facility's main building as the rest of the staff became ill. The test patient volunteers were in an adjacent building; it was down to twelve living patients. No more had come forward for several weeks.

"What was the point?" A referring doctor had asked. They weren't going to find a cure in time. Craig had not been able to persuade him.

Amy raised herself up from the treatment bed and disconnected the now empty IV. "Bigger and better every day," she said wiggling her chest at him. She kissed him; it stopped him crying. "Come on let's go and see my insides."

They walked out of the small treatment room, converted from one of the offices, and went down a floor, to an outside door. A transportable MRI scanner had been connected to a fire door with layers of plastic bio-hazard protection, and forced air conditioning hastily connected to make a semi-permanent air-lock. They walked into the truck that housed the scanner. The radiologist, Kathy, still wore her suit, although nearly all the remaining staff had stopped, after Craig had taken his off. The Swedish professor had never arrived. Craig was acting head of the research effort in the UK, with the Professors in London somewhere. Amy, without embarrassment, stripped off her top, exposing her enlarged breasts. She followed by removing her jeans and climbing onto the scanning table. "Let's get on with it," she said. Craig thought he noticed a small lump near the top of her spine, near the nape of her neck, but her hair swished back to cover it. Kathy set the machine to work. Craig retreated to the monitoring station. An hour later they had the reports. The radiologist was the only expert in town; they didn't have a consultant oncologist. The report was simple. Additional tumours visible near the spine, there was a lump, the breast ones had increased, and there were additional growths near the bowel. Amy looked at the screens without a word.

Kathy passed no comment, before apologetically saying, "I'm going to go home, I'm sorry I can't take it anymore." Her little speech was half muffled by the bio suit helmet. She took it off. She hugged Amy, kissed Craig on the cheek, and then walked out of the truck.

"Just us two then," said Amy, taking his arm and turning Craig to look at her.

"We have to send the results in."

"Stuff the results," she said, "take me to bed before it hurts too much."

When Craig awoke the following morning, he had slept at least fourteen hours. Amy was not by his side. A handwritten note was:

Craig, love,

Thank you for the last few weeks, they have kept me going, but I don't want just to waste away. The pain is already getting too much, and I don't want you to see me like that, even with my big boobs. ☺ By the time you wake up I'll be gone. Do your best for the world, I know you'll try. Tell them I tried too.

Love

Amy xxxxxx

Craig was angry, upset and crying as he rushed to dress. Where should he begin to look? Had she left the facility? When had the note been written? Why had it been written? What would she do, had she done? The questions tumbled through Craig's mind. He went to the treatment office, nothing, then to the lab, nothing. He called Hargreaves. There was no reply, he left a message, all garbled. No point taking a mobile phone with him, the network had been down for the last few days. He walked outside, a mortuary army team were loading bodies into the pit by the facilities fence; he walked towards them, trepidation building inside him. They too had dispensed with their suits and masks. They were checking a clipboard.

"Morning Craig," the senior one said.

"Morning," Craig automatically stumbled; he couldn't

remember the man's name suddenly.

"Got a slight problem," said the other.

"What?" Craig tried to focus.

"One more body than we should have. We just started for today, see, and we finished there, last night," he indicated a black plastic bag. "We were about to load this one in, when we realised we had one more than we had last night, odd."

Craig jumped down into the pit and went to the extra bag. The bag wasn't sealed from the outside, just closed, the top flap slipped inside the main part of the bag. Craig pulled the fold back. Amy lay as if asleep in the bag. She was freshly made up, her hair was brushed, and a smile was almost on her lips, but no breath escaped her. Craig's tears dropped onto her cold cheeks. He wiped them away with the palm of his hand. "Bye love," he mumbled. He replaced the fold closing the bag. The senior man helped him out of the pit.

"Who?" He looked hard at Craig.

"Amy," said Craig turning and walking away.

CHAPTER EIGHT
COBRA's Survivors

The Prime Minister sat in the COBRA meeting trying to breathe. Three hundred days since he had stood in Parliament announcing the virus that was now killing him. The swelling on his neck was visible to all; the room couldn't see the other lumps on his stomach and groin. His wife was gone, his children, one clung to life the other with his wife. The room was empty save for Tony Banks, Caroline McCoy and by video link, Hector Crossdean and John Turner, the Home Secretary. The Secretary of State for Defence was too ill to attend.

"We're using old cold war bunkers primarily," Hector Crossdean began. "We can air seal them and power is well catered for. We'll have ten in place by the end of this week, with a further fourteen in the next two weeks. They are sized differently, especially for fuel, mostly diesel. Each has multiple power supplies. The generators are on timed switches to power the freezers at least two hours per day. As the freezer rooms stay shut they will not defrost, but we have temperature sensors set as well, which will trigger the generators. They have enough fuel in their tanks at that rate for three years of daily use. The generators won't come on unless they have to. Then there are full batteries in arrays, which can do the same if the generators fail. They only have three to six months of power if they don't get recharged, which the generators should do. The batteries are also topped up by solar and wind turbines that can also drive the air locks and freezers when they generate. We've run and tested the first two locations for a week. The systems all work. They have double wiring and so on. It should work."

A similar plan was going in place in the USA, France, Canada, Germany, Holland, Sweden, and Russia amongst many others. There were occasional international communications, but it was unknown how advanced the individual nations' plans were. The Government, what was left of it, had tried to coordinate ERS frequency use to avoid interference, but it was not entirely successful. Iran could be heard on one of the French frequencies. Their President had complained a few weeks before, and the MoD had changed one of the ERS frequencies following a complaint from Norway that was down to different versions of a NATO communications manual.

"Andrew did a fantastic job with the MoD," the Prime Minister croaked. He did not need to ask how Andrew Jacobs was. He had seen him lying unconscious on a bed on one of the upper floors that morning.

"Yes, Prime Minister," Hector agreed.

"Medical supplies, Caroline?"

"Prime Minister, we don't know how long vaccinations will actually last. We have discussed this with CDC in Atlanta and the manufacturers. We have increased, sorry, further reduced, the storage temperatures for all the vaccines. The live vaccine should last up to thirty-six months, but we don't know. We have added instructions to give a second dose four weeks after the first if there are no adverse reactions. We have used this new sugar and plastic system as much as we can. Professor Hargreaves thinks it will be less of a threat than we might think, because these are survivors and they are isolated. It's perfectly possible that many other diseases will be wiped out. We have left manufacturing instructions just in case, but it will be the skills to do that, that will be difficult. The stores are being loaded as we speak. Each site has enough for ten thousand survivors just in case."

"I spoke to Kieran Graves as well," said John Turner. "He added to the wipe out theory that all the survivors would have been immunised anyway for MMR, Smallpox and so on, even if they are not naturally immune. Food is less of an issue, we've reduced frozen meat we don't think it will last, and so we've increased dry goods, boxed and sealed, then vacuum-sealed. A lot of tins and army ration packs are in there as well; we know from the Second World War that some of them can last decades. We've also added portable generators, batteries, solar panels, some wind turbines and instructions on some of the power plants and water treatment facilities."

The Prime Minister knew most of that already, but for once he wasn't in his abrupt mood. "Tony, the notification system; no more frequency issues I hope?"

"No one cares about interference planning for this system, just to hear a new message will be the key from wherever it comes, we will be broadcasting on multiple frequencies. Local signal power should overcome any problems. It is similar to the ERS, Prime Minister, but timed to start transmitting only when we decide. They have triggered the timers to test, but we don't know if it will work when they're actually needed or if anyone will be listening," he added needlessly. "Kieran Graves says two years from now, Andrew thought sooner, it's our decision."

"Sooner, eighteen months from now," said The Prime Minister, the latest projections showed a faster pace of decline of the fall of civilisation, but this outdid Roman and British empires. This was faster than dinosaur extinction by millions of years. Rats were almost gone, he'd been told, apart from in the remaining few working test labs. He wouldn't miss rats "Alternatives to the ERS?" He dragged himself back to the meeting agenda; the latest cocktail of, non-effective, drugs were impairing his concentration he knew. He was again feeling sick.

"MoD is suggesting leaving a map in several key sites under lock and key, but survivors will break in anyway. If, as Andrew has suggested, people will be in hunter-gatherer modes, scavenging, then they will search these sites, eventually find a map, and head for the nearest dump. They will be secured with a simple passcode that the ERS will transmit and will be with the maps. There are instructions in the dumps for firing up the full ERS so that other survivors can then get notified."

"Good," said The Prime Minister. It wasn't, but it was the best they could do. "Skills issues?"

The Home Secretary replied, "If we use the five thousand figures for medical skills, there should be about ten to fifteen doctors, twenty to thirty nurses, including paramedics, maybe ten dentists, a couple of vets. Andrew has suggested that these numbers will also be too high. They are all high risk at the moment, not just from the virus, but the other diseases that are starting. They'll need farmers, or good gardeners anyway. There may be a hundred who have the necessary skills at the start. Teachers," he paused, "perhaps another hundred of them. For proper water and power, they will need plumbers and electricians. Sorry, Prime Minister, I have to say that, for all we know, we could end up with five thousand soldiers or five thousand hairdressers. We hope that there will be a flat population, but it could be that only sixteen year olds survive or a particular blood group." The Home Secretary's frustration was evident. He calmed himself. "We can only plan for that."

Caroline McCoy, stepped in. "The death rates, excluding the old and the young, are split across all professions and age groups. There's nothing on blood groups. One of my analysts said that there would be a trend towards younger and fitter with higher IQ, but so far that hasn't shown up in the actual fatalities and infected."

The Prime Minister considered what he had heard. In the end, the survivors, whoever they were, would survive, or not. He could feel the nausea rising again. "Thank you everyone, please continue as best we can, now if you'll excuse me." He barely made the bathroom before the drugs did their worst.

CHAPTER NINE

COBRA Farewell

Caroline McCoy lay on her bed in the COBRA room, she could barely speak, or drink; she could feel the lumps in her throat. She looked at the diary, was it really only 420 days since that fateful Cabinet meeting? Fourteen months of chaos, well not for much longer, she thought. Her legs were swollen, as was her abdomen. She knew it wouldn't be long. She had a morphine injection ready. Tony Smith, the press secretary had given it to her. She didn't know where he had got them. He had taken his jab three weeks ago, no, maybe four weeks now. She raised herself up; it was time for the meeting if anyone called in. She clicked on the video, no one else came into the room, there was no one else down here she thought. The link powered up. She waited for five minutes. She was just about to switch off when the Cambridge Research Facility came on line. It must be Craig, she thought. Effectively, he was the CMO and head of research, now that Graves, Hargreaves, and Selkirk were gone. Craig's face and neck were swollen.

"Hello Craig," she managed. "Anything?"

"No," his voice was gravelly, and he wheezed as he tried to speak. "I think we're done, I'm sorry."

"Thank you for trying for so long," Caroline managed. "We are finished here as well, I think."

"What will you do?" Craig asked.

Caroline looked at the screen. She tried to smile. "Like most politicians, I have an exit strategy." She held up the syringe. "I think

I might go outside, I haven't been out for weeks."

"It's sunny here."

"Oh good, I hope it is here. What about you?"

"Don't worry about me, I'll be all right. I have my spot already."

"Is there anyone there with you?" Caroline was losing energy, but she didn't want to switch off just yet.

"Yes, someone is waiting for me here."

"That's good."

"Yes, it is… I… I don't know what to say." Craig struggled out his words, then he was gasping for breath.

Tears were stinging her eyes as Caroline said, "That's okay, it doesn't matter anymore, but I need to go now." She reached and disconnected. She didn't want to hear any more goodbyes. She had held the Prime Minister's hand as he took his last breath. He had fought hard, but had died a week after his eldest child, two months ago now. Hargreaves had gone before the Prime Minister. John Turner, the Home Secretary, had gone off the air before that, along with the connection to the Midlands. A network fault they were told, there was no engineer left to fix it. Scotland had come on line via the SAS's radio, but they had been silent for weeks. She didn't know how to work the radio anyway. She looked at the papers scattered around the COBRA table; a graph caught her eye. What was the date? Six weeks, no it was longer ago. The analyst had dropped it off and then said he was going home. She hadn't stopped him. The two lines showed deaths and infections still in steep upward curves. Through tears, she saw fifty-million on infections and twenty-five million on deaths, both with *est.* against the numbers for estimate. The projections were *under* estimates. She knew because so few reports came through. The army camps sent some, but the MoD had extremely few people left to collect the data, let alone add it to a report. Deaths could be twice that already. She had seen the report from the large pits around London. She had left the photos unseen, but she could imagine. One site alone had dealt with over 250,000 bodies. The graph showed the deaths catching up, over time. She pushed the slide aside.

The paper underneath was titled *Impact on Mammals*. She flipped the first page, and it had similar graphs. She remembered a briefing soon after the announcement, and then the report that the London Zoo keepers had killed their charges. Well, some of them had. Two had then committed suicide. She remembered the news coverage, the shock, the ridiculous; *something must be done* from a political commentator. Was he still alive? He had been a pain to her department even before this with his leaks and claimed expertise. She had checked. He didn't even have an O level in biology, yet he had shouted *you don't know what you're doing*, at the CMO at the infamous press conference. Maybe he had been shot during one of the riots, many had, especially outside the drug warehouse. Thirty killed she recalled, including several members of the press. An Army soldier had lost his rifle to a protester, who had then let loose on everyone. It was surprising that there hadn't been more riots and trouble. Enough, she thought, all the efforts had been pointless. It was over. She got up, sipping from a water bottle.

The Secretary of State for Health, and acting head of government Caroline McCoy made her way up the empty corridor; she wondered how long the lights would stay on. She started up the stairs. The lights flickered on above her. Of course, they were all on specific environmental circuits. There were environmental power supplies, supported by batteries, from solar panels and wind turbines. The power would last for ages. Another set of stairs, another non-working security door wide open, then the reception area, then the lobby, then the outside doors. Craig was right. It was sunny. It was eerily quiet outside; she could hear birds singing. Caroline walked across Horse Guards and into the East side of St James's Park. She was tempted to continue into the park, but she saw the carcass of a dog on the next path. A pair of fat crows had their heads buried feasting on the corpse. She returned to the empty road and then turned left along Great George Street. It was empty. She had expected crashed cars and wrecks, but there was nothing. A couple of cars, including a government Jaguar, were neatly parked at the side of the road. She listened to the singing birds. She crossed by Parliament Square, looking at the Houses of Parliament, remembering her time there, how hard she had fought to get there. The last sitting when she had given a statement to the half-empty chamber, with everyone in ridiculous surgical masks.

She walked past the entrance to Westminster tube station, the officious notice flapping from the closed gates, '*Closed until further notice - due to staff illness.*'

She recalled the train drivers threatening to strike when the State of Emergency had been called. They had walked out for a couple of days, then shamed by the press, they returned claiming to be heroically working for the good of all. Passengers had stopped using the system anyway, scared of infection. The tube drivers' action may have even slowed the virus' advance for a couple of days. That was if they hadn't all gone on a demonstration complaining about the sweeping powers implemented by the State of Emergency. The emergency powers hadn't helped; the industrial action and demonstrations hadn't helped. The unlimited resources hadn't helped. The deaths of all the volunteers testing the various test drugs hadn't helped. Nothing had.

The sudden chiming of the Clock startled her, 10:45 she saw in the Elizabeth Tower, mistakenly called Big Ben; that was the name of the bell that would ring on the hour. Some birds flew up from what looked like another dog, cat, or fox corpse lying in the centre of the road down the Victoria Embankment. There were no crowds of tourists trying to catch the perfect angle of the tower from Westminster Bridge. She crossed over onto the bridge itself. The London Eye stood motionless across the river, sunlight gleaming off the upper carriages, or pods, whatever they were called? She walked out onto the bridge to the centre of the Thames. No river traffic, although she noticed several boats were lumped together, half blocking Waterloo Bridge down river. She turned and looked back to where she had walked from. She could see a dark pail of smoke rising to the West. She knew there were pits alongside Constitution Hill. Was that where the smoke came from? Did that mean some people were still cleaning up? She could not tell.

She looked up at the clock face once more. Five minutes to eleven, she would wait until it struck; she had always loved the sound. She tried to take a deep breath, but had to stop. It hurt and made her wheeze. She heard the famous introduction to the main chimes. She looked at the syringe that she had removed from her jacket pocket; she checked it, squirted a little of the liquid out, not that it mattered. She climbed up onto the wall. She almost fell off with the first bong; startled by the sound. She injected the morphine into her bare thigh. On the tenth Bong, she let herself fall, smiling at the water as it rushed towards her; she didn't hear the eleventh.

CHAPTER TEN

The Research Facility

Craig looked at the blank video screen from the research facility HQ; the link had gone blank with Caroline's last words. No goodbye, none was needed he thought. He switched off the monitor then carefully switched off all the other equipment, leaving the incinerator for last, where he destroyed the last samples. He placed the folder with all the notes, the passwords to the systems, and a photo of himself and Amy taken a couple of days after they arrived. His last check list neatly ticked, and identifying the final resting places, lay by the side. He remained, as ever, the diligent researcher. He switched off the lights and exited the building. There was no one else around; he hadn't seen anyone for days. He walked completely around the site, looking at the flocks of birds. There was no traffic on the adjacent roads and he could see nobody looking out of the facility's windows. Devoid of humanity unlike when Amy and he had arrived by helicopter.

He thought of the death projections. He understood the statistical variations in the graphs and briefings. He doubted anyone was going to survive. Despite his own efforts, he had not been able to identify the base gene string for the virus. Maybe he had part of it but part was not enough. If they had found a remission or immune patient, they might have stood a chance, but they hadn't, and maybe there wouldn't be any. Maybe this was it for the human race. Nature made species extinct all the time throughout history, maybe this was mankind, no humankind's turn. He politically corrected himself, after all humans had managed to wipe out thousands of species. Now human beings were the next dodo or

Galapagos giant tortoise. What was that one's name? He had put it in his notes, Lonesome George, that was it.

If there were survivors, and Craig wasn't sure about Professor Jacob's plans, then it could easily end up with a few thousand people wandering around the country never meeting a mate. What if only females or males survived? Or only those over child bearing age? That would be it, even if they survived the virus, hunger, thirst or any other of the myriad things that might kill them. During one of the COBRA briefings someone had mentioned an American TV series called *Jeremiah*, and the BBC *Survivor* programmes. Craig had managed to see some episodes, but they had mammals. They could use horses for transport after the fuel ran out, and there were still thousands of survivors. The BBC's show had 95% fatalities, he had seen in the show's description. If only there would be so many. He'd put that in his notes as well. He had watched others offer up prayers and heard the calls for God's blessing. Craig was agnostic at best, and atheist normally. Mostly he had never thought about it, embedded and fulfilled in his future scientific career, delving into the depths of genetic research, the fundamentals of life and recreation. As for God, well he would find out soon enough.

He walked to the pit. He had stopped the soldiers burning and filling it in, saying that he would do it when the time came. He realised he wouldn't be able to fill it in. He didn't think anyone would care. The army had left a few weeks before, called to the central Cambridge pits to help; they had not come back. Craig had loaded the last bodies of the volunteer patients himself. He had struggled with a trolley to help carry them out one at a time. All logged, all ticked off on his sheets. He could smell the petrol soaking the ground and the bags. He found the space. His syringe was in his hand; he climbed into the bag he had prepositioned in the space. His breathing was short and painful; he gave himself no more than two days anyway.

He was an expert on oncology morbidity now, probably the world's leading authority; it would make an excellent dissertation for a PhD. He turned to face where Amy lay. He reached past her body, to where a pool of petrol had collected. He lit the fuel with a lighter he had found inside the building. The fire raced away up the pit, he blanched back from the heat and brightness of the flames. The fire would reach the end of the pit, circle around, and then it would race past the rest of the bodies either side of him, burning his feet. He injected the syringe, lay back, and waited for the darkness to come. It wasn't long before he was dreaming. He didn't feel the flames at his feet; his breath grew shorter, then finally stopped. The roar of the fire that now enveloped the whole pit and the squawk of disturbed birds were the only sounds troubling the peace of the research facility.

PART TWO

The world survived the fall of the Roman Empire and will no doubt outlast our own so much more splendid civilisation.

James Buchan

Think of the earth as a living organism that is being attacked by billions of bacteria whose numbers double every forty years. Either the host dies, or the virus dies, or both die.

Gore Vidal

There's no one place a virus goes to die - but that doesn't make its demise any less a public health victory. Throughout human history, viral diseases have had their way with us, and for just as long, we have hunted them down and done our best to wipe them out.

Jeffrey Kluger

CHAPTER ELEVEN
Gary's House

Gary Tolman was nearly eighteen on A-Day, not that he paid attention. Sixth Form College at the nearby Burton and South Derbyshire College was just about complete. He had taken all his Advanced Level A2 exams, and now waited to see if his results matched expectations for his planned degree course in civil engineering. He was planning a gap year of travel and experiences, but he wouldn't be setting off until after his results, just in case. He was alone in the house. His parents were both at work, his father directing his latest venture, a renewable energy firm based in a factory in nearby Lichfield, and his mother doing paperwork and some research at Derby University. The house, he couldn't believe this house, although they had moved in, finally, three months previously. It was a Huf house or as he liked to say *Huf-Haus*, set in its own clearing, surrounded by woods on three sides with a slope leading off the front. It was his parents' dream, and he had become caught up in the design and engineering aspects as the project slowly completed. His interest had begun from the finding of the location, nearly three years ago, to the laying down of the environmental aspects. It had inspired him to go down the engineering path, although his father's influence had helped. The house was a few miles west of Burton-upon-Trent in the heart of the Midlands. He knew his mother and father had searched for a site for years, discarding several previous locations until they had finally settled on a copse location called Henhurst Wood

The site had first been cleared of a derelict farm cottage, then the water system had been prepared. This started with rainwater collection into two 10,000-litre tanks at the top of the hill, underground, but next to the wind turbine fixings. The gravity fed system then ran into two stages of commercial level water purification, including a powered ultra-violet cleaning system. Stored water was also fed into a grey system used for the house toilets, showers, and garden water. Once used, water was either fed back into the recycling system, or toilet waste was fed into the sewage processing system that was designed for twelve people. This needed regular *sludge* cleaning for paper, or other non-biodegradable disposed items; not a job anyone looked forward to. Sludge was taken from the filters and compacted, which created fertiliser pellets. Filtered water was then sent to the base of the slope where a reed bed system provided final filtering. His friends had laughed at that bit. He had the description for a project for college. There were lots of comments about the smell, and *eughhh*'s from the girls, but it didn't smell at all, so far. The water could be pumped back up into the storage tanks if needed during a drought, or from the small stream at the end of their plot, but it was not expected to. The pumps would need to be run once a month or so, to check, but so far, despite a near drought since they moved in, the water system had worked flawlessly.

Gary's father, Henry, had deliberately over specified the systems to ensure mains level water performance. The actual water mains pipe was connected, as was the mains sewer. The planners had insisted on that, but Gary's father had switched off the water main stop-cock, reducing their metered charges to just standing charge. The water system only diverted to the main's drain if a fault occurred with the treatment system. The planners had insisted it was there, just like mains gas and electricity. The drinking water was effectively quadruple filtered from the rainwater tanks and a small spring, which was nearby, feeding into the stream and also partially feeding the tanks. Even the Department of Health had certified the system as safe for human consumption. The suppliers had it as a case study on their web sites.

Gary's parents were using the house as a showcase for sustainable living. His mother, Juliet had even gone on a TV programme to discuss the house, as the building was under way. For a brief period, the programme had made Gary a celebrity at college, as he was featured in the accompanying film for thirty-seconds, sitting in his future bedroom at his computer. One of the normally diffident girls he fancied had agreed to a date, which had not gone well when his ID was pulled in the pub. She had not come out with him the next time he asked. His *starring* role had all been faked for the cameras, as the house was not finished, but it was reality now, including a direct fibre network connection. The link sent endless data about the house to his father's company offices, and research teams at two universities. The added benefit for Gary was his Internet connection that ran at fibre speeds. The fibre cable installation had created another planning row. His father had to get way leave, for the fibre cable to be laid by persuading another landowner to grant access, which the farmer concerned was not originally willing to grant. It was finally resolved when a spur to the landowner's house was added. Another row had followed for the upgrading of the power cables and the mains water, with injunctions threatened before compensation was agreed.

His father normally described the landowner as *that arse*, before mumbling other swear words, any time he was mentioned. There had even been a stand up row at the council planning committee, when, despite the farmer's objections, permission had finally been granted. Given the farmer couldn't see any of the house, no one actually could until they came up the drive, his objections had been over ruled. The drive turned away from the house and the hill and back out onto another road.

Although the utilities were connected, the house generated its own power via an eight-kilowatt solar power array that relied on twenty of the very latest four-hundred-Watt panels, fixed to the South facing side of the roof. Most of the power generated by the array was actually fed back to the national grid, generating income for the family as part of what was called a feed in tariff. On top of the hill was a four-kilowatt wind turbine, installed on top of the water tanks up the hill. That had produced another planning row that was solved when the turbine's power was offered to the local primary school. That necessitated another cable run, and a loss of some of the generated power but only during term time. Both the power feeds, along with the mains supply, ended up in the basement, which contained a power router and then a backup battery system that could run the house for a week if everything died and the batteries were fully charged. The battery choice had caused an argument between his parents. His mother had complained about the lack of green credentials. His father wanted to be self-sufficient. In the end, his father had won, but only after compromising about some of the insulation materials in the main house. Gary's father accepted a more expensive but greener, wall filling. The basement also contained all the manual controls for the various systems, plus the computers and audio-video, AV, system. In another corner of the basement was their extensive wine cellar, which was one of his mother's other passions.

The house was enormous for the three of them; especially after they had been living in a small, terraced, three-bedroomed house for the last six months of construction, after yet another delay on the finishing. His mother refused to move in until it was all finished, including decorations and landscaping. The house itself had been finished, with the usual German efficiency, on time and budget. Ideally, his father had said, they would have had a water mill set up so that they could get hydroelectric. Geo-thermal had also been considered. They had not been able to find a suitable site, although his father's long-term aim was to get another field for geo-thermal power generation. The most suitable location was the *arse* landowner, so that would have to wait a few years. The Huf-house itself was designed to be super–efficient for energy, by taking the solar power, triple high efficiency double-glazing, under floor heating and heat exchangers. His father wanted more solar panels installed to generate more power that could be sold for additional family income. He laughingly told people that he planned a satisfying retirement on the power income.

Gary loved the house. He loved the technology, systems, and the design. He loved his parents, although he never told them that. He was a teenager after all. They had encouraged his full participation in the project from the start, and in many ways it was his house as much as theirs. He studied the engineering and watched the various workers, and specialists, install and construct the systems fittings. He had watched fascinated by the modular assembly on site, chatting with the German team in his school standard German. He had helped pour concrete for the basement and foundations, another compromise, and also helped wire in the wind turbine. His father had let him install some of the management software and set up the various heating and lighting schemes. He knew his father had checked, but he also knew he had got most of it correct. The systems then ran themselves.

Gary had a bedroom, a study, and a bathroom to himself. There were five other bedrooms including his parent's master suite. Four bedrooms were on the top floor, then there were two as guest annexes. There was the kitchen/diner open plan, leading to open spaces for lounging and the terraces. Completing the ground floor, along with a bathroom by the front door, was a cinema room, which was located between the annexes, and which seemed to be having teething troubles. The AV Company was due back to have a look later that day. That room didn't quite fit in with the open plan style of the rest of the house, but it was a feature Gary and his father had wanted; even his mother now loved the room. The house had a full CCTV security and alarm system. They had lost some electrical cabling during construction, and his mother, who wasn't used to country living, still felt a bit isolated; she had insisted on a full security system. There were only three of them normally but they had already been inundated with guests. He had been allowed a small party, when twelve friends had stayed over after a barbecue and film that did work in the cinema room; the film was fine it was the sound that kept cutting out. A dodgy cable probably. Gary thought the house needed a pool, but his father had shown him the running costs. It still needed one, Gary had argued unsuccessfully. He was working on it; there was space. The house had swallowed all their possessions, including stuff that had been in storage. There were shelves and cupboards still empty. The basement, despite all the batteries and equipment racks, could have taken a small flat and still had room. He kept his room exceptionally tidy, apart from his study's desk, at the moment, where he still needed to put away his revision books.

He was half wondering where the cinema people were. His mother had told him to look out for them. He was currently in an on-line shoot-'em-up game against someone he thought was in Japan. He was losing. His music blared from the speakers and most of the house, as he had it to himself. He occasionally watched the news, but not that day, so he missed the Prime Minister's announcement. It was only when his mother arrived home early he realised something was up. He thought that maybe he had missed the cinema people, and she was going to tell him off. He hadn't noticed the CCTV or gate bells, they should automatically flash alerts on his TV screen. He had started an explanation and apology, when she hugged him and then his father was there, and then they told him. Then they sat in front of the TV in the lounge, listening to the experts tell them how little they knew, or could do.

His mother had talked at the university with one of the medical teams before coming home. She realised that masks and so on would be useless, the virus was already out of control. She had panic shopped on the way home, getting long-term foodstuffs. She had cleared the supermarket before most people had even realised there was a problem. Her Lexus 450H was full of tins and jars. They sat and analysed the situation as far as the available information allowed. Then they had phoned distant relatives and friends and repeated much of the same conversation. They didn't know what to do, but nobody did, so they unloaded the food, filling only some of the kitchen's cupboards. Gary's parents, like most of the country, did not go into work the following day; there was a riot over bread, according to the news, outside a supermarket in town. His mother ventured out on the third day after the announcement, A-Day it was being called, to a garden centre, where she bought packets of seeds for food. She was again, ahead of the rush. Gary had helped his father dig up the newly planted lawn, creating neat rows ready for planting. He asked Gary to research green houses. Gary did not understand why, if they were all going to die what was the point?

***

His mother had got sick four months after A-Day. She casually mentioned that she had been to the university, and had been tested, then confirmed as positive. She said all that quite calmly to them after returning from another garden centre trip. This trip was to get more fertiliser, and she complained about dead dogs, rabbits and cats on the sides of the road. There was even a deer she said, the mammals were succumbing fast. Any meat for food was astronomical, and only available if you had something to barter. Even chicken couldn't easily be had, because its supply was impacted by lack of delivery drivers. By then the vegetables were growing outside the house. His father had said nothing in response, before going and needlessly checking the wind turbine. His mother had squeezed his shoulder, and then said that she would get dinner going.

Gary's mother deteriorated rapidly as the main tumour was in her lungs. The local hospital was already inundated, dealing with the normal sick and aged. The private healthcare hospital, that his parents had paid into for years, said they couldn't help anymore as all nurses and doctors were seconded under the State of Emergency rules.

CHAPTER TWELVE

Mum and Dad

Gary's father got sick a couple of weeks later; his mother by then was sleeping all the time in the lounge. She died six months after A-Day. He helped his father, who was breathing badly himself, carry her out to a grave they had dug in the woods. They wouldn't put her in a public pit despite the proclamation, ordering people to take bodies to central sites. His father had dug a second grave next to the first. They laid her in the first grave wrapped in a cloth wall-covering she had liked. They then filled in the hole. His father helped, stony faced, but struggling with the physical exertion. When they finished, they stood together and looked at the house through the trees.

"Gary, I…" his father broke down. "Put me next to her when it's my time. Promise me that," he wept.

"Yes, Dad," was all Gary could say.

Twenty days later, he did. His father had given up. Gary found the bottle of pills next to his body when he called him for breakfast. There was a note. *I'm sorry I can't go on, love Dad*, was all it said. His father had wasted away, and he was surprisingly light to carry out. Gary laid his father down, wrapped in a bed sheet, in the hole he had dug next to his mother's grave. Gary filled in that grave, the early morning frost had lifted, and he had no tears left anymore. Gary knelt and patted the earth down. He didn't want any foxes digging up the graves, although he hadn't seen any animals apart from birds for weeks, and his mother's grave had not been touched. He walked back to the empty house in the winter sunshine and passed the greenhouse they had got from the garden centre, exchanging three solar panels from his dad's factory. Money had already stopped, not officially, but people traded for what they wanted. His mother had helped set up the plants and trays.

He buried his father five days before Christmas.

His father had spent several days teaching him to drive, but he guessed he wouldn't need a test now. He could drive the automatic Lexus, and his father's smaller manual Honda. He had tried to get some fuel, but the petrol stations were closing. His father had also obtained two generators and various building supplies from a deserted builder's merchant a couple of weeks ago. His mother had looked for food wholesalers and distributors, and gone out, whilst she was able, adding to the tinned collection. One part of the house had book after book on survival techniques on the floor, along with food growing books and any other reference books she thought might help them. There was a full medical reference section, and she had raided, with another University professor, a medical store on one of her last trips out, just before the mobile phone networks packed up. His father's pills had come from the store, Gary realised; he looked at them, but shook his head. So far Gary felt fine. He had taken a test, after his father was diagnosed but, Gary was negative. The masked nurse had nodded at him. He was lucky so far; he had no expectation that he would stay that way. His father had mentioned getting a gun, but he had not done so. Gary realised now why he wanted one, maybe he would look when the time came, but so far he felt well as could be expected.

He had not seen or talked to anyone else for weeks since a cut off conversation with a great uncle who was living in Spain with no chance of returning. His grandparents on his mother's side had died years before, and his father's parents were gone before that. Both his mother and father were only children so there was no one else after his father died. Phone calls from family friends had stopped after some visits in the early days after A-Day. Gary had sent emails telling people about his mother, and then his father. There were no replies. Gary felt strange. They had both prepared him for their deaths and the crisis, with long evening discussions in the evenings as the virus spread and society slowly shut down. He felt detached. Should he be crying and sobbing? Instead, he felt strangely at peace.

***

The house had its own sound, an almost, but not quite silent, hum. It was only audible when everything was quiet, and the house was closed, like now. Gary switched on some extremely loud dub-step, he hated the genre, and only had the album because a girl he fancied said she liked it; he wondered what had happened to her. He put up with the music for fifteen minutes before he switched to one of his mother's favourite soft jazz albums. He then did weep for a while. He ate another tin of soup from the store, added to some vegetables from the garden that were in the freezer, along with the dwindling stocks of meat and fish. On Christmas Day, he listened to the Emergency Radio System, ERS, messages, eating another can of soup. He opened a bottle of wine from the cellar and silently toasted his parents, before pouring half the bottle over their graves.

The Internet connection was still occasionally working, so the router showed, even though web sites were dead, no emails, and he guessed the house was still sending data, but he doubted anyone was collecting it. He looked at the figures for generation, even today in the depths of winter it was generating three times the energy the house needed. The wind turbine was still, no wind today. There was a small weather station next to the turbine, but all the data fed into the monitoring system. He could even get a satellite weather feed from the university if he wanted; he clicked through it and got a *page not found* error message. He guessed that was gone. He read a book; he read a lot of books, all downloaded onto his e-reader and the local computer server. He checked the backups, the systems were all working correctly. He wanted to show his father the projections, before he realised he couldn't ever do that again.

***

It snowed two weeks later. Gary missed New Year, moping around the house. Unlike the previous year where the family were full of excitement planning the move from the rented house to their new home. The snow provided just a light covering, but he wanted to see what was happening. He hadn't been away from the house since his mother died. He decided to drive the Lexus into town to see if anyone was still alive. He drove out carefully, unsure on his own, and scared of damaging the car. He had just over a quarter of a tank of fuel left. On the deserted road, he drove back towards Burton. He re-tuned the radio, eventually finding one transmitting music station and then the ERS, on a.m. He passed a field where a pile of cattle and sheep were rotting. He had seen it before his mother died, limbs stuck out through the light snow covering. A huge flock of crows was feasting on the corpses. Was everybody already dead, he wondered, and why wasn't he? The ERS announced further cuts to power and water supplies in part of the country, so he guessed some people were still around. On the outskirts of town, the Paulet High School's playing field smoked. He could see army trucks, some tents, a bulldozer, and a JCB digger nearby. A few shapes could be seen in NBC kits. He thought about talking with them, so he turned off and drove over the ground. Razor wire was strung out around the perimeter.

He could see a pit with a long line of black plastic bags lying in the base. A shape waved to him to stop. "Who are you?" He was challenged through a mask, a muffled female voice.

"I'm Gary Tolman," he said."I live up the road," he vaguely pointed.

"What do you want?" She asked bluntly.

Not particularly friendly, he thought, then said, "I haven't been out for weeks. I saw you from the road. I'm looking for fuel and food."

"Are you sick?" She asked.

"No, I don't think so. My parents have died, but I'm okay."

"Good that you're not sick," she paused. "Sorry for your loss," she added quietly. "You can get a test over there." She pointed to a military green tent. "We might have some fuel for you, as well. Food, well that's easy, but test first."

"Thanks, I'm sorry, I didn't get your name?"

"Corporal Jennings, Hannah Jennings," she said.

He drove over to the tent, where an NBC suited, but not

masked, medic gave him a test without saying a word, it was quick a prick of blood on a slide, into a machine they had, some ingenious box wired up. The box went beep, and the LED green light on the front panel shone. He was okay. The medic looked at him closely. He wasn't okay. You could see the lumps in his throat. "What do you want?"

"Corporal Jennings said I might be able to get some fuel and food?"

"She did, did she? Okay, out of this tent, two tents down on the left. Food is opposite that."

Gary thanked him and walked out. In the fuel tent there were jerry cans. A suited and masked man sat at a desk checking numbers. He looked up, "Fuel?" Gary asked.

"Diesel in the Jerry cans, petrol unleaded in the Bowser, what do you need?"

"Both, thank you if I can get it?"

"No problem, where's your vehicle?"

"Outside by the medic tent," said Gary. "I'm Gary, by the way, the medic said I was green, clear."

"Smiffy, just Smiffy, you're the lucky one then, for now anyway." The man slipped off his mask, Gary could see lumps in his throat, just like his mother had on her throat.

"I haven't spoken to anyone or seen anyone for weeks," Gary explained.

"Not surprising, we see fewer every day. A lot of people hiding away, hoping. It won't help. This thing is everywhere," he said, pointing at his own throat. "Come on, I'll give you a hand." They walked back to the Lexus, "Nice car," said Smiffy.

"It was my mother's," said Gary. "She died." Smiffy nodded. There was nothing left to say. They got in the car, and Gary drove, following Smiffy's directions, to a large green tanker or Bowser as Smiffy called it. He backed up, and Smiffy took a hose from the Bowser and refuelled the Lexus. Finished, he switched off the pump.

"Don't know why they sent us unleaded. All the vehicles are diesel, so you can have it," Smiffy complained. He popped the Lexus hatch, and going behind the Bowser, returned with jerry cans. Gary followed, and they loaded four into the back. "Bring the cans back when you're done. We have more diesel as well." Gary noticed a pit filled with a large plastic rubber tank. "Crabs, I mean Air Force, set it up for us, supposed to be a central refuelling place, but very few have come. Got air fuel for choppers over there as well," he pointed across the field. "Although we haven't had a chopper for weeks. There's another dump on the other side of town. Did you want some grub? There is plenty of that in the Mess tent. It's not *Cordon Bleu*, but passable." Gary couldn't speak; he was trying to absorb what he had seen. Smiffy didn't seem to care. He continued, "Me, I've probably got a week or two before I'll be in my bed, then in one of them pits. Can't be helped," he said.

"I'm sorry," said Gary.

"Not your fault is it? Here we are." They had arrived at the Mess tent. Five trestle tables were inside the tent, with a countered kitchen at one end. Gary could hear generators outside, powering the heated lights over the food. A female was sitting down at the table nearest the counter.

"Hi Hannah," said Smiffy, "av' you met Gary?"

"Yes," said Hannah without her mask on now, "at the gate." Her hood was down, revealing a short bobbed haircut, blonde, around a tired but pretty face. Her hair was matted to her forehead.

"Grab a tray, mate," said Smiffy. Gary did and served himself some chilli with rice from the counter. "Where's chef?" Smiffy asked sitting down opposite Hannah. Gary perched on her side of the table.

"He's gone to lie down, trouble breathing he said." Hannah spoke between mouthfuls. Smiffy continued talking, explaining that there had been twelve of them deployed to the camp. It was down to ten now, and all but two, Hannah and a sergeant, who was across town at the other refuelling base, were positive. They dispensed with masks most of the time, as they hadn't had new filters for weeks anyway, and they were only supposed to last forty to fifty hours. They only put them on when someone new approached.

Two of the team were out collecting bodies. They would be back in a while.

"What about you?" Interrupted Hannah, when Smiffy finally paused for breath.

Gary explained that he lived in an isolated house, and that both his parents were gone, but he was negative or green as the medic had checked.

"The Doc told me," Hannah said. Gary presumed she meant the taciturn medic he had seen earlier. "What are you doing in town?"

"The fuel," Gary said, "some food and then a look around. I couldn't stay on my own any longer, so I think I was looking for company."

"I have to fire Pit Four," said Smiffy, "but I'm sure Hannah will keep you company." He laughed as he got up, dropping his disposable plate and cutlery into a bin.

"Bastard," Hannah said to his retreating back. "Hope you fall in and fry."

"I don't understand," said Gary.

"It doesn't matter," said Hannah. "In joke. Let's get you your food. I'm sure Chef won't mind." They cleared their trays and plates and went behind a plastic curtain that separated the dining area from the kitchen, and then more plastic to another tent crammed full of large packages of food and boxes marked as ration packs. They sorted out some stuff. They carried it back to the Lexus, loading it onto the back seat. "We have frozen meat as well," said Hannah. She walked him to a container lorry running on a generator. She swung open the door. Boxes of neatly labelled meat and fish were lined up in the container. "We're not eating as much as they expected," Hannah explained. Between them, they carried two boxes of meat and one of fish back to the car. One of the boxes was on the front. "I have to go and help on the pits now," said Hannah.

"Oh, well thanks for this, I'll bring the jerry cans back." Gary didn't want to go. Hannah had almost grey eyes he noticed. She was shorter than him by about five inches. The suit made her shapeless, but he wanted to see what shape she was.

"We'll see you then," said Hannah. She walked away towards the pits where he could see Smiffy pouring liquid from a jerry can. A lorry stopped nearby, and two men were unloading a black plastic bag. As he exited onto the road, he saw in his rear view mirrors a burst of flame and then thick black rising smoke. Gary started his drive back to the house, just as more snow fell, and by the time he was home the snow was falling heavily. He unloaded into the house. There was too much frozen stuff for the kitchen freezer, so he left it outside in the cold, for now. Maybe he would try and get another freezer from town.

The house was lovely and warm. He felt more upbeat than he had in days. He even tried to get the cinema room going. He got a blank TV signal from the satellite, but was able to get the movie server to send a signal. It looked like a dodgy cable. Well, he could get one of those as well, he didn't think the AV company would ever turn up to fix it, so he might as well give it a try. He watched a movie. By the time, he came out of the room it was nine in the evening. He wasn't hungry, and he thought the food from lunch was disagreeing with him. It was still snowing. It had to be nearly a foot deep now. He hoped the solar panels still worked. The roof was pretty steep he realised so snow should slide off. He certainly didn't want to climb up onto the roof to clear any snow. He couldn't remember if there was a ladder. He would sort out the fuel for the generators his father had wired up to the power router.

When he awoke the following morning, the snow had stopped, but there was a lot of it. He had wanted to go into town again and return the jerry cans, but in reality he wanted to see Hannah. Don't be daft he told himself, what would she see in a young immature bloke like him. A kid only eighteen, and she was what, twenty-five? He checked the house systems. All okay, the wind turbine was going in the strengthening wind. The met station showed him the wind speed and the precipitation levels. He could measure the snowfall, about eight to twelve inches if not more, he guessed looking outside. He had some breakfast, which was porridge made with water. No town today he guessed.

There was no town for another week. Three days of more intermittent snow, before a slow thaw set in. He didn't dare take the

Lexus out until he felt it was clear enough. He had no experience of driving on snow until the other day, let's face it he told himself, he barely had any experience of driving full stop. He'd passed the time sorting out food and storing stuff. He even tidied some books away. On the third day, he'd gone into his parents' room, stripped and remade the bed and cleaned up, again tidying stuff into cupboards. It would never be needed he realised. He ran the washing machine and the dishwasher as soon as the sun came out delivering a power boost. The thaw seemed to be accelerating now the sun was clearly up. He needed to sort the frozen meat out. He needed another freezer. He'd go to the Centrum One Hundred retail park in town first.

He drove into town. He thought he saw a couple of faces in houses as he drove down one street, but he couldn't be certain. He saw an army truck by the Queens Hospital entrance. The ambulances were neatly parked in a line by the side of the main hospital entrance, but he saw no one. He drove on. He turned into the Centrum One, there had been trouble there he remembered, by the supermarket. A couple of overturned burnt out cars, but otherwise it was empty. No one was around as he went to the Electrical Discount store. It was shut, but there were no shutters down. He stopped and tried the door. Locked or secured, no lights on inside. Now what? He went to the Lexus and found a tire wrench; he went back to the doors. He used the wrench to try and prize apart the main doors, no good. He supposed he might be able to bust down the doors, but he didn't want to damage the Lexus. He'd watched a character do that in a movie a while back, but it didn't look as easy in real life. There was a car maintenance shop, further along and he walked there. It was also deserted. He tried the door, it was open he realised. He pointlessly shouted, "Anyone there?" before he realised the store's door had been bent outwards. He went in. The store had been ransacked. Using the light from the windows, he realised there was stuff he could use here. There was a large car trailer on display; that was a start. He had to put it on its side to get it out the doors then rock it back level, he hooked it up, the memory of hooking up a hired trailer with jet skis flooded back. His mother laughing at his father's and his efforts to line it up. No, stop, no time for that now he told himself. He manoeuvred the trailer and hooked it up to the Lexus tow bar. He went back in the store. Power tools, tool sets, torches rechargeable ones. There were no generators or first aid kits. He found a crowbar in the tools. Spare bulbs for the Lexus and Honda, oil and oil filters, car maintenance books, brake fluid and hydraulic fluid, spark plugs, de-icer, all into a trolley then into the trailer. Cover sheets, and a plastic tarpaulin. Two fire extinguishers. He should raid a DIY store he thought.

He then moved back to the electrical store. He used the crowbar to lever open the lock, feeling it give way. He pushed and the door creaked open. There were the usual small electrical items in the front. He noticed a bread making machine. If he could get flour he thought. Stick it in the trailer he thought, no the car, he needed the space for the freezer in the trailer, although the temperature was dipping as the sun lowered. They were towards the rear. Which one, did it matter? Ex-display he saw from the price sticker. Who would honour the guarantee? He manoeuvred it to the doors and managed to squeeze it outside, sweating from the effort. Now to get it in the trailer.

"Can I help?" He jumped up shocked, spinning around. It was Hannah. "Sorry, didn't mean to startle you, we saw your car as we were going back to camp. I thought it would be you." She indicated the driver of the Army truck, sitting idling a few yards away; he hadn't heard it pull up.

"I'm, I'm… nice to see you, and yes I could do with a hand."

"Looting are you?"

"What, I didn't think, I…"

"I'm kidding, a couple of months ago we were supposed to shoot on sight, but now, what's the point?"

"I was coming to see you guys," explained Gary, as his heart rate slowed back to normal. "Honestly, I have your jerry cans."

"You better follow us back then," said Hannah. She wasn't wearing the NBC suit, but a uniform with a too bulky camouflage pattern parka coat. "Let's give you a hand with your loot first." She helped him lift the freezer onto the trailer. "What are you stealing the freezer for anyway?"

"I needed to store the meat and fish you gave me. Mine is full of vegetables," he needlessly added.

"Ah, that explains it, come on we need to go." She turned and walked back to the truck and climbed in. He followed, trying hard to remember how he should drive with the trailer behind. They drove to the small camp. Two earth mounds had replaced the dug pits, but another pit had been dug. There wasn't much of the playing field left. Gary stopped the Lexus behind the truck by the collection of tents. He swung around so he wouldn't have to reverse out. "Planning a quick getaway are we?" Hannah asked, with a smile.

"I… I don't know how to drive, reverse I mean with a trailer."

"I'm just kidding, come on let's do you a check. Doc, let's check Gary here." Gary realised that the co-driver was indeed the medic. He looked worse than before.

"Don't mind him," said Hannah. "He's always been a miserable shit, and now he can't speak, poor bastard."

Gary could have honestly said he had never met anyone like Hannah; he followed them into the medic tent. Doc pricked his finger and wiped the blood with a slide, into the machine. Ping and green.

"Lucky you, this way," said Hannah. Gary nodded his thanks to Doc, who sat down and started ticking boxes on a form with a return grunt. He was hollowed eyed and the lumps were bigger. Hannah led him to the mess tent. The lights were all off on the kitchen servers. An urn of hot water was on the side. "Coffee?" Hannah asked.

"Please, black no sugar"

"Like your men? Sorry, just kidding again, it's nice to see another face around, and one that isn't sick. Smiffy's in bed sick and Chef's gone." She had removed the Parka, which she threw across another table. She was wearing a tight olive green army sweater and green combat trousers. The top accentuated her figure. Gary felt himself begin to blush, so he looked away, although he was sure she had noticed his stare. He sat down as Hannah continued. "We haven't seen the Sarge' since you were here last, must be a week now. He's probably skipped, many have, we've heard on the comms. There's only four of us left working, and the Doc of course, but he's going…" she stopped. "We're struggling to get the bodies in the pits and the other locals left won't help. Too scared or too ill." Hannah suddenly looked vulnerable.

"I can help," said Gary suddenly. "I mean I can try and help."

"You sure? We could do with the help but it's not *nice* work?"

"I buried my parents myself," Gary said. "I can do this."

"I'm sorry," said Hannah. "I'm an orphan too. The army has been my family since I joined." They both sipped their coffee in silence for a while. "Look," Hannah said, "why not come back tomorrow, once you have unloaded your booty, and we'll see what you can do?"

"Okay, I'll see you tomorrow." Gary didn't want to be driving in the dark, which it nearly was. He got up reluctantly. He didn't really want to leave.

Hannah laughed and said, "You know your way out." He got back into the Lexus and drove away; he was sure he saw Hannah watching him go.

CHAPTER THIRTEEN

The Pits Need Help

It was dark by the time Gary got back to the house. He carefully swung the Lexus around the drive, but didn't dare start a reverse. He would have to learn how; now for the freezer. The basement had double doors that had been used to get the batteries and other heavy equipment in. He brushed off the remaining, now freezing, snow, and pulled the doors open. How would he get the freezer down? He found some cardboard. He slid the freezer off the trailer until it swung down to the ground and then he slid the freezer on the iced-over snow to the basement doors. He tipped it so that it overhung on to the cardboard trying hard not to drop it. He moved down the steps trying to keep his balance and the freezer's. Slowly he inched it down. Two steps from the bottom he lost it and it clattered the remaining six inches or so. He stood it upright and floor walked it against the wall near the wine cellar. He plugged it in; nothing happened. Had he broken it? He, of course, hadn't read the instructions. He did now. He found the master switch for some reason on the rear. He flicked it, the freezer burst into life. He went back up the stairs and retrieved the meat and fish packages, they still felt fully frozen. He doubted they would have defrosted in the shade, despite the thaw. So what, he thought, die of food poisoning instead, big deal. He loaded them into the freezer, breaking them out of the main boxes. He shut the doors on his exit and grabbed the car manuals and the few bits and bobs from the trailer. He placed them in the hall entranceway. He unhitched the trailer and walked it under the carport next to the Honda. No reverse needed he thought. He was feeling the cold. He went in the house revelling in the warmth that greeted him. He felt stiff and tired. There was a bath in the house's main bathroom, one in the master suite's bathroom, as well as baths in each of the annexes. He decided to run one. First he set his dinner to cook, a frozen lasagne he had been saving up. He stuck it in the oven. He then ran the water and took a soak; he almost dozed off before the cooker alarm echoed up the house startling him. He ate at the kitchen counter with the ERS babbling quietly in the background; he didn't think the message had changed.

The following morning he dressed for outdoor warmth. He had forgotten to drop off the jerry cans. He had used the diesel to fill the two generators. He probably needed a tank of some sort, but how and where? He thought about the *arse* landowner, remembering his father's term. Gary would go and ask if he had a tank that he could use; if he was still alive that is? First though, to the army, and Hannah; He drove out; it was icy, but there was no more snow. When he reached the camp, he drove straight in to the tents. It seemed there was no one around, and then Hannah came out of the mess tent. She had clearly been crying. "Check first," she said. No good morning in return to his greeting, then into the medical tent, but Doc was not present. Hannah pricked his finger, then the routine ping and green. "Doc's gone," she said. "He shot himself sometime last night. He's in a pit, saved us the trouble, miserable bastard that he was." She started crying. Gary didn't know what to do, so he gave her a hug. She let him hold her for a few seconds, then pulled back. "I'm okay," she sniffed, "thanks for coming, but are you ready for this?"

"Yes," he said. He hoped he was.

They went back to the mess tent. Smiffy was there, and he looked like death. "Gary mate, good of you to join our happy band, come for some burying and burning I hear." He stopped, choking with the effort of speech.

One of the other men got up, the lumps on his neck obvious, "Callaghan," he said, shaking Gary's hand, "and this is Greavesey." Gary also shook his hand.

"Pits or truck?" Callaghan asked Hannah.

"He's with me, trucks," she said.

"Okay Corp, he's yours. Don't break him," said Callaghan.

"Smiffy, don't say a damn thing," said Hannah.

"No Corporal," said Smiffy with a laugh that caused a cough.

"You should be in bed," said Greavesey in a deep Scouse accent, his first words that Gary had heard.

"Think I'll be sleeping long enough, soon enough," said Smiffy. "Come on, I'll help get the petrol ready." They got up. "Don't be too long Corp," he said, going out the tent.

Gary was lost in the fast banter between the soldiers. "Come on, we better get to the hospital." She grabbed her parka, hiding her figure that Gary was again trying not to stare at. They went out and climbed into the truck, Hannah driving. They set off, the truck revving over the ice initially before the huge tires gripped properly, and they made their way out. Gary decided that silence was the best option. Hannah leant across him and grabbed the radio. "26 mobile en-route," she said passing the handset back to Gary. There was no reply. Hannah said there hadn't been for a while, but just in case.

They arrived at the hospital and got out; there were three bodies in bags at the entrance and no one around. Hannah went back out, and she dropped the truck's tailgate down. "Come on," the bodies were each on hydraulic beds, so they wheeled them out then raised them up, Hannah showed him how, then together they pulled the bodies into the back of the truck. After all three were on board, Hannah took some black bags into the A&E reception area and dropped them on a seat. Back in the truck's cab, she took a clipboard out, and noted three in the column for that date against the Hospital A&E. There was a list with other columns per date, Gary saw, five the previous day. He looked back on the sheets as Hannah handed him the board, noting the numbers from previous days and weeks. There was another row for the hospital which had not been filled in for at least two weeks. Hannah saw him look. "We don't go anymore, it's the main entrance around the corner, no one left there, so just A&E now," she explained.

"Who?" Gary started to ask.

"Don't know, haven't seen anyone for days. There was a porter with a doctor, but no one now; someone's still alive though." They drove off. The next row on the sheet's table listed the town hall. It was the scene of his father's row at the planning committee, Gary recalled. There was a pile of six or seven bodies next to the entrance. A woman stood next to them, and another man nearby. "Oh shit," said Hannah, "it must be a kid." It was; the mother, near to death herself, had somehow got her dead child to the drop-off point. She wanted to come with them, she said. Hannah shrugged an okay. The man was a council gardener called Bill. He had been seconded to the bodies' role, now he was the only official working it seemed. He helped Gary lift the bodies into the back.

"You're that Gary aren't you?" the woman said. "Your parents have that house on TV."

"They're dead," said Gary confirming her recognition.

"Shame," she said, "I loved the look of that house. I said to Charlie only the other day…" she stopped. Who was Charlie? Gary had no idea, but he suspected that Charlie was no longer around.

Hannah said, "We better get going," and unsympathetically added, "you'll have to ride in the back I'm afraid."

"I will," said the woman climbing up beside her child and the other bodies.

"I don't have all the names," said the gardener, Bill, handing over a piece of paper.

"I don't think it matters anymore," said Hannah. They drove off going to three other pick up points, no bodies. "Fewer, every day," said Hannah. "I wish that was good news, but it probably means they are dead in their houses or too sick to bring out the other ones."

"How long have you been doing this here?" Gary asked.

"Since three days after A-Day. We set up the camp for medical originally, then after the proclamation, we had the pits. We'd already started anyway, digging them I mean, and the bags had been issued."

"How many, I mean how many have you buried?"

"Thousands, I don't know the total, the Sarge' was keeping our count, and sending it up to HQ. Thousands, it must be thousands"

"How do you, how have you, I mean?" Gary didn't know what, or how to ask.

"We do, we just do." They rode back in silence.

They turned into the camp and drove straight to the pits. Callaghan and Greavesey were waiting, no sign of Smiffy. Gary and Hannah climbed out, and then helped the woman down from the back.

"Another one," said Callaghan. "Should we?"

"Yes," said Hannah, interrupting before Callaghan could finish. They unloaded the bodies gently laying them into the pit, when it came to the child the mother started wailing, then gasping for air. Hannah turned to Gary and firmly said, "Come with me." It was an order more than a request; she walked off back towards the tents taking his arm. In the mess tent, she loudly made coffee. Gary thought he heard a small bang from the pits, but he couldn't be sure. A few minutes later, Callaghan and Greavesey walked in, nothing was said. Gary looked at the stern faces and decided to say nothing. They had a coffee or tea. Then back out to the pits. There was one more empty pit, but the other one was just about full. Gary noticed the line of black plastic bagged bodies packed tightly in the trench.

"Petrol?" Hannah said. Gary could smell it.

"Smiffy did it, Corp," said Greavesey.

"OK, let it burn," said Hannah. She stepped back with Gary from the pit, as did Callaghan.

Greavesey took out a lighter. "God bless," he said, throwing the lighter into the pit. It instantly flared and raced around the bags and bodies, Gary could feel the heat. They all stepped back further. They were upwind as the black smoke began to rise.

"We'll fill it in tomorrow," said Hannah, "that's enough for today." They walked back to the tent in silence.

Greavesey said, "I'll check on Smiffy."

Callaghan said, "I'm going for a kip."

"What about this house on TV?" Hannah asked.

"My parents' house was featured in a documentary last year before, before all this," Gary waived his hand around.

"Why?"

"It's an eco-house, special construction and so on."

"Show me it," said Hannah. "I'll follow you in a rover." She finished walking away. He heard a shout from her to Callaghan, "I'm going to Gary's house for a while." Gary didn't hear a reply.

Gary drove the Lexus back to the house with Hannah following behind in the rover. He pulled up and pressed the gate remote control transmitter in the Lexus, then they both drove through, the gate would shut automatically behind. He pulled around the bend and up the drive approach, before swinging round in front of the house. Hannah pulled up behind him. She climbed out with a whistle, "Jesus Christ, this is some place you have here; keeping this quiet?"

"No I…"

"Gary I'm pulling your leg, it's very nice. Aren't you going to invite me in?"

"Sorry, come on in." Gary triggered the door lock, using his access code.

"Wow its warm and you have electric. Where are the generators?" She quickly pulled her military coat off. Gary took it and hung it in the closet next to the front door, along with his own thick ski jacket.

Gary explained the solar, wind power and the water system. Hannah looked stunned. "You still have running water, hot water, can I have a shower?" She was joking, or was she? Gary tried not to stare at her.

"You can have a bath if you like?"

"You're kidding, right?"

"No, seriously, would you like a bath?"

She looked at him and smiled, "In a minute, show me round first, tell me about this place." Gary did. He talked about the project, to find and build the house, and how it was self-sufficient for power, water even for some food. They ended up in the basement. "Ahh, here are the stolen goods," said Hannah, "and a cellar; any good wine?" She could see over a thousand bottles she estimated.

"My mother collected it," said Gary. "We can have some if you like?"

"That would be nice, choose a bottle or two. Can you cook?"

"A bit."

"Why don't you use some of the fish we gave you, and cook something while I have that bath? I presume you have a washing machine and dryer that work as well?"

"Yes, they're in the utility area by the kitchen."

"Great, I can get this stuff properly clean and dry. Now show me this bath."

He only stopped to get some fish from the freezer, and collect two bottles of Chablis from the cellar, and then they went back up to the house. He put the wine in the fridge although it was already chilled from the cellar. He showed Hannah the washing machine and dryer.

"I need a dressing gown whilst my clothes wash and dry?"

"This way," he showed Hannah up the stairs and into the master suite. He showed her the bath. She turned on the taps; steaming water ran through almost immediately, he showed her bubble bath and salts from his mother's collection. He then collected a robe from the dressing area wardrobe. "This was my mothers," he said. "I hope it's okay."

"It's fine, thank you," said Hannah, taking off the olive green sweater to reveal an olive green stretch top. "You're not staying to watch, so stop gawping," she said. "Go on, get dinner, I'm hungry"

As Gary walked out, she deliberately took off the green stretch top, making sure he saw her black bra covered chest and back, before he got out the door. He went down to the kitchen and was washing his hands when she walked through with a pile of clothes to the washing machine. She didn't say a word.

When she walked back, the dressing gown clinging to her, she said, "Wine?"

"Sorry," he opened the bottle and poured a glass, handing it to her.

"How long for dinner?"

"Er, forty minutes, or so."

"Okay, get on with it then." She disappeared with a smile.

He prepared the food, home grown vegetables with grilled fish. He dug out some Thai spices and light soy sauce. It was a dish his mother normally prepared with fresh sea bass; he would try with frozen cod, which he defrosted in the microwave. He poured himself a glass of wine, selected his mother's soft jazz, and tried to concentrate on the dinner preparation. He laid three places at the dining table before he remembered that it was just two. He had been eating on his lap, or at the counter. He tried to find the candles, but thought that was going too far. He dimmed the house lights onto one of the pre-sets instead. He realised the music was playing throughout the house. He hoped she liked it.

He was finishing grilling the fish when she walked back in, her hair was damp; she grabbed the bottle and poured herself another glass. "I couldn't find a dryer," she said, rubbing her damp hair. "I didn't want to rummage around."

"I can get one for you?"

"No, that's okay it can dry naturally. Is the food ready? It smells terrific."

"Yes, take a seat, I'll bring it over." He finished grilling, serving the vegetables, rice and fish onto two plates, and carried them to the table, then went back for the wine. He sat, they ate hungrily; he tried not to stare as the dressing gown slowly gaped more and more open. She asked about the house. The gown gaped in shadow. The bottle finished, he was a bit tipsy.

"The time, I ought to be going," she said.

"But your clothes, they're not dried, you can't…"

"I'm kidding, come with me," she said quietly. He followed her up the stairs, and into the master bedroom. The sheets were turned down. "Warning, I tested positive this morning, I don't want you to catch it, I…" she finally stopped.

"I don't care," he said, "I haven't done this before, I never, I mean, I suppose, I didn't get the chance."

"You're kidding, right? A good looking lad like you must have had plenty of girlfriends?" She realised he wasn't kidding. "I'm sorry, I didn't mean to tease. Well, this will be…" she struggled for the right word, "… nice."

"I don't want to do anything wrong," Gary's hands were shaking.

"You won't, don't worry," said Hannah. She moved close to him and then kissed him. He slipped his hands down between them and undid the gown's belt, peeling it off her shoulders. She lifted his shirt from him, undid his jeans, and pulled down his boxers; she then pushed him back slightly and looked him up and down. "Just what I imagined," she said. "Come on." She took his hand and pulled him into his parents' bed.

"What about, er, contraception?" He asked.

"Don't be daft," she said pulling him to her.

The following morning she was again in his mother's gown when he woke up. Drizzle was falling outside the windows. "You're nearly out of coffee," she said, handing him a cup, whilst perching on the side of the bed.

"Hannah…" he started to say something.

"Don't," she said, "don't go all soppy on me, look I have the virus. I'll have a couple of months if I'm lucky; let's just make the most of it."

"But?"

"At this point you are supposed to pull me back into bed and shag me senseless," she said.

"I…"

"Oh for goodness sake," she said, pulling the gown off herself and pushing him back. He would learn she thought.

They had porridge for breakfast and then after a discussion about whether she would return to the house that evening, she retrieved her dried clothes. She had a shower as did he, then, they both got in the Landrover and drove back to the camp. On the way, Gary thought about what had happened.

"The woman, yesterday?"

"We offer them a way out. If they want it, and she wasn't the first."

"How?"

She stopped the rover, in the middle of the deserted wet road. "You really want to know?"

"Yes"

"We offer them a pistol, if they can't do it themselves, we do it for them," she said quietly.

"Have you?"

"Yes, I'm not proud of it, but they want our help. I never thought I would end up doing this. Look at what has happened to us all. I was in Helmand a few years ago. I thought that was mad, this is, this is…" She stopped, she was staring out the window of the rover.

"We had better get going," said Gary, feeling useless and hopeless.

"Yes, we had." Hannah shook her head, "Pull yourself together girl," she mumbled. She put the Landrover in gear, and they drove onwards and into the camp. Smoke still smouldered from the pit they had fired the day before. They found Callaghan and Greavesey in the mess tent.

"Look who's here," said Callaghan with a smile.

"No lip from you," said Hannah, but returning the smile. "How's Smiffy?"

"He's worse," said Greavesey, "he hasn't eaten anything either."

"I'll see him before we go out, we'll all do the trucks today I think," she said, walking out to see Smiffy.

Gary stood looking lost. "Well, did you?" Callaghan asked, clapping him on the back.

"Did I, what?" Gary said, going red and knowing full well what they meant.

"Yep he did," said Greavesey laughing.

"Well done mate," said Callaghan, "she wanted that and we all know that what the corporal wants..."

"…The corporal gets," joined in Greavesey. "Come on Gary son, we're only winding you up, let's go and get the trucks ready."

Gary spluttered, but said nothing, following the men out the tent and to the trucks. A few minutes later, Hannah joined them, then they loaded up, with Gary again in the cab with Hannah, and Callaghan and Greavesey in the truck behind. "Give you stick, did they?" Hannah asked as she reached for the radio. "26 mobile en-route," she broadcast. Gary just nodded at her.

"27 mobile en-route," the radio burst in response, making Gary jump.

"Waste of time probably," said Hannah. "Don't worry about them. They're good guys."

"It was fine, they just seemed to know, we had, you know."

"It's like that, in our job. Everyone knows everything about you; you get used to it."

They pulled into the hospital A&E; the reception was empty. The four of them stood looking around the darkened room. "The power's gone," said Greavesey, "what do you want to do?" He looked at Hannah.

"Try and find the genny, get some light then I suppose we search," she replied reluctantly.

"Won't help," said Callaghan.

"I know," said Hannah, "but let's not leave anyone behind. Whoever was doing the bodies yesterday deserves that."

"Okay, Corp," said Callaghan, "come on Greavesey let's try and find this bloody generator." They walked back out.

"There are some torches in the cab, Gary, get them."

"Yes, Corp," said Gary.

"Sorry," she put her hand to his cheek and gave him a smile. "Gary, please get me the torches."

"It's all right," Gary replied, "I understand, back in a moment." Gary went to the cab, and he found the torches in a box behind the seats, they were heavy duty ones. He walked back in. Hannah, was using a pencil torch in the gloom reading the hospital map.

"We went round here before, so I know where to go, just checking though," she said. He flicked on the torch's more powerful beam. "Let's start on the top floor, furthest away and work back down, there should be light on the wards." Just then the lights flickered, and then lit the room. A buzz of machinery and even heating began. Callaghan and Greavesey returned to a *well done*. They then started up the stairs, heading for the far end of the building.

It took three hours to go through the hospital, not that they were that thorough. The smell, and flies buzzing, told them where the bodies that hadn't been recovered lay in unmade beds, or on trolleys. One had an empty IV still attached to the decaying wrist. They ended up using the lifts and porters' trolleys. They had twenty-five by the time they were finished. They all refused to go into the maternity ward until Gary said, trying to demonstrate his bravery, that he would go, and then, Callaghan and Greavesey said they would join him.

Hannah reluctantly said, "Okay," but all three of the men said she did not have to. There were no bodies in the ward, just dead flowers, and fading cards. They were all relieved and felt a bit silly to have initially declined to go in. Callaghan found the body of a porter lying on his own trolley, in a corridor, with a single word note on his chest just saying, *sorry.*

"Why do they always apologise?" Greavesey asked. "I mean it's not their fault is it? It's not anyone's fault. It just is, shit happens! Let's get the fuck out of here." Greavesey stomped off back to the main entrance.

They spent the next thirty minutes, loading the bodies onto trolleys then down and onto the trucks. "I'll switch off the genny, no point running it now," said Callaghan. "We'll take our lot back to camp if you do the other stops," he finished.

"Thanks Cal," said Hannah. "Come on, Gary, let's get over to the Council." They drove in silence. As they pulled up outside the council building, a small group emerged, three adults and one child stood to one side of the council gardener. A pile of bodies in black bags was with them. "Oh shit!" Hannah said. "What now?" They jumped down, and, with the gardener, began loading the bodies.

"I don't think there's anyone else left," said a man. "I've got it bad already, not long I suppose, out of food as well, same as this lot. I knocked on doors as I came up. The girl over there hasn't any lumps, she says." He indicated a painfully thin girl of about six or seven with tangled brown hair, dressed in a scruffy anorak, which was too small for her, shivering in the cold. "She's been living on rainwater and rice. Her mum's in one of them bags. Others are like me. Can we get some food and warmth?" The man croaked, "Power has been off for weeks," he finished with a wheeze grabbing the side of the lorry for support.

"You'll have to get in the back, sorry," said Hannah. "What about you?" Hannah asked the council worker.

"I'll stay another day or so," he said. "I've still got some of your rations and gas canisters. See you soon." He moved back into the council building. The wind was picking up, Gary shivered.

"Come on," said Hannah, "let's check the other drops and get back." Gary helped the others get in the back of the truck.

They set off and drove around, but there were no more bodies. Gary filled in the checklist on the clipboard. They arrived back at the camp, and Hannah told the survivors to go into the mess tent and get themselves some food and coffee. Hannah then drove the truck over to the pits where Callaghan and Greavesey were unloading.

"Got quite a few more in the back," Hannah explained, "and some live ones in the mess tent. Gary stay here and help, I'll go and test that girl and make sure they get some food. Are there Parkas in the supply ISO?" Hannah asked Callaghan.

"Should be, behind the waterproofs, I think I saw a box." Hannah walked back towards the tents.

Gary started helping lift the bodies from the trucks into the pits. It took another hour, and despite the nature of the work, Gary was hungry after they finished. There was plenty of room in the pit. They hopped into the trucks with Callaghan and Greavesey, driving the two vehicles back to the camp tents. "I'll teach you how to drive it, after some food, or tomorrow," said Greavesey, as Gary sat next to him. They entered the mess tent. There was a pleasant smell coming from the kitchen, and the group sat around one of the tables. Hannah came back in.

"Okay?" she asked Gary. "I need to do your check." He followed her back out and into the medic tent. "Smiffy's unconscious," she explained, pricking his finger. Ping went the machine and green. "Only one now," she said.

"The girl?" Gary asked.

Hannah shook her head, "She's red, so it's just you now," she said. "I don't know why, but I'm glad you are." She gave him a kiss after checking that no one was watching. They walked back into the mess tent. Gary looked at the girl who was smiling, and eating what looked like a hot dog sausage in a bun. A haggard looking woman said she had found some frozen buns in a freezer and the hot dogs in a tin. They were okay, so they all had one. Hannah said, "You can all find a place to sleep, there are plenty of beds. The tents have heaters, and there are spare clothes around so help yourselves."

"Where's my mum gone?" The little girl asked sweetly.

"She's gone love, you know that," said the woman who had cooked the hot dogs.

"I know she's dead, everyone is," said the girl. "I just wanted to know where she is."

"She's out the back with the others," said Callaghan, waving in the general direction of the pits.

"Will you burn her?"

"Don't worry about that," said Hannah. "Would you like some more food?" The girl nodded, and so Gary fetched it.

One of the others coughed. It was the other man who had knocked on the house doors. He was much older; he asked, "Any pain killers?"

"I'll get some," said Greavesey. He returned a few minutes later with a box of something. It was coded not named. "Here," he said handing two pills over. "Anyone else?" All the survivors had two, except the girl, who was eating another hot dog, "Poor kid was starving," Greavesey remarked. It was getting dark.

"I should be getting back," said Gary.

"Give me a couple of minutes," said Hannah. "I'll just check Smiffy again." Gary was relieved. He hadn't wanted to ask if she would return, despite their discussion that morning. He smiled at her. Callaghan gave Gary a friendly smirk, before escorting two others to a tent next door.

Hannah returned, looking upset. "Still unconscious," she said to Greavesey. "We'll see you in the morning."

"Okay," he said, "have fun," another smirk ignored by Hannah as she put her parka back on.

"Where are you going?" The girl asked, standing up and going up to Hannah.

Hannah dropped down on one knee. "We're going to Gary's house, love."

"I want to come," the girl said.

"I don't know… um, Gary?"

"Yes, if she wants, and you're okay about it," said Gary, wanting to do the right thing.

"All right, come on then," said Hannah. "Put your coat on, it's cold out." Hannah helped the girl put her dirty anorak on. It was too small for her, and the military Farkas were too big. Another thing to sort out, thought Hannah, kids clothes. They left with polite good nights to the remaining adults and got in the rover. The girl sat in the middle. "What's your name?" Hannah asked.

"Sarah," she replied, "Sarah Matthews, and I live at 12 Bloomfield Drive. Do I live there now?"

"I'm Hannah, Sarah, and this is Gary." She ignored the second question.

"I know he's Gary, silly, we're going to his house aren't we; will I live there now?"

"I must be mad," said Hannah. "Kids, who'd have 'em?" she said to Gary. "Let's see how we get on, Sarah."

Sarah was almost asleep when they reached the house; Gary had to get out to open the gate manually, using the access code, whilst Hannah drove through. He would have to find the spare remote for the gate, he thought. They pulled up outside. Hannah carried Sarah into the house after Gary opened the door. "Get some more wine," she said. "I'll give her a bath; do you have a t-shirt she can wear, or something, whilst I wash her clothes?"

"Yes, in my bedroom."

"Your bedroom?"

"Yes, down the hall from where we were last night," he stopped and got a smile from Hannah. "You'll see the computers in my study."

Hannah carried the half asleep, Sarah up the stairs; Gary went down to the basement and collected another bottle. He returned to find Hannah sitting at the kitchen counter. "She's splashing away in some bubbles." Hannah collected a wine glass, after Gary poured it. "Pop up in a minute," said Hannah.

Gary sipped his wine, as he checked the house readings on the kitchen terminal. He checked the CCTV and saw on one of the internal views, Hannah carrying Sarah down the corridor into his room wrapped in a big towel. Gary waited then walked up the stairs. Hannah had put Sarah in Gary's double bed; she looked tiny in there. He could see she was wearing one of his far too large T-Shirts. The girl was already falling asleep. Gary stood in the doorway, and watched her drift off. Then Hannah got up and pushed him into the corridor. She walked back to the master suite bathroom and pulled the plug, she then rinsed the bath before replacing the plug and starting to fill it again. She grabbed the pile of dirty clothes. "When I come back you better be in that bath, you stink," she said walking out. Gary undressed to his boxers and carried his clothes to the clothes basket in his study. He then walked back to the master bedroom, stripped his boxers off, and climbed in the near scalding bath. Hannah had used bath salts not perfumed bubbles, he noticed. He was leaning back with his eyes closed, when he heard a "Shift, up," and Hannah was climbing in with him. They sloshed the water as they adjusted positions finally settling on him with his back to one end and her with her back to him. "Check me for lumps," she said, "seriously," deflecting his hands off her breasts where they had immediately wandered. Gary ran his fingers over her back; whilst Hannah checked her legs and front, he then checked her neck, eliciting a "That's nice," as he stroked the nape. She then took his hands. "Now you can check here," she pulled his hands onto her breasts. They spilled quite a bit of water.

They spent the evening in dressing gowns, cuddled together on a sofa watching light snow meander down outside, listening to a random selection of soft genre music on the AV system. "I checked Sarah for lumps," said Hannah, after a silence. "She doesn't have any, yet anyway."

"Neither do you," said Gary moving his hands onto her.

"You've already checked," said Hannah, but she didn't move his hands. "It doesn't mean we don't have them inside, we're both positive, and you know what that means."

"I know; I know what will happen, do we have to talk about

it?"

"Yes, we do. Gary listen," she sat up breaking the contact and turned to face him. "I need you to promise me you will do the right things when the time comes. No, don't say anything now. Don't go all soppy on me. We've had one night, and a nice bath and I'm your first proper, well, girlfriend. I need you to promise me that you won't put me in the pit, and you'll take care of Sarah as well."

"I, I promise, but you'll get better, I'm sure."

"No, Gary, I won't, but thanks for saying that. Come on, take me to bed I need to continue your training," she laughed instantly breaking the sombre mood. She undid the belt of her dressing gown letting it fall onto her arms. She wriggled suggestively up the stairs, and he followed as quickly as he could after he put his wine glass down.

Gary awoke to screaming. Hannah was already moving. It was Sarah, screaming for her mummy. Hannah was already calming her when Gary arrived and wrapped Hannah in the dressing gown. "It's just a nightmare," said Hannah, trying to calm Sarah, "you're safe here." The girl slowly quietened and, after about ten minutes, was back asleep. They returned to bed. Hannah said, "I had a younger sister, she died years ago, before this." She broke down and cried. Gary hugged her until she stopped, then they returned to bed; Gary slipped an arm around Hannah as she slept.

Gary awoke, to a poke in the chest; Sarah stood looking at him, the t-shirt was almost down to her ankles. Hannah stirred next to him; it was just getting light, helped by a layer of snow on the ground. "Are you going to be my mummy and daddy now?" Sarah asked. Hannah was waking up quickly; she pulled on the dressing gown and came around the bed.

"You must be hungry, Sarah, let's get some food shall we." Some questions are better left unanswered. "Then we can get your clothes from the dryer."

After breakfast they all went in the rover back to the camp. The snow was melting in the brightening morning, with occasional sunshine breaking through. They passed the corpse of a dog on the way. "We had a dog," said Sarah. "He died."

They arrived at the camp. Callaghan met them; one look at his face and Hannah said, "Smiffy?"

"Yep, poor bastard, we were waiting for you before we took him out."

"Thanks," said Hannah. "We can take him over together."

The other survivors were milling around, the coughing man followed them as they went to Smiffy's tent. Greavesey was there. Smiffy was already in an unsealed bag. Hannah, went up and looked at his grey face, then closed and sealed the flap. "Come on," she said. Gary stepped forward and, with Callaghan, they carried his body out to the rover. Then the small party walked and drove to the pit. The man eventually arrived wheezing and whispered something to Callaghan. Gary couldn't hear what.

Callaghan nodded at the man and just said, "Wait."

"Is my mum in there?" Sarah said. No one had realised she had come with them.

"Yes, love," said Hannah holding her hand.

"Okay," said Sarah thoughtfully, then after a brief pause she asked, "Are there hot dogs left?"

"I'll take you," Gary said. He took Sarah's hand from Hannah and started walking her back to the mess tent. He looked over his shoulder as Callaghan and Greavesey lowered Smiffy into the pit, watched by the man and Hannah. He carried on walking; when he looked back again only Callaghan, Hannah and Greavesey remained outside the pit. As they entered the mess tent to find the other two women, drinking tea, Gary heard what he now recognised was a single shot. Both women looked up but, Gary covered their questioning looks with a, "Morning, is there more tea?"

Five minutes later, the others returned, the man wasn't mentioned. Hannah said, "We'll go on the route, we need to get some clothes for Sarah and some other stuff. I guess we all could do with some clothes and things. There's a big clothes store in the retail park, I think."

"The High Street has an outdoor camping shop. They'll

have clothes for her as well," said one of the women.

The other said, "I'll have a lie down if you don't mind, not feeling too good. You lot go, I'll be all right on my own. I'll make some lunch. I can rustle up a good stew, I should think, before I lie down."

"Right," said Hannah, "let's just take rovers, I don't think we'll need the trucks."

They climbed up Hannah, Gary and Sarah in one rover, with Callaghan driving next to the woman, Greavesey hopped in the back of the other rover. "30 mobile en-route," Hannah broadcast.

"31, likewise," came the reply.

They went to the High Street first. Many of the shops were open and had been looted, including the outdoor fitters, but when they went inside, most of the clothes racks remained. There was a stink coming from the back, two dogs, and a fox carcass were rotting. They hurriedly grabbed a couple of ski jackets for Sarah and helped themselves to gloves hats and anything else they thought of, before guiding Sarah out of the shop. Hannah returned and pushed past the dogs and fox to the rear storeroom, then she had to go back to the Landrover to grab a torch. Back in the storeroom with Callaghan she found what she was looking for, water sterilisation tablets, gas cookers, and canister's and branded mountaineering ration packs. Hannah, Callaghan, and Gary then carried the boxes out, filling the rear of the rovers. They then travelled across town via the council building. The gardener was not around. Out to the retail park, they passed the scene of Gary's previous excursion. They forced open the entrance, to the clothing store. It was almost untouched, with racks of clothes that would never be worn. The woman, Hannah and Sarah, went in search of children's, and women's clothes, whilst Callaghan, Greavesey, and Gary browsed around the men's section. Gary took a couple of packs of boxers and some socks from a shelf. The other two didn't bother.

Callaghan said, "Gary, listen mate, need to ask you something?"

"What?" Gary said, concerned.

"Me and Greavesey are probably going to split soon, but we need to know Hannah will be okay? She's in charge, but that doesn't mean much anymore. With you here to take care of her when she gets sick, we can leave and head back south, see what's happened to my own lot."

"Now, you're leaving now? But you two are positive as well," Gary whispered. His concern was obvious.

"No, not yet, we'll help with the others. The two women won't last long, we reckon, so we'll go after that. Don't think there are many left in the town. You're still green; so you're okay, for quite a while, we reckon'. When I… when we, get properly sick, well Mr. 9 mm will…will take care of that." He tapped his Parka pocket. Gary hadn't realised he was armed. "So what do you think?"

"I, I… yes, of course, whatever you want, I'll try and look after her."

"You won't put her in the pit will you. She hates it, she hides it but…"

"Hides what?" Hannah said, approaching with the others. They were pushing a trolley stacked with stuff, much of it in girly pink, Gary noticed.

"Nothing," said Callaghan, "just thinking about getting a pair of chinos for the dance on Saturday."

Hannah thought about demanding to know what they had been saying, but thought better of it. "Let's get this stuff back," she said.

"We have to pay," said Sarah.

"No, we don't love," said the woman. "We've already paid plenty."

They drove back to the camp. When they entered they could smell the stew. They went in search of the woman they had left behind. They found her half way to the pits, collapsed and gone. The woman took Sarah back to the tent, whilst Hannah, watched as Callaghan, Greavesey, and Gary carried the body to the edge of the pits, got a bag from one of the trucks, and then gently lowered her down.

"She said she wanted to lie down. She knew, when she sent us out," said Hannah.

"Yes, Corp," said Greavesey, "she knew."

They went back to the tent, but no one felt like eating. "Look," said Gary, "why don't we go to my house, I have spare bedrooms and power and showers and so on."

"That's very nice young man, are you sure your parents won't mind?"

"It's Gary, my parents are gone, Mrs?"

"Mrs. Brown, but please call me Doris, I should have said yesterday, before that poor lady. I didn't even know her name… Well I'll get the stew."

The six of them once again climbed into the rovers, having checked that the generators were topped up, and the armoury was secure. Callaghan emerged from there with an SA80 rifle, two pistols, and several boxes of ammunition. "Don't suppose you have these?" Gary was asked.

"No, I don't know how to shoot either."

"It's okay, Corp will teach you, it's her proper job after all." Hannah just smiled. Callaghan carried them into his rover.

As they arrived at the house, the others gave suitable expressions, "Jesus Christ," from Callaghan.

"Must be a rich bastard," from Greavesey.

"I thought I saw this house on TV," came from Doris.

"There are bathrooms and showers upstairs," said Gary, proud of the impact the house had on others, "and the two annexes have rooms and bathrooms. There's the master bedroom and two others up there plus…."

"They can't have my room," said Sarah.

"Sarah has my old room," explained Gary.

"I can't manage the stairs," said Doris. "I'll take an annexe. Is there a bath in there as well? You can tell me all about the house after, now someone get the stew before it gets cold, and put it in the kitchen on a low heat."

"We'll leave upstairs to you if the other annexe is okay?" Callaghan indicated the stairs.

"There's only one bed there," Gary explained.

"You are an innocent," said Hannah laughing. "They're together, I thought you realised."

"Well, bless my soul," said Doris. "Each to his own, I suppose. Hannah dear could you help me in with my things from the car." Hannah did. Gary carried the stew into the kitchen. He could hear Callaghan and Greavesey laughing; well that's a turn up he thought. He put the stew pot on the electric hob and stuck it on a low heat.

Callaghan went back out to the rover and came back in carrying the weapons. "You need to put these somewhere safe along with the ammo, although we carry our pistols, as you know."

"The basement for now, I guess. It's back behind you through the white door, and down the steps. There are shelves there."

"Noticed your gate and door security on codes and remotes, CCTV I presume?"

"Yes, inside in the corridors, and outside. It covers the gate, front entrance and rear. Not that we have many callers. No one but you guys for months."

"I know, but you can never be too careful, which is why we have these," he waved the weapons. "I'll stick them downstairs." Callaghan went down. He returned a few minutes later with a couple of bottles of red. "Grabbed these, hope that's okay? I figured we could have them with dinner."

"Thanks, that's great, it will save me getting them." Callaghan strode off to the Annexe. Gary started preparing the vegetables. Sarah found him down there as she walked in wearing a pink outfit, with the labels still hanging out. The top was on back to front.

"What are you doing?"

"I'm getting dinner," Gary said.

"Is this a den?" She was looking at the basement door.

"No, that's the basement, where we keep the equipment and so on. You need to ask before you go down." Gary would need to get a lock; the house was not child friendly.

Hannah arrived, smiling at them both. "Let's sort your outfit out," Hannah said, picking up Sarah. "You set the table," she said to Gary. She then walked away from the kitchen and back up the stairs, "Why don't you show me your outfits," Gary heard her say.

Doris came in. "This house is lovely. I'm going to have a bath, and then I'll be back to help with dinner, love, is that okay?" Gary felt that he had lost control, but he liked having everyone around.

Callaghan and Greavesey strode back into the kitchen. "Hey mate," said Greavesey, "didn't mean to embarrass you, thought you realised, given we weren't…" He stopped with a look from Callaghan.

"No, *I'm sorry*, I just hadn't realised and I'm not thinking straight, I mean properly." Gary caught his own implication. "I mean with Hannah and…"

"She turns heads that one," said Callaghan, smiling at Gary's embarrassment.

"Yes… I'll open the wine and let it breath," said Gary, trying to change the subject.

"I'll grab a shower first then," said Callaghan, going back towards the other annexe.

Greavesey smiled at his back. "Need a hand?"

"You can help chop veggies, they're in the freezer over there." They discussed how Gary grew his own vegetables, Gary pointing out the vegetable patch on what used to be the back lawn. They chopped, for the most part in silence. Gary laid out six places and put china plates on warm. It was dusk and the house auto lighting system sparked into life. Hannah came back in wearing jeans and a t-shirt rather than uniform, with Sarah now correctly dressed in the pink outfit without the labels.

"Is there TV?" Sarah asked.

"There are some kids movies on the system I think," said Gary, he broke off from chopping and peeling, to fiddle with one of the controllers. He showed Sarah to a seat in front of one of the TVs. It burst into life with one of the Toy Story films.

"Great," said Sarah, "I love Woodie."

"So do I," said Callaghan. He was wrapped in a towel around his waist. "I couldn't trouble you for some clothes, could I Gary? Should have gotten some in that store." There was a bulge in his neck, which he tried to hide with one hand.

"I don't think mine will fit you, they may Greavesey, I think my dad's might. It's this way." Greavesey and Callaghan followed him up the stairs. He opened his room's wardrobe, and said to Greavesey, "Help yourself, there's underwear and so on in the drawers." He did the same in the Master bedroom with his father's wardrobe. There were some new women's clothes scattered on the bed.

"Thanks mate," he said.

Gary left him to it, "Jeans, shirt and boxers, is that okay?" Greavesey asked, following him down the stairs.

"Yes, that's fine, I can always get some more. I'll put your uniforms in the washer if you want?"

"Thanks, Gary, I mean it, for everything, your help and so on, you'd do all right in the job, you know." Gary took that as a worthy complement. "Better grab a shower if that bastard hasn't used all the water."

Doris was sitting with Sarah watching Toy Story. She had also changed into fresh clothes, and the blouse she wore showed the bulges in her neck. Gary turned away and went into the kitchen area. Hannah was dropping vegetables into a pan. She came up to him put her arms around his neck and kissed him.

"Hey you two get a room," said Callaghan, coming back

into the kitchen wearing chinos and a shirt.

"We will," said Hannah breaking away. "Now pour me a glass of what I'm sure will be another delicious bottle of wine, then get your gear and put it in the washer through there," she pointed. "Get Greavesey's as well, it stinks."

"Yes, Corporal, three bags full Corporal, anything else Corporal?" Callaghan said pouring some wine.

"You can f…" Hannah stopped as Sarah stood in front of her. Callaghan just smiled and left to get the washing. "What's the matter Sarah?"

"My neck hurts, can I get a drink?" Gary gave Hannah a look.

"There's some lemonade in the pantry cupboard on the left, I think," said Gary.

They delayed the food, by which time they were all sitting with Sarah watching Toy Story. They then all adjourned to the dining table, Sarah sitting between Hannah and Gary. Then the questions started about the house, just as Hannah had asked the previous day. There was no dessert, which disappointed Sarah, but she was looking tired, so Hannah took her up to bed, promising to read her a story, or make one up as there were no children's books as far as Gary could recall. Doris asked for some painkillers, and Callaghan said he had some. He went and retrieved them and Doris took them with a sip of wine, "Well that will send me off to sleep, the last lot did. I'll say good night." She tottered, a little unsteadily, off towards her annexe as Hannah came back down.

"Out like a light," said Hannah. They sat chatting for another hour.

"I'm looking forward to a proper bed," said Greavesey, stretching.

"Clear off, you two, and keep the noise down," she laughed.

"What about you?" Callaghan said. Gary felt warm being included in their chatter. The two men rose and walked off to the annex, taking the remains of the bottle and their glasses with them.

Gary looked at Hannah, "I've something to show you," she

said. "Come on." She started walking up the stairs, "Come on, I won't bite, much." Gary followed her into the master bedroom. She shut the door. "Teeth brush first," she said. They did, in the adjacent sinks in the en-suite. "Now strip to your boxers," she said. He did as he was told. She told him to sit on the bed. She casually pulled off her t-shirt, revealing a lacy red bra. Then she lowered her jeans, revealing a matching pair of panties. She turned round in a spin. "You like them?"

"Ye'… yes," he stammered.

"You better take them off me then," she said, falling on top of him.

There was screaming and shouting as Gary woke from a deep sleep, for the second night running. He fought disorientation before realising it was Sarah screaming. He got up and raced to her room, just as Greavesey and Callaghan, both naked, came running up the stairs, both holding pistols ready for a fight. "It's okay, darling," said Hannah, appearing whilst tying her dressing gown. She went to comfort Sarah. "Guys you might want to put some clothes on, you're scaring Sarah." Gary looked at the other two. They all blushed. Callaghan and Greavesey turned and walked back down the stairs. Gary returned to the bedroom. Hannah came back in after ten minutes and climbed back into bed, snuggling up to Gary. "That was pretty funny actually, especially the looks on your faces when you realised you were all naked; great views."

The following morning, Hannah was up first and in the kitchen with Sarah, when Gary walked in. Hannah was in jeans again, this time with a sweater. "I'm taking a day off," she said.

"No problem," said Gary. Callaghan and Greavesey marched into the kitchen, dressed in dry, freshly pressed uniforms. When had they done that, Gary wondered? He realised someone was missing. With dread he asked, "Is Doris okay?"

"Yes," said Hannah, "she's staying in bed for a while. I've taken her a cup of tea; she said she wasn't hungry, there's porridge ready. Gary, you're low on oats for your porridge, and you've no flour. We might have some in the camp store, and your meat will run out unless you get chickens and so on. You need a proper inventory and food plan. I thought I could help with that." Hannah stopped, realising she was ordering people about when they weren't under orders, apart from Cal and Greavesey. "Sorry, I was in auto-pilot, even you two, I think we're done with that, no more Corporal, no point."

"Yes, Corporal, of course Corporal," both Callaghan and Greavesey had leapt to attention.

Hannah shook her head. They all sat and discussed the day; they wanted a tour of the house and site. The men said they would go and get some clothes and bits after checking the camp. They would call in at the Council building and see if they could find the gardener who hadn't appeared the day before. Hannah suggested checking a farm for chickens or oats and wheat.

"Need to find out what else you might need for bread," she said to Gary. He caught the implication of you rather than we.

"If I'm Green still," he said, by way of a reply.

"We can bring the checker back if you want?" Greavesey said.

"Yes, do that," said Hannah.

"Yes, Corporal," they both said again.

"Bastards," said Hannah, but she was smiling.

They cleared the breakfast things away into the dishwasher. Hannah went and told Doris what was happening. Then they donned their coats. The day was bright, sunny, and cold. Gary explained that the solar panels didn't need sunshine just light, but clearly the bright light helped. They walked up to the turbine, that barely moved on the still day. "Welcome to the problem of wind power," said Gary. He then showed them the water tanks and explained how that system worked. They walked back towards the house; they stopped at his parent's graves.

"Your parents?" Hannah asked.

"Yes," said Gary quietly.

"A good spot," she said.

"Are *parents* your mummy and daddy?" Sarah asked, taking

his hand in hers.

"Yes," Gary couldn't say anything else. He was suddenly overwhelmed with the sense of loss, not just for his parents, but friends and fellow students, even his old teachers. Were they all gone already? He squeezed Sarah's hand. How was she managing to cope with her mother gone? What about the others, their families, friends colleagues, all going or already gone? It was overwhelming if he thought about it, but then he realised it was not, because he didn't often think about it, even in the short time since he had lost his parents.

"Come on," said Greavesey, "let's see those smelly reed beds Gary told us about." He and Callaghan took one of Sarah's hands each and swung her up into the sky to giggles of joy. They walked down the slope leaving Hannah and Gary.

Hannah hugged him, but said nothing, letting him compose himself. "Sorry," he said, "sometimes, I..."

"I know," she said, "it's okay, really it is, and we *all* have those moments." She kissed him.

After a while, he said, "I'm okay, come on." He started following the others down the slope. The reed beds weren't *that* interesting as Gary knew, and they didn't smell, much to Sarah's disappointment. They walked back to the house. Callaghan and Greavesey said they would get going and do the tour. They would hunt out a radio set as well if they could find one to put in the house.

"Greavesey's speciality is supposed to include comms," Callaghan said, "which is why he's so talkative."

Greavesey, issued an expletive, then said, "Sorry," in case Sarah had heard. She hadn't, she was watching a very large flock of geese honking overhead. The two men then climbed in the rover and set off. Hannah, Gary and Sarah, went back in the house. Doris had got up, looking awful, but she brushed their concerns away. She was pleased to see that Callaghan or Greavesey had left some pills for her.

Hannah asked, "Doris, will you be all right watching Sarah for a while? Gary and I need to go and get some things."

"Yes, dear, we'll be fine, Gary love can you put one of those films on for her?"

"Toy Story, Toy Story," shouted Sarah.

"Toy Story it is," said Gary. Once Sarah was settled, and Doris had a cup of tea, he and Hannah left the house.

"Hitch up your trailer to the rover," said Hannah.

"We can use the Lexus if you want?"

"No, let's keep it semi-official, plus then we'll have the radio."

Gary pulled the trailer forward; there were still a couple of bits he hadn't unloaded, which he dumped next to the little Honda in the carport. He climbed in next to Hannah.

"30 mobile. Going farming."

There was a brief pause before "31, Roger, at the Council, will update later."

"30 Roger," Hannah put the handset down, and then said, "let's see your local farmer." Gary directed her from the main road, looping around the base of the hill, back away from the town and then pulling down a single-track lane. They pulled in front of a rambling farmhouse and out buildings. Hannah pressed the rover's horn. A large flock of birds flew up from behind the house, further disturbing the silence. They climbed out. They went to the farmhouse door and knocked. Hannah then tried the door, but it was locked.

"Around the back," she said. Her hand was in her jacket pocket; she pulled out a pistol.

"I didn't realise you had that?" Gary said.

"All the time, under my pillow as well." Gary stopped and looked surprised. "You might have been a psycho-rapist for all I knew, my choice in men has not always been good you know." She was smiling at him. "Come on, careful I'll go first." Gary wasn't armed, so he let her. He felt his heart rate pick up. They reached the back door; Gary could see an empty dark kitchen. The rear door was locked when Hannah tried it. "Oh well," said Hannah.

She smashed the glass in the back door with the butt of the pistol. "Haven't done this for a while," she commented, reaching in and unlocking the door. Gary just looked astonished. "I had a different upbringing from you I think," said Hannah by way of an explanation. "Anyone here?" she suddenly shouted, making Gary jump. "No one here but us chickens," she joked in a silly voice, pointing out of the kitchen window across the garden to a pen.

"You made me jump," said Gary breathing again.

"I know, sorry," she said, but she wasn't. She loved to tease him. She looked at him hard. She loved more than that. Pull yourself together girl, he's just a lad really, too young for you. She snapped herself out of it, concentrate! She put the gun back in her pocket; she could smell the stink from here. "Can you smell it Gary? That sweet, sickly smell?"

"Yes, what is it?" Gary realised he had smelt it before, by the pits. "Oh," he said, "shouldn't we?"

"No, leave it, let's get out of here; see what's outside." They went back out, pushing the door closed but not locking it. "Your chickens," said Hannah, "no foxes of course, and they seem to have managed to escape and keep pecking for food. Looks like half a dozen or so, you'll need more for meat, but you can get eggs." They found the coop and there were plenty of uncollected eggs, but how old they were they couldn't tell. Some were broken, "Birds I guess," said Hannah. "You'll need a cage or something and a coop back at the house. They'll be OK for now, unless you want one for dinner?"

"No, let's see what else we can find."

The first barn was full of rotting hay, the second barn was empty and opened out to a yard filled with rotting cattle corpses. There were dead rats, dogs, mice, and foxes. A couple of crows, were still picking their way through, they didn't stir at their approach. They backed out and around; they entered another section and found a tractor, and a civilian land rover, "Could be useful for you," said Hannah, again emphasising and reminding Gary that it was only him. They had seen a plough and other equipment in the yard. Gary didn't know where the fields were or which fields belonged to the farm, not that it would matter soon, he guessed. They again retreated, and before Gary had a chance to make a comment, Hannah pulled open another barn door, and said, “Bingo.” It was a grain store. In three stalls, were piles of grain; in one corner was a small mill. Next to it was a half-filled bag of what looked like flour.

“Can we use it?” Gary asked.

“I don’t know, it looks like flour, but it could be rotten. Rats or mice haven’t had it, I guess, there’s poison over there.” Hannah pointed at a container of poison on a bench, “Mind you they’re all gone as well, I guess. Don’t know about bugs, but it looks clean.”

“Which grain is wheat for the flour?”

“No idea, we’ll have to check in a book, you’ve got loads, or we can check the town library.” They found some jars, and put some grain from each pile into different jars. They then collected the half sack of flour and carried the items back to the rover. The flour sack went into the trailer. “One more barn,” said Hannah. They walked towards a door on the left of the small courtyard. The door was padlocked. Gary jogged back to the land rover and returned with a crow bar. He prized the lock off the old wood. “Make a thief of you yet,” Hannah smiled at him. The door splintered open. In the barn were two chainsaws, a quad bike, a generator and then through an internal door, more equipment. There was a pallet of nitrogen fertiliser, marked seed wheat, another pallet of seed barley, and then more fertiliser. There were ten pallets in all, neatly laid out on the barn’s floor. The end of the barn had large closed double doors. “Looks like, you are farming,” said Hannah. She approached the bags marked seed wheat. They were of a Hessian type, but looked undamaged. From her hip, she pulled out a large hunting knife, which Gary had also failed to notice.

“I didn’t know you had the knife or gun,” he said.

“If you had kept your eyes moving rather than locked on these,” she wiggled her breasts at him, “then you’d notice more.”

“I’m sorry, I didn’t mean.”

“Stop saying you’re sorry, anyway I liked you looking.” She sidled up to him and gave him a kiss. She broke away after a while.

"Later, big boy," she said, squeezing part of his anatomy. "Let's see what wheat looks like." She stuck the knife into one of the bags. "Okay," she said holding up a rounded kernel, "that's wheat; we have lots of that next door, and more to plant here." She then repeated the exercise with the barley, holding up the grain whilst he nodded. "No oats though, so no sowing them just yet," she patted his cheek.

"Hannah."

"Yes?"

"Can you please put down your knife and gun?"

"Yes, but why?" Gary stopped her talking with his mouth, he pushed her up against one of the pallets, pushing his hands inside her coat, then her sweater. She resisted for only a few seconds.

"I knew you'd be a psycho-rapist," she said as they rearranged clothing. "Bit cold for that though, and don't say sorry!" She was smiling. They walked back out holding hands to the Landrover. They climbed in.

"30 returning to the house," she broadcast, not expecting a reply.

"31 getting the clothes, with plus one pax. Back in 45 put the kettle on, out." Greavesey's accent was still distinctive over the radio.

"What's a *pax*?" Gary asked.

"They have an extra passenger. Come on let's get back, exercise makes me hungry," she smiled at him.

Sarah was buzzing around the house playing with a paper plane, when they returned. There were pens and bits of paper everywhere in the TV area. Doris was sitting in the kitchen looking tired, there was some soup bubbling on the stove; it smelt good. Gary was carrying the half sack of flour.

"Fresh flour, if my eyes don't deceive me," said Doris.

"Don't know how fresh it is, but we need to give it a try," Gary said. He walked out of the kitchen and, a few seconds later, returned with the boxed bread maker. He opened it up. There was a recipe book inside. "Yeast we need yeast and salt and sugar and…"

"In here," said Hannah. She held up a small yellow packet from one of his mother's cupboards.

The other Landrover appeared. Gary hadn't buzzed them in, so how had they got through the gate. They also walked in through the front door with various boxes and another man, the gardener from the council building. "How did you get in?"

"Through the gate and door?" Callaghan interrupted. "Simple, we watched you type the codes."

"This is Bill, you've already met, I think, we thought he should be here with us," said Greavesey.

"I hope it's okay me coming, I'm not too good, but I can still help out with stuff," he said.

"It's fine; good to have you here." said Gary. "I'm Gary, this is Hannah and Sarah and Doris."

"Hello again," said Bill, "names to faces. The guys said I could get a shower or a bath and change into my new clothes." He held up a large carrier bag.

"Bill, welcome," said Hannah shaking his hand."Sarah and I will show you to your room. Did you bring the checker?" she asked Callaghan.

"Yes, Corp," he replied. They were all serious now. "I'll bring it in," he said, walking back out.

"Sorry, Bill this way, Gary's still green, I mean, he's negative for the virus you see."

Bill looked surprised. "But we'll infect you! You should have a mask and suit and so on."

"It doesn't matter," said Gary, "it really doesn't."

Bill reluctantly fell silent, and he then followed Hannah and Sarah up the stairs. Sarah, who had stayed quiet, started talking as they disappeared from view. "That's my room, that is Gary and Hannah's, and you can have that one."

Gary began to tidy up the lounge area. Doris told him, "Don't fuss, I'll do it, but can you sort out another film or something for Sarah?" Sarah had come back down with Hannah, having shown Bill his room. "Not *Toy Story*," Doris added. Gary looked on the system. There was a Disney section. Maybe *The Little Mermaid* would do, or *Beauty and the Beast*? He went back into the kitchen area where Hannah had already gone, followed by the others. Callaghan was plugging the machine in on the worktop counter. Hannah was standing next to it.

Hannah said, "Doris can you take Sarah into the lounge whilst we test Gary, please?"

"But I want to watch," said Sarah petulantly.

"Another time," said Doris, leading her by the hand. "Now show me that drawing you were doing."

"Come on," said Hannah to Gary. She took his middle finger, avoiding his gaze. She pricked it and wiped his finger onto a slide that Greavesey handed her. Gary knew the routine, but there was a real tension in the air. Hannah passed the slide to Callaghan who dropped it into the scanner, the machine buzzed and vibrated on the counter. Hannah looked away, then Ping, Green. "Thank God," Hannah mumbled. She walked out the room.

"Well done mate, you're still Green, amazing," said Greavesey. Gary didn't know what to say.

"All right?" Doris asked leaning in.

"Clear," said Callaghan, switching off the scanner. "Good thing too," he slapped Gary on the back. "Let's get some lunch, I have some defrosting rolls with me, and that soup smells great."

They gathered at the table and ate soup with defrosted bread rolls. Doris read the bread recipe book. Bill, shaved and dressed in clean clothes, had joined them. The swelling was evident on his neck, but he was smiling, "Running water, toilets and everything," he said shaking his head, "and now restaurant service. What more does a man need?"

They sat and chatted. Bill explained his job as a lead council gardener, and said that he'd love to take a look at Gary's vegetable patch. Sarah wanted to help as well. No one had any objection. "We can go and try and mill some more flour, if we can get a genny, wired in," said Hannah, "or we can search some other farms for oats." They agreed. The four of them would go back to the farm, leaving Doris, Bill, and Sarah to prepare dinner and look at the vegetables. Gary showed Bill where the meat was in the freezer, before Greavesey remembered they had more in the land rover and in the ISO freezer at the camp.

CHAPTER FOURTEEN

Garden and Illness

The next two weeks followed a regular pattern, of scavenging around farms and shops; Bill took over the garden, struggling more and more each day with his breath. Doris did the kitchen and food when she was able, but slowly spent more time sitting, or in bed. Sarah mostly stayed in the house with them, but occasionally went on trips with Hannah and Gary, depending on where they were going.

They threw the first load of flour away when the bread didn't taste right, much to everyone's disappointment because the aroma was lovely. They milled new flour, and that was fine. Another week into their search, they found a farm with oats. That was milled back at the *Arse Farm*, as it became known, after Gary told them the story. Bill knew a bit about chickens and sketched out a run and coop. Callaghan and Greavesey returned from one excursion in the Army truck with a garden shed in pieces, chicken wire, and other bits of wood, luckily with the instructions. They created the coop from the shed following Bill's guidance. The next day they returned with a mini JCB, and half a dozen different chickens to add to the ten they had found at the *Arse Farm*. They needed a cockerel. Each morning Callaghan tested Gary; Hannah couldn't watch, nearly always finding something else to do. Sarah complained more often of pains in her neck and began to cough, a cold, they hoped, but it didn't respond to cough medicine. Together they would finish the day in the cinema room enjoying the escapism of a movie, one for Sarah, normally Disney, and then one for the adults. The system held over 1,000 films to choose from, plus dozens of TV series. They drank wine and occasionally talked before heading off to respective bedrooms. Sarah occasionally woke up, but now she walked into the master bedroom and got in with Gary and Hannah, twice disturbing them, which Hannah just laughed at, and Sarah called serious cuddles.

After a spell of heavy rain, the weather finally brightened in mid-February, although Bill said winter was not done yet. Bill had revamped the vegetable patch. He raised the vegetable beds and, on a trip with Callaghan and Greavesey, came back with another greenhouse, cloches, more seeds, compost bags, and a host of other bits and pieces. Another trip, and a large shed was added, with a rotavator and other equipment stored inside. The original shed, which held little more than a lawn mower and had been neatly positioned out of sight of the house, was moved to join the other outbuildings that now comprised two greenhouses, a big shed, the little shed, and the chicken coop. These were all set up adjacent to the main lawn. Gary thought about the weeks of effort that the landscapers had put into the garden before his mother had been satisfied. Now, there were sheds, greenhouses, no lawn and raised beds, equipment, canes and bird scarers, to keep them off the seeds. Bill also planted two apple trees, and two pear trees, along with raspberry and gooseberry bushes. Gary pointed out that there would be apples and other fruit in farms, but Bill insisted he should have some nearby. When Bill's illness got too much, the lumps clearly visible on his neck, he would sit and talk to Doris, or teach Sarah. In the evenings, he drew up plans and wrote instructions on planting for Gary, pointing out a large gardening manual where more information could be found. The book had been another retrieval from the garden centre.

Doris had asked to sit outside in the sunshine. She was so sick that she had not been out of bed for two days. After Gary's ritual blood check had delivered a ping and green, and Hannah had allowed herself to breathe, Gary and Greavesey had carried her out to a bench seat where she could watch Bill and Sarah raking in some compost. Greavesey and Callaghan went off to do the camp checks. Gary was sorting washing, whilst Hannah cleared the kitchen. During one trip, Hannah had found a small tea and coffee shop and raided it, bringing back packets of filter coffee and beans. She had just made a pot of fresh coffee, and the kitchen was full of the smell of roasted and ground beans. She took two cups outside, first to Bill, then she walked back towards Doris. Sarah was sitting talking to her. It was then that Hannah realised what she was saying.

"Bye, bye, Doris, you have a good sleep now." Sarah was patting Doris' hand. Hannah called Gary and Bill. Doris had survived 272 days since the announcement. Hannah saw a bit of paper sticking out of Doris' coat pocket, she pulled it out, read it, and then wordlessly handed it to Gary.

"Come on Sarah," said Hannah, "we need to get ready to go out."

Gary read the note and gave it to Bill, and then he walked up the slope, wordlessly, towards his parent's graves.

Bill read:

Dear Hannah, Bill, Gary, Cal, G, and little Sarah,

I'm done now. I'd like to thank you for my last few weeks, where I have found a new family in this lovely house. It's time now, to be with my real family. My husband, Harry and daughter Sharon went to the pits a month or so ago, I lose track of time these days. I want to be with them, now. Please take me there. Do the best you can for each other and whoever's left, I know you'll try.

Love

Doris Brown xxxx

Bill folded the note and put it in his pocket. He walked into the house; Hannah was coming back down the stairs, dressed in uniform. "I'll radio the others," she said, going out to the Landrover, "then we'll all go, okay?" When she had returned, she said, "Sarah, love..." Sarah had come back down stairs wearing her big coat. "Go find Gary, he's up the hill with his mum and dad, I think. Ask him to bring Doris to the rover for me." Sarah ran off shouting for Gary. Hannah turned to Bill, "Help me wrap her in this." Hannah had a plain white sheet. They did so. When Gary had come back down the hill, he picked up Doris. She weighed almost nothing, Gary thought, and he carried her to the back of the Landrover. He then lifted Sarah in. Bill went and sat in the front with Hannah, wheezing and coughing. Hannah put the Landrover into gear, and they drove to the camp. Hannah parked adjacent to the half-filled pit. Callaghan and Greavesey stood waiting, a jerry can of petrol on the muddy ground next to them.

"Corporal," they both said in greeting.

"Give Gary a hand," she said back.

Gary helped pass Doris' body out of the Landrover. Sarah jumped down as Bill came round, wheezing, from the front passenger seat; Sarah held his hand. Callaghan and Greavesey carried the body over and placed it in a black plastic bag, and they then lowered the bag into the pit. They stood in silence for a few moments.

"Hannah, Gary, please take Sarah back to the house," said Bill, he gave them a long look.

"No!" Hannah and Gary said together.

"Yes," said Bill, "it's my time, I can barely breathe and walk. I've had a good innings, and I'm not going to be trouble for the rest of you." He lowered himself down on one knee and hugged Sarah. "You go with Hannah and Gary, little one. Make sure you water them plants, just like I showed you," he said.

"Are you staying here with Doris?" Sarah asked.

"Yes, love, I'll keep her company." Bill stood with Gary's help. He then shook his hand and held his shoulder for a while. Hannah just shook her head, took Sarah's hand, and got back in the rover. Gary joined her, placing Sarah between them.

Hannah, grabbed the radio, "30 mobile, en-route to the house," she broadcast. They heard the squawk from the speaker in the other rover. They drove slowly away, neither of them checking in the mirror. Gary didn't look at Hannah, but he thought he heard her sob. When they arrived back at the house, she went straight up stairs, leaving Gary to bring Sarah inside and take off her coat.

"Shall I water the plants now?" Sarah asked quietly.

"No, not now, why don't I put a movie on for you?"

An hour later Callaghan and Greavesey returned in a rover,

and one of the trucks, they had some equipment with them. They unloaded the truck and immediately began erecting the components of a radio mast, which they bolted to the end of one of the sheds. There was a reel of cable in the truck, which Greavesey kicked out. He then asked Gary, "Run that into the basement, will you?" They worked steadily. Sarah came out and watched them. After two hours, they had the lines in, they then walked into the kitchen; Hannah was in there preparing a meal, still dressed in uniform.

"All right, Corp?" Callaghan asked.

"Yes," was all Hannah said.

They wired up the transceiver in the kitchen. Then, Callaghan tested the set with Greavesey in the Landrover, they gave the radio a call-sign of *Golf Hotel*, for, Gary's House, they explained. It worked.

"Should have done this a while back," said Greavesey. "Anyway, we'll take the truck back."

"After lunch," said Hannah, serving five bowls onto the kitchen table. They sat in silence.

Callaghan and Greavesey announced they would go and mill some flour after they had taken the truck back, and asked whether Sarah would like to come with them. "Yes, I like going to the farm, *Arse Farm*," Sarah said.

Hannah had to smile; it broke the tension, "Go get your coat then." Sarah ran off up the stairs. Hannah looked around the faces of the three men sitting at the table. "I'm all right, I just needed a while."

"Sure thing, Corp," said Greavesey, standing up. "Come on Cal." The two men left the kitchen, Callaghan picking up Sarah from a jump off the last few steps. They heard the engines start, then they heard, "31, mobile en-route camp," followed by, "26 mobile likewise," crackle from the radio.

Hannah grabbed the microphone and responded, "*Golf Hotel* copied, out." She turned to Gary and said, "I need a walk, and then I'll be fine, coming?"

"Yes."

CHAPTER FIFTEEN

Personal Farewells

The weeks slipped by. Hannah taught Gary how to shoot very seriously, and insisted he practice with the SA80 and the pistol. Greavesey added to the weapons with a shotgun and nearly four hundred cartridges. He had found that on a farming scavenge. They wanted to find a hunting rifle. They knew there was a gunsmith in Derby, but they hadn't ventured that far yet. Callaghan showed Gary how to drive the trucks. He wouldn't pass a test, but it was good enough, he said. They had a hilarious couple of hours one afternoon, laughing at Gary trying, and mostly failing, to reverse with a trailer, using the Landrover first, causing several dents, then finally the Lexus.

At the end of March, in bed, Gary felt a small lump on the bottom of Hannah's left breast. Hannah, said, "I know" and lifted his hand further up, "but don't stop."

Sarah's neck was swollen badly on one side by then, and she was coughing a lot. She didn't want to go out at all; even to water the plants in the vegetable patch, where green shoots were springing up. She would watch Gary or one of the others from an inside seat, before turning back to watch a Disney movie again. Callaghan gave her half a pill to help her sleep, but she was clearly in a lot of pain sometimes, especially after a coughing fit. She ate little and just sipped at water.

Callaghan and Greavesey were also clearly ill, and only capable of short trips to the camp. Hannah and Gary went on any scavenging parties. The week before, they had come across two bodies in the street, both in black plastic bags. How they had gotten there and who had put them there, they didn't know. They beeped the Landrover horn, but no one came out. They loaded the bodies into the rover and drove back to the pits, placing them in. Gary then set fire to the pit. It wasn't full, but they had prepared another one nearby. They went back into the HQ tent. Hannah collected maps and some frequency codebooks from a safe. They then headed back to the house.

At dinner that night, after Gary had put Sarah to bed, he returned to the kitchen, to find a tense conversation between, Callaghan, Greavesey, and Hannah. "What's up?"

"Greavesey and Callaghan are leaving," said Hannah.

"I know you mentioned it a while back, but I thought you'd changed your minds?" Gary said.

"I know we did," said Greavesey, "but I haven't seen Buck House and the Houses of Parliament since I was a kid, except on TV of course. We thought we'd have a drive down and check out the sights before…" He stopped, caught in his own story making.

"We won't go till after…" Callaghan looked upwards.

"Never really got on with kids before," said Greavesey, "but she's a diamond."

They didn't have long to wait. Two days later, Sarah died. Gary and Hannah had woken up to silence rather than her coughing; they found her lying on her side finally sleeping peacefully. They buried her in a small grave next to Gary's Mum and Dad. Unbeknown to Gary, Bill had planted bulbs on top of their graves and daffodils were starting to bloom. Hannah placed her in the grave, and Gary filled it in. "I'll find a nice rose, or something for her, later," Gary said. Hannah stood in silence, tears running down her face. Callaghan and Greavesey both looked away, not wanting to show their tears. Gary didn't care; he pulled Hannah to him and wept. Callaghan and Greavesey eventually moved away, back to the house.

That night, they sat around the kitchen table; none of them were eating anything. Greavesey went to his annex and came back with a bottle of 30-year-old malt whisky. "Found this in one of those Whisky shops, think we better have it now, don't want it to go off or anything." He poured out four glasses. "To little Sarah and all the others, God rest their souls." They raised their glasses and drank. Gary wasn't keen on whisky the last time he'd tried some at a friend's birthday party, but he felt its burn and warm glow this time. He thought, that's good. They drank most of the bottle with barely a word between them.

The following day, Hannah and Gary got up to find Callaghan and Greavesey already breakfasted and ready to go out on a scavenging trip. "Won't be long," Callaghan said, "got a few things to collect."

"We can go if you need stuff?" Gary said, conscious of their wheezing, and the lumps on both their necks.

"No mate, we can manage this one, see you in a bit."

"You're not…" said Hannah, suddenly scared.

"No, Corp, tomorrow maybe, we think, just got to get some stuff from the Camp, check it and maybe some other bits and pieces." Greavesey squeezed her shoulder. "Stick some of that fresh coffee on. We'll be back for that."

Gary went off and did some pottering in the garden; he could see more daffodils out, and other flowers. Bill had planted or moved lots. His mother would have been pleased, he thought. He avoided the fresh grave and walked up to the wind turbine. He returned when he heard the blare of rock music, hurrying down to the house. Callaghan and Greavesey had returned driving a bright white Range Rover. They were both in good spirits. Hannah came out of the house, and despite herself had to smile. They switched the car off, and they all went into the house. After coffee, where they explained they had found the car dealership on the other side of town, Callaghan and Greavesey started loading the Range Rover. They already had Jerry cans of diesel in the back. They added some food from the house, and Gary saw two SA80's in the back, as well. "Can't be too careful," Greavesey said.

Hannah had gone for a walk she said, but she returned and helped Gary prepare dinner. Gary found a good bottle of wine to drink with the last fish from the freezer. "There's none left in the

ISO," said Callaghan, "you'll have to catch your own in future." They sat down and ate. They then watched a movie, finishing another bottle of wine. It was going to be *I am Legend*, but Hannah requested *Independence Day* instead, and they spent the movie making sarcastic comments about the plot and acting. Greavesey and Callaghan had put on a good show of vitality, but by ten o'clock they were both clearly tired and feeling sick. They went off to bed. Hannah and Gary cleared up and then also went to bed. As had become customary, Gary checked her for lumps. Her breasts now had three, and there was a small swelling on the left side of her neck. When he touched her, she pushed him onto his back and straddled him, holding his hands to her breasts throughout. They fell asleep with her still on top of him.

When they got up they found Callaghan and Greavesey ready to go.

"Thought we would make an early start, avoid the traffic," said Greavesey, with a wheeze. The efforts of the previous day had taken their toll. "Come on Cal mate, best be off." He approached Gary and gave him a kiss straight on the lips, to Gary's shock. "I'll tell you what son," he said, "if the Corp' hadn't grabbed you I'd have you myself, still got a good look that time on the stairs." He released Gary then hugged Hannah saying nothing.

Callaghan shook Gary's hand then pulled him in for a hug. "You take care of her now, all the way, okay?"

"I will," said Gary welling up.

"Corporal, it's been an honour and a privilege to serve with you." Callaghan stood at attention, Hannah grabbed him and hugged him, then they were outside, then the Range Rover was started, then they were pulling down the drive. They could still hear the music after the car disappeared. They strained to hear it for a long time. It was 322 days since A-Day.

"Just us now," said Hannah, turning to the house, "let's do your check."

CHAPTER SIXTEEN

Gary and Hannah

The spring turned into early summer. The vegetables grew; they had everything they needed except for Hannah's health, which inextricably worsened, although Hannah tried to hide it. On the 9th June, Gary came back from the camp, where he'd gone to check things at her insistence, to find a dinner set, with a bottle of champagne on the table. "Shower, shave, clean clothes and dinner is in twenty minutes," she said. She was wearing the dressing gown; he could see flashes of red underwear. Her hair was tied back. He hadn't realised how long it was getting, as was his own. He did as he was told. When he returned, Hannah was dressed in a skirt and top. Her hair was brushed out, she wore makeup and he could smell perfume. He'd never seen her in a skirt before. She had opened the champagne and poured out the glasses. She handed one to him. "Happy birthday," she said.

"I'd forgotten it was, I don't even know when yours is, or how old you are?"

"My name is Hannah Lucy Jennings. I'll be 27 in September." She shrugged at the last part. "I was born in Dagenham, but I was fostered out or orphaned or whatever, with my younger sister Kate. She died fifteen years ago in August, she was seven, leukaemia." Gary went to say something. She stopped him with two fingers on his mouth. "I joined the army at eighteen, and it's been my life since, until this. I never thought I would meet anyone like you. I guess it wouldn't have happened, but for the virus. Gary Henry Tolman, I can honestly say that I have never fallen so hard for anyone in my life." She breathed deep. "I've never told anyone this before or felt like this before, I, I love you." She looked at him hard. "I can't believe I've said it now." She paused. "No, you don't have to say anything, I'm not expecting that. I was a bit of a tearaway before the Army, in trouble, and so on. I've been a bit of a slut during my time, hence, the comments from the guys. That goes with the territory for a girl in the job."

He shut her up this time, "Hannah, I love you too, almost since that first day I saw you."

"What in my NBC suit? You must be kinky," she kicked him under the table. "You were so innocent, and I stole that away," she said misty eyed. "Anyway, I wanted to celebrate your birthday, and us being together for as long we have. Don't…" she said, stopping him interrupting her. "We need a serious discussion. I'm going to die. We both know that, the lumps are getting worse, and it's getting harder to breathe. It was so hard with Doris, Bill, little Sarah," she paused again. "I thought I was coping okay at the camp. Coming here to live with them made it far harder, but much, much, better. Since the guys left," Hannah paused again, "well, since the guys left I've been feeling pretty miserable for myself, and that's not been fair on you. I need another promise from you."

"What, what do you need?"

"I need you to promise you'll carry on after; after I'm gone. There will be other Greens out there," her arm waived, "there must be! You need to find them. Hopefully, one will be a lovely young lady and you can use all the techniques I've taught you to impress her. Maybe, have kids, and start the whole human race up again."

Gary again tried to interrupt, "I only want you."

"I need that promise, along with the promise about the pits. I can't go there. Promise me Gary, promise me love."

"I promise to try, and not the pits." His voice was barely a whisper.

"Right, speech over. Now, I seem to recall you quite liked the red underwear, so you better come and see if you still do." She got up and sauntered away as she went up the stairs. Her blouse came off then her skirt. He still liked the red.

***

It had been hot and warm for several days in early August. Hannah had been listless and barely eating. Her neck was swollen, along with her abdomen and breasts. She tried to help Gary with the daily routine, but sometimes Gary let her sleep until midday, only to get told off. During dinner, Hannah said she wanted to go to the seaside the next day, if the weather was still good. The following morning, Gary had packed a picnic of fresh vegetables, a bottle of wine, some fruit, strawberries, and raspberries from the plants in the garden. He had even defrosted some of the last of his ham, to go with fresh hard-boiled eggs and a fresh loaf from the bread machine. He had found a wicker picnic basket in one of the cupboards, dusted it off, and now he loaded it into the back of the Lexus. He had been to the camp yesterday and topped up fuel, and collected a spare jerry can, just in case. Hannah was wearing a sundress, and a hat. Her shoulders were red from the Sun yesterday, but she said, "I don't care," in a croak, as she was finding it hard to speak. He put two fold-up chairs, towels, and blankets in the back. Hannah had walked slowly and gotten into the front seat, where she held a road atlas. The Lexus' GPS still worked, the satellites were still up and transmitting, but neither Gary nor Hannah had any idea for how long they would last.

Hannah had taught Gary how to map read as part of his training, along with weapons drills and anything else she could think of that he might need. This had included an exceptionally embarrassing, for Gary that was, discussion of women and menstrual cycles. Hannah had to explain why she didn't have periods, or why she hadn't had any since she'd been in Afghanistan. Stress the doctors had said. That explained a lot, thought Gary. He had been too embarrassed to ask when she first came to live with him, apart from the brief contraception discussion on their first night together.

Once they were ready, Gary set off. Hannah had insisted on an SA80 and a pistol, which looked incongruous on the back seat. They had not travelled this distance before. They set out. Gary was a bit out of practice with the Lexus, despite the refuelling top up, as he normally used the Landrover because of the radio, where he could keep in contact with the house, when he was away. Not that he went far. A trip to the camp, where he had found detailed instructions left by Cal and Greavesey on the generators, the Bowsers, and so on. All the generators were off now. The freezer ISO was empty, and the last of the boxed meats was in the basement. They had chickens, and Gary knew he would have to find a cockerel, to breed from them. Hannah had shown him how to kill, and then pluck one. She had learned that on an army survival course years before. She was out of practice, but they managed. They had twenty live chickens left. They produced too many eggs, and the excess went to waste, despite trying different methods of freezing, and cooking.

Gary turned the car away from the nearest town, heading for the motorway on the deserted streets. Grass was growing in many road gutters and the verges were encroaching onto the road way. It took nearly two hours to get to the coast. The motorway was deserted; the roads were deserted. Hannah dozed most of the way. They reached the coastal town of Colwyn Bay and manoeuvred off the A55 North Wales Expressway through the streets that were empty, save for parked cars. They were not abandoned slap shod, but parked neatly next to empty, lifeless houses with overgrown gardens. He could see a few shops with smashed windows, but most were intact. Heat haze was rising on the roads. Gary had glimpses of the sea a few miles out, but Hannah was asleep. Gary pulled up next to a no parking sign facing a narrow promenade; he then bumped up over the pavement, which jolted Hannah awake. Her first view was of blue sea with light waves breaking onto a deserted brown sand beach. She beamed, her first real smile in days, Gary thought. Gary unloaded the car whilst Hannah waited at his insistence. He laid out the blankets, set up the chairs, poured wine, and opened the wicker basket. He then came back to the car and escorted Hannah down.

"Oh Gary love," she said, "that's perfect, just perfect." She sat in one of the chairs, sipped her wine, and nibbled at the food.

"Damn," said Gary.

"What is it?"

"I forgot swimming costumes."

"I don't think anyone will notice, you go ahead, I'm going to sit and watch you, maybe make some rude comments."

Gary stripped and walked out into the sea. Then, he realised how cold it was. There were suitably rude comments from Hannah about the effect of cold on men, but after a playful run back, he walked and then dived in. He swam for ten minutes and then came back to Hannah. She stood waiting with a towel warmed by the sun. He pulled his boxers back on but stayed sunbathing.

"Don't you get sunburnt," said Hannah. It was unlikely, she thought. Gary was bronzed from working outside. He was every inch the rugged man. God he was sexy, she thought. Long blonde hair and more muscled since their first night together. They hadn't had sex for several weeks; she just felt too ill. It had hurt too much the last time, although she had tried to hide that from Gary. He had realised though, and stopped, claiming he was tired. It even hurt to cuddle, because her breasts ached from the lumps. She was braless in the dress, but they still hurt just to touch. They chatted about the weather, about the birds and about what needed doing in the garden. Gary had another swim. They ate the food, well Gary did, she just nibbled and drank some wine.

They leaned the deck chairs back, and Gary announced "I'll have a snooze, sleep off the wine. Don't want to drink, and drive."

"Okay, I'll have a snooze as well, I love you."

"You too," he murmured.

She watched him doze off. It was time, she thought. She leaned over and kissed him. He mumbled something in his sleep. She sat back and retrieved the pills that Callaghan had left her months ago. She hesitated, "No," she told herself, "I won't be any more of a burden. I don't want him to have to carry me to the toilet and so on." She smiled at how he would be embarrassed. She lifted her hand to the neck tumour, "I don't want him to see me like this either," and she knew it was slowly disfiguring her face as well, pulling the skin, giving her a lopsided expression. She opened the pills one by one. Callaghan had said ten should do it; she took fifteen in between sips of wine. She settled back, placing her glass in the wicker basket. She looked at the sea, and she saw a flock of seagulls circling a spot inland; she thought she could vaguely hear their calls. She watched a small black bird with a long tail, she didn't know its name, it was pecking where the waves were breaking; the tide was coming in she thought. She looked at Gary; she smiled and turned her view back to the sea. She closed her eyes. She slept.

Gary stirred, he could feel the sun burning his forearm; he moved and opened his eyes. The tide had come in; the waves were louder. He looked at Hannah and said, ' Sorry love, I slept longer than I meant to," before he realised she was sleeping too. He would pack up before waking her. He cleared up the picnic and carried his chair and the basket back to the car. He slipped on his jeans and T-Shirt. He needed a new one, he thought, his clothes were tight on his upper body he realised, must be the muscles. At least his hair was shorter now, Hannah had cut it back the previous week, but it was still long. He looked down at Hannah; hers was almost to her waist he realised and blonder from the sun. He walked back down and kneeled in front of her, not wanting to startle her, she was smiling he noticed.

"Hannah darling," he said, shaking her hand. Her skin was warm in the sun. He shook her hand again, "Hannah," he spoke more loudly. Her hand slipped down. The pill packet fell on the sand. "No," he whispered to himself, despair rushing in. "Not yet, not yet," he cried. He sat for quite a while holding her hand watching the sun drift lazily towards the sea. "Come on," he said, "I'll take you home." He lifted her from the seat and carried her to the car placing her in the passenger seat. He put her safety belt on. He shut her door, he left her deckchair on the beach, her sun hat had come off, and was blown in the sea breeze into a wave. He climbed into the driver's side and started the engine.

He drove back to the house. He occasionally said something to Hannah about the route, or the places they drove past, but mostly he drove in silence. When he pulled up outside the glass front of the Huf-house, the sun had finally dipped, and dusk was falling. He carried Hannah to the spot where three graves lay covered in summer flowers. He laid her down to one side. He then fetched a spade and began to dig in the soft earth beside them. After an hour, he felt that the hole was deep and large enough. He fetched a floral wrap he had given to Hannah after one scavenging trip. She had worn it most evenings to protect her from the slight evening chill when they sat outside. He carefully placed it around her shoulders. He then lifted her and placed her in the grave. He kissed her now cold lips, the smile still in place, before placing the last part of the wrap over her face. He then filled the grave. He would plant some bulbs, and flowers tomorrow he thought. It was dark, and the quarter moon was setting. The night was warm. He could hear the wind turbine slowly rotate further up the hill. There had been birdsong earlier, but they were quiet now. Everything was quiet now. He sat on the earth for a while watching the moon slowly sinking, then disappearing behind the trees and the hill. The stars looked unusually bright, he thought, probably just his eyes getting accustomed to the darkness. He'd ask Hannah. She would talk to him about night vision and so on. He stopped himself. He walked back to the house. He'd sort out the car tomorrow. He went upstairs. There was a collection of A4 printouts and a note on his pillow. He would read that tomorrow, he thought. He lay down on the bed. He hugged the dressing gown, smelling her. He tried to sleep. It was 448 days since A-Day, and he was alone.

CHAPTER SEVENTEEN

Alone

In early September, Gary decided to search for survivors in houses. He'd started on Baker Street, going from house to house, breaking in as needed. He found three bodies in ten houses, with one in a back garden; an almost skeleton. Only the clothes betrayed a woman's body, or what was left of it. In each house, he checked store cupboards, taking what was left in tins packets, bottles, and storage jars. The Lexus and trailer were packed by the time he returned to the house. The following day he returned with the truck and loaded the decaying bodies into bags and then onto the lorry. He took them to the camp and placed them in the pits. He couldn't do that for the whole town, there could be hundreds of bodies still in houses. He tried two other streets, with similar results. Two children and a mother in a small bedroom in a standard semi-detached house were the last. He carefully loaded their bodies into bags and then into the back of the truck and drove to the camp. He lowered them into the pit, this one was only a quarter filled. No more, he thought as he stood in the pit. His hand rested on the 9 mm pistol at his side. A group of crows, what was the collective term? A *murder* he suddenly remembered. Where had he recalled that from? Some trivia quiz or a school lesson. He looked at the crows and at a pair of magpies sitting on a fence fifty metres away. *One for sorrow two for joy*, he remembered the start of the rhyme, not the rest of it; he could try to look it up later. *Two for joy* then, what joy? He was alive, but there was little joy.

He looked down at the three new black bags in the pit, next to the others he had placed in there. He noticed a couple of peck marks in the older bags. He would not allow that. He climbed out and fetched petrol from the camp bowser. He fired the pit watching with grim satisfaction the crow *murder* fly off. The magpies had already gone. The smoke was billowing up into the overcast sky by the time he drove away, back to his home. After he walked back into the house and he had washed his hands from the mud from the pit, he looked at the empty wine bottles and other recyclable tins and boxes in their respective bins outside the utility room. He loaded them into one of the Army trucks and headed off into the town, driving to the recycling centre. He had dumped them into the respective bins when he thought how ridiculous it was. No one was going to collect the large skips. Each marked as *Garden Waste, Household Rubbish, Glass.* There would be no more landfill either. Mum might have approved of that, if it hadn't meant there were no more people to create the waste. He felt hopeless again.

He drove the truck to the business park and rifled through the supermarket distribution warehouse once more, collecting more boxes of supplies. No food that had been looted long ago, but he had cleaning supplies, detergent, soap, plus cloths and toilet paper, even water filters for the fridge and dust bags for the vacuum cleaner. He wanted the house stocked ready for the winter. He went from planning for the future, to handling the 9 mm, thinking about nothing. The box of pills in the basement, left behind by Callaghan that Hannah, had used also attracted his attention. A bottle of good wine or a bottle of malt and a dozen capsules and he could slip away quietly.

***

It was late afternoon as Gary contemplated the hole he had dug. Ten days of near continuous rain, drizzle and occasional high winds suited his mood. The solar panels had struggled for days to generate power, well below their normal rates due to the heavy overcast skies. The wind turbine had contributed, but he had used the generators on two occasions in the past week, just as a precaution to make sure the batteries stayed charged. Not that he used much power. He refrained from using many of the systems in the house that used high energy, like the iron. Not that he liked ironing. There was no one to see his creased jeans and shirts. The heavy sweater he was wearing now, could dry in the house. He was bored and depressed, and the weather did not help. It was mid-October, the deciduous trees in the woods around the house had shed most of their leaves, which lay as a slick carpet across paths and the garden. The hole was deep enough. He stopped digging. He was still torn between his promise to Hannah and his own feelings of despair. The four graves were covered in moss and old flowers. One rose bud, three-quarter opened, remained on Sarah's rose that he and Hannah had planted back in May. The other flowers had finished for the winter. He knew he could plant winter bedding as Bill had left details in his notebook, but he wasn't sure if he would, he wasn't sure about anything.

"Sorry love," he mumbled at her grave, "I don't know if I can do this anymore. I'm not sick, well I don't think I am." Gary had not checked for days. He could hear what Hannah would have said, including the expletives she would use. He could imagine her stern expression, and then it softening with a hand on his cheek, a sly tease, or joke, just as she had during July as they both realised she was running out of time.

"You promised," he heard her say.

"I know, but…"

"But what? No *buts*," she would have laughed and then smacked his backside to emphasise her joke.

"No buts, love," he agreed. Then, she would have punched his shoulder and they would have carried on whatever they were doing, preparing a meal, planting some crops, cleaning, washing, or just sitting, and reading. He glanced back down to the house, imagining her sitting watching him, occasionally reading a book, as she had in those last few weeks when she was too ill to help in the garden.

Gary looked down at the hole once more. Not yet then, but what was the point? He carried the spade back to the nearest shed, leaving the hole empty and unfilled. Who would fill the hole in anyway? His body would be picked at by the ever present crows. Not that he would care, there was no one left to care. Food for the birds, just like the other corpses he had found outside. He climbed up outside the hole. Just then the sky cleared in the West. A shaft of sunlight lit up the otherwise dull surroundings. The windows from the rear terrace sparkled with rain droplets; Gary could almost sense the solar panels bursting into life. Not yet he thought. "I'll carry on, darling," he spoke to Hannah's grave. He walked back to the house, and then looked back at the hole and the four graves. The sunlight filtered through the trees onto each of them. It was a good spot. Morbid he knew, but it was his favourite place in the garden. He felt the sun on his back and felt warmed in body and spirit, although the chill breeze was a promise of the winter to come. I need to prepare, he thought, get ready properly. Tomorrow, he told himself.

A week later Gary had filled in the hole, cursing himself for his sentimentality and failure to uphold his promise to Hannah. He thoroughly cleaned and tidied the house, including removing old clothes from the cupboards. The bright autumn sunlight generated enough power for the washing machine and drier. He emptied all the rooms and, after washing and drying, even ironing, he folded the old clothes and stored them in the basement. He even toured around the local shops and retail park updating his wardrobe and throwing out his, too small, worn clothes. He had certainly grown in the time since A-Day. Hannah had told him he needed bigger shirts. He smiled at the recollection of her hands on his chest and arms. He shook himself clear of the memory. He assembled more storage shelves in the basement and found a vacuum packer in a local store. He read in one of the reference books how vacuum packing would preserve food and other goods. He would give it a try.

He found a sewing machine and added a knitting machine and some wool although he had no idea how to sew or knit. Something to do in the winter months he thought. The material shop also had fasteners and zips and so on. He boxed up bits and pieces, although he suspected he would have no need of any of it. He drove to another cafe looking for coffee stores and managed to loot a couple of boxes, but it wasn't a flavour he particularly liked. The local *Costa* and *Starbucks* in the town were both looted. Their glass windows lay in pieces on the deserted street. He would have to drive further afield, search in other towns and even cities. If he were going to do those trips, he needed to plan them, prepare where he wanted to go. There was no point just idly driving around wasting fuel. He could search all the houses in town, but that would take months just for a few tins or rotten supplies. He refrained from drinking alcohol, confining himself to the odd glass of wine or a malt whiskey. The wine stores in town were looted clean, he could break into some of the larger houses. Maybe they would have cellars, but what he really needed to find, for food and alcohol, were distribution warehouses. He started collecting receipts, delivery notes, and invoices from shops looking for addresses, but most information would be computerised and communications would have been electronic, so how would he find out? He thought smaller shops might be more likely to have hard copies, but that meant offices, and breaking into filling cabinets. Well, he had nothing else to do, now his crops were in and stored in the basement. He took detailed town maps and plotted his expeditions on them, using his old study to pin the maps up on the wall. In an outdoor expedition store he collected every map he could find, as well as the handheld GPS navigation systems. He grabbed a couple of bikes on one trip and placed them in the basement, ready for when the fuel ran out. He even cycled into town and back, but he didn't enjoy the hills or the time it took. He couldn't carry much either.

***

He was not short of food. He had taken to doing a monthly two-day trip away to scavenge. He took the land rover or the Lexus with the trailer. He always had provisions and equipment on a trip. He carried a sleeping bag, and a tent, not that a tent was needed. He could always stay in an empty house. Many turned out to have decayed bodies somewhere inside. The smell would normally give them away, just like the farm. He always had a water jerry can, spare fuel jerry can, the weapons, a camping stove, first aid kit, a camera, a spade for a latrine and whatever directions he could find. He tried to target his runs, looking on maps for business parks. He was mainly after food wholesalers, or distribution centres, not for frozen food. That would be rotten or gone, but for canned meat. Maybe rice or lentils, if insects hadn't eaten them. He missed meat. He had chicken, even a couple of times duck and goose. He had eventually managed to shoot them with the shotgun; he had missed a lot, but he slowly got better. He had stocks of more wine and whisky looted from larger houses, when he found them. He climbed hills with the vehicles, sometimes at night, trying to see whether he could see lights. He still hadn't obtained a proper hunting rifle to hunt more easily. The goose he had shot had made him sick, for two days.

His first trip away had been a week after Hannah's death, the warm weather had broken with a terrific thunderstorm, and then it had turned colder and wet. He was miserable in the house. He still hadn't read Hannah's letters. They were piled on the kitchen table. Whilst it rained he finally forced himself to start reading. There was a covering note, he found that hard to read, but he took that with him everywhere. Then, there was a series of briefs that was what she called them. The first one was called *Survivors*, like the rest it was littered with smiley faces, diagrams and pictures, all neatly printed out from his laser printer. "When had she done that?"

SURVIVORS - PART 1

You're Green; therefore, you are either:

A) Completely immune

B) You've had it and got better; remission I think it's called, but I could be wrong.

C) Exceptionally resistant.

My guess is A), possibly B) although I can see no signs, I have checked ☺. If it's C), well you know what will happen! If you are the only one left, that would mean you are a one in 65 million.

I know you are special, you are ☺, but one in sixty-five million?

When we set up the camp, just after A-Day, there was lots of talk about survivors. One of the officers was talking to one of the RAF pilots, when they were still flying in; they said that the odds were officially set at 99.99% fatalities. I've worked that out, there should be 6,500 survivors in the UK alone, maybe more if there are some B)s around.

You need to find other survivors, many will not have been as lucky as we were with food and so on especially during the winter, but even if it was awful I think there would still be 5,000 or so left. If you add in longer term C)s as well then there could be many more around. People survive all sorts of things; you have survived this. So stop sitting around moping. Get out there and find them, but take care, remember, they will have had to do difficult things to survive and not everyone is as friendly as me☺.

Some will want to shoot first and ask questions later as we used to say about combat.

You can teach the others lots, you've grown up so much since that first day in the camp! ☺

Look for other farms or things, smoke from house chimneys, wind turbines like yours. Leave notes if you find camps like the one in town. There will be fuel there, which will attract survivors like our one should. They might find you of course, wouldn't that be good!

When you find them, rebuild a better world. That means children, and thinking about society and the community you can build. It sounds crazy, but those weeks we had with Doris, Bill, Cal, Greavesey, and little Sarah were some of the happiest of my life. It was the way we worked together and helped each other. That is what I want you to create. First you have to look and find those people. You can do it, what are you sitting around for. Get on with it and that's an order ☺!

CHAPTER EIGHTEEN
The Warehouse

On that first longer trip, he had gone only for a long day, not overnight. He had gone further on the trip to the Northwest coast, but that first time he had headed inland to one of the larger towns, Rugby. He was looking for a business park on the outskirts of town near to major motorway junctions. He had found it after fifteen minutes lost on a ring road system; he was map reading and had found the businesses listed in a hard copy of the Yellow Pages. He had also checked in the looted supermarket office, looking for invoices and shipping notes. In desperation, he had stopped in the middle of the motorway and sorted his position out. He wished he had bought the Lexus, as the GPS was still working. After re-orientating himself and ignoring a road exit, not on the map that had confused him, he took an exit into a series of huge warehouses. He found the one he was looking for. It took him twenty minutes to break in, only to get inside, and then see a door open on the other side of the building. Check next time, he told himself. Hannah would have shouted something military at him. He hunted around the warehouse for the best part of an hour, finding only some tins of sweet corn. He took a dozen, but the place looked to have been ransacked, or it had not been restocked before everything had stopped. He tried the building next door. He had to break in via a jemmied office door. The warehouse was half-full of new TVs, and other electrical goods all in different cages within the floor space. He should have a spare Blu-Ray player, he thought. Another cage housed laptops; he jemmied the lock, and found the highest specification he could see. He took two. He loaded that lot back in the Landrover. If the movie system failed, he could always come and get another one. The third warehouse he tried had household goods, so he stocked up on detergent, washing powder, toilet paper, pest sprays, dishwasher tablets. He could and had, found these closer to home, but it was good to know where more could be found. He marked the location on his map of the estate.

The fourth warehouse he had to drive to, and it appeared untouched. He tried the doors and found one open. *Bingo*, as Hannah would have said. He could smell rotten food, and the floor was littered with ants and other bugs. There was a freezer section he could see, no point going there. That was where the smell was. He wandered around. There were boxes of cans, as well as sacks of rice. Some were open, he noticed. He found the rear doors. They were electric, no good without power, but there was a fire door. He pushed it open with a large bang, startling a flock of pigeons. He brought the Landrover and trailer around. He loaded up cans of ham, some beef stew, and the rice. The trailer was packed, so he added more stocks to the back of the rover. The pigeons that had returned suddenly flew up again startling him. He looked around, feeling the hairs on the back of his neck suddenly stand up. There was nothing there, just a fox carcass, the eyeless skull staring back at him.

He almost didn't notice the animal carcasses in the fields, not anymore. Hannah and he had seen a group of horses dead in a field a few months before she died; their bloated bodies providing a feast for some crows and an enormous cloud of flies. That had upset them both, for some reason. They had seen plenty of dead sheep, cattle, and pigs on their trips, but the horses had been hard to take. Gary looked around, conscious of the pistol in his pocket, his hand rested on it, and the SA80 in the rover, which he wished was on its lanyard around his neck. The feeling eventually passed, so he finished loading and shut the fire door. He would come back in a few weeks he thought. He went to the Landrover and took out a plastic covered notice he had created, more of Hannah's instructions to find survivors. It directed people to the camp, not the house.

Greavesey had explained, when they had added the additional sensors to his security system, "You don't want everybody turning up uninvited, there could easily be some dodgy blokes about."

He stuck the notice to the fire door and then drove around, disturbing the pigeons again, and stuck another notice to the door he had first entered. He then drove home carefully, towing the trailer, desperate to see another vehicle or some sign of life, but despite the journey there was nothing. Even the motorway service station was deserted and windswept, the only signs that humans had ever existed, except for the buildings, were the plastic bags blowing in the breeze. After driving in on a whim, he drove straight out without stopping. He could have searched, but he had no more room in the trailer. Maybe, another time?

***

His last trip had been over a month ago. He had stayed away from the house for two nights as he travelled west to, then along, the coast, starting near Lancaster and heading to Formby. He had skirted the edge of Preston, before heading inland through the towns of Wigan, then Warrington. He saw occasional smoke rising from different locations, but when he did investigate, it wasn't pits; it was burning houses. He slept overnight in warehouses that he found. He did not see anyone alive, but he did see pits at the two army camps he couldn't bring himself to fill them in. He retrieved fuel from some. There were no army personnel around, and the ISO containers were either locked or opened and empty. He didn't actually need any food, as he was just sticking up his notices, and seeing what was about. A trip a few months before had finally netted him a cockerel and some more chickens. The cockerel had pecked him viciously as he tried to get it in the cage. He had returned to the house to collect the cage then gone back to the farm where he found it, north of Burton. Now, the damn thing was crowing at five in the morning. Still, he seemed happy enough; there had been two clutches of chicks already. He thinned out the population by adding to the meat collection. The population was also hit by the arrival in the skies of a sparrow hawk or something. He'd found the chicken feathers one morning and thought fox, but there weren't any of those. Hannah's logic on humans should apply to the other mammals as well he thought; there would be survivors, but where? He had seen the sparrow hawk the following day, grabbing a chick. He thought about getting the shotgun, but he watched its graceful flight and let it be.

His evening reading at the moment was on bees, fishing, and fish farms. He wanted some honey, as well as the improved pollination that bees would bring. He had thought about fishing, but he didn't know what or where to catch it. That meant more books to research and then practise, or a longer trip to a salmon farm; if that still had any fish alive. He presumed he could learn to use a net, but he feared trying boats, especially at sea. He didn't know anything about fishing, but he knew he would have to learn. His final topic of research at the moment was organic pest deterrent. He knew pesticides weren't a long-term answer, although he had plenty for the time being. Insects had ravaged his gooseberry crop, and some caterpillars had gotten to some of his lettuces. He planted more flowers and some Hostas to tempt slugs and caterpillars away, but it probably just increased their numbers. He had a constant battle to keep insects, and ants especially, out of the greenhouses. A concrete base would help. They had not laid one, when the greenhouses had been set up; yet another task on his list.

Gary spent most evenings reading or planning projects with to-do lists. In the long nights of the winter, he occasionally watched a movie, but even that activity declined. He forced himself through some of the stored TV series, but realised the sights, and sound of civilisation made him depressed, regardless of the story line. He would pause the film or programme on the pictures of crowd scenes, or busy shopping centres, malls as the mostly American characters called them. Looking at the traffic jams in the scenes, he couldn't reconcile that picture to the empty roads and motorways he travelled on. He finally stopped at a scene in a TV episode showing neighbours washing cars and exchanging relationship stories. There were nearly twenty people in the scene, with kids playing ball, and cars driving by in the suburban street. Driving into town the deserted street only added to the strange feeling. Instead, Gary mainly switched the system to music and selected instrumentals, frequently off his mother's soft jazz, playlist. Even music lyrics were hard to listen to. He tried classical and could cope until he heard a sentimental piece. He tried opera but had to stop with some of the Arias, due to their emotion, even if he couldn't understand the foreign language. He played the odd computer game, but he missed the on-line challenge. He read his reference books in the lounge in hard copy, or those that he had on his ebook reader. From there, he could concentrate on his research and plans. The days passed. He was lonely and sad and continually argued with himself about carrying on. His promise to Hannah was harder everyday. He worked on the garden, and the house. He checked the grounds and tidied back the attempts of nature to cover his efforts. He went to the *Arse Farm* outbuildings, avoiding the house, carrying out maintenance tasks on the equipment. He cleaned and prepared for the spring, if he decided to live that long.

Part Three

Earth is abundant with plentiful resources. Our practice of rationing resources through monetary control is no longer relevant and is counter-productive to our survival.

Jacque Fresco

We've arranged a civilisation in which most crucial elements profoundly depend on science and technology.

Carl Sagan

In Italy, on the breaking up of the Roman Empire, society might be said to be resolved into its original elements, into hostile atoms, whose only movement was that of mutual repulsion.

Edward Everett

And while the law of competition may be sometimes hard for the individual, it is best for the race, because it ensures the survival of the fittest in every department.

Andrew Carnegie

CHAPTER NINETEEN

A New Start

Gary Tolman took the leaf remains from the kitchen. He walked them up to the far end of what used to be a manicured lawn. He lifted the lid on the third compost bin. He shut the lid and checked that the water irrigation system was drip-feeding to the raised beds correctly. Bill had provided plans for him, and he had implemented them in March. Now in the warmth of July it saved him an hour or so every day in watering duties. He checked the nets over the strawberries and raspberries. He had learnt the previous summer that birds could destroy a crop. There were huge flocks of all types around. The nets at least kept them off his garden. He would make preserves with the fruit later or freeze them. Not as nice as fresh, he had told Hannah that during his evening chat at her graveside. He guessed he was a bit mad, but it was the only time he actually spoke. He walked lower on the site towards the entrance to *Arse Farm* that he had created by cutting through a hedge. The field on the other side of the hedge had been a meadow for cattle or sheep; Gary presumed, although he couldn't recall seeing any. It did give him a quicker way to the barns and so on. He had not grown nor tried to grow, any barley or wheat. He was planning that for next year. He had been practising with ploughs, tractors, and the other equipment. He had spent a day cycling to another farm, where he had found a combine harvester on a Landrover, scavenging trip. He had cycled back to that farm and then driven the beast, with the bicycle strapped to the driver's cabin, somehow to *Arse Farm.* He had put it in the barn. He would need to figure out what all the controls did, but he would have time after he planted. He was tempted to practice on other farms where crops that had gone to seed, had self-seeded and then grown, but he hadn't tried yet. The flocks of birds were feasting on those. He still had flour, milled by Cal and Greavesey, stored in the basement, not that he often made bread; there was just him after all. Gary finished checking the lower reed beds and the entrance to *Arse Farm.* He thought that area would be good for beehives if he could set some up. He thought the meadow would also be a good spot to grow some more fruit trees. He had seen some in a garden centre that were still growing if he could replant them. He walked back up to the house; he'd just check one of the generator's feeds he thought, when he saw them.

Three figures were in silhouette near the wind turbine. He stopped and stared and blinked through the morning sun. The figures moved towards him. He checked his pocket; no pistol, it was in the house. He didn't carry it around the house. The spare was in the basement, along with the shotgun, and SA80s. He was going to turn and get it when he saw that it was a black woman and two girls; he started to relax. Birds flew out of the trees as the strangers approached. Then, he saw the woman had a rifle, it wasn't pointed at him, but it wasn't pointed away either.

"Morning," Gary croaked, his own voice shocking him.

"You on your own?" The black woman, with a hostile and demanding tone of voice.

Gary didn't know whether to answer or not. The woman was quickly looking backwards and forwards towards the house. The two younger women were twins, maybe thirteen, or fourteen, Gary thought. "Not very friendly," Gary said, "walking onto someone's property pointing a gun at them."

"I'm not pointing it, at you, am I?" the woman said. "This your place, then?"

Gary thought he could answer that. "Yes, it's my parent's house."

"They around still?" The woman was still trying to get an answer to her first question. The girls hung back, saying nothing.

Gary decided to take a risk, "Look, why don't you come in the house, I have fresh coffee, and bread." Gary thought the girls looked thin. The girls immediately looked at the woman, pleading with their eyes.

There was a pause which seemed to drag on. "Okay, but don't try anything."

They walked around the vegetable patch to the rear terrace entrance and then into the kitchen. Gary's pistol was on the side closest to the front door. He ignored it and went to the coffee machine. "How do you take it?"

The woman noticed the pistol and realised the young man could easily have gone for it. She lowered the rifle further. "Black, no sugar, girls?"

"Never had coffee," one of the girls said.

"I have raspberry and strawberry juice smoothie, made this morning," said Gary. He opened the fridge and took out the jug. He grabbed two glasses and poured the juice out placing them on the table. He then poured coffee into two cups, adding creamer for himself; needed to add that to the list for the next trip, he thought absentmindedly. He placed the coffees on the kitchen table. The woman and the two girls had not moved. "Bread," said Gary; he opened a tin and pulled out a loaf that the machine had produced overnight, he'd put it on a timer, so that it was fresh and warm for his breakfast. "No butter, I'm experimenting with vegetable oil, but I can't figure it out yet." He grabbed a knife from the kitchen collection; he noticed the rifle rise in his direction. He cut several slices, ignoring the inference, and he then placed the knife in the dishwasher. It was ready to run; solar power was pumping into the house, so he switched it on. He was showing off, he knew but he was also trying to diffuse the tension.

Gary sat at the table. He grabbed a slice of bread and sipped his coffee. "It's good," he announced, eating a mouthful. The woman pulled a chair back, and the rifle lowered pointed at the floor, now that the knife was away. She sat down, well back from the table. The two girls went round behind her and sat. They reached for the bread, then the juice. The bread disappeared. The woman was in her mid-thirties, Gary guessed. She was tall, her jet black hair was beaded and platted. She was wearing combat trousers a dark t-shirt and a jacket. The girls had platted blonde hair. They were dressed in jeans, dirty yellow t-shirt on the one, and a red t-shirt on the other again they had jackets. They had no backpacks, or anything else with them. Were there more people with them, or were they set up away from the house? Why had they come in from the wind turbine direction? Gary had lots of questions, but he kept his silence. The girls finished their bread. The woman was finishing hers. The juices were gone. "Would you like some more? I have other food as well."

"Who are you?" The woman asked, still trying to get information from him.

"I'm Gary Tolman, and this is my home."

"Who else is here?" She asked again. This could get annoying Gary thought.

"Just me, at the moment," he added, realising he'd answered her question.

She asked, "You clean?" Gary looked confused. The woman indicated the military checker on the kitchen worktop near the pistol.

"Last time I checked, two days ago, yes." Gary had gotten out of the habit of daily checks.

"Check us," she said.

Gary switched on the machine, turning his back on the pistol. He took a clean slide and held it out as he had watched and been shown how to do by Callaghan, Hannah and Greavesey. "You need to prick your fingers," Gary said.

"We know," said the woman, she removed a hunting knife from one pocket and pricked her own finger. She handed the knife to one of the girls before wiping her now empty hand's bleeding finger on the slide that Gary handed to her. She took it at arms-length; her other hand kept hold of the rifle. If Gary wanted, he could easily have knocked the rifle away. He didn't try. The machine bleeped telling Gary it was ready for tests. Gary took the slide from the woman and then placed it into the machine. He passed another slide to the first girl who had the knife, the yellow t-shirt girl; the machine pinged, green. The woman breathed out hard. Gary removed and cleaned the slide, running it under a tap, then wiping it dry and handing it to the girl in the red t-shirt, he took the slide from the first girl who had handed the knife to her sister. That was if they were twins; they looked identical. The second slide went into the machine. They waited before a ping, and the green light. The third slide quickly followed. Ping and green result. "Now you," said the woman. Gary again rinsed then wiped the slide, then the second girl gave him the knife. She realised immediately what she had done.

"It's okay," said Gary. He pricked his middle finger and immediately laid the knife on the kitchen table. He saw the rifle lower from the corner of his eye. He placed the slide in the machine; he had the usual wait. For the first time in nearly a year, he wanted a green. Ping and then green. He breathed again. He took the slides rinsed them both then placed them back on the machine, he switched the machine off. "Do you want that food?" He asked. He got a quick yes from both girls. "I have chicken, and homemade tomato pasta," he said, "or, there are eggs, various veg' what would you like?" He opened the fridge wide so they could see. The girls couldn't contain themselves any longer; they leaped around. "You can microwave the pasta, and chicken, two minutes per plate," he added. The girls almost pushed each other to grab the bowl and offered plates. There was enough for three, the girls realised. They looked at the woman, she nodded, but there was a hint of a smile, to them anyway. It vanished when she saw Gary looking.

"You?" The red-shirted girl asked.

"I'm fine, thanks. You guys go ahead," he coughed. "Sorry I haven't spoken for a while. I'll get some cutlery out." He went into a draw again, noting the tension in the woman. He removed three spoons and forks and laid them on the table. The microwave pinged; the kitchen filled with the smell of hot pasta sauce. "I'll get some water." Gary filled a jug from the cold tap and put out fresh glasses. The microwave pinged again. The yellow-shirted girl placed the first two plates on the table. Then went and sat down, she waited for her sister. The microwave pinged again. Gary had watched them all whilst the clock ticked down all three times. The girls were relaxing, but the woman was right on the edge. The red-shirted girl took the last plate and placed it down. Gary manoeuvred with her round the table as she placed it in front of the woman; Gary was there with the pistol at the side of her head. "I'll take the rifle," he said. The woman looked angry, but slowly handed the rifle to him. "Don't touch the knife," he added to the girls, he sensed one of them was about to grab it. He took the rifle and placed it on the floor, just outside the kitchen area. He went back to the table and took the knife and placed it by the rifle. All the time he covered the woman, and the girls with the pistol. He came back into the kitchen proper. He lifted the pistol and unloaded it, to the woman's astonishment. "Your pasta is getting cold," he said, placing the pistol back on the kitchen counter by the checking machine. He then went and refilled his coffee cup. "I have chores," he said. "I'll be out back where you saw me first."

He walked out carrying his cup. In fact, he walked past the veggie patch and up to the graves. He had placed a wooden bench there earlier in the spring so he could sit with Hannah, Sarah, and his parents when he came up to talk most evenings. He could smell the flowers there. He sat and asked Hannah if he had screwed up, he didn't honestly care, but he had promised her so he would try. His coffee was nearly gone when he saw the woman approaching, her jacket was off and she wasn't carrying the rifle.

"I'm Valerie, Val," she said. There was no apology, there never would be. "The girls are Kelly and Cass, not Cassie, red shirt is Cass."

"Gary."

"You said." She looked at the graves, but didn't ask. "Nice spot. Been here long?"

"We moved in about three months before A-Day. My parents built it, I helped." Valerie didn't look convinced. Gary took a closer look. He could see a long scar on her right arm. She was about five feet ten, and the t-shirt was well filled. She was inspecting him as well. What did she see, he wondered? Tall, he knew that, long blonde hair in a ponytail, clean shaven, Hannah's orders, and dressed in clean, but worn, work jeans and shirt. Gary was just twenty. He guessed the sun, and outdoor life made him look older. "How did you find me?"

"We were driving in last night, making for a military camp in town for fuel, I hoped. We saw an electric light; it turned out to be a school. We stayed there overnight then we followed a power cable up a hill, and we saw the turbine, when we walked up and saw you."

"I see. We had to supply power to the school to get permission to build the turbine, didn't realise it was still running."

"You have solar as well I see."

"Yes"

"Running water?"

"Yes, you saw, the house was built to a design from my father. My mother added all the green conservation bits like the recycled clean water system."

"Sewage?"

"We have flushing toilets, a filtration system cleans up that and the other dirty water." He didn't think the time was right to explain how the water reed system worked.

"I haven't sat on a working loo for months."

"Be my guest," said Gary. Valerie smiled for the first time at him; it lit up her face.

"I'm fine for now, thanks."

"It will beat holes in the ground and spades." Gary said needlessly. "I can show you around if you like, or are you heading off?"

"Don't have any place to be for a while," she said. Gary detected the hint of an accent, Caribbean he guessed, but he wasn't sure. He walked back towards the house. As he approached, he saw Cass with the rifle aimed at him. He looked at Valerie. "It's okay," she said. The girl lowered the rifle. Kelly came out and handed the knife back to Valerie. She put it in a scabbard on her hip. "Gary is going to show us around. You need to wash your faces, you both have tomato sauce on them and on your t-shirts," she added sternly. They both smiled in return.

Gary gave them the tour of the house, with the exception of the basement; Val said another time. They ended up back in the kitchen, where Gary unloaded the dishwasher. He packed away his cutlery and crockery and the few pans he had used; he only had to run it once a week. As soon as it was empty, he took the plates, cutlery, glasses and mugs and loaded them away, saying in passing he would run it later. The girls came back from one of the annexe bathrooms with clean faces, "Hot water, flushing toilet," said Kelly to Val.

"Yes, Gary told me," said Val.

"Do the bath and shower work as well?" Kelly said, tentatively to Gary.

"Of course, the whole house works." Gary asked Val, "What will you do now?" .

"Go get that fuel then find somewhere to stay."

"You can stay here if you want?" Gary wanted them to stay.

"Can we Val, can we stay here? We can have a bath. There's food and…" The girls' voices were scrambled together.

"Ssshh," said Val holding up her hand. "Let me think about it. Fuel first." There was a discussion about logistics, and maps. Val pulled a folded map from her jacket. It lay by the front door, along with the rifle. "You're not on this map," she said.

Gary could see the primary school and the camp at Paget County High School marked with an X and the letter F. "No," he said, "the house was only finished just before A-Day. I guess it didn't make any maps. That," he pointed to *Arse Farm*, "is the farm shown here on the map, and here's the school. The house is about here," he pointed to an area of woods shown on the Ordnance Survey Map.

"But you have a road? Where's that?" Val asked.

"Just here, we had to build it away from the farm, the *arse*, sorry the farmer who lived there wouldn't give us access, so we had to build down this way instead. If you go along the road, from the school, and into town, you'd miss the entrance unless you were looking for it. Which way did you come?"

Val ignored the question, "Can you take us back to the school?"

"Of course, I was going to the camp later to check anyway."

"Why?"

"I was with some army folks before they…before they died or left," he stumbled. "They sorted me out with a few things, and I helped them on the camp. I check to see if messages have been left, run the generators and get fuel when I need it."

Val looked at the checking machine and the radio. "Did you do the pits?" Val asked.

"A bit, why?"

"Just asking," she gave him a look; he couldn't decipher what it meant. "Okay, let's get going."

They took the Lexus, Gary explaining that he wanted to top up with unleaded. He pressed the gate open button, and it closed automatically once they were clear. The twins sat in the back, and Val sat with the rifle propped against the passenger door. She looked tense again. Gary carefully drove out and turned away from town, back around the hill, and pulled up a few minutes later at the primary school. He couldn't see a vehicle and looked at Val quizzically.

"Over there," she said, pointing at a 4x4 under a military camouflage net next to the trees. Gary drove over. "We'll follow you to the camp, just give us a few minutes to get packed up."

All three got out of the Lexus. Gary watched Val direct Kelly into the nearest school building; he could see a bulb on in the corridor. Cass and Val pulled off the net revealing the Nissan Pathfinder. It had no number plates; Gary guessed Val had *acquired* it from a showroom. Kelly returned with three back packs, which were loaded into the back of the vehicle along with the net; she then went back into the school followed by Cass, and they came out with what looked like garden loungers and sleeping bags. Val did a quick walk around. She then said something to the girls; they got in the vehicle. Val pulled the door to the school closed. She got in the driver's seat, and Gary heard the Nissan's diesel start. Gary turned around, and they drove out, following Gary's Lexus to the camp. He drove past the remaining empty pit; he had used a JCB a year ago partially to fill in the last used one, where Doris and Bill had gone. Gary pulled up by the unleaded fuel Bowser, and he directed Val to stop the Lexus next to the rubberised tank and dispenser. He came over to the Nissan; Val had got out with some plastic tubing, but looked lost, the girls stayed in the vehicle.

"How..." she started, "we used jerry cans and siphoning before, not from a tank."

"Give me a minute," he said, feeling pleased with himself for some reason. Gary went towards the camp tents, noticing a couple of flailing tie ropes. He would have to fix those he thought. A couple of minutes later Val heard generators start, the camps electricity came to life, she could see lights inside the tents and air conditioning vents started blowing. Lights lit up on the control panel by the tank. Gary walked back with a smile on his face. "Would madam like unleaded or diesel?" he joked. Val gave him a withering look that wiped the grin off his face. What was her problem? Gary thought. He grabbed the dispensing hose and handed it to Val. She undid the fuelling cap. "How much do you need?" he asked.

"Fifty litres or so," no smile or please.

Gary filled the Nissan and Val watched as Gary filled the Lexus from the unleaded Bowser. He then switched the truck off and walked back into the camp, shutting down the generators after first checking the tents. There was nothing there; he knew there wouldn't be. He returned to the Lexus. Val had already driven the Nissan onto the road. Gary got in the Lexus and went out back past the empty pit onto the road. He pulled up by the Nissan. "Are you coming back?" He asked Val through the open windows, his voice seemed loud on the empty road with just the idling sound of the two vehicles; the Lexus was nearly silent.

"We are going to look around," said Val. "Need to get some clothes for the girls; they keep growing out of theirs."

"There's a retail park with a big clothes store that way," Gary pointed away from the route back to the house.

"Thanks."

"I meant after?"

"I know," she was silent; the girls looked pale, and had not gotten out, or said a word, since they arrived at the camp. "We'll see," was all Val said.

"Well, you know where I'll be and how to find me."

"Yes."

Gary didn't understand any of this, he craved human company, but human company didn't want to be with him, it seemed. He put the Lexus in gear and with a nod of his head he drove slowly away. In the mirror, he watched the Nissan turn and then drive off in the other direction. He returned to the house, feeling lost and alone, more alone than he had for months.

CHAPTER TWENTY

They Return

That afternoon he returned to his chores. At seven, he finally entered the house and prepared some more pasta with a few bits of grilled chicken. He picked at the meal, not really hungry. He had several bottles of malt whisky lined up, he was experimenting with which one he liked. He was tempted, but he knew that if he started tonight, he would never finish. It was still light outside even at nine. He thought about going and having a chat with Hannah. Maybe later he thought. Instead, he got out her pack and reread her *Survivors* brief. "Sorry love," he said out loud, "I can't force them." At ten, he went to bed.

The following day he had planned to get ready for an expedition to try to get a beehive. He reread the instructions for doing so, more than three miles, otherwise, the bees may try to return; he knew where there were some. He should move in winter, but he hadn't thought of it then. There was a wasp's nest near the turbine, which is why he had planned the hives to be near the entrance to *Arse Farm*. He knew he would put it off. He hoped the girls would return, and he didn't want to be too far away if they did. Too optimistic, he told himself. His throat was sore just from the little talking they had done or had he caught a cold. He hadn't had one since, well since before A-Day, he realised. He had some cough medicine left over from Sarah he remembered; he'd check the medical cabinet for Strepsils. Later he thought; instead he got the mini digger and prepared a trench for the fruit trues he planned by the farm entrance. He layered the trench with compost from his own bins, and added some compost from the garden centre's bags.

He wouldn't plant until September, he thought, so the compost could rot down. He knew there was manure on the farm as well, but he hadn't used that yet. The farm. He had put off clearing the house; he knew the body was still upstairs. He had only been back in the house once to find keys for the tractor and other vehicles. He could do that he thought, he was in the mood.

He drove the mini digger down to the farmhouse; he dug a grave behind the building. He entered through the back door and went up the stairs. There was still a bit of a smell. He braced himself for what the corpse was like, his imagination running wild. The body was lying on top of the bed, which was infested with ants and other bugs; flies buzzed. Gary pushed open a window letting some air into the warm room, and the flies out; a small cloud of them escaped. The body itself was a partial skeleton. Gary returned downstairs and collected a black bag that had been left in the back of the rover. He went back upstairs. Birds flew from the windowsill; they had been attracted by the burst of insects. He managed, with some effort, to get the body into the bag, together with sheets and many of the insect maggots lying underneath. The bag was surprisingly light. He took the body downstairs out of the kitchen door and laid it into the grave. He immediately filled it in using the digger. He dug another pit, by digging up the small overgrown lawn, behind the kitchen door. He went back and stripped the rest of the bed down to its base. He dragged the mattress and rotten bedding down and placed it in the pit. He then drove the small digger up to the house. He returned, driving the Landrover with a can of petrol. He poured petrol over the bedding and then stepped back, throwing a disposable lighter into the hole. It burst into flame.

He returned to the farm's kitchen and emptied cupboards and the fridge, throwing the old packets onto the bonfire. He knew there was a pile of cattle and sheep to be done as well, but he couldn't face that today. He went back to the bedroom and pulled the window partially closed, it could air for a few days, he thought. He went back out and pulled shut the kitchen rear door, he made sure that the bonfire couldn't spread; it was already dying down. He drove back up to the house feeling filthy and sick. He stripped off his dirty, smelly clothes outside; he wanted to burn them.

"Well, that's a sight you don't see every day." Val was sitting by the main entrance, dressed in a plain grey t-shirt and jeans. Gary covered himself with his hands, "Don't mind me I've seen it all before, but the girls are a different matter." There was a smirk on Val's face, as she looked him up and down.

"Where?" Gary spun around turning beetroot.

"They're in the car at the gate; we couldn't get in." Gary turned and recovered his jeans then turned and faced Val again, his crimson expression slowly decreasing. "Nice butt as well," she said. "Look, we were a bit rude last time, and the camp, well the camp is something we'll tell you about later. I'm not very good at this. The girls, I mean us, would like to stay for a while if that's okay with you?"

Gary looked from Val back towards the gate; he could see the twins standing by the Nissan. "Yes, that's okay," he managed; he welled up unexpectedly and turned away from Val, embarrassed again. He opened the door to the Lexus and pressed the remote, he could see the gate begin to swing open, surprising the twins. He collected his clothes and put them in a pile by the side of the door. He entered the door's code. "I need to shower. I've been, I've been, it doesn't matter, I need that shower. Look, help yourselves, there's food in the fridge." He propped the front door open with an empty vase.

"Thanks," said Val. She touched his arm and gave him a stare. "Yes, you do need that shower," she added, "you stink!" She walked away back towards the girls who were walking up the drive.

Gary headed upstairs. He took a long shower and then dressed in long khaki shorts and a light blue polo shirt. He came back down and heard talking in the kitchen, which stopped when he walked in. There was bread and fruit on the table, mostly eaten. He could see eggshells by the cooker and microwave. A tin of ham was open as well. The girls were sitting where they had been before. They wore new t-shirts again with slogans on he couldn't quite read, he had no idea, without the colour scheme who was Kelly and who was Cass. Val was standing by the coffee machine as it gurgled to its finish. "Hi," he said, the girls looked embarrassed.

They murmured a quiet, "Hi," back. He saw the briefing pile

on the table with Hannah's letter on top. "We're sorry," said one of the girls, "we didn't mean to pry, it was on the table, and we couldn't help but read it." Gary looked from the girls to Val and back again; he then wordlessly collected the pile of briefs and the letter. He folded the letter and put it in his shorts' pocket, he then took the pile of briefs up to his old bedroom study, placed it in his desk's drawer and shut it. Gary walked back down the stairs, and out onto the rear terrace. He carried on up the hill and started hoeing a part of the veggie patch, ready to plant something, he couldn't remember what. Ten minutes later, Val walked up. She carried a cup of coffee and a sandwich on a plate. He took them, he was hungry he realised. He was sweating again, probably stank again. The temperature was climbing this afternoon. He went and sat by the graves. Val followed him.

"She loved you very much," she said, sitting by him.

"Yes, she did … I… I loved her too." The tears were in his eyes; he had placed his coffee down and, unknowingly his hand rested on her grave.

Val placed her hand on his bare knee. "I'm sorry, the girls are sorry. They are cleaning up the kitchen. I've told them you'll inspect it; it was immaculate when we walked in. Can we still stay?"

Gary hadn't even considered that they might leave again; he didn't want that. "I have to finish the hoeing, then..."

"No, you don't, I was watching, you've hoed the same place three times," she said lightly and with a trace of humour in her expression. "Come back in when you've finished your coffee and sandwich. We'd like to talk to you." She got up and made her way back towards the house. Gary ate in silence, then drank his coffee. He carried his plate and mug into the kitchen. It was clean and tidy. He put his plate and mug in the dishwasher; it didn't need running yet. He took a deep breath and walked into the lounge area. The twins were sitting on the main sofa opposite Val. Gary looked at them. He took a seat on the floor. "Kelly," said Val.

"I'm Kelly Grace Masterton; I was fourteen two weeks ago. We lived outside London with our parents and younger brother. They died six months after A-Day, our brother was before that," she paused before continuing. "We, we managed to get by, thanks to a nearby farm, until Val found us." Kelly was wearing a T-shirt with the words *Comedy Farce* on it.

"I'm Cassandra, Cass please, Joanne Masterton and I'm thirty minutes older than Kelly. We don't like pits, and we're really sorry about your letter. Is that Hannah?" she pointed at a photo. Cass wore a t-shirt with *Branded* on it.

"Not now Cass," said Val. "I'm Valerie Jones, no middle name, I'm from Grenada originally; I came to the UK six years before A-Day to work as a nurse. I was in London, to start with, but I couldn't afford housing, so I moved to the South coast. When the Virus hit, I was seconded to Southampton hospital… I managed to survive. When the hospital stopped, I started travelling around, hunting for food. The cities were grim, and some bad, and difficult stuff happened," she hesitated.

Gary wondered what had happened to them.

Val continued, "I found the girls and we've been travelling around ever since. We came this way to see if we could find the girls' grandparents. They live, lived, twenty miles north of here, that's where we've been since we saw you; no luck the house was deserted. We've been short of food for weeks, so thank you for sharing last time and this time, it was wrong of us to read your stuff." She looked at the twins. "If you give us a chance to stay," there was pleading in her question, "we'll tell you about some of the things that have happened to us." They were all looking at him.

His turn Gary thought, so he took a deep breath. "I'm Gary Henry Tolman, Henry was my dad's name. I lived here with my parents; we moved in only a few months before A-Day. They died, I didn't, some others came and stayed for a while… they all died or left to die." He thought of Cal and Greavesey. "Hannah stayed with me until she died; it was nearly a year ago now, in August," he paused. "The letter is, well you know what it is, and she left me the briefs as well. I've been on my own since. You are the first people I have spoken to or seen since then. I'm sorry I reacted so, so childishly, I'm not used to people, I suppose. Hannah would have told me off for being silly. I hope you will stay for as long as you want."

Val walked over, and Gary stood. She held out her hand.

"Nice to meet you Gary," she said. Gary shook her hand. The girls followed and formally shook hands as well.

"Is that Hannah?" Cass asked.

"Cass, I said leave it," said Val.

"It's okay," said Gary, telling himself again to grow up, and stop being so sentimental. "Yes, yes, that's Hannah, with Sarah, Doris, Bill and at the back are Callaghan and Greavesey." He pointed out the face on the group photo. Kelly was looking at a single picture of Hannah.

"She's very pretty," she said. "Who is this?" It was a photo of his parents, with him, taken on holiday six years ago. They smiled out from the past.

"That's my parents, Henry and Juliet with me a while back."

"Wow, you've changed," said Kelly.

"Enough," said Val, "let's get sorted out." They all went out to the Nissan; the driveway was crowded with vehicles, the Landrover, Lexus, digger, trailer, Gary's father's Honda, virtually unused, plus a quad bike and now the Nissan. Gary helped the girls carry backpacks, and other bags into the house, Val carried the rifle. "Can you put this somewhere safe?" Val asked, handing it to Gary.

"Basement all right?"

"No, can I put it in a room."

"Upstairs," said Gary, "unless you want to use a guest annexe?"

"This place is like a hotel," said Cass.

Gary was beginning to be able to distinguish their voices; Cass' was slightly deeper. "You can choose," he said. He showed the annexes first on either side of the house. Each had their own en-suite and shower over a bath. They then went upstairs. He pointed down the corridor at the master suite. "That is my parents', I mean my room, this used to be mine, and Sarah had it when she was here." He swallowed hard again. "There are two other bedrooms up here," he showed them; they had views over the garden. They had been around the house quickly before, but this seemed more important. "Those two have en-suite showers, there is a main bathroom with a bath," he pointed it out. "Cupboards and so on, quite a few are empty."

"Can we have the rooms up here?" Kelly asked.

"Yes, please," said Cass looking at Val first then Gary. Gary shrugged.

"Okay," said Val, "I'll take the rear annexe then if that's Okay, Gary?" she said.

"That's fine, great, there's a cupboard by the door where you can store that," he indicated the rifle. It had been back in Val's hand during the tour.

"Sorry," she shrugged, "habit."

The twins had a brief argument about left and right room choice before switching twice, then agreeing. Gary couldn't tell who was who without the T-shirts to guide him; their voices overran each other, so he lost his voice detection. Gary left them to it, "I'll let you settle in; I'll pick some fresh lettuce for dinner."

Gary was in the kitchen area when Val came in, she had changed into a blue blouse and a pair of black slacks; she was barefoot. She immediately started helping him prepare dinner. "There's wine in the basement if you want to get a bottle."

"I can't go down there, I'm sorry, no don't ask."

"Okay, take over here, I'll get some." Gary was still in his shorts and polo shirt. He opened the door to the basement and went down. He was fiddling with the bottles when he heard a sound behind him. One of the twins was down with him.

"It's huge, what is all this stuff?" He thought it was Cass. She was dressed in a green polo shirt and light jeans. Her hair was strawberry blonde beyond her shoulders, and had been un-platted.

"That's the house management system, including the entertainment system, and that's power generation, and heating. We have the cellar and then storage." Cass saw the two SA80s, the shotgun and a pistol on a bench and backed away. "There's flour and rolled oats for porridge, some other food stuffs I found," he pointed at the boxes of tinned meat, and sacks of rice. He thought they would need more soon, especially with extra mouths to feed. He said, "Can you grab me some rice from that sack, there's a scoop inside." Cass broke her stare away from the weapons. She collected the rice in the scoop, which was a plastic ice cream container. She walked back up the basement stairs. Gary followed and shut the basement door. Kelly was in the kitchen; she had a plain white t-shirt on with jeans as well. Her hair was different as well, it was now in a ponytail.

"We borrowed a hair dryer from your room, hope you don't mind?"

"That's okay," he said. The girls weren't girls, Gary realised, they were young women, and he would have to be careful with his looks.

"Can we have some wine?" Cass asked Val.

"Yes, can we?" Kelly pleaded.

"I don't know, you're a bit young," she said.

"My parent's used to give me with some with water when we were on holiday in France…" Gary stopped.

"Okay, I suppose it's all right then."

They had dinner; they talked a little, but not much. After they had cleared up, they loaded the dishwasher. Cass told Val and Kelly that Gary had an entertainment system. They all entered the cinema room to see how it worked. Gary showed them what was available and what the various control panels did around the house. They could get their own choice of music in their rooms or the same music throughout the house or watch a film or video on the various TVs around the house. The main cinema room had a projector, and screen supported by a surround sound system. Gary then had to demonstrate, which in turn led to the blaring out of different music selections in different parts of the house or zones. The girls complained about the lack of their type of music and mentioned bands Gary had not heard of. They all fell silent, realising that no new music would ever be made. Gary said they could get some CDs from a warehouse he knew and then load them onto the system. The girls asked for a pen, and paper so they could start a list, and they asked about a piano so they could practice. Val said it could wait till tomorrow. They found a movie that the girls wanted to watch on the system, a rom-com. He left them to it, saying he wanted to check the grounds. He left them in the cinema room and went and poured himself a malt whisky, a bit peaty, he thought, but it was growing on him. He walked up to the bench. He spoke with Hannah for a few minutes before he realised Val was watching him.

"You do that often, talk to her, I mean?"

"Most evenings," Gary said, "a bit mad I know." Gary wasn't embarrassed about his chats.

"What's that you're drinking?" Val asked, taking the glass and smelling, then sipping the drink.

"Malt whisky I'm trying that one."

"Bit peaty for my liking," said Val.

"Me too," said Gary. They were quiet for a few minutes, listening to the sounds of birds and insects.

"Can't hear that film at all."

"It's sound proofed, so that the room doesn't disturb the house."

"What if someone comes to the door or gate?"

"CCTV cuts in when the bell is buzzed, and since my army friends were here, if sensors are triggered."

Val nodded, "About the girls," she said cautiously.

"What about them?"

"You'll have to be careful with them, they are very impressionable, and they have been through a lot."

"I don't understand?"

"Just be careful, you are the first male role model they will have seen in ages, and some of the men they have met since the virus started have not been like that. If they want you to know, they will tell you. Just don't get too," Val struggled for the right word, "involved with them."

"I'll be careful," he paused. "What about you, the basement?"

"Not yet but maybe, one day." She cut him off with a slight shiver, and she stood, breaking their moment. "I'm getting cold; I'm going in." Gary didn't think it was cold.

"I'll be in soon; I'll just finish my drink." Val knew his drink was finished, but she knew he wanted time out with, she guessed, Hannah, maybe his parents. She'd ask about the fourth grave another time. She left him.

"Well, love," Gary started once he was alone, "here they are, don't know if they'll stay, but at least they came back." He took out her letter from his shorts; he knew what it said by heart anyway. It was getting dark, clouds beginning to mask the sky. He skipped the first part and then in her handwriting rather than the typed brief:

I haven't got long left now, love, if the weather's okay tomorrow we'll go to the seaside. One day, if my survivor brief is correct, you'll have the chance to meet new people and fall in love again, I hope. Don't reject them, give them a chance, give them my hope.

"I'll try love, I'll try." He got up, hearing an owl hoot… what? He listened again, an owl, what would it eat? He listened hard, and he suddenly felt cold as well. Maybe he had dreamed it.

Over the next few days, Gary introduced the three newcomers to the house's systems and his working routine. On the third day, he left them alone in his house whilst he went to the camp and to replace the jeans he had eventually burnt after the farm trip. He left them for more than three hours. He took the Land Rover, using it as an opportunity to try out the radio as well. He toured the town, killing time after he had checked the camp. He put one of his notices up on the windswept council building. He collected an electronic keyboard from the retail park, the biggest one he could find. The twins had mentioned that they had taken lessons. He wanted to find them a proper piano, but he had no idea how to tune one or get it into the house. He would need help. The keyboard was a start. He thought about driving over to the Derby

University campus. He'd not been there since his mother's diagnosis. He thought there would be some good books in the library, if he could get in; a job for another day. His task list was long, and growing. Hannah had left a full list of things on his computer as well. He parked up for a few minutes feeling a chill; he should have worn a sweater. What happened to the summer, he thought? He drove back. There was an atmosphere when he walked into the kitchen. Val just shook her head at him, but clearly both the twins had been crying. He dropped off his jeans upstairs, and he took a sweatshirt from his room and came back down. "Show me the farm," said Val bluntly, taking his arm. He pulled on the sweatshirt.

They again took the Land Rover down to the farm. Val asked about the trench and he explained about the plan for the fruit trees and bees. He showed her the equipment, the grain stores, the mill and she could see the cattle and sheep pile. She noticed the grave outside the kitchen door and the hole where she could see the metal springs of a mattress. "I was cleaning up when you first arrived, that's why I stripped off, I was dirty from, from the body," he finished.

"Certainly gave me an eyeful." Gary felt himself blush again. "I talked to the girls about moving on again," Val continued. "They don't want to go, but I don't want us to outstay our welcome. It's that time of the month as well, for them, they're, suffering a bit from PMT, they're young, they don't know how to handle it properly."

Gary was determined not to be embarrassed about that. "Why do you want to go?" He decided to concentrate on something he might understand.

"I don't want to outstay our welcome, as I said. You have a routine, and we are disturbing it, you've survived well…"

"Val," he interrupted, "don't you wonder why I'm still here. You've seen the graves; I have the means to finish it. I've been hanging on, waiting for people." He paused, "When you left the first time, I almost finished it. Please don't go; I need help I can't do this alone," he pleaded.

She looked at him, "Your survivor plan?"

"It was Hannah's plan, I don't know if it's true or possible, but you and the twins turning up are a start, and a huge relief."

"Her note said children, what about that?"

"I don't know, I guess if we find enough people children will happen."

"What about you, do you want children?"

"I haven't thought about it really, but when…" he paused again; he had to stop doing that. Sarah, Hannah, and the others were gone. "We had a young girl here, Sarah, she's in the picture; it was like I imagined having a child is like."

"Is she the fourth grave, with Hannah and your parents?"

"Yes, but how did you know?"

"Gary you are one of the most open people I have ever met, and despite this, this disaster, you have a touch of innocence about you. I like that." She paused for a while, lost in her own thoughts. "I want to have a child," she suddenly said.

"But, how, I mean who?"

"Hannah was right about you. I am sorry I read her letter and the briefs, without asking you first, but I do want to read them again, properly; that girl spoke a lot of sense. They tell me about you and her, don't you see? The child, well you may be the only capable man left, there's not much choice; I'm kidding." She punched his arm playfully. "Look, I'm thirty-five, time is running out. If you're fertile, then, well I have a chance of motherhood again."

"Again?"

"Yes, I lost a child to the virus, and her father, not that I was with him." Ella, thought Val.

"I'm sorry, I didn't know."

"Save your apologies for things you have done or might do, it happened, I'd rather not talk about it." The hard edge was back in her voice. "Anyway," she shook herself out of her mood. "I need to know that you will commit to the child, if we are lucky. I think you are too young, what are you twenty-two, or three?"

"I'm just twenty," he said quietly.

"Even worse, it doesn't matter, it can't matter, you have to promise, and I mean really promise that you'll help take care of us all, me, the child, the twins. Pregnancy can be dangerous, especially now, I won't be able to help you. You and the girls will have to do everything. Can you make that promise; that commitment?"

"Yes," he said, no equivocation, no hesitation, it was what Hannah would have wanted, what he wanted. "I promise."

"That's okay then," her eyes never left him; her penetrating gaze was reading his soul, he felt. Even Hannah hadn't looked at him that hard.

"How?"

"How do you think?"

"I mean, when? I don't know what I mean."

"I'll let you know, don't worry. Look this isn't love. I don't need you all romantic, and loving. I just need you ready! I hope that I'm attractive enough for you after Hannah." She wiggled her hips at him, and half twirled.

"Errrr yes, of course, I, I..."

"I hope you do get jokes," she said. "Look we'll get by, I'm sure we'll manage." She did genuinely smile this time. "Come on, the girls will think I've killed you or worse."

Gary couldn't think what worse was, "One thing though."

"Yes, what?"

"The basement, you need to tell me."

"I will, but not yet, okay?"

"Okay."

They returned in the Land Rover. The girls were both standing outside arms folded, looking very stern, waiting for them. Maybe they'd heard the engine coming back, or had watched the exchange. One of them had a pair of binoculars around her neck.

"Well?" Kelly asked. Gary guessed it was her. "Are we staying?"

"Yes," said Val.

"And?" Cass said, the binoculars bouncing against her chest.

"Yes," said Val.

"Yippee," said the girls, hugging Val and then to his surprise hugging Gary. They stayed.

CHAPTER TWENTY-ONE

Consummated

Gary had to wait several weeks to consummate the arrangement; he was beginning to think it wouldn't happen. During the wait, he did an expedition on his own, to the first food store he'd found near Rugby. As he packed to go, the girls became tense. He went through the security systems again, and then he sat and cleaned the SA80 and the pistol. He remembered the feeling he had gotten the last time he had been there. This time, he would go clearly armed, and not leave his arms in the rover. He didn't tell the girls why he was on edge, but they realised that he was. He tried the SA80's sling as Hannah had shown him, pulling the rifle into the firing position. Val and the twins had heard him that afternoon; off in the woods test firing. He drank no alcohol before going to bed early, barely touching a dish that the twins had tried out, using tinned meat. He took the rover and trailer again. He wanted to check out the other warehouses on the site. He tried the radio regularly as he departed, estimating they had thirty miles range before the landscape blocked the signal. Then, it was quiet on his trip. He would not stay over as it was only sixty miles or so, but he still took his full setup. He was given a hug from the twins before he went off. Val had just nodded, looking annoyed. When he arrived, he parked at the fire exit as before. He looked around. The weather was fairly dismal again. The summer was a damp squib compared to the previous summer. He didn't get the feeling he had before. He pulled open the fire door. His poster was still there, it was fading, so he replaced it. The warehouse had been used; he could see. A lot of boxes were gone. There were still plenty in the shadows. He found a note attached to one of the boxes:

Take what you need, but please leave us enough to live on. We've seen your poster we may come sometime, but not yet.

R *and* L

Gary looked around quickly and stupidly, but there was no one. He scribbled a reply on the bottom:

Thanks, there are four of us now, I'll come back, don't know when but I'll go to other sites to leave as much for you here as possible, we have power and water. We have radio, channel 23 UHF 234.6 MHz

Gary

He took only two boxes of meat tins, and a box of *Uncle Ben's* Rice boxes; he realised what they were after peeling open the top, he hoped it had survived. He checked other boxes, but he didn't want to take anything. He checked the other warehouses. One was full of books, CDs, and other discs. He had the twins list with him just in case. He found about half of the titles, of course there were hundreds of copies of each. The last warehouse held furniture, the warehouse roof was leaking, and he could smell mould. He would leave it as he had found other warehouses with furniture. He returned to the rover. He decided to drive the long way around the town's ring road, just to see what he could see.

He was almost back at his motorway junction for the M1 when he saw it. He braked hard; he couldn't believe what he was seeing. He turned around on the dual carriageway and backed up to the exit of the ring road, weaving across a couple of junctions. Fields replaced the warehouse and light-industry units. Yes, there it was, he was not mad or seeing things, there it was, a sheep grazing in the field. Gary could see sheep corpses, or what were left of them, near a gate, but there was an *alive* sheep, its fleece was thick and filthy, but it was there. He parked by the gate. It took him only ten minutes to catch it, by which time he was covered in mud and probably sheep dung, but he didn't care. He had a sheep! He had roped it, and then pulled and lifted it onto the trailer, where he tied it down. It would be uncomfortable, and had complained, but now it just lay or sat on the trailer. He pulled up some grass and placed it on the trailer. The sheep looked at him, with what he thought was utter disgust. Gary didn't care, he had a sheep! He steadily drove back to the house. He started calling on the radio at forty miles, but he didn't get a reply until nearly twenty-five miles to go.

"Golf Hotel receiving 30; is all okay? Over." One of the twins was replying. Gary couldn't tell which one it was, he still struggled with that. The twins deliberately tried to confuse him; often they succeeded. They would swap clothes halfway through the day so that they could look exasperated at him when he discovered from their voices what they had done. Unless they were mimicking that as well; he wouldn't put it past them.

"All okay and you won't believe what I have found, over."

The only reply he received was, "Did you get our CDs?"

"Some," he said, "see you in forty-five, out." The rain had finally stopped when he drove up through the gate. Val and the twins waited by the front entrance as he pulled to a stop. He bounded out of the vehicle expecting a hug.

"What the hell happened to you," said Val, "are you hurt?"

"I'm fine, I've..."

"Where are our CDs?" Cass, he thought.

"Why are you so muddy?" Kelly asked, he guessed as usual.

"I found a sheep, I caught a sheep, look!" He pointed at the tied sheep in the trailer.

"What?" Val said.

"Oh and maybe two more survivors," he added.

Another "What?"

He unloaded the sheep off the trailer and tied it up in the rear garden. Then, Val told him to strip outside, just to his boxers this time. Then, he went for a shower. Over dinner, dressed in clean clothes, he explained what had happened. All the time the sheep was forlornly looking at them through the house window. He then had to show the twins how to load the CDs onto the music system. He did have a couple of small cuts on his arms and a graze on his knee, from his tangle with the sheep, which Val then insisted on treating with disinfectant and not particularly kindly. The twins disappeared to their rooms to try out their new music collections, competing with each other for volume until Val shouted, unkindly, at them to turn it down. Just as his mother had done at him before the collapse, before A-Day, before the fall of civilisation. Gary thought Val's shouting was funny. Val did not and jabbed a sore graze with disinfectant.

"Ow, that hurts, what's got into you, what's the matter?"

"You," she said, "how could you?"

"How could I what? What have I done?" Gary sensed he had screwed up.

"You went off; you went off without a thought about us, our plan, what if you had an accident or something, then what would I have done? You promised me!" She was trying to keep her voice down, "You promised to give me a child, and then you just wander off, without a care in the world." Val sobbed.

"I'm sorry," Gary realised his mistake although he felt he was being harshly treated. If she felt like that, why hadn't she stopped him, or tried to get pregnant before now.

He kept his cool, learning from his father's approach to his mum; "Don't argue, agree it's all your fault," his dad had told him.

"I didn't think; I'd almost forgotten our chat. I'm sorry, but I'm back now. If you want, we could?"

"Not a chance, I'm having a bath, you clear up your mess." She walked off to the annexe.

It was two weeks later before it finally happened; first Val had barely spoken with him as he built a sheep fence just inside the farm orchard. There had been a practical discussion about what to do with it. "Find more," Gary said before he realised that would mean a trip away again.

"Get wool," one of the twins suggested.

"I'll need to shear it," said Gary. He found out how in a book, but he lacked the necessary equipment. He found it in the farm. By the time, he'd tied the sheep up and made his first effort, the sheep looked like a demented poodle. Val had finally smiled at him after that. The sheep seemed happier now though. The twins decided they would work on a wool project. They took the wool, and reading another research book, said they needed a spinner to do it properly. They then cleaned the wool with detergent and hung it up to dry.

It was mid-August; Gary had been morose the week before, the anniversary of Hannah's death. The twins had tried to cheer him up that day by swapping clothes at least four times until Val told them, "Leave him be." At dusk, he had taken a half bottle of malt up to Hannah's grave, it was all gone by the time Val fetched him in at midnight. The weather was nowhere near as good as it had been the year before.

The following morning, Gary had a hangover for the first time in his life, but he responded to teasing from the twins and his mood began to lift. A week later, he had brought the last fresh strawberries in; they would deal with them in the morning. The twins were on cooking duty. As he washed up, Val just said, "Tonight," to him, and gave him a look. The twins decided they wanted a movie, but finally went to bed. Gary didn't go out to Hannah. He sipped a malt, as did Val, whilst they watched some mindless film for the second or third time. "Shower," said Val, "I'll be fifteen minutes."

Gary went upstairs having sealed the house and done the security checks. He showered and shaved and got naked into bed. He was scared; he'd only ever been with Hannah. Don't think about Hannah, he told himself, think about something, anything. It was another twenty minutes before his door was pushed open. Val came into the room closing the door quietly behind her. He had left the light on. He always had with Hannah. Stop he told himself, stop. Val turned the light off, she was wearing a long white t-shirt he noticed, one of his, and he'd wondered where that had gone. She pulled the covers back. He could barely see her. Her black skin was hidden in the dark; she pulled the t-shirt off and lay down on top of him. He could feel her breasts against his chest; he went to kiss her thinking that would be right. "No," she whispered turning her face away. She began to move on top of him, but he wasn't responding. "What's wrong?"

"I can't just do this," he realised. "Just give me some more time?"

She took his hands and placed them on her breasts sitting astride him, she moved again. He began to respond. "That's it," she said, "that's right." It wasn't, and she rolled off of him. She lay on her back, as did he, their sweat quickly cooling.

"Val," he started very quietly, "I can't just do this mechanically, you may not love me or anything, but I need some affection."

"That's... *very* honest."

"Hannah told me to be honest in bed, and to ask a woman what she wants as well, you won't tell me or anything." Gary sat up trying to see Val's face in the dark.

"Angelic Hannah again! She's like a constant watch on me, a constant comparison." Val reigned in her anger. No, not anger, more inadequacy, she lowered her voice, "I'm not Hannah. I can't be her, please don't compare me to her, just give me what you promised." Val got up and left the bedroom.

Gary pulled the sheet over himself and tried to sleep, cursing himself for his failings, angry with Val and even Hannah. What did he know about women and what they wanted? What did he know about human relationships? He was twenty from a wealthy middle-class home, living a privileged protected existence. Even since A-Day he had been protected. The house and his parent's plans and even the understanding they had of what was going to happen. Then there had been Hannah, Cal, and Greavesey, with their guidance, and training. Yes, he knew death, but it was still sheltered. He had to live for the living, not for Hannah, and he had to stop bringing her name into every conversation. He would try.

The following day was tense; the twins sensed something had happened. Kelly agreed to accompany Gary to the half-dilapidated garden centre. Gary took the Lexus and the trailer instead of the Rover. There was a brief discussion about no radio, before Val shrugged and said he could do what he wanted, he would anyhow. Cass stayed with Val, working on the wool. Kelly started quizzing him as soon as they were on the way. "What's up with you two again?" Kelly asked.

"We had a disagreement that's all, we're fine," Gary replied.

"She's mad at you about something, like the radio."

"It's not the radio."

"It must be something serious. She's grumpy as hell. She had a real go at me over my room."

"Then keep it tidy!"

Kelly realised Gary would not be sympathetic about tidiness. Val called it borderline OCD, whatever that meant, she thought she remembered hearing the term at school, but that was a long time ago; over two years. "See you're tetchy as well."

"Sorry, look it's personal, can we talk about something else? We have to get these trees." They were silent for a while. They drove towards the camp, Gary slowed. "I should check everything's okay," he said.

"Please don't," Kelly had gone pale.

"Why?" Gary glanced at her expression. "Okay then," he sped up and headed for the Garden Centre. Kelly breathed hard. "I don't understand. I mean, why don't you want me to go in?"

"Its personal," Kelly pushed a CD into the Lexus' music system turning away from him.

"I'm sorry, but it's one of my jobs to go there, and as we were going past, I thought I'd…"

"You both treat us like kids."

"Well, you are only..."

"We're not kids anymore! Jane Grey was only 15 when she was Queen, for fucks sake." Kelly and Cass were reading several history books. Val would have told her off about her language, the movies were not helping. "We wish you both would stop treating us like that." There was no conversation in the vehicle for a while; their mutual silence was only disturbed by the sound of the CD. Gary pulled into the garden centre and drove through to where the banks of trees and shrubs could be seen. Neither of them went to get out. "Is your row with Val about us?" Kelly eventually asked.

"No, it's about the future."

"Val want's a baby doesn't she?"

"How do you know?"

"We would hear her sometimes, crying when we were on the road, she wouldn't say, she doesn't say much. She has a baby's picture in her stuff." Gary decided it was not the right time to tell Kelly off about prying. "She wants another baby, and time's running out, she's getting older, so *that* is what the row's about, isn't it?" Kelly looked at him, an air of triumph about her. "Won't you do it with her? Why not? She's pretty she has a good figure, she's not too old." Gary was bright red.

"I don't think you should be saying this stuff."

"Don't be silly what do you think Cass and I talk to each other about. You're the only man about and eventually…" She looked at him with a slight smile.

Gary went redder if that was possible. "Kelly stop, look this is between Val and I, it doesn't involve you or Cass."

"Yes, it does," said Kelly. "We read Hannah's survivor brief, remember. We have to start the Human Race again; that means children for all of us. We don't mind, by the way." She smiled at him again.

Was that a seductive smile? Gary thought, he mustn't think that way. "Jesus Christ, you are the limit Kelly. Look, it's personal. As I said, it's not that I won't. It's just not that easy, I mean, I..."

"The men in the camp didn't have any problems." Kelly suddenly had tears in her eyes.

"What men? What camp? Tell me about the camp?" said Gary quietly, he took Kelly's hand and squeezed it, and she shuddered, not at his touch but at the memory. She began to tell him, drizzle started on the windscreen.

"The camp was called Fox Farm," Kelly started. "We'd seen signs for it for miles. We were walking, trying to find food but going, I suppose, towards London in November last year. We were running out of food. We'd tried to get some from a supermarket, but it had already been looted, there was no food left. We got some apples from a tree, and we carried some more in our bags, and we had some water from rain in plastic bottles but that was it. An army vehicle came along the road, you know, the ones with the canvas backs, like at the camp. When it stopped a soldier, asked us if we were okay and if we were heading for Fox Farm. We could see lumps on his neck, so we knew he was sick. He said that they were from there and that they could give us a ride if we wanted. We didn't say anything, whether the man realised we were girls I don't know, we didn't look much like girls; we wore hats and jackets."

"Anyway we said okay, so he told us to climb in the back. There were two soldiers already inside and a pile of bodies in plastic bags. Those soldiers gave us a Mars bar each. We hadn't had any food, other than apples, for ages. So we grabbed it and we ignored the bodies in the truck. When we arrived at the camp, there was some shouting, but we couldn't see what about, because the back canvas was down. When they opened it up, all we could see was a huge pit. We thought they were going to put us in it! They didn't of course, but there were thousands of black plastic bags in the bottom of it, two or three deep in places." Kelly's head was in her hands. "There were other trucks with soldiers unloading bodies just throwing them in the pit. When Mum and Dad died, our neighbour carried them out for us onto the street. We watched the army truck come down the road and pick them up. We thought that this was where they would have ended up. Thrown into a pit like rubbish bags." Kelly was quiet for a little while.

She eventually carried on, "We could see smoke coming from another pit, and there was a big mound further along as well. *Death Pit Central* is what one of the soldiers called it. Anyway he sent us towards a tent, so we walked over. We were glad to get away from the pit. A man, another soldier, took our names and ages and then, in another tent, we were given some hot food and then we were shown to a barn. It was full of other people, all ages, men, women, and some children. The others were all sick. There were cesspits behind the barn, and there was water from a pipe. It wasn't too bad, I suppose."

Gary might disagree. "Is that where Val found you?" he

interrupted. He needed to breathe and break the spell as well; it also gave Kelly a chance to blow her nose.

"That was later. I suppose the camp got quieter over the next month or so. Anyway, there were fewer soldiers about, and less food again, despite the number of people getting fewer in the barn. We didn't have much to do but look after the sick ones, we'd help them to the toilets, the cesspits, when they needed to go, but they were all ill and dying. When they did die, soldiers would come in, or some of the barn adults would carry the body out to the pits, even we helped take them outside the barn." Kelly stopped again tears trickling down her face. "When we'd first arrived, we heard and saw helicopters as well as the trucks, but after, probably eight weeks, it had pretty much stopped. It was quiet, apart from the moans from the ill ones. We heard the odd gun shot as well, one of the men told us what the bangs were. There was a group of buildings and tents across the other side of the camp from us. We were told it was the HQ, and we didn't need to go there, so we didn't. Later, I think one of the soldiers… he must have, realised we weren't ill; he had a big swelling on the side of his neck. Anyway, one afternoon he came and collected us. He said he wanted to check for the virus. So we moved across to the other side." Kelly stopped and took another deep breath.

"The pits, we walked past all the open pits, they were full of bodies no bags, just tumbled. We did holocaust day at school, and they showed us the black and white pictures from the concentration camps. This was colour and the smell and the numbers of bodies. There were bulldozers parked near the top, it was, it was…" She turned into his shoulder and sobbed hard.

"Let's get the fruit trees. You can tell me more when you're ready," Gary said, horrified by what he had already heard. They got out of the car and spent the next fifteen minutes selecting six fruit trees, two apples, pears, and Victoria plum saplings.

"We had Victoria plums in our garden," said Kelly. "Can we get some more bulbs as well for the spring?"

They scoured around the centre and added some roses and other shrubs to the collection in the trailer. Gary added some of the last compost bags as well. He would have to go further afield if he wanted more, which reminded him that he couldn't go far until Val was… He would have to deal with that soon. Kelly was back in the Lexus; he went to start the car.

“No, wait,” she said, “I need to finish, you need to know, and then you can tell me about Val and Hannah, okay?” Gary wasn't sure about the last bit, but nodded his compliance. “When we got to the HQ, we were taken to a medical tent and given a test like your machine. They were amazed we were green. So were we, I mean we didn't know either. There was a discussion about us, then they stuck us up some stairs in a barracks room; there were beds in there all empty.” There was a long silence. Kelly just looked down at her hands. Kelly couldn't say about the next bit, refused to remember the next bit, she had promised Cass, they had promised each other; they would never say. “Val found us a while later. Val will need to tell you about what happened to her and the others.” Gary was confused. What had happened to Val? He missed the hint that something else might have happened to the twins. Kelly was continuing, “We heard lots of noises, and we were scared, we even heard screams, but we had food and shelter, and… we were green. That's why we hate the camp and the pits, I hate them, Cass and I hate them, so does Val.”

"I didn't know; I'm sorry I took you there that first time."

"It was bad, we didn't know you; didn't know if we could trust you. Val said we had to be very careful, and then you took us to a camp with pits and you were just like the soldiers, you just ignored them, it scared us all, so we decided to leave."

"So the Grandparents were…"

"We did go to see, but we knew they wouldn't have made it, but we had to get away. Once we were on the road we talked about it; about you and decided to come back, and we found you naked on the doorstep." Kelly smiled, and Gary blushed again. The atmosphere was broken. "So tell… have you, you know, with Val, is she?"

"I…"

"You promised?"

"I did no such thing, I"

"I told you…"

"Okay, yes, but no, we tried, and no she's not pregnant."

"Why not?"

"Look we've only just started and…" This was excruciatingly embarrassing, thought Gary.

"Last night, last night was the first time wasn't it?"

"Yes," confessed Gary.

"So why's she angry with you?"

"I," he paused, "look it's complicated, and personal, I mentioned Hannah and..."

"Are all boys idiots?" Gary looked shocked. "If you bothered to watch some of our films, you might know that mentioning an ex in bed, is not a great way to build a relationship. Have you apologised?" Gary felt as if he were in a film himself. Here was a fourteen-year old girl, no a young woman, teaching him about relationships. He was supposed to be a grown man. "You better get us home now, wait till I tell Cass, she'll be mad at you as well. Is that why you came out, to run away?"

"No, I needed to get the trees. I, I don't know; yes, probably," he admitted. He started the car; he thought that the next bit would be equally embarrassing. It was. When he parked, Kelly immediately went to find Cass. Gary went to find Val; she was reading the reference book on bees.

"I need to talk to you," he said as the girls walked into the lounge area, "alone," he added. He pulled Val to her feet and virtually dragged her back to the car. They drove down to the trench he had prepared. Val looked furious. He kissed her, he didn't let her pull away, she went to slap him, he stopped her. "Listen," he said, "I'm very sorry about last night. I didn't do that properly or treat you right. I'm an idiot, so Kelly tells me, she's probably right, no don't say anything, Kelly knows and so does Cass by now. Anyway, I promised you down here before that I would help you have a child and look after you, and then I behave like an idiot. Look if you want to stab me with that knife, your hand is resting on, then go ahead. You are a beautiful woman; any man would be glad to have you in his bed. I'd like you in mine, if you'll give it another try, just; no, it's my fault, you just; just be you."

"I thought it might be prejudice, you being white and me being black and..."

"No, why would you think that? I love your colour; I mean it's not important. I'm screwing this up again, aren't I?"

There was a half-smile on Val's mouth, "And you told Kelly, all this?"

"No, well some I guess, she asked, and she seemed to know about you wanting to have a child, we had a long talk. She told me a bit about Fox Farm."

"What did she tell you?" The smile vanished.

Gary held up his hands, why was this so difficult he wondered? "Only about their part, the pits and I understand about the camp now. Kelly said I would have to ask you about your time there, I presume that's the basement? You don't have to tell me now. Tell me when you are ready," then he paused. Val looked at him hard as she had before. "I'm going to plant these trees now. I'd like you to help, but if you want to shout at me or use that knife, then… Oh stuff it!" He gave her another kiss, looked her in the eye, and then walked around the vehicle. He grabbed a sapling and carried it back to the trench. He went back to the trailer and picked another. He avoided Val's gaze. When he went for the third sapling, she was carrying one of the others back. They spent an hour planting the saplings. He would need to water them in later he realised, have to bring some in a jerry can.

"You need to water these in," said Val.

"I was just thinking that."

"After lunch," she said, and he nodded. When they returned to the house, the girls were waiting in the kitchen. Sandwiches were on the table, and fresh coffee was in the pot.

"I won," said Cass, grabbing the last homemade oat cookie from a tin.

"Won what?" Val asked.

"Kelly bet me that Gary would be dead or beaten up. I said no, just minor injuries." Both the girls smirked.

Val tried to look cross, but in the end joined in the smirk at Gary's expression. She went and hugged both the girls. "I see I'm going to have to have a serious conversation with you two."

Val came to Gary's room that night and every night for two weeks. She would not stay to sleep, but they managed. She was cross after the first month, as her period came, and she wasn't pregnant. There was another discussion with the girls. They had decided to become experts on pregnancy, pulling books from the library during a visit, which now joined the growing library in the house. A week later, Val returned to his bed, and they started again. The whole house knew the timings of Val's ovulation, checked by temperature, and what stage they were at, and whether Val and he had been together. Gary got used to the discussion amongst the women. He knew Val's period was due, but he agreed with her that he should make a trip to get the beehives in before winter. If she weren't pregnant, they would try next month, Val would be thirty-six then, she said.

He had located the beehives by simply checking yellow pages for honey merchants. With the girls, he headed out, leaving Val to mend a part of the fence that the sheep had tried to destroy to get at some fresh grass. Gary and the twins returned with two hives. Gary was dressed in a military NBC suit, to try to stop being stung; he had been. He was unloading with help from the girls who were standing back. The hives' entrance hatches were shut, but the hives were a bit rotten, so the odd bee had escaped. Val came walking down the pathway. She was carrying what looked like a stick. She showed it to Gary. Pregnant read the sign. Val kissed him in front of the girls. There were excited screams from them. Gary beamed; he was going to be a father!

***

Val was thirty-seven or thirty-eight weeks pregnant, and very fed up. The baby was due mid-May according to the calendar, and her own, and the twins calculations. Val felt fat, and her ankles ached. The girls had been practising routines with her, but she was dreading the birth. She knew what could go wrong, and she had not had an easy birth with her first child. She felt a twinge, probably another *Braxton Hicks*. She was sitting, more like lying, on a garden lounger with a glass of water; she missed wine and the malt whisky she shared with Gary. Her pregnancy had gone well. Despite her ankles, she was fit and well, no morning sickness that she could recall, no spasms, and no scares from bleeding. The house was prepared, and had been for a few weeks. She had joined an expedition to pick up everything that the baby might need according to Kelly's list. Kelly had developed the list habit over the past six months. She used Hannah's briefs as the basis. It was obvious to everyone else, but Kelly, that Hannah was her role model, even though she had never met her. The girls were learning to drive all the vehicles, and Gary had taught them all how to shoot with the SA80 as well as the shotgun and pistol. He had followed the training he got from Hannah and in one of her briefing papers, directing him on such matters as range safety and target distances. Gary seldom, if ever, mentioned her. Val knew that was deliberate on his part and for her sake. It didn't stop the twins mentioning her. They were fifteen and gorgeous, Val thought, long blonde hair, tall, fit, and healthy helped by working in the outdoors. They worked just as hard as Gary and had helped him plough a field, and then plant the seed wheat in *Arse Farm*. Gary had eventually told them the tale and the name. The crop was slowly turning yellow ripening for harvest. The winter had been mild, with almost no snow, and the vegetables and fruit were well on their way to bountiful crops.

Gary had done one two-day trip, away on his own. She and the girls had fretted endlessly. He had gone to a fish factory on the Northeast coast, via two other business parks. He had taken the Lexus and trailer; he said for the comfort. He would be out of range of the radio anyway. He had returned with boxes of canned sardines and tuna, plus some ham, and beef in tins. He had also found a fish farm, with huge tanks of dead salmon, he said. The tinned fish had gone down well with fresh pasta. He also thought he had seen another sheep on a hill but couldn't be certain. He had left posters in six locations. He hadn't been back to the first warehouses; he wanted to return. After the baby, Val had said, and Gary had agreed.

She wanted Gary near now. She sighed, another twinge, she

thought. She could see Gary and the twins up the garden, laying a water hose. Gary wanted to extend from the rain tanks down to the fruit trees and even *Arse Farm*. He talked about taking power there as well and maybe laying some conduit. They had discussed it last night over dinner. They could go the other way to the primary school as well, the power line to that was already open. Gary had taken them all to his father's office, factory, and warehouse. There were two hundred solar panels in the warehouse. Gary had plans, Hannah's plans, Val knew, but plans nonetheless. Gary also knew where the wind turbines were, as he had been there with his father during the planning of the house. She felt another twinge. This was harder, Oh shit, she thought, it's started. She called out to Gary.

***

Val was dreaming. She was dreaming of her daughter, her daughter's smile, the dream turned, as dreams do. Suddenly, she was in the basement. She was screaming and shouting, and then she was awake, the baby was screaming, not her. God she was tired, she thought. It was just three weeks since Henry Gary had arrived with little fuss, she thought. No panics, no last minute emergencies, seven hours of labour, with her providing instructions to the girls and Gary. Gary had been great. He had stayed calm and not run away like Ella's father. She could name Ella now she thought, her little girl. Henry was raising the roof; he would have the whole house awake. She had stayed in the annexe and Henry's cot was there. She picked him up. Breast-feeding had been the only slight problem at first; she hadn't done that with Ella, rushing to get back to work so that she could earn her living. Henry latched on and gurgled, she looked down on him a light covering of black hair, but he was pale skinned. Cass mentioned that he looked like Gary, Val couldn't tell yet. She looked outside, dawn was breaking; it looked as if it would be a lovely day. She dozed off.

***

Three months into her pregnancy, Val had told Gary about the basement. As soon as she had become pregnant she had stopped visiting him in his bedroom. Tension had built until he took her for one of their chats by the fruit trees. His excuse was to plan the ploughing, but she knew he wanted to talk. For some reason he found it easier there. After a brief chat about the fruit trees, she said, "Out with it, what's up?"

"You," he said.

"Me, what have I done?"

"Nothing, that's the problem, since you got pregnant you haven't been near me?"

"I, I'm sorry," Val was a bit lost. "We agreed we'd get a baby, she patted her stomach, and that…"

"So you just thought that would be it? I miss you, all right? I miss the sex as well."

"I see, I, well I didn't think you would want me now, after all you were only doing it, because you promised me."

"I didn't do it for just that, not after… Anyway, I miss you, being with you, and not just the sex, the talking the…"

"Okay I get the picture, so you want me to come back to your bed?"

"Yes."

"I should get you to beg." Gary realised she was teasing him; she had a sly sense of humour.

They slept as a couple for three more months until Val said she was too fat. She was also embarrassed when the girls would come in with breakfast in bed. They had stopped sneaking around after Cass or had it been Kelly, told them they were silly and added, to both their embarrassments, that they could be heard making love as well. Gary had choked over his coffee. Val demonstrated that dark skin could go red. They had slowly stopped having sex anyway. They were both concerned for the baby, and they both knew that it would be fine, but they spent most evenings just talking before falling asleep. Working the land was hard work, so sleeping always came easy. One evening Val just started talking, they were both lying looking up at the stars.

***

"I found Fox Farm in January, eighteen months after A-Day, the dates just blur; I came across a sign. Before that, I had worked at the hospital, but nearly everyone was gone. I needed food. I tried cars, and I walked around the edge of London. I didn't like cities. Southampton was bad when I left there. When I walked into the camp, it was like hell on earth. Kelly told you about the pits. I told them on the gate, there were only a couple of soldiers about by then, that I was a nurse and that I wanted food, I hadn't eaten for days, I was weak and cold. They were both sick. I could see from their necks. They said I had to see the sergeant; I walked past the pits and went in. He was creepy, short dark hair, bulge on his neck. He looked me up and down, and I felt unclean. He asked me if I was sick. I said I didn't think so. He did the blood check I was green, I'd had one at the hospital, but it was still nice to know. I said I wanted some food and rest. He just nodded, and one of the other soldiers had come into the room," Val was breathing heavily Gary noticed. He put a hand on her stomach.

"You don't have to," he said.

"I do, I do have to," she replied, placing her hand on his. "I suddenly felt afraid, the twins were probably up the stairs even then, but I didn't know that. The other soldier asked what I would do for the food. I didn't realise what he meant. He then said I could think about it a while. He grabbed my arm, he was stronger than me, and he was armed. I didn't know what was happening. He took me to a door; there were steps down, a big basement. It was dark and dingy and stank. Must have been fifteen women down there in the dark, but they were all silent, no hellos, nothing. I could vaguely see that they were all ill. I tried to talk to them, but they said nothing back. I'd only been down there about fifteen minutes when the door opened again. Two girls of about twenty, one was Asian, one white were, well really, thrown down the steps. They were topless, as well, but both were clearly ill. Their backs were bruised, they had lumps on their breasts, they weren't really crying, though. I tried to help them. I asked them what had happened, and they just looked at me."

"I'd been in that basement maybe two hours. I'd just been sssh'd by people whenever I tried to ask what was happening. I wasn't the oldest in the basement, but I was the only one I could see who was healthy." Val leaned over to the bedside table, and sipped some water; her voice had become flat and monotone. "The door opened, and the same soldier who had pushed me down there told me to come up. I walked up; he pointed me past the stairs and into a side room. The sergeant was there sitting on a bed, his shirt was off, another soldier stood by the side. They… they raped me, all three of them, they did whatever they wanted. What could I do? They were armed and stronger men, they hit me if I tried to stop them. They cut me on my arm when I refused to do something." Gary knew the scar, he held her to him; she sobbed a little. "Anyway, after a while they were done, they let me get dressed although most of my clothes were torn. They took me out of the room into another room and there was some food with another soldier. He pulled off my top before he gave me some sort of stew… I had to sit, half-naked, whilst I ate. That was the way it went."

"We had buckets in the basement for toilets. The women around me slowly got worse. When one died, the soldiers came down and carried her out. Sometimes two women would be taken up, and only one would return. We only got food if we went with them, when they wanted. Sometimes it was two days or more before they called for one of us; we were desperate to be called, to get food. They would throw water in bottles down every now and then. I was not ill, so I got called more and more… They would call two or even three of us up and compare our bodies. They laughed at the other girl's breasts as the lumps increased in size. I could see the pain they were in; when I said something I was slapped and humiliated. I… I kept quiet, what could I do? They made us…" she stopped. "It carried on, but then less often, the last time I was called up there, it was just the sergeant, he looked very ill. I wanted him dead. He told me to strip what little I had on, once we were in the room. I said no, he came towards me and I hit him on his neck right on his tumour. It must have exploded inside or something, he went down. I grabbed his pistol and I… I shot him in the face."

Gary jerked up in the bed. Val's dull monotone had lulled him, even whilst he was horrified.

"I shot him Gary, from as close as I am to you, the girls don't know that. They don't know most of it… They know I was raped, but not the rest. I thought some others would come running when the shot went off, but nothing happened. I pulled his body away from the door where he'd fallen. I found some clothes in the room and put them on. I opened the door. I had the pistol in my hand, I would have shot anyone who came in, but no one did. I opened the door to the basement, there was another light by the entrance that I switched on. I could finally see the basement properly. It wasn't a sight I ever want to see again... I went back down there to try and get the others out, but only five of them could walk and I helped them up the stairs into the food room. We helped ourselves to what we could find. I was watching the doors and scared someone would come at any moment. One of the other women asked me where the soldiers were. I just said, 'dead.' She just nodded at me; she was too weak to talk I suppose, or too shocked. When I went back into the corridor, I heard voices from up the stairs; it was the twins. They said they hadn't been touched, and as far as I could see, then, they hadn't. I don't think that's true, but they haven't said anything different. They hadn't been fed for two days either. So they came down, they didn't know me from Adam. I was dirty, smelly, wearing thrown together army gear, and carrying a pistol. I must have looked scarier than the soldiers. We stayed in the building a few days, I checked outside. There were some soldiers on the far side. An occasional truck sound and the odd shot but no one came over to the building. There was no one left alive in the basement, the girls helped carry out a couple of the living ones, we took them upstairs; they died there."

"Kelly didn't tell me that," Gary spoke for the first time in ages.

"No, I'm sure there's lots they didn't tell you, another time maybe. I need a whisky."

Gary could see the tear tracks on her cheeks "I'll get you one," he went to move.

"No, it's just wishful thinking; not with the baby." She took his hand and put it back on her stomach then moved it up to her breast. She pulled him down on top of her.

"Are you sure?" She shut him up with a kiss.

CHAPTER TWENTY-TWO

Early Morning Arrivals

Val awoke to the sound of consternation in the house. Henry was still asleep. Gary was running, coming out of the basement in just his boxers, the SA80 sling was going on over his neck. Kelly followed him out with a pistol; she was just in a T-shirt, then Cass wearing just a t-shirt, as well, with the Shotgun and another pistol, which she gave to Val. Val tucked her breast back into the nightdress, she realised she had walked out like that, no one noticed. Gary was focused on the TV screen. There was a vehicle at the gate. There were four indistinct figures walking up the drive. They were all armed. Val went back into her annex, she grabbed Henry, and then the rifle from the door side cupboard, and she ran up the stairs, somehow not dropping either of them. "Kelly, Cass," said Gary, "upstairs with Val. Cass check the back cameras, on my study TV." They went without a word, responding without their normal backchat. Gary carefully opened the front door lying on the ground and inching round using the SA80's sight. His heart raced. He suddenly wished the house wasn't all glass; he hoped the girls were well back.

"That's far enough," he shouted. The group stopped. "Put down your weapons and put your hands up," Gary shouted again. There was a quick discussion amongst the group, then they started forward again. The shot was massively loud in the doorway, the cartridge spun away and bounced on the tiles, the shot echoed in the still air. Gary could instantly smell the cordite, the bullet pinged off the drive three feet to the right of the first person, exactly where he had aimed; he redirected his aim to the lead person. He had stopped along with the others.

"Don't shoot," one of them said. Their weapons were laid down, and hands were raised.

Gary wasn't convinced. "Strip," he shouted. There was another discussion. The jackets came off, the jeans went down, he realised through the sights he had a fifty-year old man, an older woman, another thirty-year old woman, and a boy. Gary guessed his age as fourteen. When they were down to their underwear, he shouted, "Stop. Cass, Kelly?" Gary called over his shoulder into the house.

"Yes," they replied.

"Down here." When they arrived, he said to Kelly, "Take the SA, and give me the pistol. Cass, move over behind the rover and cover me. Kelly, if they try anything; shoot first…"

"Ask questions later," she answered.

"Good girl," they moved into position. Cass ran out behind the rover, giving Gary a view of her naked bottom as she crouched, watching the front.

Kelly said, "You may want to tuck yourself in first." Gary looked down and did so. He walked slowly out toward the group, the grit of the drive digging into his feet, he was careful to leave a line for Kelly with the SA80 and Cass with the shotgun, wishing she had grabbed the other SA80 instead. He approached the group. He told them to step back, they did, away from their clothes and the weapons. He checked, but he could not see any hidden holsters or knife sheaths. The air was cool, but Gary wasn't cold. His heart raced. The older woman was shivering in her underwear.

"You must be Gary," said the man. "I'm Rodger, R, the boy is Liam, L, the lady is Celia and..."

"I'm Miriam." The woman was Asian. "Can we put our hands down? We mean you no harm."

"Yes," said Gary, "walk forward towards the house."

"Our clothes?" the older woman said, Celia. If that was really her name?

"Later," he said. Gary didn't know whether there were weapons hidden in the clothes. They moved forward. Cass stood up behind the rover, there was a whistle from Kelly and Cass used one hand to pull her t-shirt down, her modesty protected only from view, by the rover. "In the door, turn left into the kitchen, take a seat, keep your hands on the table." Gary followed them in, Kelly also. "Anyone else with you?" Gary realised he'd asked too late.

"No," said the man, "just us."

Gary wasn't sure of the answer. "Cass, check the sensors, and go put some jeans on. Val?"

"Yes," he heard her shout back.

"Keep checking the drive."

"Okay."

"If you're lying, you'll get the first bullet," Gary said to the man Rodger.

"I'm not."

Gary pressed the pistol to the Asian woman's head, as she was closest. "Is he?"

"No," she jumped, "it's just us."

Cass arrived back wearing jeans, although Gary couldn't see that; he had backed off, but still kept the pistol pointed at the group. Kelly was by his side, "Kelly, you go now," he ordered.

"Okay," she said.

Cass said, "I think they're okay. You're scaring them." Gary lowered the pistol. There was an audible sense or gasp, of relief from the four-seated persons, and maybe Gary himself.

Val arrived with Henry in one arm and the rifle in the other. "It's okay, Gary, they're okay. Hello Celia," she said.

Celia had been a Human Resources administrator at Val's first hospital. Val needed quite a bit of processing done when she first arrived from Grenada and Celia had helped sort out the paperwork. Val hadn't seen her for nearly four years or more. Val hadn't recognised her at first, she had been too worried about the approach of the strangers. Now, they hugged. Gary had shaken his head in disbelief and gone to put some clothes on, after he had told Cass to collect the weapons from outside and check the clothes, he had finally allowed Val's welcome to be extended. The weapons were in a pile outside. Gary still had a pistol with him but in a holster he was now wearing belted to his jeans. The twins had taken the SA80, the shotgun, and the remaining pistol back into the basement and Val had given Gary the rifle to put back in the cupboard. When he finally returned to the kitchen, the twins made him sit between them. Val had kissed his cheek and given him Henry to hold. They had all dressed except for Val. She was still wearing a dressing gown. Henry slept. Coffee and tea were served. Toast was in the toaster. They were running short of tea. Kelly had a piece of paper out as usual and Gary said, "Tea," to her, she showed it to him, already on the list. Gary was immensely proud of the girls for the way they had acted that morning.

"Look, really sorry we startled you like that," Rodger started an explanation, with an apology, which Gary did not feel was truly meant. Gary had really taken a dislike to the man. "The last house we approached, well it wasn't good; they tried to steal all our food. We weren't sure if we had the right place as it's not on the road maps. Liam and I," he indicated the teenage boy who had started devouring toast, much to Cass's amusement, "well, we've been meaning to come for a while, but Liam wanted to search for his aunt and uncle first. No luck of course. We did winter holed up on a farm near the warehouses in Rugby, where we left the note. We found Miriam and Celia earlier this year. Thought we might see you at the warehouse, but we can't watch every day. We left another note for you just in case. When you hadn't come by the spring, we thought we would set out. Had trouble getting fuel for the car, ended up siphoning, anyway here we are. We saw you a while back before that loading in the warehouse, but we didn't have any weapons then. We saw that you did, so we left you alone."

Gary nodded, wondering why Rodger had given such a long explanation. There was something wrong with the story. The weapons, he had not had weapons on display that he could recall. How had they found the house? He had left directions and the address on his poster for the camp not the house. He was even more on guard, but he said nothing. Kelly kicked him under the table.

"A bit embarrassing all that with the clothes," said Miriam. "You had me really scared for a while."

"Your son?" Celia asked, "Can I hold him."

"He's Val's and mine," said Gary. Val took the baby from Gary and handed him to Celia.

"I can't remember the last time I had a baby to hold, he's adorable."

"Gary?" Cass said.

"I'm going to check the chickens," said Gary, still suspicious. He went and checked their car on the roundabout route.

"He'll be okay," said Val. "He's a bit nervous and protective, and the last time people turned up at his house he had a gun pointed at him."

"Who was that?" Liam asked.

"Me," Val said, no one laughed.

"Actually the last time we turned up, he had less clothes on than this morning," said Kelly, and that did get a laugh.

Gary returned to several conversations going on at once. He grabbed a mug of coffee and walked back out to the bench. Val found him there a few minutes later. The girls were watching Henry.

"What's up?" She went and sat next to him.

"I screwed up."

"What do you mean you were brilliant? Our hero?" She put an arm around him and kissed his cheek.

"I didn't check for others."

"There weren't any."

"If there had been, we could be dead or worse. Stupid mistake, could have been fatal. They had a shotgun in the car as well, didn't search there either."

"So what, you're not the only one here, we could have said something as well."

"It's my job. I promised to protect you all, and I nearly messed up. Hannah would have got it right."

Val was exasperated. "Hannah is dead Gary, you're sitting next to her, she would have been very proud this morning, I was very proud this morning, the girls, well, that's going to be another problem soon." She mumbled the last bit. "You did what you should have done, and you did remember and check. It was just later than was perfect in your eyes, not mine. I hadn't even thought of there being more people. I was too surprised there were *any* people. Not only that, but you set the alarms last night, and you didn't sleep through them when they went off. You took *immediate decisive action*, as one of Hannah's damn briefs says."

"Four more Gary! You realise that must mean there are more out there as well." Val was surprised how much she wanted there to be more people, maybe she had bought into Hannah's dream or plan as well? "Now stop being stupid, you took a risk with us, look how that worked out, this will too. I know Celia, it's amazing she's here, but she wouldn't be with them if they were a risk to us. Now bring the rest of those eggs, I think we are going to get through some food."

"I don't trust him, Rodger that is. Don't know why, but something's wrong."

"Okay, but we didn't trust each other at first either, did we?"

"No," Gary had to agree, as Val walked back towards the house. Gary did return and listened to the conversations, including the story of how they had found the sheep that could be seen grazing in its pen near the *Arse Farm* gate. Val and the twins could only draw Gary into the conversation when the house systems and history were discussed. Then, the conversation turned to what now?

"Gary has a plan, well, we all have a plan," said Kelly.

"Yes," said Cass, or was it the other way round today; their fast dress had left them both wearing plain white t-shirts and jeans, their blonde hair tied back in identical pony, tails. God, what did he look like? He hadn't shaved for a few days, and he knew his hair was long again; also tied back. He knew he was bigger than any of them in the room, but no one was short, except maybe Liam the boy, but he was still young.

The twins had wanted to check Gary's height; Val was tall, as well as the twins, Val was what, five feet-eight, and the twins taller. They had grown since they arrived. He was six feet-five? The house was deceiving, as his parents had wanted big doors and ceilings. The basement was high because of the full height computer racks, 42U plus stands whatever that worked out at. He was drifting.

"Gary," said Kelly, kicking him.

"What? Sorry I was thinking"

"A dangerous sign," Cass said. He could tell it was going to be one of those days when they teased him all day, if he weren't careful.

"Miriam asked you about the plan, but you're in another world."

"We need to check," Gary said.

"Check what?" Rodger said defensively.

"For the virus," said Gary, getting up and switching on the Checker.

"But we're all still alive, everyone who had the virus is dead," Rodger said.

What was his problem? Gary wondered. There was something about him that Gary instantly disliked. He didn't buy his story about the warehouse the first time. Gary recalled that his weapons had been in the car, and he'd had that feeling that he was being watched. How had they found the house he asked himself again? A sixth sense or something at the warehouse. He had the feeling again now. Gary tried to clear his mind. "I'll go first," Gary said.

"We check regularly," said Val, sensing that Gary was concerned about something, and trying to defuse the tension that had crept back into the room. Gary took a needle from a sterilised solution near the Checker, Val had set up the system; the knife was messy and dramatic. She had also gotten a set of slides to go with a host of extra medical supplies they had looted from a GP's surgery, the drugs were long gone, but sterilisers and so on had still been there. The medical kit, set up by his parents, was now much bigger.

Gary placed his slide in the Checker after it had beeped its readiness. Ping and green. Kelly, Cass, and Val followed. Val then checked little Henry; she did it as a demonstration, as she had checked only yesterday evening. She then handed Henry, who had cried with the prick of the needle, to Kelly. Miriam then volunteered; then Celia, then Liam. The machine ponged, and a red light came on. Gary hadn't heard a pong since Hannah, Cal, and Greavesey had demonstrated it. There was silence. "Rodger," said Gary.

"I'm Red as well," he said.

"Up!" Val said. She had grabbed the pistol out of Gary's holster and was pointing it at Rodger and Liam. Liam looked as though he was going to cry. "Out," Val ordered. They walked out of the rear entrance. "Down that way," she pointed to the path towards the farm. "Sit there," she told them. Gary and the others had followed her out.

"Val, what are you going to do?" Celia asked.

"Did you know Celia? Miriam?"

"No," said Miriam, "we thought they were clean, green, they said they were."

"How could you?" Val shouted at them, "You come to our house armed, and infected! You might have infected Henry already, I should shoot you on the spot!"

"Don't be ridiculous," said Rodger, in a panicky voice. "Look, we're both well. We haven't been ill at all. We've said we're sorry about this morning, it was a mistake, but you can't shoot us. The disease is genetic, they said, so if Henry is yours and Gary's son, then he'll have your genes, and he'll be okay as well."

"Val, he's right," whispered Gary. "I think we're immune and Henry should be as well. As Miriam and Celia are green, they must be as well. We've all been exposed to reds before, and yet we haven't got ill."

"Are you prepared to take that risk with Henry?" Val said harshly.

"We already have, when they came into the house."

Val lowered the gun. "I need to think," she said. She gave the pistol to Gary. "Okay, they can stay, but not in the house, they can use the farm if they want to stay. Celia and Miriam can stay in the house."

Rodger and Liam stood up. Gary could see the sweat on Rodger's brow, and Liam was silent, too quiet that kid, thought Gary. Rodger went to say something. Gary leaned in close and whispered in his ear, "I don't trust you, and I'll be watching you, one step out of line or another lie and I'll pull the trigger myself, understand?"

"Yes, but"

"No buts, understand?"

"Yes," Rodger eventually stammered. Gary didn't believe him.

Gary walked back to the house. He collected the new arrivals' weapons and put them in a cabinet in the basement. He locked the basement door. The pistol was still on his hip. When he returned, Val was waiting for him, the twins hovered behind her. Kelly still carried Henry, and they both gave him a half smile. Rodger and Liam were also walking back to the car.

"Miriam, can have your old room Gary, and Celia is in the other annexe. They are getting their stuff from their car. I've told Rodger and Liam to take their car round to the farm, via the main road. They can sort themselves out. We'll have dinner outside, I don't want them back in the house until we know Henry's all right, maybe a few days if they stay."

"They could be *B)*s or *C)*s," said Kelly, "if we are all *A)*s?"

Val had almost forgotten Hannah's designations. "We'll have to see, thanks Gary," she said and gave him a quick kiss. "I should trust your instinct more." The twins whistled. "You two have chores I think." She took Henry from Kelly. "I need to feed Henry before he starts screaming and get dressed." She was still in her dressing gown.

"Yes, Val," the twins said in unison. Gary was reminded of Callaghan and Greavesey responding to Hannah.

Gary watched them head off, the twins to the wind turbine to check the tanks. Gary went to help Miriam and Celia with their stuff. He also wanted to watch what Rodger and Liam did when they found out he had already removed the shotgun from their vehicle. Celia and Miriam were already coming back to the house. They each had a backpack and a sports bag. The vehicle was backing up away from the gate; it was a Toyota of some sort.

"Gary," Miriam started, "we really didn't know, and this morning was…"

"Rodger's idea," Gary finished.

"Yes, but how did you know?"

"A good guess I suppose." Gary stared after the retreating Toyota. He could feel Rodger stare back, or was it just his imagination. "Come on ladies," he said, "let's get you sorted." He took the two sports bags and led them back into the house. Gary returned to his chores. He then walked down towards the farm. He checked the bees and the fruit trees. He walked over to the wheat field, checking the crop. It was well past noon, and the sun was making a huge effort to turn the day into a perfect summer one. He walked to the farmhouse; he could see the Toyota parked in the yard. Rodger came out of the house as he approached.

"There's running water in the hose there," Gary said. "I've been planning on power, but I'll need help for that."

"Got it all planned haven't you?" Rodger said.

Gary decided to try to not get annoyed. "Rodger, this can go two ways, you can put up with the inconvenience for now and help with our plans, or you can go elsewhere. It's up to you and Liam which you choose. If you choose to stay, then you have to help."

"Who decides what gets done?"

"We all agree."

"Yeah sure you do; one happy family now, with a couple more in your harem?"

Gary held back his anger. "The previous guy who lived here was an arse; he's under the pile in the back garden over there. If you want to join him, well, we've had that discussion. I'm, no, we, are giving you a chance. You can share our food, water, and even power eventually, or you can go back on the road and scavenge. Personally I could do with the help for harvest and so on, but if you choose to leave then so be it. We'll survive. Dinner will be at seven. I suggest you get sorted and cleaned up. If you want hot water there are gas canisters around, and a gas barbecue in one of the barns. There's diesel in the jerry cans by the tractor if you want to go." Gary walked away, hoping he hadn't missed another weapon in his quick search; the hair on the back of his neck prickling the whole way, but he refused to turn around.

Dinner was served on the terrace. It was *help-yourself* from the veggie and salad buffet, plus chicken, eggs and some tuna mixed with pasta. There was fruit salad and some pineapple from tins, and the fresh fruit from the garden. Rodger and Liam had arrived, and were seated together at one end. Val was with Henry, asleep in a caboose at the other end. Gary ate standing up. There was water, but no wine. The twins had wanted to celebrate the new arrivals with some champagne, but Val had given a very firm, "No." There was none of the normal fun of the conversations they usually had. Celia and Val had held a long conversation that afternoon, whilst Val showed her the greenhouses. Miriam said she had some training as a chef and had set about preparing the dinner and checking out the kitchen stores. She had also been a singer, she said, and part time actress. She was attractive, Gary thought, tall, and very thin, wasn't everyone? She had fine cheekbones, and her hair was cropped roughly short. She had a tattoo on the inside of her left wrist, of a swallow, Gary thought. Miriam caught him looking and smiled. More complications, Gary thought. Val had also seen the exchange of looks. Celia was fifty-two, but she looked older, her hair had turned mostly grey, it was shoulder length and again hacked to that length. Val kept her hair neat and braided.

"Liam," he said, trying to get some answers from him rather

than Rodger, "how did you meet Rodger?"

"I found him on the road, thirsty and starving," said Rodger. "Gave him some food and water and he came along with me. Six months or so after A-Day"

"I asked Liam," said Gary.

"What he said," said Liam, not looking up from his plate.

"When did you meet up with them?" Kelly asked Miriam. Gary gave Kelly a look "What?" she mouthed confused.

"Oh, about four months ago," Miriam was oblivious to Gary's look at Kelly. "Celia and I met before the winter, near Winchester. There was an army camp there, where we got food. We met Rodger and Liam outside Bedford. We had found a warehouse, and we were in there when they arrived." Miriam fell quiet.

Celia, said, "The army chaps were really good, poor souls. They were going out and collecting bodies, whilst they were ill themselves. The pits were awful, but what else could be done, so many dead. You saw the hospitals Val, you know what that was like." Val's view of the army was different Gary knew.

"I did too," said Gary deciding to leave it for tonight. "Better get cleared up," he said and started collecting plates. The twins got up and helped. Rodger and Liam just sat. Miriam collected left over food onto one plate. Celia collected glasses. When Gary returned, Val was standing.

"Rodger and Liam want a shower or a bath, I said tomorrow."

"Yes, tomorrow would be better, the water system won't have enough now," Gary lied.

"That's what I thought," said Val, agreeing with Gary's lie.

"Well, we'll head back to our *accommodation* then," said Rodger. "Come on Liam." They got up with only a glance back from Liam. Gary watched them walk down the track till they vanished into the dusk. Celia came back out.

"Where have Rodger and Liam gone?" Celia asked.

"Back to the farm," replied Val.

"They didn't say good night; that was rude."

"Yes, it was," said Val looking into the dusk as well.

The others returned, and they finished clearing up. Gary told them he would check the grounds and close-up. Val and the girls knew he would be setting the security up. Gary had another setup he wanted done. He rummaged around in a shed and found a spare motion triggered floodlight. There was one on the front of the house and by the gate, this one he would put covering the track. When he re-entered the house he checked the CCTV cameras were working.

"Celia and Miriam have gone to bed," Val said. The twins came and said good night and also went up. It had been a long day with an abrupt waking.

Val asked him kindly, "Are you going to bed, or for a chat with Hannah? Henry's ready for another round of food." The baby was snuffling and starting to cry. "You can stay and talk to me."

"No, thanks," he smiled and touched her cheek, "I have one, or two other things I need to check on first."

"I'd like to have another you know," she said, cupping his face in reply to his caress.

"That would be nice," he said, getting her meaning, "tonight?"

"No, sorry, I meant in a while, once things have settled down, would that be okay?"

"Yes," he said. He gave her a kiss, as Henry decided that he really was hungry. Gary could smell that he needed changing as well. He kissed Henry. "Shall I change him?"

"No, I'll sort him out, a bath, feed and then sleep; you finish what you need to do." Gary closed her annex door and walked back outside.

CHAPTER TWENTY-THREE

Rodger

Val burst awake when she heard the shots, two or three. She was up, grabbing the rifle. Kelly was already coming down the stairs followed by Cass. Both of them with pistols and both at least dressed with a bit more decorum than the previous morning. There was no sign of Gary. It was still dark. The house lights had come on triggered by their movements; that system was normally off, Val realised. The doors to the house were still shut. Where was Gary?

"What's going on?" Miriam asked as she came to the top of the stairs, pulling on a shirt and jeans.

"I heard shots," said Celia, coming out of the front annex in a plain nightie. "There are floodlights on down the track. I saw from my window." Val pushed past her to look. She could see a figure, in shadow, standing looking at a lump on the ground.

"Stay here," she said to them all. "I'll go check."

"No," said Cass, "you're needed for Henry, your milk, we'll go! Kelly, cover me!"

They left the annex before Val could say anything. The front door opened and Val watched the girls move out, using the vehicles as cover, pistols out in front of them. Why did they have pistols? Where had they learned this stuff? They watched in silence as the girls approached the shape. They heard a muffled shout, the figure's hands went up, then down, then the girls were hugging someone. He turned. A cap was taken off a head. She could see the blond ponytails of all three. They walked back to the house. They came through the front door. Gary was unrecognisable from his normal appearance, except the ponytail. His face was muddied, he wore camouflaged jacket and trousers, and an SA80 was slung from his neck. The twins were hanging onto him; he was shaking like a leaf. He went and sat down on one of the sofas.

"Rodger," said Cass or Kelly, Val wasn't sure for once. Val nodded at them as they went to sit down on either side. Gary stood up.

"Make safe," he said to them. "Should have done that outside." He went through the drill as Hannah had taught him and he had taught the twins; they did the drills with the pistols. "Clear, clear," Gary said to them then showed the SA80 to Kelly, Val realised.

"Clear," she said. Val watched each reload the weapons. Gary then sat down again. The girls sat either side of him.

Celia and Miriam had stood back but then a babble of questions, which Gary ignored.

"Front door locked?" He asked Val, looking up. She went and checked. He switched the TV on and tuned to the CCTV. They saw Val at the door, then moments later she was back in the lounge.

"Liam?" Miriam pressed.

"No," said Kelly, "just Rodger."

"I didn't see him," said Gary, "just that arse. Oh shit, what have I done, I've…"

"You've done the right thing," said Val. She went and poured him a malt. She could hear Henry starting to cry. Gary took the malt from her, he was still shaking, he sipped at it; Cass took it from him and had a sip then passed it to Kelly.

"Yuk," she said after a sip passing it back to Gary. He sipped again.

Celia and Miriam went and sat down, "I think I need one of those," said Celia, noticing the brandy and pouring herself one. Miriam took a whisky; Val helped herself, as well. Gary got up and sprinted for the downstairs bathroom. When he came out Cass had got him some water, he drank half the glass then took the malt. It was getting light. The birds could be heard. Val had fetched Henry and she was feeding him.

"Okay?" Val asked.

"Yes," he said, the shaking had stopped. "I didn't give him a chance, I saw him coming, and when the light tripped I fired."

"But how did you know he would try something?" Celia asked.

"I didn't, I mean, I thought he might, there was something, I don't know…"

"Leave it now," said Val switching breasts without embarrassment. Miriam gave a stare, Gary didn't even notice.

"What about Liam?" Cass asked.

"We wait and watch," said Gary. He had redirected one of the CCTV cameras the previous evening to look down the track along with the floodlight he had set up. After that he had re-dressed in combat gear. Then, he had gone to the twin's rooms. He gave them a pistol each with strict instructions on what to do if the automatic lights came on in the house. "Just in case," he told them. He had kissed them each on the forehead and said he would be outside. He then left them and smeared his face and hands in mud.

Waiting next to one of the sheds, he had nearly dozed off several times. Gary kept himself awake by running conversations through his head with Hannah, Cal, and Greavesey; he imagined that they were there with him. Back when they had been really there, they had told war stories a couple of times about Afghanistan and patrols. Gary made himself think that was what he was doing, an ambush.

He had thought he had fallen asleep when he saw the figure coming up the track, he could see a pistol in one hand and a knife in the other. He had levelled the SA80 sights and made sure he was ready. He could have shot straight away, but he wanted to be absolutely clear. The lights had burst on, and there he was, Rodger, startled by the lights shining into his eyes. He had fired the automatic burst before he realised. Rodger was propelled backwards and went down. Gary had waited a few moments checking the area, then he got up. He walked down to the body, he'd just reached it when Kelly shouted or was it Cass, "Hands up."

He put his hands up and managed an, "It's me." Then, they were hugging him and pulling off his hat and then they were walking back.

Gary felt utterly exhausted, he must have dozed; he woke with a start. Liam was coming up the track. One of the twins flicked the system to full screen, yes, definitely Liam. They watched him stop, then approach the body then he was shouting screaming and kicking the body. They could hear it from the house.

Gary was up and rushing down, Val was right behind him with Miriam. Gary pulled Liam away wrapping his big arms around the teenager. He was shouting "Bastard, bastard," uncontrollably, whilst sobbing. They pulled him away. Rodger's body lay in a pool of drying blood, face down on the dirt track, his back was mostly missing; they could all smell the stench of his intestines, which were part of the mess on the track and beyond. Val bent down and pulled a pistol from his right hand, she pulled him over; his lifeless eyes stared up. His left hand still held the knife. She closed his eyes, Miriam was being sick against a fruit tree. There were three entry wounds in the middle of his chest.

"We'll bury him later, back to the house now," said Val, putting an arm around Liam as she extracted him from Gary's arms. Gary pointed him up the track before he let go. Val started walking. Gary helped Miriam up, she hugged close to him, he could feel her body through her thin shirt, he felt desire flood through him; he was then disgusted with himself. He pulled away from her grasp. Had she noticed?

"Come on, I need a coffee," he said.

The twins were waiting at the door. Gary walked through to the kitchen. Liam was sitting sobbing with Celia and Val. Val waived him out. Gary said, "I'm getting changed, stick this back in the basement," he said handing the SA80 to Cass.

"I'll clean it first," she said smiling. She took it from him and did a perfect check and unload drill.

"Yes, do that, thanks."

"Miriam, you okay?" Kelly said. "I have a clean shirt that

colour if you want one?"

"Yes," said Miriam in a bit of a daze. She hadn't realised she had gotten vomit on it. She automatically pulled the top off; she was braless. Gary couldn't help but look.

"Come on," said Kelly, pushing the shirt back against Miriam's breasts, "lets clean you up." She guided Miriam up the stairs.

"Henry?" Gary said absentmindedly, still with the image of Miriam's breasts in his mind.

Cass had watched the whole thing; she seemed amused; "He's fine, fast asleep, go shower and change. You look like, Rambo or something." Cass and Kelly now alternated war movies with Rom Coms. They treated the Rambo series as comedies.

Gary spent quite a while in the shower; he got the shakes again, but turned the water to cold until shivers replaced the shakes. He wrapped a towel around himself as he walked out of the en-suite; he jumped as he saw Val sitting on his bed still in her nightie. She stood and walked up to him, "You missed a bit," she said licking her fingers and rubbing his forehead. Her hand trailed down his stomach. "You feel cold," her hand undid the towel; she stepped back. She lifted the nightie up and off. Her breasts were heavier than he remembered. He'd never seen her completely naked in daylight. Even when she had been giving birth to Henry, the twins had protected her modesty a little. "I'll warm you up." Her arms wrapped around him.

"What about the…"

"If anyone comes in, I'll shoot them." Gary believed her.

***

It was mid-afternoon when Gary woke up; he was alone. He got up and looked out of the window. He could see the twins in the garden. It was a very warm day. The twins were in bikini tops and shorts. He dressed in a polo shirt and shorts. He looked out of the other side of the house; the body was gone from the track.

He went downstairs. Miriam was in the kitchen, preparing a meal. He realised he was starving. Breakfast and lunch missed and last night's dinner was, well, he was hungry. Miriam turned and saw him. She smiled, "Val, Celia and Liam have gone to the farm to, to… they've gone to bury Rodger. The smile went for a moment, I couldn't go; anyway, sorry about earlier, the being sick, and so on. You must be hungry, can you wait for dinner, or I can get you a sandwich?"

"I'll wait thanks, I need to do my chores; I'm behind today. I've been sleeping." He saw her smirk. "I'll check the girls. Where's Henry?"

"Just here, he's fine, go on." Henry was fast asleep in a baby chair by her feet.

Gary walked out to the twins. They saw him coming but carried on their work.

"If it isn't our very own Casanova, finally risen from his bed." Kelly said cheekily.

"Less of your cheek."

"Or what, you'll spank us? That could be fun." Cass coquettishly remarked. Gary realised they were flirting as well.

"Behave," he said trying to be stern. "I wanted to thank you both for this morning and yesterday morning. You did great."

"You did, you mean," said Cass. They both walked up to him and gave him a hug; he tried not to be distracted by their bikini-topped bodies in his arms.

"Enough," he said, "get back to work, I need to find Val." He resisted the urge to smack their bottoms.

"Yes *Sir*," said Kelly, picking up a rake.

He walked away shaking his head. He walked back down the garden, round the house, and towards the track. He had reached the entrance to *Arse Farm* when he saw Val, Celia and Liam coming back. Liam was driving the small digger, badly, but driving it. He waited for their arrival; he could see a dark patch of dirt on the track but no other sign of the events of that morning. Liam pulled up next to Gary; he studiously avoided looking at the track.

"Okay?" Gary asked.

"Yes, Val showed me how to use the digger, you don't mind do you?"

"No, that's fine."

Val rescued the conversation before it almost started. "You slept well?"

"Er, yes, thanks, you've sorted out?"

"Yes, next to… Well, it's done," Val stated with a degree of finality.

"Thanks, I didn't mean for you to sort it out on your own."

"You needed to rest," a hint of a smile, "and it needed doing. Liam agreed to help Celia and me."

"Thanks, all of you. I was going to check the wheat. I'll have to combine soon."

"It can wait," said Val, "we all need to talk and sort stuff out. Liam needs a space; he can't stay at the farm on his own."

Liam looked uncomfortable, Gary wasn't sure he would like the talk either. They walked back to the house, Gary asking Liam if he minded leaving the digger by the entrance, he didn't want the digger banging into other vehicles by the house. Gary had a quick check on the beehives, watched by Liam. They walked back up. They went round the rear. Cass and Kelly were spraying each other with the hosepipe; it was such a picture of innocent fun. Val started to tell them off when the hose was redirected at her then toward Gary who jumped back. He ran round the outside of its arc and turned it off. "Another spanking I fear," said Cass, smirking at Gary, had Val heard? He hoped not.

"You two go and get dressed for dinner," said Val. "I'll need to change as well; you two girls will be the death of me I'm sure." Gary had escaped the water. He re-coiled the hose and put away the tools the girls had been using. He checked the chickens and realised that Liam was watching him closely.

"I check the grounds each evening," he said. "I start at the turbine at the top and work my way down. A bit out of routine today, but…" He ran out of ideas.

"Can I see the turbine?" Liam asked.

"Sure."

"How much power does it produce? We did a project at school on turbines, and we went to see one of the wind farms…" They walked up the hill, Gary trying to answer the flood of questions.

After dinner, there was wine this time. Gary helped clear up, whilst Kelly and Cass were in their rooms. Val was bathing, then feeding Henry. Miriam had accepted praise for the dinner and was sipping a glass of wine, watching Gary. Celia was helping with the baby. Liam had been shown Gary's computer and was busy playing a game, Gary thought he would enjoy playing games on the big screen in the cinema room; he hadn't done that since, well since before this had all started. Val walked back in. "Little so and so is finally asleep. Celia is having a bath. Is there any more of that wine left?" Miriam poured some into a glass. "Thanks," said Val. They chatted. Miriam would share Celia's annex unless the twins shared, which would not go down well as they were used to their own rooms. Val and Gary said they would re-organise chores in the morning and just see how they got along.

Two weeks passed, two weeks of working and scavenging. Gary did a daily run, alone, to the camp and would pick up whatever anybody needed. He was pleased to get out of the house, as it still felt tense. Val was ignoring him completely bedroom wise, she was most often seen with Miriam chatting in the kitchen, which had turned into Miriam's fiefdom. It seemed to be always untidy, Gary thought. It was the same with the lounge, with three teenagers constantly leaving things around. Outside Celia had taken on the greenhouses. Gary felt that his trips into town were his only alone time; even his bench chats would have Celia or Val or Miriam coming to interrupt him or yet another question from Liam.

Gary finished loading the dishwasher and clearing away, an almost nightly attempt on his part to create some order. He noticed Miriam and Val sitting at the kitchen table "I'll just go and..." Gary started to say.

"Sit down Gary," said Val, "we three need a discussion

before the girls come back down."

"I'm not sure I like the sound of that," Gary said nervously.

"Miriam has moved in with me."

"What, I thought the twins could share, to give Celia the space."

"That's not what I mean; I mean Miriam will be with me." Gary realised what she meant.

"But, but…" he struggled. "I mean us, the other morning and so on."

"Gary, Gary… I like being with you, I do, and that morning was, well anyway; I haven't really liked men for years, the farm, well we've talked about Fox Farm. That just made things clearer for me." Val was struggling too. "I still want another child if we can, and maybe Miriam," Val turned to look at Miriam.

"One day, yes but, not yet. If you would help that would be great. Val and I have talked about it. Honesty, Miriam, honesty," she told herself out loud. "We need a new world Gary, one where people aren't afraid of conventions and silly prejudices. I hope you're not prejudiced that way, I know you aren't racially." She looked at Val, "Look, we've barely got to know each other, any of us, and yes this is quick, but there's so few people left." She took a gulp of wine and a deep breath. "I've been with men before, too many. I, well, we've all done things we wish we hadn't. We need to be open and clear for the next generation, the girls, Henry, Liam. Wow that was a speech, sorry."

"I don't understand. I mean you've only just met; how do you know, I mean, it's not my business really but…"

"Celia knew me before, remember, and she told Miriam. Celia is a gem by the way; she's talked to Liam now Rodger isn't around. You do realise he's only just twelve?" said Val. The subject seemed to have been changed and Val was checking the kitchen entrance in case anyone else came in. "Liam was abused by Rodger you realise, sexually abused I mean," she spoke very quietly.

"But you and Celia were with him for months, why didn't you?" Gary fired at Miriam harshly.

"What, stop him? We didn't know; not for sure, we suspected, but nothing happened. Rodger would take Liam off on scavenging trips." Her reply had started angry, but died. "We should have known; we should have stopped it, but…"

"It's over now thanks to you," said Val to Gary. He looked down. He still couldn't believe he had pulled the trigger. "Liam's a scared boy who is also positive with the virus. He needs our help. Look, you don't mention it unless he says something to you, okay? His feelings are all over the place; Rodger fed him and looked after him as well as… Anyway, we'll all need to tread carefully."

"What about Kelly and Cass?" Gary asked. "What do they know?"

"They know about us," she held Miriam's hand again. "We told them they didn't need to give up a room. They will ask about Liam if they haven't already guessed. It's you I'm worried about."

"Me, why?"

"The girls, I can see them with you. I'm not blind Gary." Gary went to protest. "It's okay," her other hand was on his now. "I know, nothing has happened," she thought, *yet*, "but it's going to get complicated. They don't know whether you're their brother, father, or action hero after the last few weeks. They're teenage girls, yes grown up teenage girls, I can see as well, but you are the only boy around. You have needs as well, I know." She squeezed his hand. "I can't stop what is going to happen, I have no right to, even if I wanted to, but not yet; they don't think so, but they are still too young."

"I understand, I do; I'll be careful, maybe I should move out?"

"Now you're being stupid, this is your house, your home. I, no we, don't want you to do that..."

"Do what?" Cass said coming into the room, followed by Kelly a few steps behind.

"Gary, you look like you could do with a malt," said Val. "I need to talk to the girls." Gary took the hint. He went into the lounge area and collected a malt whisky; he then went up the garden and took his spot next to Hannah's grave. He thought he heard raised voices, but as he told Hannah, it was probably for the best. He thought Val might come out and join him, but no one did. Lights clicked off upstairs, he noticed, then came on and went off in the rear annexe. He thought he heard Henry cry, but then all he was left with was the odd bird chirping and the cluck of a bedding down chicken. There was the briefest of baa's from the sheep. He took out Hannah's letter.

> *You knew I was red, you knew I would eventually die, just like little Sarah and the others. I've seen you looking at me so you know truth when you see it. Don't be afraid of it. I'm writing this wishing I could be with you as you grow up. God you'll break hearts. Rambling a bit, it hurts so much sometimes. I don't have anything left to say or write love, you'll be up in a minute, worried about me, caring for me. I'm so lucky you drove in that day. I love you, more than anything I have ever loved. I don't know how to put the words down I want to say. My beautiful, handsome, lover. If there is a heaven I'll be waiting for you, if I get in!*
>
> *Goodbye my love.*
>
> *Hannah xxxxxxxxx*

For once Gary didn't cry reading the letter; that was better he thought. He still felt comforted, and he could imagine Hannah saying those things; no that was wrong. She was too forthright when she was speaking, just like Val had been earlier. He carefully folded the letter and put it away. Maybe he should go off for a while, find other things to do; but he knew he couldn't, there was so much to do. He would have to live with it, be more distant from the girls, tread carefully around Liam; help with Henry; be a *father* to Henry and whatever else he was asked to do. If only Rodger had been okay, he could have done with the help. The twins were great, and would help more and more, but another man. Gary realised how much he missed his father, he automatically looked at his grave and then his mother's. Now, he had Liam, to guide as well. What did he know about being a father, or brother, and he wasn't any sort of action hero? If he had acted like a movie star hero, Rodger would never have had the pistol or the knife. Gary scolded himself for his poor implementation. He wondered if he could have done things differently? What did Rodger think he was doing? Not just that night but on that first morning? Approaching the house armed like that. They all had been armed Gary remembered. Had Rodger had control over them as well, or had he persuaded them. There was that story about the house, was that true, was that justification?

Gary instinctively knew that he would have been killed that night, but what about the previous morning. Rodger couldn't have known about the girls and Val or could he? Gary was certain now he had done the right thing, but the others, the girls? Gary didn't know, couldn't know what Rodger had planned, he just knew it would not have been good. It was done now, right or wrong, correct, or not. He could ask Liam, if he could get him to talk, would he know? What about Celia and Miriam? That was a question for another day he thought, now it was time to lock up. He checked around the house, resetting cameras and sensors; he went into the house and locked up. He went up to bed, undressed. He speculated as to whether he would ever see Val in the bed again. That morning, after Rodger, had been special. He read for a while, without taking in what he was reading; his ears listening for noises. He got up and walked down passing rooms. The twin's bedroom doors were shut; in his old room he could see Liam asleep. He returned to the lounge, and he switched on the CCTV, and sat watching.

Val found him there the following morning. He was gently snoring, no not snoring, just deep breathing. Henry had woken her and Miriam, and then they had heard the cockerel announce the dawn as well. She went back into the annexe and took the duvet off the bed, placing it over Gary, lying in his boxers. She saw the pistol in his hand; she took it from him and placed it on a shelf. She watched him for a while, and then joined Miriam with Henry in the kitchen, Miriam had the coffee on; Celia was there a few minutes later. She started the toast. Liam came down. He drank some strawberry and raspberry juice. Kelly came in, already dressed in jeans and T-shirt, with barely a look at Val or Miriam. She drank a juice and went straight out to the chickens. Cass arrived, her hair still wet from the shower. She had a polo shirt and jeans on; the look she gave Val could have killed. She went straight out, Val watched her go into one of the sheds and come out wearing the beekeepers' kit, they had obtained a couple of months before. Val watched her walk down the track. Cass stopped to look at the sheep and then continued to the hives.

Val wondered how long the silent treatment would last. The conversation the previous evening had been intense. Val had told them to stop flashing their bodies at Gary, to have more self-respect, that they were almost behaving like sluts. That it wasn't fair on Gary. Harsh words had been exchanged back, about Val, her behaviour with Gary; then getting together with Miriam who was the slut, Kelly had shouted, before storming out. Cass had stayed to get the rules on dress, no more bikini tops cuddling up to Gary. Cass had been embarrassed and cross, and had shouted about Val having her tits out all the time, and what about Miriam stripping off. Miriam had spluttered she hadn't realised she had done that; that awful morning. The word hypocrites had been used. Celia had tried to calm things. Val had tried to be calmer and said that they all needed to act with more decorum; that had been to Cass's departing back; with threats of "I'm leaving first chance I get." It had not gone well.

Val remembered an argument with her own mother. She had come back into the house in Grenada after an evening out with a boy; when she had nearly gone *all the way*. The happiness of the date turned to shame and anger in a few minutes. Had she over reacted? She would apologise later, once they had worked off some energy. She wasn't good at apologies, never had been, and since Fox Farm she found it harder. She shook her head and put some jam onto her toast.

"They'll calm down soon enough," said Celia.

"I hope so," said Val. Henry began to let the world know he wasn't happy either. Gary wandered in looking blurry-eyed. He picked up Henry.

"Hey fella, what's up?"

"Gary, give Henry to me, and go and get dressed," said Val harshly. Gary's boxers were gaping open.

"Oh sorry," he said handing Henry to Val. He left.

"Val," said Miriam, "take it easy you bit his head off."

Gary dressed after a shower, he even shaved, his hair was too long he thought. He would get one of the girls to cut it back, it took too long to dry. He checked outside, not as warm yet, as yesterday. He noted Kelly at the chicken coop in jeans and then watched Cass coming back from the beehives, no honey yet, it was unlikely this summer unless the bees adapted really well. Maybe they could take a trip out to the honey farm. They had left more hives there. She was in jeans as well, Gary noticed. I'll stick with shorts even if they don't, he thought. Need to get the combine ready later. Wheat should be ready in a few days if the sun keeps going. That was what he was trying to read last night. A guide to wheat yields, in a farming reference book. He then needed to check on how much he needed to keep back to replant. Then there was the route through a hedge to the other fields belonging to another farmer. Used to belong, Gary corrected himself. If he cut through he could try harvesting another field. That was wild-grown oats, he had realised a few weeks ago. He would need good filters to clear out the rubbish.

Then there was power to the farm. He needed to get some high voltage power cable, and set up some panels or run a feed down. He'd check the figures to see what their current use was; with extra people and so on he wasn't sure if the system on the house would cope. Actually, it was more a battery problem. Where could he get more batteries? Lots to do, his neck ached from sleeping, he suddenly was scared; his neck ached. Was that a tumour? He checked in the mirror, nothing. He would do a machine check when no one was around. He distractedly walked back downstairs, his head spinning. He ate some toast and jam, drank a coffee and began tidying up. He was about to amble outside with almost no words to anyone.

"Gary," Val snapped him out of his reverie. What was her problem today, time of the month? Who knew? He was drifting again, "Gary! Are you with us today? Look, the girls are in a bit of a strop after my chat with them last night, so you may want to talk to them. Miriam, Celia and I are going to sort house stuff out, so can you take Liam with you on your chores and give him some more routine ones to do, okay?"

"Yes, that's fine, I need a Kelly list, had some ideas."

"Go and sort it then, we'll clear up."

"Make sure you run the dishwasher, and check the salt levels, I meant to do it yesterday."

"Gary, go! Liam! Don't just sit there! Go brush your teeth and help Gary!" Val thought she sounded like a fish wife, or worse, her mother. She sat back down, Celia put her hand on her shoulder, and Miriam held her hand. "Please don't tell me I've screwed this up."

"They'll be fine, we'll all be fine, you see," said Celia.

"Where's the dishwasher salt kept?" Miriam asked, thinking that practical things would be a good way of proving that.

***

"Hey," said Gary approaching Cass and Kelly. They were standing by the shed where Cass was putting away the bee keeping kit. "Any honey yet?"

They both spun round at him; arms folded, "What did she say to you?" Cass demanded.

"Do you think we're sluts too?" Kelly followed suit.

"Hey what's the matter? What do you mean? Why are you shouting at me? Look calm down, you'll scare the chickens." He tried a joke.

"It's not funny, you didn't hear what she said to us," Kelly was almost crying.

"Who said? Who called you that?"

"Val! Who do you think?" Cass exclaimed.

"I'm sure she didn't say that; why would she say that?"

"All because we gave you a hug in our bikinis the other day, she says we're throwing ourselves at you." Kelly was sobbing now.

"I'm sure that's not what she meant, I had a chat with Val last night, when she told me about her and Miriam. She didn't call you that, she just said I needed to be care..." Gary realised he did need to be careful. "It doesn't matter, you are not sluts, you're my, my friends. We're all like a family together, the last couple of days have been mad, Val's tired. She has Henry to think of, and us, and now there is Celia, and Miriam, and Liam to think of as well."

"Why did they have to come? Everything was fine before they came." Kelly had stopped sobbing.

"We wanted more people to come Kelly," said Gary softly, he could see Liam heading his way. "Now, I'm sure we can sort this misunderstanding with Val out."

The next few days were taken up by with Gary working flat out on preparations for the harvest. Gary had Liam as a shadow nearly all the time. Meal times in the evenings, when everyone ate together, were tense. The twins would eat and drink, say please, and thank you, but then leave as soon as they could for their rooms, they wouldn't even stay for a cuddle with Henry. They did their chores, but Gary struggled to get a word out of them. Celia took to working in the greenhouse and veg plot, and she seemed to be getting somewhere, but Miriam was ignored, and Val got short, one word answers. Then, Gary announced at dinner that the following day it was harvest time, and he would need a lot of help.

"Can I drive the combine?" Liam asked.

"You can help me, yes," said Gary. "I need Kelly or Cass on the tractor and trailer for the grain. Val I'll need you on the other tractor for the straw, it needs to be turned into neat lines; we need that bailed as soon as we can if we want bedding ready for livestock."

"What livestock?" Miriam asked.

"I know, but I am sure we will find some soon, we have one sheep, and there *must* be more and really, I want some cows. We're getting low on meat. When we find some, I don't want to be hunting around for winter bedding. We'll have the fun of clearing the carcasses anyway. If the straw is bailed, it shouldn't rot as easily or we can stack it. When the grain gets back to the farm, it needs to be filtered and cleaned again. The combine won't be clean enough; that needs the filters running. Cass, Kelly, up to you which way round you divide it. Celia, can you look after Henry, we can all be down on the farm, but I'd give other things to do if we had time. I don't want to push our luck on the weather by waiting."

Gary's list of orders and instructions had been met in near silence except for Miriam's question. Gary had decided he had enough. "One more thing," Gary was angry with all of them. "Val, you'll apologise to the girls. Girls you'll apologise to Val. I don't care who said what, or why, but I'm sick of this atmosphere. I'm supposed to be the immature one. The only way we are going to survive next winter is if we cooperate, now. I am going to check the grounds, then get an early night. Liam, you're with me. The rest of you kiss and make up, or whatever." For emphasis, Gary slammed his glass onto the table, got up before anyone could argue. He heard Liam struggle to get up quickly enough to catch up.

"Well! That was unnecessary, I..." Val looked about ready to shout.

"Val," said Celia, "he's right, Miriam, this is between Val and the twins, help me get Henry ready for bed." She did a similar fast exit taking Henry from Val's grasp. Val stared open mouthed.

The twins looked at each other, and then at Val, and then back at each other. "I'm sorry I shouted at you," said Cass.

"So am I," said Kelly.

"You're not sluts, I'm, I'm sorry I said that. I am just worried about you and Gary and all of us..."

"We like Gary a lot and one day, well, he is the only bloke around," said Kelly.

"I know, and he's getting more, I don't know, more in charge," said Cass.

"I know," said Val, "we'll have to knock him back in line…" Val smiled for the first time in days, "Whilst letting him think he is in charge." The atmosphere was cleared. When the twins went to bed there were proper good nights. Celia said that it sounded like *The Waltons*, but the twins didn't know what she was talking about, neither did Gary; Liam was already asleep. Gary listened from his room, satisfied. He re-read the farming guide.

CHAPTER TWENTY-FOUR

The Previous Time

Gary had known Liam wanted to talk to him for a few days. He'd started to say something and then stopped on a couple of occasions. The previous evening, they had started to do the security checks together when Cass had joined them. Now, they were together at the water tanks. They had just completed the worst job Gary could think of clearing the sludge from the water system. It used to be the worst job, Gary realised that was until he had done the pits. That had taken an hour of explanations as well as another hour of just work. Now, having cleaned up, Gary and Liam were checking the water tanks. It had been dry for several weeks and Gary, always wanting to worry about something, wanted to ensure the tanks were still okay. He and Liam checked each of them in turn. They were all at just over half capacity. Nothing to worry about just yet, Gary knew.

"Gary."

"Yes, Liam," Gary tried not to sound too exasperated, expecting yet another question on how the water system worked, or what size the pipe needed to be for an exfiltration. The previous day it had been about how much honey the bees could make and could they make candles from the bees wax or what about polish. The day before that it had been on what type of blades were best for the combine and what would happen when the grease for the lubrication system on the combine ran out. Liam had watched Gary fill a grease gun and pump the gel into the exposed nipples on the underside of the harvester, before Gary let Liam have a try on another section, watching the grease ooze out of the exposed joint when the task was complete. Liam's ability to ask endless questions seemed to know no bounds, and Gary had to constantly stop himself from getting annoyed. It didn't help that Liam could thrash him on most computer games as well.

"I need to tell you something, but I don't want you to get cross."

"I don't get cross."

"Yes, you do, especially when we haven't tidied up."

"Well, okay, but that's not cross that's just frustrated, and if you just tidied up without me having to say something… Sorry I won't get cross."

"Promise?"

"Promise."

"We were here before," Liam said quietly.

"I know we've been here lots of times. I..."

"That's not what I mean, R… R… Rodger and me," Gary was listening intently, now. "We, we, saw the light, it was after the warehouse. We followed you then, but lost you, so Rodger said we would search and find you, but we couldn't so we wrote the note in the warehouse, stayed there a while, but you didn't come back. A few weeks later we were searching again, then we saw a light down there," he pointed to the primary school.

That light, thought Gary, is more trouble than it's worth, he recalled Val and the twins using it to find him.

"We followed the cable duct up the hill, but it was dark, and Rodger went off on his own. He often did. It was dark, I said that, I was scared; he would hoot like an owl when he was coming back, he did that time, but then he said he hadn't seen anything. Anyway we stayed in the school and the following day we drove away. We didn't see the drive entrance. I think we must have missed it. We drove back south and went to another warehouse Rodger knew, he always seemed to know where they were. Then, it was the winter and we stayed in a house and then, and then we, we met Miriam and Celia."

Gary tried to remember the day Val, and the twins had reappeared. He had heard an owl; had that been Rodger, but why had he gone away? Why hadn't they called out and joined them then? Liam didn't seem to know. Gary couldn't ask Rodger.

"There's more," said Liam. He took a deep breath. "That night, the night you killed him"

"Yes"

"He said, well he said that he was going to get the house and women that afternoon when we were in the farm on our own before dinner. He told me to stay behind and that if I said anything before I would regret it. I was scared so I kept quiet. He said that he deserved it, that you were too young, and he said he should have done it before. I hadn't realised we were in the same place until that morning, and Rodger told me not to answer any questions at all and definitely not to mention we had been here before. He made me promise; he hurt me until I promised. I'm sorry, I should have told you before."

"You've told me now," said Gary softly. Gary felt vindicated by his actions, but concerned about Liam. He rested his hand on Liam's shoulder and asked, "The other house, Rodger said, the reason you were all armed, was that true?"

"No, not completely, I don't know really, he lied all the time about what he did. He lied to Miriam and Celia. That house was near Bedford, he left me one morning and went there; he'd been and looked at it before, I think, a few weeks before. I, I heard shots, then a noise and then he was back with food and things. He said they had shot at him when he went to say hello. He said that was why we needed to be careful coming to this house. Miriam and Celia didn't want to, they didn't understand why we were coming so early, but Rodger said that it was the safest thing to do and that we should all carry guns. He had to teach Celia how to hold one. He could be very, very, I don't know, you had to do what he said. Please don't tell the others, please?"

"I won't." Gary wouldn't, but he knew there was more for Liam to tell, one day. He could hear one of the twins shouting for dinner. They strolled back to the house in silence.

CHAPTER TWENTY-FIVE

New Guests

Val sat on the rear terrace outside the kitchen, enjoying the September sunshine whilst listening to the mid-afternoon bird chatter. She could see Liam with the twins beyond the fruit trees, digging the cable run by the side of the water. Gary had laid a concrete plinth ready for a barracks or big shed; accommodation, Gary said, for when people came. The harvest had been better than Gary's pessimistic thoughts. The grain store still looked light, he said, compared to when he had first visited the farm with Hannah. It was one of the rare occasions he mentioned her name. It did not stop Kelly or Cass doing so, but Gary rarely did when Val was around. Gary had split the crop into wheat for seed for next year's planting, and the rest that he had allowed to be milled for flour. The quality of the grain was definitely worse, but the flour was still okay. Miriam had kneaded and then baked fresh bread using the first batch of flour in the oven instead of the bread machine, she had also used her own yeast, which she had started a couple of weeks ago, saying that they couldn't rely on dry packet yeast forever. This was also true of every other dry ingredient; Miriam had effectively become the main chef and provision requester. They were on strict coffee rations, and they were out of rice. Flour might become scarce after winter. They were all right for eggs, and chicken was their main meat, when they ate meat, which was rare. Miriam had drawn up a list with Kelly, and set out, via a spreadsheet, how long each provision would last. Gary had gone into the town to check the camp with Celia.

Val knew Gary was worried. She also knew that he saw

himself as chief protector and provider, and that it was his responsibility to solve these problems. Hannah's briefs, and letter, were what he based this on. She also knew he was sexually frustrated with her; she had not been with him since that morning after Rodger or *Arse2* as Cass now called him. She had wanted to explain to Gary why she was with Miriam, and why so quickly. She had started several times, but he was clearly upset, no matter how many times he said he was fine with it. He worked so hard, she thought, all his energy went into the buildings and the plans. She'd gone down to *Arse Farm* and watched him attack a hedge, cutting a path through to another farm's fields. He'd been at it for hours and didn't stop until he had a smooth clear path. Maybe he really was a bit OCD. He hated the kitchen now that Miriam had taken over and whenever he walked in, he immediately started putting stuff in cupboards or the dishwasher. It was the same with the lounge, or the cinema room, where he would get cross with Liam, or the girls, if they were left untidy.

He didn't shout, he would just say, "Would you *please* put this stuff away."

Again she didn't help there. Henry's needs came first and changing mats, new diapers, as she called them, nappies as everyone else called them, were ready all over the house. They had to be washed as well; no disposable ones. That had been a shock to her system, but the only practical way. There was no rubbish collection or landfill. So disposables were not used. The washing machine was constantly on. Gary said they should get a second and a second dryer. Provided the sun was out they had the power, or they could use the two lines out the back.

One of Gary's routine chores was to dispose of what rubbish they did create, and he would take stuff off to the old council recycling centre every two weeks or so. He had a plan for paper and glass if they could ever find a recycling factory or know how to work it. Val didn't think they would create a landfill issue if they just buried it on a tip. Val also knew that her row with the girls had also changed *his* relationship with them. He would not allow himself time on his own with them. If that happened, whilst they were doing the daily routine, Gary would find something else to do, or go, and get Liam.

Liam followed Gary around, whenever he could. Learning all the time, and Gary letting him. The latest project was learning to drive the cars, which the girls were doing as well. That seemed odd to Val, thinking how young they were, but they had to be grown up now. Liam's thirteenth birthday had only just passed. On the surface, he appeared fine, but the impact of Rodger's abuse could still be seen. Liam didn't say much, and if he told Gary anything, Gary didn't say. Liam only burst into life when he was playing a computer game, especially against the twins or Gary, or when he and Gary were discussing power and water systems.

Gary, mused Val, they no longer had their bench chats by Hannah's grave. Last week she had tried to join him twice for a malt whisky, and each time he had finished his drink quickly and gone to finish his security checks. She knew that was her fault as well, because of Miriam. No, it wasn't because of Miriam. It was her, and it wasn't just Fox Farm either. She had been gay for at least five years before A-Day, as Celia had known. She wasn't gay because of the sex; she was gay because she preferred women. The sex with Gary had been fine, no that was unfair, sometimes it had been good, but since Fox Farm... It was difficult; she shuddered at the memory; she still hadn't told Gary everything.

When Val left Fox Farm with the girls, she had found a health clinic that still had supplies and gave herself a full check. Embarrassingly for them all, she had then checked the twins. They had to wait a couple of days whilst Val rediscovered how to do the tests, carry them out, and wait for the results. She used a car inverter to power equipment when it was needed. The twins said they hadn't been touched; however, Val could see bruising on their thighs and arms, they were clear of any sexual diseases though. Amazingly Val found she was also clear, although HIV was a possibility; she hadn't told anyone that. She didn't know how to do the HIV test, if a test were even possible. Still she was green. Henry gurgled beside her, he was green; she had checked him that morning. Gary was green, he checked himself daily, she only knew because she heard the ping. The girls were green yesterday as was Celia. Miriam had checked that morning.

Miriam, that was another conversation and problem coming. She had told Val that she did want a child, as did Val again. So would Gary? He had agreed with Val before, but now, she didn't know, and she didn't want to ask. She knew Gary was preparing for a long trip to try to get provisions, but mainly to find other people, other survivors. There had been a discussion, really an argument about it last night. He was talking about a week. The argument was about who would go with him. The twins wanted to go, and Liam wanted to go. Gary thought he should go on his own. Val didn't know what to think. Maybe Celia would get something out of Gary.

Celia, she was feeling a bit lost, Val supposed, although she noticed Gary would stay for a chat on the bench with her. Val was surprised how envious that made her feel. Celia didn't say what they talked about, and neither did Gary; Celia had always been a good listener. Val had told Celia the basics about Fox Farm, and she was great with Henry.

Celia had lost her husband and adult daughter to the virus. Her daughter had just gotten engaged; they would have been married, the year after A-Day. Celia said that she had been looking forward to retirement and grandchildren. Now, she was working hard, but Henry wasn't hers. Then there were the twins. It wouldn't be long before one or both of them made a play for Gary. How would he react? How would she react? Val just hoped it would be a while yet, but she knew hormones would drive something to happen. Maybe if Gary could be persuaded to be with Miriam, that would keep his head away from the twins, and Val still wanted another child and Gary had agreed that he would. Maybe between her and Miriam, they could keep Gary distracted for a while and get children too. At least until the twins were a bit older. Val felt deeply cynical and guilty with herself for thinking so coldly. Henry needed changing again, she realised, and she had her chores to do as well. The greenhouse tomatoes needed picking.

***

Gary had gone to the camp with Celia. Celia didn't seem to mind. Two weeks before, Gary had spent a morning filling in the empty pit and the rest of the half-filled pit. He had also taken down some of the tents and packed them away. Miriam had helped him that day, along with Celia. He had checked the generators and the fuel levels in the Bowser and tank. He estimated he had a year's worth of diesel left, but unleaded was almost gone; unless he could get more from a petrol station tank or go to another camp and find a Bowser. Two other places he'd visited had diesel, not a lot, but no unleaded. The Lexus would have to go, and the little Honda, which the Twins and Liam were learning to drive in, it was a constant happy memory of his mother and father. He would need power and knowledge to use a garage; another project on his list. Maybe one of the generators could be wired-in to power it up long enough to refuel the Bowser. After the fuel checks, he looked to see whether anyone had been there or if a note had been left for him to discover. He hadn't expected to find anybody, or anything, and he wasn't disappointed. The radio was still there switched off, but with instructions, for anyone who did turn up, on how to switch it on, and how to run the small generator that powered it. The instructions also warned that they might not get a response during daylight hours, as the house wasn't always listening. Less true these days with Miriam or Val nearly always in there, with Henry of course.

On the journey over in the land rover, Celia had again raised the question of Miriam and Val. It was like listening to his mother, and perhaps that was the role she thought she was fulfilling. Gary would also not be surprised if Val and Miriam had put Celia up to it. Gary knew she had lost her husband and daughter. Maybe she thought of Gary as her son, in some ways. It was a pleasant feeling Gary realised, but this Val and Miriam thing was complicated. His own emotions were all over the place. He was hurt by Val's actions, more hurt than he said. He was frustrated by losing the affection as well as sex. He was also hurt by the implied behaviour around the twins, he felt guilty as well, because he did sometimes think about the twins that way, and then forced himself to stop. His only recourse was to keep his distance from all of them. Liam was fine, but he was a boy, a virus positive, abused boy. Gary was slowly coaxing him out of his shell, but that was hard work. Gary knew he sometimes let his frustrations show, in his terse responses.

Why couldn't they keep the bloody house tidy, he thought? That would keep his annoyance levels down, just thinking about it raised his ire. The good news was that the girls and Liam were taking on lots of jobs now, which meant he had more time for project planning and what little scavenging they did. He'd built the accommodation plinth, not because he thought 20 people would suddenly turn up, but because it was a visible project for everyone to see, and it meant that they thought that he was still dreaming of a new society. In reality, Gary thought, they were doomed.

In his darkest moments walking the grounds or sitting with Hannah, he would think about where all the people had gone? He would look at the spot where he had filled in the hole. Had the others noticed the patch of earth not covered in flowers, if they had, nothing had been said? He supposed that all of them had been through similar experiences. How had Val and the twins got through Fox Farm? Liam through the abuse with Rodger, and who knew what Miriam and Celia had come through? All of that was after losing family and friends, no one seemed to talk about that; was it too painful? Gary realised he rarely talked about his parents, yet the house should remind him, every day. Their grave should. He pictured his mother, but the picture in his mind was of the holiday photo, not the months before she died. That was like a dream, just like the period after Hannah. He struggled to remember any of that.

He wondered what his mother or father would say? Here he was, living with five women, a father of a lovely boy. I bet they want me to go with Miriam or with Val again, he thought turning his thoughts back to the Celia conversation. That would clear one bit of frustration he thought; but, there was always another but, it would add to the house crowding and the food needed. They needed more people, and Gary needed another man to talk to. They needed more crops and food stores and that would need more effort to grow and collect.

Why hadn't they found more survivors? Why was Liam red but still alive, were there more like him? He was mostly worried about food. The chickens were their only source of meat, unless he hunted geese and duck. He had read a chicken reference book, and was scared they would all succumb to bird flu or some other ailment. That would leave them without eggs or chickens. Mind you, getting rid of that cockerel wouldn't be a bad thing. Damn thing seemed to want to attack him every time he ventured in the coop and run. Still, the girls didn't get attacked, so they took care of that chore, or Celia did.

Celia, he dragged his racing mind back to their conversation, really several conversations. It had started all right, with enquiries about his health, and then he had asked her to get to the point. He'd just changed gear badly and crunched the gearbox on the rover. Then, he'd delayed the conversation as they reached the camp, and he'd done the checks. They had planned to go into the town, and do a final search of the shops, just in case there was anything missed. They could get some winter clothes for Liam, Miriam, and Celia. Gary wondered if one of the cafes on the high street might still have coffee stocks hiding somewhere he hadn't already looked at least a dozen times. Today, for some reason, the pistol on his hip was rubbing his thigh. He still thought he had a neck problem. It occasionally ached, but he was green so it couldn't be that. He checked his neck again; it had become a habit. He also made sure Liam checked himself for any lumps. He was drifting again. They were in the rover and he had barely noticed. Celia…

"Yes, sorry Celia, I was paying attention I just missed that last bit."

"Gary you are..."

"Handsome, heroic, um?"

"A pain; look this is important and you keep avoiding the discussion."

"It's not an easy discussion to have, is it?"

"Gary I'm not your mother let alone your father, but sometimes I think I have to be. I don't know what the best thing to do is; or how to solve this problem, where everyone is happy… Now, I sound like an episode from Corrie."

"Never watched it…"

"Stop avoiding the subject, what are you going to do?"

"Get these clothes for starters then..."

Celia smacked him on the thigh and couldn't stop herself from smiling. She felt that this was the true Gary, not the one she had seen since they had arrived that fateful morning. This was the Gary that the twins knew and Val knew. She wanted to see that Gary, he reminded her so much of her husband, John, God bless him. Her daughter's fiancé was similar; maybe that was why

Lorraine had fallen for him. Now, she was drifting, smiling but with a deeper sadness. "Gary, will you give them what they want?"

"I don't know what they want."

"Yes, you do, Val wants another child, and Miriam wants a child. They want you to give them one. They just haven't asked you yet, but they will soon. There would be a lot of men who would be happy to do that."

"I'm not them! I'm not like the men Val knew at Fox Farm, or the men Miriam knew before, as a singer or whatever she was. I'm not some sort of stud human, around only to; well you know what. They only want me for one purpose. Then after that, there's nothing. I get the extra responsibility, the extra mouths to feed, the space."

"We'll all help with that."

"I know, and I know you do. I barely have to do anything for Henry, even if I want to. He's my son, but I've only given him a bath once. Once! Back before this all happened there were constant stories on the TV about absent fathers, it was one of my mother's rants, I'm not absent, but I barely get a look in." Gary could feel the resentment and anger building. "As long as I take care of Liam, everyone is happy. Poor kid, we're all just waiting for him to get sick or breakdown or take after Rodger."

"Don't get angry; that won't help."

"I'm sorry, I'm just frustrated, I thought Val and I... Well after Hannah. Oh I don't know what I mean or want. Yes, I suppose I will give them what they want if I can. If we survive long enough to do that, if there's enough food to get by."

"What about the twins?"

"What about them? Not them as well?" Gary half wanted them, and half needed to keep his distance.

"No, I don't mean that," Celia knew it was inevitable. Who else was there? Liam, but Kelly and Cass would never let that happen, Liam was red. The girls were even wary of being with him, which was very unfair. Celia also knew what Val had said to the girls, and that it was wrong of her. She also knew that sooner or later, one or more, likely both, of them would make a play for Gary, and then sparks could fly. "What I meant was, since the row."

"I didn't row with anyone."

"I know you didn't, no one is blaming you,"

"Val is!"

"No, she isn't, not really, she's just trying to protect the girls. They're only fifteen; it's not even legal." Celia realised how stupid that sounded. "Sorry that sounded silly, what's legal anymore? You haven't driven on the correct side of the road once."

"Sorry," said Gary pulling over. They were at the high street.

"That doesn't matter. I'm not saying this very well. You… well when we arrived, I couldn't believe how close you were with the girls and Val, now you avoid them. Don't disagree, you know you do. I think Miriam, Liam and I, and Rodger even, have caused that."

"You haven't caused that, it was that stupid row that did that; Val did that. Now every time I go near them I have to think, is that too much attention? Did I touch them wrongly? Encourage them, lead them on in some way? I'm on tenterhooks the whole time, just in case I over step whatever mark Val may have in her head. I'm fed up with it. Even yesterday evening, I'm trying to plan an expedition… The best people to come with me would be the twins, but if I take them Val will think I've taken them away to have my *wicked way* with them. For God's sake! As if I would force them or anything." He was angry again and was about to continue, when he saw it. A car, no, two 4x4s parked in the street. "What the?"

Celia had been looking at him, not the street, "What's the matter?" She turned and looked, "Oh my God, people."

There were seven of them. There was a brief moment of potential confrontation. Gary got out of the car maybe thirty metres away. Three came out of the two cars, and four came out of the shop, already holding winter coats. Gary noticed one reaching for a rifle in a car; he noticed a couple of pistols on two of the men. Two men, one twenties, one forties, the younger man was black. Two teenagers he thought, younger, smaller, sexless. They had moved to the back of the furthest 4x4, having come out of the shop, away from him. Celia was still in the car, calling on the radio back to the house. Three women he could see, one in her twenties, her hand on one of the man's arms; one in her forties he guessed, she wore a head scarf, another one, older than Celia, hanging back. They were all tall, he realised. He was probably taller than the men, but only just. Gary decided to gamble; he reached for his holster, noting the sudden move in his watchers. He undid it and then placed it in the car, telling Celia to wait. He ignored the torrent of messages coming from the radio's speaker. He was now in his normal summer clothes of polo shirt and shorts with flip flops. He walked towards the group. "Hi, I'm Gary," he said, extending his hand.

"You clean?" The head scarfed woman, not hostile, but not friendly. He could see a child's car seat in the back of the first 4x4; a child of about two was asleep in the seat.

Eight, Gary thought. Eight! Hannah, why did I doubt you? "Yes, I'm clean, as of this morning's check."

The younger woman asked, "You have a Checker?"

"Yes."

"You army?" An accent he couldn't place, from one of the men.

"No, look, I'm in shock a bit, I wasn't expecting to see anybody else, especially so many, I..."

"This your poster?" The black man questioned waving one of Gary's posters.

"Yes," Gary lowered his hand. Please, he thought, please let this go right.

"The woman, she clean?" The head scarfed woman pointed at Celia.

"Celia, yes."

"Good," said the woman.

"Your child?" Gary indicated the child in the 4x4.

"Yes," said the woman.

"Are you clean?" Gary thought, two can play that game. He noticed the younger woman smile as well. "Only I have a child at home..." There was a hesitation; they looked at each other. They didn't know.

"We're on our way to the camp across town. We'll check there," the older man stated.

"That's the checker I have." There were looks at each other again.

"Fuel all gone as well?" The older man asked, sounding annoyed.

"No, there's diesel, aviation fuel, and about 150 litres of unleaded, if you can use the equipment."

"Diesel's fine. You're on radio?" The black man indicated the Landrover.

"Our home, my parent's, I mean my house. Celia is telling the others."

"Other's, there are more of you?" The younger woman seemed pleased.

"Yes, a few. There are six back there, plus Celia and me, including my son, he's three months old." Gary realised that he'd given away his, their, strength, sorry Hannah he told himself. Cal or Greavesey would have kicked him. It was time for another gamble. "Look, you're nervous, I'm nervous; you need fuel, and a health check. We're going to head back home, you can follow or not, up to you?"

"We can get fuel later, Joe," said the younger woman to the older man.

"One thing," said Gary, "we have a red teenager with us. He's not sick, but he has the virus."

"We have two like that at home as well," said the younger woman. "I'm Kathy," she said coming forward and shaking his hand. Ten, at least ten, Gary thought.

The screech of tyres could be heard from the end of the street as the Lexus shot into view. Val was driving, Gary barely registered, before it stopped, and the twins disembarked with SA80s at the ready.

"Hold it, hold it," shouted Gary at them, "it's okay." Kelly and Cass slowly lowered their weapons, and Gary realised the younger black man lowered his. Wherever that had come from?

"Jesus Christ," said the younger man, "that's one hell of a cavalry." He carefully placed his shotgun into the passenger seat of the front 4x4. "I'm Andy," he said sticking his hand out for Gary to shake, "pleased to meet you Gary."

There was a round of names and introductions, explanations, and discussions. The twins, wary at first, hung back until the teenage girl, Diane, from the rear 4x4 asked whether they had a similar winter coat. She was a year or two younger than the twins, Gary thought. The boy was thirteen, Chris, he said; taller than Liam thought Gary. The journey to the house was delayed whilst the twins picked out winter coats with Diane. Their old ones would be too small for the coming winter. Val also said hello, but was very wary. Celia was chatting to the older woman Rose, and the head scarfed woman who was Zaynah. The child was two and a half years old and called Spike.

Gary suggested, "You can stay at the farm," now there was water there. "If you want or are you heading back?"

"We'll stay," Joe said, after a quick discussion. There was power provided by a generator, Gary had completed that task ready for the solar feed to come in. They could come up the house to meet everyone. Gary walked back to the Lexus with Val and the twins; the SA80's hanging from straps around their necks, when they got to the car. Gary gave Val a hug, and a kiss on the lips; he then did the same with a slightly lighter kiss with each of the girls. They looked shocked, and a bit embarrassed at first, then smiled, no beamed at him.

"Thank you," he said, "thank you, all of you, for riding to the rescue. It scared the hell out of me, and them."

Val looked like she was going to be cross at the hug and kiss, then pleased and then cross again. In the end, she smiled. "Come on you two, let's get back; Miriam and Liam will be going nuts unless Celia has told them." Gary walked back to the rover, and the convoy of four cars set off. The Lexus went back to the house via the drive, whereas Gary took the route to the farm, answering Miriam's questions via the radio. Gary showed them the farmhouse, the generator, and the water supply. He pointed the route up the track to the house, which couldn't quite be seen. He told them to come up when they were ready.

Rose said, "I'm ready now," as were the two teenagers, Diane and Chris. So those three climbed in the back of the rover, and Gary drove up to the top of the track, and then crossed back to the drive. The house got the usual wows, then the walk around, and then the meeting with Miriam. Henry was back in Val's arms. There was a warm smile from Val for Gary on his return, and another smile from Liam. Gary realised this felt so different from when they he had awoken with Rodger, Miriam, Celia and Liam coming up the drive in the dawn. Val had the checking kit ready inside the kitchen area, all three were green; the twins checked themselves as well. Liam walked away. Gary went and told him about the other reds, he nodded in response, and Gary squeezed his shoulder,

"Why don't you show, Diane and Chris the games on the movie screen, chores can wait?" That met with eager consent, Gary warning him to, "Go easy," on his new competitors. The twins were already talking music to Diane when the suggestion was made; the girls both looked at him for permission. "Yes, you two as well, as long as dinner is okay, Miriam will need some help if they stay for dinner." The girls hugged him, twice in one day he thought. Gary noticed the others walking up the track; they were carrying a box. The box turned out to be fresh fish, a mix of flounder, bass, and turbot. There would be plenty for dinner after all. Miriam jumped for joy. Food was discussed; yes, they would stay. Showers, toilets, baths were discussed offered and accepted. Gary accepted the chaos, the disruption. Food followed, wine was opened and shared.

Joe explained that the group was twenty strong in total. They lived on the East coast near Hornsea in a group of cottages nearly two hours away from the house. They had some vegetables, diesel generators, chickens and ducks. They had created rainwater tanks and used Agas for heating and hot water. They had found each other via notices that Joe had put out. They knew of two other groups, one north of Hornsea near Whitby and one south near Sutton-on-Sea, but no one in-land until they had found one of Gary's posters. They wanted the full story of the sheep from Gary. The child who was toddling around, watched carefully by Zaynah, was not Joe's; although Joe made clear he and Zaynah were together. The usual stories of survival followed and, one by one, the other guests went and were checked by Val, on the checker. The last check was the child Spike. There was an audible sense of relief when ping and green resulted. The Hornsea group's checker had stopped working six months earlier.

Joe and Gary found themselves wandering up the hill towards the turbine, for once Liam was not trailing. He seemed to be in a continuous death match with the other teenagers, with laughter coming from the cinema, and frequent cries of cheating.

"Gary, I'm going to be very frank with you and I hope you will with me? I don't think any of us can afford not to be"

"I agree," Gary nodded.

"How old are you anyway?"

"I'm twenty-one, you?"

Joe shook his head; he mumbled, "So young," then said, "I'm forty-two. You've done fantastically well, so far."

"Thanks, but I had a head start, my parents and this house. Best of all I had excellent teachers, the army group we mentioned at dinner"

"Even so you made it"

"We all did."

"That's true, but I've been with people all the time, you had, what a year on your own?"

"A bit under, until Val and the twins showed up."

"You and Val together?"

"Yes, I mean no, not really, she wanted a child so... It's complicated. She's with Miriam." Gary really didn't want to talk about this; he recalled the conversation with Celia earlier.

"Ah!"

"Must be complicated with your setup as well?" Gary thought, wanting to deflect the conversation the other way.

"Yes, it is, but I'm kind of outside the procreation discussion. I had the snip before A-Day. Spike's not mine, but I've stepped into that father role. Zaynah and I met early on; we found others and ended up on the coast. Andy has a small harem," Joe shook his head in wonderment. "He has Kathy *and* two more pregnant back on the coast. What about here?"

"As I said, it's complicated, sorry don't mean to be er…" Gary struggled for the right word, "unforthcoming," he settled on. "It's just not sorted out yet, and there's a lot that's happened since Celia, Miriam and Liam arrived. There was another man Rodger."

"The fresh grave at the farm?"

Had someone said something, Gary speculated? "Yes, he, well let's say, he decided not to be friendly."

"You took care of it?" Joe was reassessing Gary again.

"Yes, not proud of it, but it was going to be him or me, more likely us. He, well, he wasn't a good man, let's leave it at that." Gary was struggling with the right words.

Joe nodded, "Had a small group come by three months ago, all men, scavenging, but they demanded food, and then tried to take it. We buried them as well."

"I see."

"Is that why your cavalry are so well prepared?"

"Yes, I suppose so. They even scared me today, like something out of a movie, sorry about that." Gary couldn't help but smile though, his girls riding to the rescue. "My army friends taught me some basic stuff, and I've taught the girls, it has come in handy, but I don't have to like it."

"One of the other communities, south of us, had a run in with a bigger group. That didn't go well, food was taken and the women were… Well, they were raped we think, not had much contact since."

"Shit, that's not good, I had no idea; didn't they have weapons."

"Some of the men in the attacking group were all in combat gear, and they had SA80s, like you have. We have only shotguns, pistols, and a couple of hunting rifles. One thing we could do with, weapons." There was a half question there.

Gary knew where some were, and how to get them. "Earlier you said *so far*, what did you mean?"

"Yes, that's really what I want to talk about. Someone mentioned that you had a plan for humanity or something?"

"Not as grand as that, and it's more a dream I made with… It doesn't matter. It was a way of taking what we've done here and expanding. In reality were slowly failing. Yes, I know we look fine but one disaster and who knows. The fuel will eventually run out, and then we'll be back to the middle ages, but without horses to move around. Unless we can get power and so on going."

"I agree that it's going to get harder and harder, food will always be difficult, you've done great with flour, we have been scavenging stocks, but knowledge and how to do stuff is just as important. You have a sheared sheep! We trade with the other communities, but its scavenged stuff we trade, as we all have fish and vegetables. What we don't have and will run out of, with the diesel, is power. That's where I think we can help each other."

"What do you mean?"

"We can trade with each other. There must be solar panels around, and you know how to set them up." Gary knew where over two hundred were. "Val said that you are going to power the farm?"

"Yes, that's the plan, if I can make it work; I only know what my dad taught me, and how this house works. I did help a little bit installing, but that took several builders and so on. I don't have that manpower available, there's only us."

"Gary we have people, here's what I'm thinking. We'll head back tomorrow and return with a team, say six of us to help you do the farm, and anything extra you can think of. In return, you help us set up solar back on the coast, maybe help us plan water better as well. Then when we're done you can come back with fresh fish and, when we have power, frozen. We can freeze it there. Maybe get longer-range radio working. One of the men back at the coast, Trevor, says we need VHF or short wave or something, but without power none of that will work. With power, we could even... Well, let's see what we can do. Speech over, what do you think?"

Gary had listened intently. They were standing up near the turbine, which gently turned; it was dark. Joe had not been able to see Gary's face as he talked. "See that?" Gary said, looking back at the house, it seemed to have lights on everywhere. Music could be heard from some of the rooms, and Gary guessed someone was demonstrating the sound system. If there were neighbours, there would be complaints.

"It's a fabulous house."

"Thanks, but that's not what I meant. I mean, the last time this house was so full of people was just after we moved in, before A-Day. I've heard more laughter this evening and seen more smiles than I can remember in a long time. You wanted frank talk Joe, well here it is. If we don't do what you say, we'll all be dead, maybe two years maybe longer, but we'll slowly die out, despite the children. We don't generate enough food; a bad winter could destroy all our crops. We have no livestock except for chickens and one pathetic lonely sheep. It's possible we'll get by but what about disease, all those childhood ailments that the new generation might catch? What about storms and accidents? Your plan, well your plan is our plan, Hannah's plan, and it's my plan. Yes, I want to cooperate, but one thing?"

"What?" Joe didn't know who Hannah was, or what Gary was talking about, but he knew their vegetables weren't enough; they needed farms and flour. Just a couple of sacks for bread would be a major boost to morale.

"Val made me promise her when we discussed having Henry, that I would look after them; that I would take care of all of them. I don't need you to promise that, but I do need a promise, that you will do all you can to make this plan work? I don't know you and you don't know me, but I think your promise will mean something. I want to find the surviving sheep and cattle and pigs and most importantly, more people. There will be people who don't want to help, or who, like that arse Rodger and the group you mentioned. They will want to take and not help. I, we, us… we all need to prevent that, show that working together we can survive. We can get back some of what's gone. I want your help with that, your promise with that."

Joe thought Gary was a bit mad, weren't they all? He'd known him less than twelve hours, yet he had a feeling that this was the most important promise he'd ever made in his life. He was divorced, his children and ex-wife both lost he thought, no sign of them anyway. Here, he was being asked by a twenty-one year old to promise to commit to what? A dream maybe, with some bits planned. Yet he knew, he instinctively understood that Gary needed this. Maybe they all needed this. Joe had spent a lot of time abroad; he had been in the USA on A-Day, getting back just before the financial system went into its final crash. Were similar discussions and plans being made by survivors in other parts of the world? Gary was looking at him, time for speculation later.

"Gary I'm not sure I fully understand what you want from me, but I will promise you this. I will do everything in my power to help us all survive; no, not just that, to flourish. It feels as though we've been barely treading water for years as a society, even before A-Day. We have a chance; if we work together, to recover, even to have a better life. Once upon a time, I would get stressed if my Cappuccino wasn't made right; now I only worry about where we could get water. I think you and I, and more importantly, *we*, all could work together well. I want to try that. I *promise* to try that?" Was that enough? Joe used to do big speeches for sales pitches. He felt that this was far more important.

Gary stuck out his hand. Joe shook it. It felt silly and yet right. It felt unnecessary, but at the same time completely necessary. Gary said, "I think I can help with the weapons, and some flour, and …"

Joe stopped him, "Hold up a second, do you ever stop? That would be great, but what I need now is a pee in one of your posh bathrooms and then a drink. We can work this out in the morning. I saw one of the lists that, who was it Cass or Kelly, had?

Doesn't matter, this feels weird, no offence, but I feel like I've just made a bigger commitment than marriage. How old did you say you were?" Joe slapped Gary on his back. "Let's get a drink and tell the others."

CHAPTER TWENTY-SIX

To The Coast

Gary drove the army truck, loaded with sixty solar panels. Celia sat next to him. Following behind, were the twins with Liam in the land rover. They were towing a trailer loaded with jerry cans of diesel, a cage containing the cockerel and under a tarpaulin, half a dozen sacks of flour along with some starter yeast. They were going to switch cockerels to stop inbreeding in their respective coops. Gary was following the two 4x4s containing Joe and his crew as he called them.

The crew had arrived as planned two days after Joe, Andy, Rose, Kathy, Zaynah and Spike, had gone back to the Coast. Chris and Diane had asked to stay, which they had, with Chris sharing Liam's room and Diane in with one of the twins. Chores had been done, but only after Val had pushed a bit. Day to day routine was blown anyway as Gary planned for the return visit and what the crew would do. Joe had returned with more fish, now in the freezer, some different veg, Andy, Kathy, and three new people. One was a red. She was a thirty-five-year old woman called Helen. She had red hair as well, which is how she joked about it. She had a long chat with Liam five minutes after she arrived. Another was a thirty-year old Asian man called Gart. Gary wasn't sure of the spelling, but that's how the name sounded. The final member of the crew was a huge, stocky Irishman, called Murphy. Murphy had been a builder, to no one's surprise, except for Gary. He had missed out on Irish jokes for some reason.

Murphy said, "More of a JCB driver on construction sites,

although brick-laying was part of my art. Even a bit of plumbing."

Gary had seen Joe off on their first return trip to the coast at Hornsea, with a trip to the camp. He had unlocked the key safe with the combination Hannah had left him. He had then taken the keys to a rusting padlock on an ISO container; inside remained the camp's armoury. Twenty SA80 rifles sat in neat racks, alongside cleaning kits, and, behind another lock, ammunition, and slings. Gary issued out six to Joe's astonishment with accompanying kits. Other than the fish and the hospitality of the previous day, and over a breakfast of scrambled eggs on fresh toast, this was the first demonstration of their agreement. Gary then issued two more pistols. There was an issue log book at the front of the ISO and Gary carefully noted the six rifles, five hundred rounds of 5.56 mm, two pistols and a hundred rounds of 9 mm, in the log issued to Joe, *Hornsea* his name came after Cpl Hannah Watkins for four. Two had gone with Cal and Greavesey. Joe had signed for receipt before he realised how silly it was. Then, they had refuelled from the diesel dump. They shook hands again, and the visitors had headed off on their journey back to the coast, with Gary asking them to look out for sheep or cattle on their way.

It had taken Joe nearly fifty miles before he stopped shaking his head. Joe struggled to understand how an eighteen-year old had survived. No, that was unfair, not just survived, but thrived despite his concerns. Zaynah had told him that Gary was expected to be a father again soon, to Miriam as well as Val. She also said that she was sure the twins would follow once they were old enough. Joe loved Zaynah dearly, but her Muslim upbringing and morals sometimes led her to ignore the reality of the survivors' situation. She would grumble about Andy until Joe reminded her that polygamy was a Muslim tradition. Not in her family she had retorted. Joe could only smile at her until she relented and smiled back. She was also impressed by what she had seen. Flushing toilets, running mains water, electricity on tap without having to worry about generator fuel. She wanted that back.

When Joe's crew had arrived back at the house via the farm entrance, they found Gary had been out and collected two large garden sheds he planned to use for the accommodation hut, if they could help him figure out how to do it. But more importantly, and the primary purpose, there were thirty 400 watt solar panels, stacked neatly by the farm. Cable drums ready and aluminium poles already partially laid out. The task of planning the layout had gone to the teenagers, using Gary's father's software, just as Gary had helped his father prepare the house array nearly five years before. With six extra pairs of hands, the array had gone up quickly. The inverters were a different matter, necessitating two trips to his father's factory to pick up bits of equipment that Gary had neglected or forgotten. He was angry with himself. Kelly was in the land rover with him, when instead of heading for the factory, he turned into the camp to refuel; he hadn't said they were going. He felt her tense, then relax. She could only see earth mounds, instead of the pits, "When did you do that?"

"A while back, with Miriam and Celia. Sorry, I should have told you."

"Thanks for doing it. I, we… Its better this way, less memories."

"Good," he said, "now the fuel."

"Show me how to do it," said Kelly.

Back at *Arse Farm*, Gary added in the missing components, a switch this time, a meter last time. Kelly made sure both were on one of her lists, ready to take to the coast, along with spare inverters and components. They also pre-loaded a new computer to run the local monitoring software. There was still the issue of batteries for the farm and the coast. Gary had checked the house system and calculated what would be needed, but he was not sure how the batteries were connected. He did not know what capacity he required. He hoped they could use car or other vehicle batteries, after all it was what the one's in the house's basement looked like. He knew at some stage they would have to go and get more otherwise the power system intended for the coast, and now in the farm would be daylight only.

Now, it was time to switch the farm's system on. The main feed entered into the farm on the fuse board near the kitchen. Click, lights flashed then went steady. The fridge in the kitchen of the farmhouse started whirring. Lights went on, two relays on the fuse board popped. No one knew what they supplied as the board wasn't marked. Murphy came running in from one of the barns. "Jesus! You sacred the life out of me when the lights went on."

Now, the farm had power, next was water, and sewage. Gary had already laid the water to outside, now they needed to dig in rainwater collection, filter treatment, Ultra Violet cleaning and recycling. They would need pumps as well. That took the following days. Joe's crew plus the house workers were split across the sites. The farm's kitchen was replaced, new furniture was added from a retail park store, and even a lick of paint decorated all the rooms. The four bedrooms, all of which were a good size, were equipped with new double beds. The kitchen glass that Hannah had broken was repaired. The farm was not the house, but it was habitable and comfortable. The final task was the accommodation block. It was easily wired for power with a double feed from the house and the farm, and was in reach of water. Murphy and one of the team disappeared for half a day and came back with bathrooms, showers, and WC's, which the two of them then set up overnight, determined to finish quickly. The block could easily sleep up to twenty residents, on the installed bunk beds.

Murphy's plumbing skills were much better than he claimed. Gary took a trip into town and returned with a case of Irish Whisky as a special thank you. Helen, with help from the twins, had also ploughed another field. She had a bit of farming background, but wouldn't expand on that. Andy was the team's mechanic, and he was diverted onto car, tractor, and associated maintenance, helped as needed by Gart. All of the house's and farm's vehicles got an overhaul and after a couple of trips away with a generator they returned with new tyres, where they were needed and more spares to go in the farm's barns. Andy had broken into a tyre service place on the retail park that Gary had ignored.

On their final night, the group gathered in the house. The late summer had broken. The wind howled, and rain pelted down. They sat around the house sipping wine or whisky, after eating an amazing fish dish that Miriam had created. They all planned the return trip and who would go. Gary knew who it should be, but he was expecting a row with Val. He had tried to have a private conversation with her, but there were too many people about. The last afternoon Gary and Andy had taken an Army truck to his

Dad's factory and preloaded it with the solar equipment and panels ready for the coastal journey. They had then returned via the camp and topped up the fuel. Gary looked concerned at the tank's meters, they had gotten through quite a bit in the last few days with all the trips, diggers, and top ups. They had to find more, or Gary's hope for a year's worth of supply was hopelessly optimistic. The farm would use less for the barn generators, but the more they farmed the more they would need machinery driven and, therefore, more fuel. The rain and wind could be heard above the sound from the cinema door, where the teenagers had lain claim again for another movie or gaming session. Gary wanted that talk with Val, but also needed to talk to Joe.

"Fuel, is not going to last, I know we want to trade, but that will burn fuel more, so we need to be careful unless we can get it out of garages."

"We tried that, but the fuel was contaminated or simply gone. A lot of garages never got resupplied once the virus hit."

"Still we need to try; I don't know how to do that."

"Nice to know there's something you don't know," he laughed. "I've never seen so many reference books in someone's home. Anyway, Andy can show you; there hasn't been time this trip."

Andy heard his name mentioned, "Show what?"

"Gary's worried about fuel, we've used a lot of his diesel the last week or so."

"He's got plenty?"

"No, that's the problem," Gary explained, "I'm down to maybe six months' supply if we're careful." The other adults were all listening now.

"You've got loads," said Andy realising that Gary didn't know. A big grin was on his face; he was a pretty competitive person at heart, and had been intimidated by the house and what Gary had achieved. Gary just looked confused. Andy put him out of his misery. "Jet fuel," he said.

"Jet fuel?" Joe and Gary both asked.

Gart continued stepping into the conversation, "Yep, if its jet fuel, then it's basically diesel; you'll need to add some additive; that's normally a lubricant for the engine."

Andy took up the explanation, "Landrovers, military ones and military trucks, probably won't care, but modern car diesels will. You add it to each tank in the vehicle, but otherwise it's the same stuff; some people swear by it, my mate…" Andy stopped himself, "… anyway, you can use jet fuel, if it is jet fuel?"

"What do you mean?" Gary was on the edge of his seat.

"Some fuel used in planes is Av Gas. If you drive a classic car, 1950s or earlier that might use it, but not unleaded vehicles, Av Gas is leaded, and high octane. If it's Av Gas, it'll be useless, mind you, unless you want to fly a small plane."

"What did the army use it for at your camp? Did they say?" Gart asked.

"Helicopters, but I didn't see any there, I saw some before I ever went there, flying back and forth." Gary was trying to remember if anything had been said.

"Training helicopters, you know the ones you can learn in, have piston engines, they'll take Av Gas, but bigger ones tend to have turbine jets, that'll be Aviation fuel, jet fuel, and that is what I think you've got."

Kathy came and sat on Andy's lap, "I never knew you knew, so much about helicopters."

"Man of mystery me," he said giving her a kiss.

"Andy, if you're right, then we have a couple of years supply at the camp and maybe at the other camp as well."

"There's another one?" Joe asked. That hadn't been mentioned before.

"Yes, it's on the other side of town. As far as I know it had only aviation, and some diesel, but that's gone. It never got setup properly, it was back in that first winter; they were already dying you see." They all fell silent, remembering.

"It sounds like you have one fewer problem than you

thought, Gary my friend," said Joe. "We can check tomorrow or later. I had no idea about the fuel either. No wonder none of you have mentioned it. I presume that's how we have been getting by."

"Yep from a few months now, mind you there is a problem, that's pumping it, they normally refuel tankers, and then the tankers do the planes. So getting it out of the tanks does take some fiddling, but it's straightforward after that."

"There's another Bowser tanker at the camp, I've never thought of it because I thought we couldn't use it."

As soon as the rain stopped, Kathy dragged Andy away to congratulate him on his cleverness. They walked back to the farm. Joe and Gart followed soon after. Murphy and Helen were both asleep in the cinema room after the teenagers had gone to bed. Gary sat in the lounge with Celia, Miriam, and Val. Here it comes, he thought, Gary had almost forgotten the conversation with Celia on the day they had met Joe and the rest. Now, he had a feeling it was time for that discussion. At least the twins had gone to bed.

"Gary," started Celia. Gary had been expecting Val. "Who do you need to go with you tomorrow?"

Gary looked backwards and forwards, "I won't need much help there; it's more who could do with a trip and help out on the way back. Only I can drive the truck back, although Cass and the others have been learning; Cass is furthest along. So I guess it's the twins, and Liam will want to come, but only if they want to; if necessary I'll go alone."

"Val, what do you think?" Celia asked. Gary thought they had planned this as well.

"I agree, Gary, they should all go, but I'd like Celia to go as well." She looked at Gary. "If that's okay with you?" This was like fencing, Gary guessed, not that he'd ever tried.

"Will you be okay with Miriam and Henry for a few days?"

"Yes, we'll survive. I mean we can cope for a few days, but there's one thing we need from you before you go."

"The twins will be fine if that's what you're worried about?" Gary could feel his anger rising.

"I know they will." Val was talking very softly, not confrontationally. "And that's not why I want Celia to go either, I do trust you with them. No, it's us; that's the problem." She indicated Miriam and herself. "We want…"

"I know what you want." Gary felt himself blush. "Sorry, that came out harder than I meant. I understand what you and Miriam need and want; I'm just not sure I'm the right man for the job. There are the others now, I mean other candidates."

"Gary, we don't know them," said Miriam. "I realise that I have changed what you had with Val. I didn't mean to. It's just the way it is. We haven't spent a lot of time together, not like you and Val have, but I know you are a good man. I've seen you be a good man, and that is what I want as a father for my child."

"Gary, I know this is not how life used to be; the normal way of things, but we have to live how things are now. We agreed before Henry how this would work, and I'm so sorry…"

"Val you don't have to…"

"Yes, I do," she reached for his hand. "Gary, I am so sorry for how I've treated you and the girls. It was selfish, and yes I had my reasons, but I think we have to, all of us, behave differently. When that radio message came through from Celia saying you were facing an armed group on your own… I know it's turned out okay, but none of us knew that at the time. I realised how much you mean to me, and the girls, to all of us. That's why I'm nervous again about you going off."

"You've no idea how pleased I was to see you all at that moment, not because it was dangerous, but because you came with the girls."

"I know, I know," Val squeezed his hand. "Now you have to take Miriam to bed?"

"What? I thought it was you?" Gary was flushed again. He stole a quick look at Miriam. She was blushing as well. He couldn't look Celia in the eye, but she seemed to be laughing behind her hand.

"Wrong time, its right for Miriam, we've been doing the charts just like we did for me." Gary remembered the discussions.

"It has to be tonight or we'll miss the cycle, and you'll be off and something… It has to be tonight; to start with."

"Just count yourself lucky I'm beyond all that," said Celia. "Thirty years younger and well…"

Gary was so embarrassed. "I don't know what to say, okay, yes, I will whatever… I'm going to check the grounds and lock up."

Val said, "I'll come with you; I'll need to do it when you're away."

They strolled out. Val took his arm but they said nothing. He made sure lights clicked on and he checked the coop. The ground smelled of the rain. The wind had dropped, but it was chilly. They came back in, locking doors behind them. He hoped Helen and Murphy were out for the night; the house lights would come on if they moved. Val said goodnight and gave him a kiss before heading into her annex. He thought he heard Henry stirring. He'd just checked on Helen and Murphy when he noticed Miriam moving quickly upstairs. This was going to happen, Gary realised.

Gary thought about Miriam. He thought about her when she'd stripped her t-shirt off. She was already in his bed when he came into the room; the sheet tucked around her. She was on a different side of the bed from Val. Gary hadn't redone a duvet; it was too warm he felt, so he only had the sheet. Miriam watched him go into the bathroom. He used the loo, washed, brushed his teeth, and shaved. He undressed and came out in his boxers dropping his dirty clothes in the wash basket. He went to switch off the light.

"You can leave it on if you want."

"That's okay," he said, switching it off. He climbed into bed. He slipped his boxers off. He rolled onto his side and looked at Miriam, he felt her hand on his side. It would be okay, he realised. It was.

***

Driving in the truck on the way to the coast, Gary allowed his thoughts to drift.

"You're quiet," Celia stated.

"Sorry, just thinking things through… Do the girls know? I mean about what happened last night?"

"You and Miriam you mean?"

"Yes, look this is not easy to talk about, for me anyway, it's bad enough with all you women discussing menstrual cycles and ovulation schedules, let alone that waxing session you all had. Liam and I didn't know where to go. Had all that with Val, it's just got worse with Miriam as well."

"And me, and don't say it's not so. To answer your question, no I don't think they know, so you might want to tell them before we get back, not now."

Gary grabbed the truck's radio. "26, 30 over"

"26, Go," Kelly replied. He could see Cass driving in the mirror, over the last few weeks they had started styling their hair differently.

"Know any songs about sheep hunting?"

"No."

"Keep your eyes open. I'm feeling lucky today, 30 out."

Kelly looked at Cass; Cass glanced at Kelly, "Miriam or Val?" Cass said.

"Has to be Miriam, wrong time for Val," said Kelly.

"What are you two on about?" Diane asked, leaning forward with Liam.

"Nothing," they said smiling at each other. "Watch out for sheep or cattle."

CHAPTER TWENTY-SEVEN

On The Coast

They were at the coast for five days in all. Murphy and Joe had shown him around. Andy had talked about fuel and vehicles. They had a discussion about fishing, and using something bigger. There were several small fishing boats available with nets to go out to sea. Andy had gotten engines working, but no one had gone very far from shore and results had not been good. They showed Gary, the twins and Liam how to beach fish, but the weather was much colder and despite the joy of the seeing the shoreline, Gary thought of Hannah on the beach. He turned melancholy, despite the twins threatening to throw him into the surf. The solar array was soon wired up and when it switched on there were huge cheers. Gary had hidden three bottles of champagne in the truck, which he then presented to Joe. Zaynah, hugged him, then apologised for her immodesty, then she hugged him again. She wouldn't drink. Andy's two pregnant ladies, Sylvia and Danni, took the twins under their wing, getting them involved and asking questions about the house, which everyone wanted to see. The visitors had overstated it, Gary said modestly, secretly pleased and proud that his parent's home still attracted attention. On their last night, they were all crowded into a knocked through lounge between two of the cottages. That had happened whilst Joe had been away, and under Zaynah's direction. She liked open plan she said. Murphy had specially sought out a single malt just for Gary.

"So what's next?" Joe asked the room, revelling in the crowd of happy faces and unrestricted electricity, during daylight anyway.

"Communications would be good," said Liam. He was really coming out of his shell since his chat with Helen, and he sat with Diane. They seemed close.

"Facebook, Skype," said Kelly, "oh, to have them back." She and Cass were sitting on the floor next to Gary. They were both sipping wine as well. Val would have said something, but no one seemed to mind.

"We did get by without them before you know," said Rose. She was sitting next to Celia.

"How easy would that be, to set up a network?" Gary asked.

"Wireless would be possible, if we could relay the signal, but it's a long way and lots of hills," said Trevor; one of the new people Gary had met. He was about forty, and he was also the other red.

"But data connections were everywhere, surely they would just work?" Murphy asked.

"No," said Trevor, "you need the BT exchanges; then the relay points, then the data centres, all working." BT had provided most houses with a copper telephone connection and consequently, any broadband access via their local exchanges.

"If they all had power?" Joe commentated.

"Don't have that much solar or wind. We don't even know where the data centres are, or which ones are the right ones," Trevor replied, and the room sombrely listened.

"You had fibre at the house and the farm, I noticed Gary?" Joe continued hoping there was more positive news.

"Yes," said Gary, "but it was all set up by one of the Internet cable companies. I hadn't thought a lot about it. We could get more fibre I'm sure, but I don't know how to do that."

"That will work for short distances, again if there is power," said Trevor. The room fell silent.

"Radios," said Chris, "can't we use radios; you have them in the rover and truck."

"We do and one in the house and at the camp. There will be others at other camps as well. They are UHF, and we tested them out to thirty miles or so."

"That depends on the antenna height I suppose." Gart joined the conversation.

"The ERS goes much further than that, or did, I haven't heard it for months," said Celia.

"Power," said Joe, "it keeps coming back to power. Another research project, I think, for the radios that is; and we need to solve the battery issue if we want power at night like now." They were running the room lights on generators.

"The battery issue is solvable, I think," said Gary. "I just need to get the information from my father's office. In the meantime, we'll have to messenger, maybe a weekly run back and forth. There's always room to stay at either end."

"I'm definitely going back to the house," said Rose, "the bath was great and proper loos."

"Me too," said Helen, "still we'll have that soon enough, if Murphy pulls his finger out?"

"What have I done?" Murphy had been playing with Spike. Zaynah picked him up. "Couple of days I should think for the sewage."

"This is a plumber speaking, so best count on a week," said Andy, laughter from the adults, Murphy just smiled.

Helen said, "Enough of this hilarity, I want to know about your briefs, from Hannah weren't they?"

"What?" Gary said surprised.

"Sorry," said Kelly, "I thought they should have a copy. Don't worry, I removed most of the personal stuff."

"Kelly you had…" Gary stopped, of course she did, he didn't have the right to the information and no one else. "Sorry you are right, please excuse me everyone. I better explain; Hannah was very close to me. Before she died," he paused, "she had written a series of briefs which Kelly seems to have brought with her. The briefs cover all sorts of stuff that Hannah had thought about."

"Is that where the *A*, *B,* and *C*s come from?" Helen asked.

"Yes, *A*s were Hannah's theory of people who are immune from the virus, *B*s were people who had recovered or were in remission and *C*s were those who were red or green, I suppose, but still going," Cass replied before Gary could.

"Like us," said Liam.

"Yes, sorry Liam, like you Helen and Trevor, but it could be any of us. Everyone was healthy once, before the virus that is. You three are still healthy, even though you are red."

"That reminds me," Joe said, "we must get another Checker."

"What I want to know is about part two of Hannah's survivor brief," said Helen. "I understand her working out the survivor numbers, God I hope there are more than that but, it's children I'm concerned about. She looked at the pregnant Sylvia and Danni. Look everyone here knows, but you don't. Murphy and I are together, but I won't bring an infected child into this world. I can't do that, not after…" She stopped. Tears were running down her cheeks, Murphy was at her side in a second.

"It's okay, love," he said.

"Sorry," said Helen after a few seconds of embarrassed silence. "I lost my children." She visibly pulled herself together. "Tell me what you think about part two of the Survivor Brief." Gary knew it and could picture every word.

SURVIVORS PART 2

Healthy Kids

So, when these lovely ladies fall for your charms, the issue of children will come up ☺Joke as well!

Your mum, seems like a lovely lady, wish I'd met her, has left a couple of genetic research books in the library. I don't understand a lot of it, but the basics are that we will end up with a matrix of possible outcomes depending on whether the virus gene is dominant or not. So, if it's dominant we get one set of results, and if it isn't, we get another. I guess we don't know which. If we just used red or green then there are four results each way. So eight in total, see my spreadsheet for a full run down but here's the basic. Ladies first of course!

Dominant virus:

Green Female + Green Male = Green child

Green Female + Red Male = Red Child

Red Female + Green Male = Red Child

Red Female + Red Male = Red Child

Non-Dominant Virus:

Green Female + Green Male = Green child

Green Female + Red Male = Green Child

Red Female + Green Male = Green Child

Red Female + Red Male = Red Child

The books make it clear that it's not quite as simple as that, there are suppressed genes, and male dominant but not female, and so on. Baldness skips generations it seems. I'm sure all the researchers and scientists were working on this, but they had one disadvantage, they didn't have or didn't know who the A)s were. We might know now, if I'm not wrong about you, love, and there are others.

I've played around on the spreadsheet with variations going up to 16 combinations if I've got the formulas right, and then any B)s might act as Red or Green in the calculations and variations. This stuff gets complicated very quickly. You were coming back and I haven't had the time to do it again. You'll find it in the folder with my pictures and these briefs.

So, my instructions are, find a green and have fun!

CHAPTER TWENTY-EIGHT
Discussion

Kelly finished the explanation; Gary had drifted, listening to her, but really listening to Hannah in his head. "She was army?" Joe asked.

"Yes, she wasn't an expert or anything, she knew that, she just thought about it."

"So what does that mean?" Helen asked.

"It would be a risk, dependent on which gene is dominant," said Kelly; she had read the books. Kelly provided a brief explanation of the further variations she had found in the spreadsheet, and her own thoughts on the matter. "I think the virus is dominant in most cases, in terms of disease progression. What it doesn't explain, genetically speaking, is how two reds can produce a green? That is what has happened in our cases, Helen, Trevor, and Liam excepted. Unless we are all Cs with a delayed outcome, how depressing is that? We have no mother and child, or father, and child pairs, or grandparent with a grandchild for that matter. We have one set of siblings, well twins, Cass and me, we just don't know enough," Kelly looked sad.

"We all know that identical twins are special," Celia commented, to smiles from Cass and Kelly.

"Thanks Celia," Kelly said, "but the gene combination from our mum and dad should have worked for our brother, or other people's siblings but hasn't, clearly." Gary thought how grown up she sounded. "It's clear that a survival combination is rare even with the virus as a red, but I don't know if Hannah's formula and combinations are right or not."

"I can check the calculations," Danni said trying to lift the atmosphere. "I was training to be a maths teacher when, well I had a year to go. I was pretty hot on spreadsheets."

"I don't understand," said Chris. That led to a discussion about teaching and education and another need to share capabilities. Danni was the most qualified, although Celia had once worked as a teaching assistant, years before.

"We need proper lessons and so on," said Joe. Kelly and Cass groaned and put their heads in their hands.

"I don't mean school, well I do, but different, the new children will have to learn to read and write and add up, but we need lots of practical stuff as well. Like Murphy teaching plumbing and bricklaying. I think we should all have to do, say an hour a day, learning someone else's skills."

"Gary has been teaching me about the turbines and things, but I don't understand the maths very well," said Liam.

"You should have said," said Gary, "I'll cover it, or Danni can help you."

"After the baby," said Danni, "I could come to the house."

"Val's a nurse of course," Celia said. "Maybe she should come here to help with the babies, just in case." There followed another round of discussions about medical matters that put everyone on edge, especially when Kelly mentioned another short brief from Hannah on illnesses.

"She thought of nearly everything that girl," Joe was impressed. "Good point on measles and rubella, even mumps and chicken pox. I suppose we have to hope that they have all been killed off with the virus. We would all have been immunised or had them as children."

"I never got any of them," said Rose. She was the oldest. "My mother put me in contact, but nothing." They quickly established that nobody there had suffered from the diseases or illnesses. "Is that a link?" Rose asked. "What does that mean for the new children, they can't be immunised unless they could develop the vaccines again? What about dentists?" Rose finished with another question.

"What about them?" Celia said.

"We don't have any."

"No, but," Celia stopped, and then she asked the room, "does anyone have any fillings?" No one had, the teenagers were too young, but had not needed or complained about toothache. They brushed their teeth; they all did. Gary had been for a check-up just before A-Day, but he had never needed treatment.

"Another link possibly," said Rose. "Glasses, I have reading glasses, but no one has eyesight glasses."

"That could be because they couldn't see to find food," Murphy had a morbid sense of humour sometimes.

"They would still be around," said Helen smacking him. "But we all have normal eyesight I suppose, it seems like a link."

"Height," said Gary, he explained his theory.

Gart agreed, "I noticed that as well, but does that make people As, or Cs?" No one could agree whether it did or not.

They mutually stopped talking about it after Andy said, "Life's risky, remember how we would watch kids in Africa dying of simply cured illnesses. We're like Africa now, only there's no UN or charities coming to our rescue. It could be worse, that's my philosophy anyway. There was typhoid in London; I remember a warning broadcast after the water stopped. Typhoid for God's sake! Then there was Stonehenge, but that wasn't illness that was, I don't know what that was."

Several people asked, "Stonehenge?"

"You didn't hear?"

"Hear what?"

"There were thousands they said, thousands."

"There were," said Liam, running out of the room.

Gary chased after him, almost falling over Kelly and Cass in his hurry.

"What did I say?" Andy asked.

"We don't know, we don't know a lot about Liam," said Celia. "He was, no that's not for me to say, but I don't know what sparked that."

"I do," said Diane, "we were playing a game, just us two back at the house, when Stonehenge came on the screen. I said I'd never been, when he didn't say anything I saw he was crying. He didn't say anything, he just got up and left, I asked him later, but, well he's a boy. They don't like saying anything."

Gary caught up with Liam. He was trying not to sob. "You okay? Look you don't have to tell me if you don't want to, but if you do; well I'm here. If not now… Then when *you* want to."

"It's where Rodger found me, well us."

"I see."

"No, it's not that," Liam took a huge breath. "My parents took me there, we were all of us red, my parents my little sister; all of us. Our Church, we all went to Church, said that the virus was *divine retribution*; I don't know what that means. They said we should all connect with God again. So we all went to Stonehenge, I don't know why, there were thousands of people there. I was just a kid; we had to park the car miles away in a field and then walk in. After we arrived, some people came round and gave us a drink to have at the right time, they called it, appointment or appointed, I don't know. I wanted to go to the loo, but there were people everywhere. Mum said not to worry, and that I wouldn't want to go after we had the drink. Then, a speech started and then a man said it was time. My mum and dad hugged us; then they said we should drink. My mum helped my sister drink, she was only three, you see. My dad kissed my mum, and I think they just missed me. They had taken their drinks, people were lying down, there was a lot of crying, and then my sister was lying down, and my mum and my dad. I still had my drink, I didn't know what to do, I…" He was sobbing again. "Rodger found us later."

"I had no idea, Liam," said Gary.

"I wish you had told me," said Diane coming forward, she

had been listening. She hugged Liam and took him back into the house, "I'll get you some water."

Gary returned to the room; there were quizzical looks. Gary explained Stonehenge, realising there was no explanation. That ended the evening.

***

They set off back, leaving behind a working solar array and the layout ready for a powered sewage system. The truck was lighter, and they had boxes of fresh fish in the back, along with some potatoes. Liam was with the twins, and Celia was with Gary. Gary had an alternate route home mapped out. They had been travelling for forty-five minutes when Celia decided she needed to talk.

"I can't believe that happened; Stonehenge, I mean," said Celia.

"No, but there were a lot of, well a lot of suicides, I suppose."

"I know," she said patting his thigh. "Still, things are looking brighter even the weather." It was bright and sunny, but cold. "What do you think about the children and the risks, red and green, I mean?"

"I think we need all the people we can get," replied Gary. "I told Joe that this morning, they want me to go to another of the coastal set ups to the north of them; Whitby I think. Set up another solar array there; supposed to be another ten survivors at least, Joe said. If we worry about who might catch a virus, we might as well all do a bloody Stonehenge! Sorry, don't mean to sound harsh, but we all forget that we're only green at the moment, people caught the virus, and went red, Hannah did. She wasn't red for months before I met her. We could all be Cs really. Just waiting to catch it or develop it."

"I don't think so. I think your Hannah was right. I think those of us, those that are left, we are mostly *As*. We have some *Cs* but no *Bs* that we know of. What's that?"

Gary had taken them off the main road and they were heading up into hills, he wanted to see what was around, Gary slowed the truck then stopped. The girls were on the radio immediately.

"26, what's the matter why have you stopped?"

"30 look out your left front window, half way up the hill"

"I see them, are they what I think they are?"

"Yep, sheep, maybe half a dozen."

It took them fifteen minutes to drive close, and find the bottom of the field they were in. They checked to see whether the sheep belonged to anyone, but judging by the thickness of their coats they were looking after themselves. It took two hours to round them up, and then, one by one, get them in the back of the truck; there was a ram that was not amused at all by the process. Gary and Liam had to use all their strength to get him in the back. They realised that the sheep were different ages. Finally, they had seven sheep in the back of the truck. Gary was once again covered in sheep droppings and mud, along with Liam. The plaintive baas of all the sheep had finally subsided a bit. They had moved the fresh fish into the rover's trailer, where the new cockerel was in the cage looking unhappy. Hopefully, he would cheer up when he met his new companions. When they finally had it all sorted out, they looked pleased with themselves all the way home. Chattering on the radio until, as they neared the house Val joined in once they were in range. She had been worried as they were late.

It was almost dark, and the temperature was dropping on a clear evening when they finally arrived back. Gary went via the farm, pulling up by the lonely sheep. Were they the same breed, Gary wondered? He didn't know, and couldn't really tell in the gathering gloom, he didn't know whether it would matter for breeding either. Val with a kiss and a sniff of bad smell, carrying Henry, Miriam with a coy smile of greeting, and the twins all walked down to join Celia and Gary. Gary reversed the truck through the gate of the sheep paddock. He and Liam then dropped the back tail gate down of the army truck. The sheep were huddled at the far end. The truck stank of sheep, wet wool, and sheep droppings; or was that just Gary? How to get them out, he considered? The ram decided for him, jumping out of the truck followed by the others. Gary was fearful of a break or an injury, but the soft ground clearly broke their jumps and falls. The ram immediately headed for their single sheep who cowered in one corner. The ram was onto the ewe's back in seconds.

"Wow he's keen," said Cass.

"Does that mean the others are already pregnant do you think?"

"Five months, from breeding to birth, in the farming book," said Kelly. They shut the gate after Gary pulled the truck forward. They walked back up to the house. "Unload, now?" Kelly asked.

"No," said Val, "Miriam, and I will do that, you all need to get out of those filthy clothes, I mean all of you, you as well Celia. You're covered in sheep's mess and mud. Not in the house, round the back and strip off there, before you go in." They were too cold and tired, to be embarrassed, so they followed orders. Gary carried the cockerel round the back and released him into the coop. He heard a great deal of squawking and clucking. Gary guessed the hens were meeting their new master. By the time he got back, the twins were just finishing undressing before they went into the house, in just their underwear. Had they deliberately stayed out? Damn, he remembered he hadn't said anything about Miriam.

He stripped off his jacket, shirt, and jeans, leaving them with the pile of other clothes. He then went inside and upstairs to the en-suite. He could hear showers and baths running. By the time he got in the shower, the hot water had run down, he thought, maybe the house did have limits? He finished in cold water, shivering the whole time. He was shivering when he wrapped a towel around himself. Val was sitting on the bed.

"It went well?"

"Yes, they want you to go over to help nurse when the babies come. I'm sorry Val, I'm really tired, if you're here for…"

"No," she looked embarrassed for a change. "I just wanted to chat, but I'll let you get dressed and have some dinner."

"Not fish I hope, we've just had that for five days straight."

"You okay, you're still shivering?"

"Yes, just tired I think."

Val left and Gary dressed, still feeling cold. He went down for dinner, but barely ate. He was now hot. Val produced a thermometer and everyone looked concerned when Val announced 101° as his temperature. Val effectively ordered him to bed after a blood check, ping green, so it wasn't that; they knew that anyway. The virus symptoms didn't have a fever. Gary slept in bed all the next day, Val and the twins bought up soup and water. He slept most of the next day as well. He slept right through the following night after he had managed to eat some more soup with some bread.

The following morning he forced himself to get up; he ambled down to the kitchen, in a t-shirt, and jeans, but was dragged away from there and sat in the lounge. Val bought him some toast and herbal tea, which had replaced coffee. "Toxoplasmosis or Chlamydophila abortus," said Val, "both fevers caught from sheep. We don't know for sure, but they both can be dangerous to pregnant women. That is why Miriam has kept away; otherwise, you would have been straight back to work," a smile from Val.

"Is she?"

"Too early yet, give it a few more days, especially as I'm not sure how long the testing kits last. If she misses her next period then we can hope." For once Gary wasn't embarrassed by the chat.

"What's happened, while I've been…?"

"Lying around?" Val smiled at him. "Liam, and the twins have sheared the new flock, not completely just cleaning them up, and then they hosed them down with washing up liquid and some disinfectant. Don't worry, I had them wear surgical masks and then I hosed them down. I'm joking about the last bit, but we've been taking care. You won't recognise them, the sheep that is. The wool, well Kelly is a determined girl, she says she will spin it. She found some addresses for wool suppliers in a yellow pages directory in the library. She also went and refuelled with Cass; on their own, at the camp. She says the Bowser there is Jet Fuel as far as they can tell. Best way, she says, is to test it on a vehicle we don't need. Cass says there are several diesels in the dealership, or we could use the

Nissan."

"What's Liam up to?"

"He's fine, I heard about Stonehenge," she shivered. "He says he wants to go to a radio shack or somewhere, something about VHF radios. He's been reading up. He went to the library as well. He says he knows what we need; we just have to go there. He keeps talking about Diane as well."

"Not surprised, they were always together."

"You don't mean…"

"No, but I guess I'll have to have *the chat* with him."

"Celia already has. Don't look surprised. Gary, you can't do this all yourself, I know you have a very strong sense of what a man should do, but we outnumber you, women that is, four to three, and that's with Henry. The ratio is the same on the coast."

"Okay, okay, I have no idea what to say to him anyway, I can barely say, wait till you're married, can I? Anyway, I better get on with some chores."

"Nope, you're not going anywhere. Your temperature is down to nearly normal, but I need you to rest just in case. If you must do something plan power systems, or update one of Kelly's project lists. Stay inside out of the cold and tomorrow we'll see how you are."

"Yes, nurse," he said. She playfully smacked him, then hugged him.

"Don't get ill again, you scared us." She was suddenly very serious. "We can't lose you Gary, love." She placed her hand on his cheek. "Now, Henry needs a feed."

Love, she had called him love; "he's not crying."

"No, but these," she pointed to her breasts, "tell me he does."

"Oh," said Gary, realising he could still be embarrassed.

***

Miriam announced she was pregnant in mid-October "1245

days after A-Day," she said. They had toasted the news with champagne. Diane was back along with Andy, Rose, and Kathy.

Kathy had spent half the afternoon going through the ovulation charts with Val. So far she was not pregnant, despite Andy and her "trying really hard," she said, to lots of laughs. They knew it wasn't Andy. He had two waiting at the coast. Miriam had sipped a little champagne.

Andy admired the cellar. "It'll need a stock up in a year or two"; he then teased. "We'll have to plan a French expedition," he said, before realising how difficult that would be. No *Eurotunnel*, no ferries, no planes, the sense of loss built up, only relieved when Kathy shouted to come up and stop drinking the cellar dry themselves.

Back in the lounge they planned a trip to an electrical store nearly fifty miles away, where they hoped to find radio equipment. Every Yellow Pages they could find, was in the house now. The shelves in the lounge no longer had a minimalist design; they were packed. Andy was flicking through some. Liam had done a great job organising and planning what was needed. Gary and the twins, and now Andy, had checked the list for antenna sizes and wavelengths, but as far as they could tell Liam had it right. Rose was reading up on midwifery. What they really wanted though was for Val to go back with them. That was the subject of discussion. Val was reluctant to leave the house; she rarely left it, even to go to town for clothes. In a whispered conversation with Gary, he got the other reason, tonight was her turn. Miriam and Celia clearly knew; Gary wouldn't be surprised if everyone knew except for him, including the sheep. The ram had calmed down and seemed mightily pleased with himself. Gary, and Liam with the twins, erected a second pen for him. Gary still didn't feel 100% after the sheep bug, but it was a warning they all needed.

"What do you think, Val?" Kathy suddenly asked, "About Helen and Murphy, I mean, you're the closest we have to a medical expert, do you think they should have a child?"

Val considered her answer, "I'm not an expert, but if they want a child they should have one." She looked down at Henry asleep in his chair. "We don't know enough about the virus either way to say what the outcome might be. Yes, Henry here is green," she paused, "but that's at the moment, he could be a *C* as Hannah called it, we all could be. If Helen can face losing another child, for any reason, not just the virus then she should."

"Will you come back with us and tell her that and some others."

"Yes, I'll come with you."

As it was, they delayed their return for a further day. The electrical store was a goldmine of radio equipment and antennas. They ended up with five ICOM and five Kenwood HF/VHF/UHF base stations, twenty matching mobile units, and a bonus, of thirty handheld VHF radios plus various attenuators, antennas and accessories. They split model types. Gary and Andy made sure the site was secure so that they could come back for spares if needed. By the time they were finished, they decided to return to the house and fit the equipment to the vehicles and the house. Val would take the Nissan, so that got done second, after the first VHF base station. Gary insisted that the kitchen stayed as a kitchen, it already had the Checker, and the UHF radio cluttering it up, so it was wired into the utility room and the existing UHF military unit was moved. External speakers were wired into the radios. Gary said if they laid a cable or two down to the basement, he could add it to the sound system. That took another chunk of time to complete, adding to Andy's frustration. That was until Gary demonstrated that it would mean the radio could be heard all over the house, including in bedrooms at night. Antenna cable was laid back out to the roof where Gary would add a permanent antenna to match the UHF one that Greavesey and Cal had fitted. Liam produced a call sign list. The House was still *Golf Hotel* the Nissan became *Golf Victor One*. The coastal community would have *Charlie Hotel*, with *Charlie* Call signs for the vehicles. There was a common frequency to talk between base stations, and then a local UHF frequency for routine area movements. Vehicles on the trip between could go on either VHF frequency. Other communities could be added as needed, once they had a base station and mobiles.

"Like Australia," Kathy said. She remembered a TV documentary about bush radio even being used for schools. They were all annoyed by not having sorted the radios out before, it was over three years since A-Day and yet there was still stuff they hadn't thought of. Nearly the whole of the extra day had gone by the time Andy said to Gary.

"The Lexus, you'll have to change it?"

"I know, and the Honda."

"Yep, you'll have to switch to diesel." Andy then drove Gary and the twins out to a couple of the town's showrooms. They scoured the lots before picking out another brand-new Nissan Pathfinder and a demo Toyota Land Cruiser LC5 from a different showroom, both 4x4s, and both diesels. They had to destroy a key safe in the Toyota dealership to get in; there were plenty of vehicles in the showroom. The Nissan's keys were hanging with the others in an office cabinet. They then spent an hour replacing tyres on both vehicles as they had flat spotted. Andy checked out everything else. They had to jump start the batteries, then fuel them initially from jerry cans, making a mess of the dusty but dry showroom floors. Finally, they arrived back at the house where the others had become worried.

Val made a second trip to Gary's bed that night, but she was gone by the time Gary awoke. It was raining hard when she set off for the coast. Gary, the twins, Miriam, and Celia stayed behind. Liam, Henry and Val left loaded with fruit, more flour, and Henry's supply needs. Val had hugged the girls and Celia, but then hugged Miriam and Gary together, before giving them a kiss each. She then climbed into the Nissan with Liam and followed the coastal visitors down the drive.

CHAPTER TWENTY-NINE

Birthday

Kelly and Cass Masterton had celebrated their sixteenth birthday with their new family around them. There were presents from the coast, bought by Helen and Murphy. They had announced they wanted to move into the farm, now that Helen was pregnant. Diane and Chris were with them. Andy had travelled over to do a routine vehicle maintenance check, pick up some more mobile radios, and then head back, to his two children and a finally pregnant Kathy. Gary had joked with him that the only reason he had come over was to get some sleep away from two babies and Kathy. Andy hadn't disagreed. Gary knew he would be in need of sleep soon as well. Miriam was six months into her pregnancy and Val was two months into hers, it had taken longer this time.

The twins had insisted on having a party, so people had to dress smartly, which had necessitated a couple of trips to various shops in town and then other towns. Then, they had to go again, but with Chris and Diane. Val and Miriam also had to go, Miriam for a maternity outfit, and Val because she didn't have a dress, which the twins insisted all the ladies had to wear. Gary was told to get a smart suit, as well as Liam, and then Chris, Murphy and Andy. Helen tried a maternity outfit that Miriam had, but it was the wrong size. Helen was shorter, so she had to go as well.

Food for the party was limited, but Gary and Miriam allowed some tins to be opened for the special occasion. There was fresh fish and even some chicken. Gary had looked at the four lambs that had survived but said no. They needed a bigger flock.

Some early veg was available from the greenhouses, but the party only showed how meagre their supplies were. Gary wanted to do a big greenhouse project or find one they could power that was near enough to farm.

The winter had been very harsh. After a very wet autumn, there followed a long period of freezing conditions, then snow that lay around the house and farm. On two days, the house's solar system generated nothing at all because the snow fell so thickly and even lay on the steep roofed panels, necessitating a ladder and a delicate push off before the laying snow froze solid. The turbine had slowed as well. Ice had formed, and again Gary and Liam had spent an hour knocking it off. Consequently, the house, for the first time, had used the generators to, not only keep the batteries topped up, but to supply the house with normal power.

When Gary checked the empty farm, a pipe had burst. Murphy had come and fixed the pipe once the roads were deemed safe enough to travel. The solar array on the farm was covered in snow and generated nothing for days, and resulted in two broken panels. They would have to be replaced. Two further arrays were planned for the other coastal communities at Whitby and Sutton-on-Sea. The main array at Hornsea also needed more power. They wanted to add another house to the grouping. In all 132 of the spare 200 panels were allocated. Gary explained that they should have a life of twenty years, but the inverters were a bigger problem. They could burn out faster. He needed more spares, and their availability would limit the number of possible arrays that could be built. The plan was for a major scavenging trip with trucks to two factories. That was scheduled for a month's time. They hoped to get wind turbines as well, plus cables and other components. Between the two communities, they had target locations planned. One was near the radio equipment shop, and they had decided to empty it.

"We have to solve the battery problem," Gary said, which would mean a longer trip.

"Not till spring," Val replied. The weather and roads could not be forecast. Trips to the coast were stopped for nearly a month; they even had snow there for a few days.

The sheep had given birth to eight lambs in all, but three were still born, and one died in the snow, before Gary and the others could get them inside one of the farm's barns. Gary kicked himself for not doing it earlier. One of the mothers also died. They now had one ram, six adult ewes, and four lambs. If they were lucky, they would breed again that summer, but no one knew if they would, or if the lambs would survive. Gary suspected the virus was to blame, but they didn't know if that meant the ram or a particular ewe was red.

Helen was now in charge of the farm plans, laying out which fields they should target. Potatoes were planned for one section; if they could get enough seed ones by raiding gardens and allotments. They checked, but no farms grew them in the area; another expedition needed. Most market gardening had been in Lincolnshire and they hoped to find, not just food sources, but more survivors. Kelly had created a list of potential trade items, including frozen fish, solar arrays, information on sewage systems, skills exchanges, and radios. All-in-all they thought three trucks and two four by fours should head off, all with radios. They would be armed, just in case, and this was now the source of the largest disagreement. The armed group that had attacked the Sutton community, was thought to come from Lincolnshire, or maybe further south. If they were still alive, and functioning they may have to fight in or out. No one wanted that, so they would scout ahead with one of the 4x4s and then, move in only when they thought it was safe. The expedition was planned and ready for another day. Tonight though it was party time.

***

The weather was dry, and therefore the rear terrace became a dance floor for the teenagers, and anyone they could drag up, which was everyone, including Miriam, Helen and Val. Gary had no idea how to dance, but no one seemed to care as the girl's choice of music blasted over the house and surrounds. There were some slow dances mixed in and Gary was told by the twins to dance with Val, Miriam, Celia and finally each of them, where they teased him mercilessly about his lack of footwork. Celia said that they should all learn how to dance properly. Rose knew apparently, and Sylvia had taken lessons. Finally, at midnight, Val insisted, they quietened everything down, the doors were shut. Chris was playing a game against Andy on the cinema screen. Diane and Liam were cuddling and smooching on the couch until Helen and Murphy called her away and along with Andy and Chris, they headed back to the farm. Celia and Miriam with Gary were cleaning up. Val was sorting out Henry. Liam said he would go to bed, he was clearly disappointed Diane wasn't still around. Gary said he should stay and help to clear up, but Miriam said it was okay as they were nearly done. The twins were outside doing the checks, they said.

Gary was feeling a bit tipsy having mixed champagne, wine, and then a whisky. Andy had tried the malt along with Murphy. Andy said he didn't like whisky. This was great news as far as Murphy and Gary were concerned. Val had sniffed it but refused even a sip, patting her stomach, and saying not with baby. Miriam beamed at everyone. Celia clucked around like the mother hen she had rapidly become. Not that she would say so, but she organised the running of the house with Val. Gary did the projects and the heavy manual work alongside the girls. Miriam was in charge of all food provisions. Liam had radios and power planning. The twins looked after chickens, sheep, the vegetable patch, and the greenhouses where Celia, planned the planting. She already had plans underway for a wider diversity of vegetables. Val and Miriam called goodnight as did Celia. Gary could see the twins sitting up the garden, chatting away.

Gary called to them "Come on in, it's late and cold."

"In a minute," one of them said.

"Okay, make sure you lock up, I'm going to bed."

"Okay."

Gary went into his bathroom, brushed his teeth, washed, and undressed. He carried his clothes out, his suit on its hanger. The twins sat side by side on the end of his bed. Their party dresses were similar, apart from colour. They were both strapless. Kelly was in pale blue, matching her eyes, her long blonde hair in a ponytail. Cass had gone for red; her hair was loose but freshly brushed.

"We've been talking to Hannah," said Cass.

"We've agreed that it's time," said Kelly.

"Time for what?" Gary asked naively.

"Don't be silly," said Cass, "you just have to decide who's first?"

"You don't mean? But Val, Miriam they…?"

"This is between us, not them, we told them yesterday anyway. So you have to choose?"

"I can't choose I…"

"That's what we figured as well, so we'll have to do this together." They both stood. Cass collected his suit and hung it in the wardrobe; Kelly took his dirty clothes and put them in the wash basket. Gary stood with his mouth open. They then turned their backs, one at a time to each other, whilst the other unzipped their respective dresses. They were both braless as the dresses fell away. Kelly pulled her hair out of the ponytail ties.

"I, I don't know how this will work, I…"

"Shh" one of them said, "we've been planning this for ages, and we know you know *what* to do, we've planned *how* we're going to do it, we think we'll cope." She leaned in and kissed him, then waited as the other one did the same. "I think you'll manage," said the first pulling him back onto the bed. He did.

CHAPTER THIRTY

The Expedition

It was four years since A-Day, when they finally set out on the big expedition. In the end, they had three trucks, two empty, apart from jerry cans of fuel, the third loaded with trade items including twelve solar panels and fixing equipment. They also loaded fresh fish and what fruits and vegetables they could spare. There was also freshly sheared wool; the entire flock had been done, with Liam and Murphy handling the duties, despite Helen wanting to help. Val had objected because of the pregnancy risk. Helen said she had done it growing up. In the end, they compromised, Liam and Murphy actually did the handling, with Helen shouting instructions from outside the pen. The eleven fleeces were then cleaned and checked. Four of them were on one of the lorries. They hoped that some of the ewes were pregnant again.

There were three 4x4s accompanying the trucks. Each vehicle had two people, one SA80, and two pistols. Gary had insisted on one whole days' worth of shooting practice before they went. It had almost ended in a row with Joe and Trevor; who thought he was being paranoid, until Gary had explained about Rodger, and raised the Sutton attack again. Each vehicle had a transceiver UHF, and VHF, plus one truck, and one of the 4x4s had a second transceiver on the joint house and coast VHF frequency.

Their first stop on the expedition, after loading the panels from Gary's father's factory, was the radio shop in Tamworth, which they cleaned out, hoping there would be opportunities for trade. This took less than a day. They had agreed at Val's insistence to only drive during daylight, and they picked out potential stops for each night. Gary could drive one of the trucks, as could Joe and Murphy. Gary had Liam with him, Murphy had Joe, and Andy had Gart. In the 4x4s were Kelly with Celia, Cass with Diane, and two newcomers to the house from the coast, George and Sandra. They could both also drive the trucks. They had moved down to Hornsea from Whitby to learn about the solar and water systems, in preparation for their own systems. They were both green and in their forties. There had been a row about Diane coming, mostly because Chris wanted to as well. That on top of the row about Diane being too young, but Liam insisted she should come, and Diane wanted to go. Chris was, instead, left in charge of the house and farm security. There were three pregnant women left at the house with Rose. She stayed behind to help Val and Miriam with Henry. She also made sure, Murphy told them, that Helen didn't go mad. Liam and Trevor had also set up a laptop in each 4x4, all on a wireless network.

The furthest point south on the planned expedition was the battery suppliers, located on an industrial park near the junction of the M40 and the A3 near Cobham. They then planned to drive north east and approach Lincolnshire via the west of Suffolk and Cambridgeshire. They didn't want to risk the M25 to the east of London, as they didn't know what the bridge was like or the tunnel, so they realised that they would have to go through the centre of London. They planned a whole day for that journey, not knowing what they might find. Gary also had his eye on a coffee distributor to the northeast of London, so that was the target after Cobham. Gary wanted to split the convoy so that they could search a broader area looking for people, but he had been overruled. The lead 4x4 would go off in front and scout the road, but no more than a couple of miles ahead.

The radio shop was on the outskirts of Tamworth, and they travelled cross-country, and from there they picked up the M42 then the M40 running south. The route had been another compromise. Gary wanted to use minor roads to search for livestock and people. They finally agreed to search only on the way back; so motorways would be used on the outbound part. The road surface even on motorways was breaking up with grass growing in some lanes, and the verges pushing out across the hard shoulder and onto the main lanes. Their first night stop was set for the M25 junction with the A3. It took them a further three hours to get there. The journey south was full of radio chatter about what they were seeing, or not seeing, in between comments passed about everyone's sex life, especially Gary and the twins.

That news was common knowledge the morning after the twin's party, it seemed. Val said nothing at breakfast to him, when he diplomatically left the bedroom, before the twins. Miriam smiled at him only commenting that her baby was kicking. Celia smiled and said she would check the chickens. Liam was not awake. Val then disappeared upstairs, Cass told him later, to check they were okay, which they were, she said only a little bit sore; they could still embarrass him.

The twins had moved that first morning into the master bedroom, taking over wardrobes and re-arranging the dressing table and bathroom toiletries. Diane and Chris now used the twins' former rooms when they stayed. Whether Diane had been in her room, or Liam's, was not entirely clear, and Gary didn't feel he should ask. Eventually, he had said something to the twins one morning, and Kelly had laughed and said, "Not yet, but soon."

There seemed to Gary to be entire conversations and plans that went on that he had no knowledge of. He overheard one discussion between the twins and Val about breeding programmes, but they had shut up the moment he walked in, claiming to be talking about the sheep. Neither of the twins were pregnant, as far as he knew. It had only been a month since they had joined him that first night. They were trying. The girls would decide who was physically first on any given night, and Gary couldn't tell them apart in bed at all. Gary didn't care anymore what anybody else thought. He loved them equally and completely. He loved the fact that they stayed with him in bed instead of sneaking out in the early hours, as Val and Miriam had done. He still felt uncomfortable about the situation though, until Celia sat with him on Hannah's bench one evening, her with a brandy, him with his usual malt.

“Why are you worried?” Celia asked him.

“I don’t know, it’s what other people think and the girls

themselves; is it fair on them?"

"Have they complained?"

"No, not as far as I know anyway. Have they to you or Val?"

"No, so what's your problem then?"

"I don't know, I suppose it's, Val, Miriam, you, and what about Liam and then Joe's lot?" Gary tried to think of a reason.

"Gary, you are silly. You and the girls were meant to be, we all knew that, years ago, they love you, everyone can see. Don't get hung up on some silly moral code from before. I hope we're all well past that, I mean look at Andy! Who should say if it's wrong or right? Do you think it's right?"

"Yes, but…"

"Yes, but, nothing! Most men would dream of being in your position with Val and Miriam, let alone the twins."

"Rodger said I was building a Harem."

"Did he? He was an arse!"

"*Arse2*," they both laughed, which is where Cass found them.

"You're late for bed." Gary again tried not to be embarrassed.

Celia just kissed his cheek, and said, "I'll lock up, you have other duties." Cass and Celia then giggled in their female conspiratorial way, Gary thought.

***

The hotel they planned to stay at that first night of the expedition was the Hilton. They turned off the A3 after leaving the M25, then onto the Hilton's driveway. Before they left the A3, they could see mounds and pits in Painshill Park. The radio chatter dropped as it had around Heathrow. The last time Gary had driven with his parents past Heathrow; the stream of jets had been continuous. As soon as they were all parked up at the Hilton the twins were clinging to him, Cass said it looked like Fox Farm. George and Sandra were in the lead 4x4, and they had already reported that there were old cars in the car park. The entrance was wide open, and the reception area was a nesting site for a flock of sparrows. Three of them scouted the North wing and two the South, hand held radios tuned in. The room doors were all opened.

"Must have unlocked when the power finally died," said Trevor over the radio. He called a few minutes later saying, "Not this wing."

When they had gathered back in reception he told Gary and Joe he had found multiple bodies on the ground floor of the North wing. Instead, they took their overnight equipment into the South wing. Gary was about to share a room with Liam, when the twins pulled him away, for Gary to watch Diane join Liam. Liam looked as surprised as Gary did a month before. Gary didn't see how the others spread out. The vehicles were secured as best they could. All weapons were in rooms, they discussed having watches, but they thought they would be safe enough. Trevor and Gary then decided to set a string and can trap, across the door entrance to the South wing. The sheets and towels were mouldy, but the mattresses were fine. They got a gas burner going out the front and heated water, then some food. They were using some of the few army ration boxes taken from a couple of the camps. They had discussed raiding a military base to find more if they were there to be found still. They had spades to make the basic latrines that were then dug. Gary and the girls realised, as did the others, how much they hated being away from the house or the coast. Many of the others had spent months living rough, with no proper toilets and water scavenged where they could find it. Gary had only had a few nights without modern conveniences, this was worse than a Duke of Edinburgh Award scheme camp he had been on, he thought. After they had eaten, they packed up. It was dark, and they were relying on torches to visit the latrines before the trap would be set, just in case. Gary suggested to Joe that they check the kitchens and stores in the morning. By the time he got back to the room, the girls had stripped the bed and joined their three sleeping bags together. He unslung the SA80 and laid it by another on the bureau, before joining his lovers.

Gary woke in the middle of the night; he thought he had heard something. He went to the window and looked out. He saw a fox licking the area where they had washed the army mess tins and cooking utensils. He woke the girls. They thought he wanted something else before they walked over and watched the fox. "Another survivor," said Cass, pulling him and Kelly back to the bed. The following morning the fox was the talk of the group, although Cass and Kelly spent some time with Diane. Liam said he wanted to talk to Gary. Before Gary could get that chat, Cass told him that it hadn't gone well between Diane and Liam. Liam had cried, and Diane thought it was her. Gary was sensible enough to ask if Diane knew about Rodger. Cass said she didn't think so, not everything anyway.

Gary grabbed Liam and said to Joe, "You guys get ready to move. Liam and I will check the hotel kitchens and stores." They walked through the hotel, still quite dark despite the early summer daylight coming through the windows.

"Gary," Liam said, as soon as they were through a set of doors heading towards the restaurant, and then the kitchens. "I've messed it up with Diane."

"I doubt that, look sit; tell me; how?" They sat on a pair of restaurant chairs as if waiting for a waiter that would never come. Liam even fiddled with the menu.

"Yes, I have, we were going to, you know, but, I couldn't. I couldn't stop thinking of Ro…Rodger."

"Does Diane know?"

"That Rodger is dead, yes she does." He looked down at his hands.

"You know I didn't mean that." Gary looked at him until he looked up.

"You've known, you've known all this time what he did to me?" Liam was fighting to control his emotions.

"Yes, Liam, I knew after you told Val and Celia. I didn't say anything because, well because I wanted you to tell me yourself, if you wanted to, and when you wanted to." Liam was looking at him with blank expression. "Look," Gary continued, "I'm useless at this stuff. I'm always misjudging the girls, and Val, and Miriam. I'm always getting emotional stuff wrong."

"You seem to do all right?" There was a hint of a smile.

"That's because the girls conspire against me to get what *they* want. I think you need to tell Diane what happened; at least part of it. I think she'll try and understand, and that will help when you're together. I'm not an expert, but there seem to be very few secrets around, and the fewer there are, the better things are, as far as I can tell."

"There were four of us, three boys and a girl. Rodger took us all from Stonehenge."

"You don't have to tell me now unless you want to, but the others are waiting, you can tell me in the truck or maybe you should just tell Diane."

"But she'll hate me."

"No, she won't. If she feels for you like the twins feel for me, she'll understand, and she'll want to help. Just give her a chance. Listen, after I lost Hannah, I thought I could never, you know, be with someone again and now look."

"Okay, I'll talk with Diane later. The twins won't have said anything to her, will they?"

"I hope not. Come on, let's check the back." He certainly hoped so, and if they had, he hoped Diane was as smart as they were, and would not say anything until Liam told her. Gary wished, not for the first time, that he were better at dealing with emotional issues.

In the kitchen, they found a shut freezer door, which they didn't bother with, and a storeroom. They had to strain to pull open the door, but they managed it. "*Bingo*," said Gary.

"What?" Liam asked.

"Sorry, something Hannah used to say." Inside the nearly airtight storeroom was box after box of food goods, rice, flour, marmalade, soup, tins of all types, baked beans, and four boxes of filter coffee, three of tea, two of powdered milk. Gary called the others on the radio; he'd ignored an earlier call telling them to wait.

Joe and Kelly came running through.

"Is it Christmas?" Joe said.

"I'll add hotels to my target list," said Kelly, giving Gary a hug, then Liam, then Joe.

It took them twenty minutes to unload the store, and another twenty minutes to pack up after tea was made with powdered milk. Over tea, Gary spoke with the twins. No, they had not said anything about Rodger to Diane, but yes, Diane had told them what had happened the night before. Gary then suggested that Diane ride with Liam and Cass join him. Cass started to protest before Kelly gave her a kick, and she immediately realised what she should do. They then sat and waited whilst George and Sandra took the lead once again. Everyone was back and serious, ready for the search. George and Sandra radioed back that they were at the warehouse, and the convoy arrived a couple of minutes later. Cass had avoided looking at more mounds and pits as they drove in.

There was a line of burnt houses opposite the business park off Portsmouth Road. They had all seen burnt buildings over the years; what caused the fires was unclear. In the early days, it was probably electrical faults, or mains gas, or smoking, but there was no fire brigade or service members fit to respond. Now, it was either, gas canisters exploding, lightning strikes, or an outside chance of survivors setting fire. They didn't know which. As they stood outside the factory, discussing how to break in, George remarked that he had been in Newcastle nearly a year after A-Day, and whole swathes of the city had been burning. Two red's, now gone, had told him that a pit had gotten out of control and then a tanker and fuel dump had gone up, but he didn't know if that was true.

They turned their attention to the battery factory. Andy and Joe forced the lock, using a crow bar to the office door. After a couple of minutes, the warehouse door opened. "*Bingo*," Liam said smiling at Gary. Diane had been smiling, holding his arm as they approached the door. Gary had noticed, as had the twins. *Bingo* it was. The warehouse was three quarters full of the batteries, cabinets, cabling and most important of all wiring diagrams and manuals. Whilst the others loaded as much as they could, with Joe talking about spreading weight around, Gary was sent with Kelly to search the office for other information.

Gary at first objected, only to be told off by Celia, "Gary, we need your knowledge, not your muscles." Then to the amusement of the others, "And, stop trying to do everything, as usual."

In the office, Gary and Kelly found invoices and receipts, plus contact details for other solar suppliers, including a note from his own father. Kelly watched him carefully fold the note and put it in his pocket. There were contact details for turbine manufactures including hydro-turbines, something on Gary's wish list. The battery company was in the business of renewable energy, so had the details of nearly everyone they might need. They also supplied complete systems to different locations. When Gary and Kelly had returned, loaded down with paperwork, there was a discussion, more a dispute going on, about truck weight.

"We need space for trades," Joe insisted.

Trevor and Andy wanted to take what they had and head straight back. Gary got asked what he thought. He didn't like being put on the spot or treated as a leader. Celia stepped in sensing, as usual, Gary's uncomfortable state of mind.

"Can we use car batteries instead of these ones?"

"Yes, I suppose so," said Trevor.

"Then, I think we should take fewer batteries and leave the space, as Joe says. The other point is fuel. If we do another trip like this, then we're going to use a lot of fuel. I know we are okay for now, but it won't last forever. We need to find others and set up trading to get food; our fuel should be used for that. Speech over," she said with a smile.

"Can't argue with that," said Andy. They proceeded to unload some of the batteries, which reduced the weight. By the time they were ready to move, it was two in the afternoon. They were ready for food, but if they delayed for that they would be late at the next stop.

"Okay," said Sandra, "I'll issue out some food, and we'll eat en-route." They had bread and some tinned fish, quickly scraped into sandwiches. Water bottles were topped up from Jerry cans. They had previously agreed not to cross London without a full day to do it in, so the next target was a warehouse distribution park.

They drove to Kingston in convoy, George and Sandra again leading the way. As they drove in, they noticed the entrance to a large water treatment works, and then a recreation ground devoid of mounds or pits. George and Sandra called in, the business park was ransacked so; they agreed to drive on to the *TraveLodge* in the centre of Kingston. They met up there. They did the rooms routine again, but they still had a couple of hours of daylight left.

"There are signs for a shopping centre up there," said Cass.

"There's the high street shops as well, think we should do a sweep?" Andy suggested.

"I'm done sweeping," said George.

"Me too," said Sandra. "We can stay and watch the trucks if you want to go look?"

"We'll stay as well," said Diane, although Liam looked disappointed. Gary didn't think he would be disappointed for long. He recognised the look on Diane's face.

They left the three trucks and one 4x4 and took the other 4x4s with them splitting up between the two vehicles. They drove along and across the pedestrianised pavement that was slowly being overgrown with grass. They stopped outside a *SuperDrug* next to an *M&S*. Both were smashed up. They searched inside anyway using torches. In the *M&S* they broke into a rear storeroom, only to find a rear door wide open. The *SuperDrug* was better, as they found medical supplies in the pharmacy storeroom, after they broke it down, using a rope and a Toyota to pull the door off. There were various bottles of shampoos, toothpaste, and soap still on the dispensary. The girls also grabbed boxes of tampons and other feminine hygiene products. They even added a couple of hair dryers and straighteners to the haul. They stored the stuff in the back of the Toyota. They pulled up to the *Bentall* centre, but nobody really wanted to venture in. By the junction with the A308, they found a *Waitrose*.

"Worth a try?" suggested Joe. The shelves were empty, so they tried the back storerooms. They had been raided and cleaned out. They checked a couple of other shops before all mounting up in the vehicles and heading back to the *TraveLodge*. Sandra and George were busy preparing food.

"Didn't pick up a takeaway then?" Sandra joked.

"No. Where are Diane and Liam?" Gary asked.

"Checking the rooms," said George with a wink. They reappeared for dinner, looking embarrassed, but happy, before they disappeared straight off again.

Joe and Andy sat with Gary. "Don't think we're going to find much here," Joe sounded resigned to the disappointment.

"No, it's all pretty much cleared out," Andy agreed.

"Don't know how anyone could have survived without food and water." Gary considered how bad it must have been in the big cities, with large populations clearly fighting over resources. There had been bullet holes, or what looked like bullet holes on some walls. There were even a few rusting cartridge cases near one shop.

"The Thames isn't far, but I wouldn't fancy drinking that, not without one of your filtration systems," George commented joining the other men.

"Probably clean now, no pollution left." Joe speculated.

"Rotting corpses excepted," Andy added.

"Even them, they're probably gone," said Gary. "Did you see that treatment plant, if we could power one of those, well then…"

"Keep dreaming. Anyway, I think an early start for tomorrow, not sure I'm going to enjoy seeing the sights." Joe's comments triggered the packing up of the cooking stuff and the distribution of the remaining group to their rooms.

CHAPTER THIRTY-ONE
To Hyde Park

The following morning Gary and Cass agreed to take the lead vehicle, with George and Sandra taking over the truck. Kelly and Cass had flipped a coin to see who would go with Gary; it was the only use for coins these days. Aside from the Northeast business park they had two other stops planned. One purely to see the centre of London, and second, a military camp which was always in the news in the first few days after A-Day, set up in Hyde Park. They drove in along the A3205. They could see parked cars on deserted streets, and occasional mounds in open spaces. They were using the map, but Cass had also programmed the Toyota's GPS, which told them to turn around when they ignored the one way signs by Lambeth Palace. The rest of the convoy was only half a mile behind as they wanted to be closer going through the deserted city.

They turned onto Westminster Bridge and stopped in the centre of the bridge's span over the River Thames. They looked at the famous landmark on the other side of the river. The clock had stopped at three-thirty-five for some reason. The river itself was muddy brown and swirling from the tide. There were no boats visible, they could see no smoke. The others arrived in a roar of engines that disturbed flocks of birds. They all disembarked and stood almost in silence, except for the ticking engines, as they looked around at the famous landmarks devoid of people.

Joe said, "Guess the Government bunkers and so on, what did they call it… COBRA are around. Could be worth a look."

"Do you really want to?" Gary asked.

"No, not really, might find more information on contingency plans and so on, but what good would it do. We need doctors, electricians, plumbers, builders, and mostly farmers, not where they stuck some politician in a bunker. Reckon they're all gone as well anyway. There's been nothing on ERS for years."

"Let's carry on then, this is just depressing, last time I was here you couldn't move on the pavement, and my Mum and I queued for an hour to get on the London Eye," Gary said. They looked at the still wheel; several boxes seemed to have broken glass. Cass and Kelly swapped roles; the only give away of the change to any watchers was in their hair styling, pigtails versus ponytail. So Kelly and Gary set off, followed a minute later by the rest, for the short journey to Hyde Park via Bird Cage Walk. Then around Buckingham Palace and up Constitution Hill, the park littered by mounds. Gary drove into Hyde Park and pulled up by the side of some Portakabins and half collapsed tents, just north east of the Serpentine Lake. There were mounds further into the park, and some pits, which Kelly tried her best to ignore. The others arrived following a quick radio call.

They checked the cabins and tents, just litter and whiteboards covered in meaningless numbers, until Gary said, "They were the same as at the Camp in Burton. The big numbers with *k* after them is the body count."

Cass, Kelly and Diane, shuddered and walked out. Sandra flicked through some filing cabinets. They had some maps marked with other camp locations. They spread them out and had a look what was around. A further filing cabinet held additional area maps, again marking sites. They had all discovered similar maps for local areas, but this showed national maps. That would be useful. One of the maps had Fox Farm on it. Gary looked at the name. The others, except for Celia and the twins, didn't know about it, as far as he knew. They folded the maps back up, and Joe took them out to one of the trucks.

Liam called from outside, "There's some fuel in one of the tanks behind the cabins." They needed to get a generator running to use it, if it were still safe to use. They had a portable generator in a truck, which should be able to power it, if they could wire it up. They were hunting around when they found a power feed cable leading to a larger generator loaded on a flatbed trailer. Now that was worth having.

Andy surveyed it. "Tyres and brakes will need changing," he explained. They then had a discussion about what to do. That generator could power whole buildings or, as in this case, sites. It was too valuable to leave. They poured some diesel from their Jerry cans into the generator's fuel tank. How could they start it? They went back into the offices, searching until George radioed and shouted he had a manual, found in another office, marked *Commanding Officer* with *Colonel Carter-Bowles* underneath. Five minutes later the generator was fired up, with a roar of exhaust smoke and noise that sent birds scurrying from the park's trees including a flock of what looked like parakeets. The generator then settled down. There was an *Apply Power* lever and, when Andy moved it over, lights including floodlights burst into life. The generator was rated at 200kVA. Gary thought it was similar to the one at the hospital back in town.

They made a decision to spend the night there. There was the possibility, however remote, that the noise and lights might attract any survivors, although they all suspected there weren't any, unless it was scavengers like them. They decided to do a full search of the camp. They found one box of tinned bake beans which would get added to their stores and make a good tea.

"Baked Beans on toast?" Kelly suggested, to all round agreement, and a couple of missed references by Gary, Cass, Kelly, Liam, and Diane to something called *Blazing Saddles* which had Joe and Celia laughing. Cass and Kelly said that they would cook, if Liam and Diane would sort bread and set up another burner for toast. Liam and Diane agreed, before anyone realised that they had found working toasters in a mess tent. Gary, George, Sandra, Joe, Andy, Celia, Gart, and Murphy found seats in a cabin next to the one marked CO. It was clearly a briefing room of some sort. They looked to re-plan their route, back. With the trailer and generator, they would make slower progress, the weight of it was near the towing capacity for one of the Army trucks. They thought about getting an HGV tractor instead, but that would mean another vehicle, and getting one sorted. Andy was going in search of tyres and brakes for the trailer, and it would take some time to get it ready for the road. They might be stuck there for a most of a day sorting it out.

"Plenty of nice hotels to break into," said Murphy, "always fancied staying at *The Dorchester*."

They agreed they would go over and stay there, once Andy returned. He would go with Gart in one of the 4x4s to find tyres. They could send two vehicles, but Andy said he would be fine with just Gart and a couple of friendly SA80s. Not that anyone expected to see anybody. It was clear the area was deserted. Suddenly there was a scream.

They all grabbed their laid down weapons and rushed outside to be met with "It's okay, it's okay." It was Diane, once relieved of toasting duties, she and Liam had sneaked off to another part of the camp, in search of a suitable space to continue their newly consummated interest in each other. They had found a tent with camp beds and gone inside to find three bodies. By the time the others arrived, they had calmed down.

"Sorry," said Diane, "we were just looking around when we found them." The group of tents was behind a set of overgrown trees. That was why they had been missed, in the first search.

"Let's search properly," said Joe, annoyed with himself for not doing so before. "Andy and Gart, you get going otherwise, it will be dark and too late for *check-in* at *The Dorchester*, and you two," he turned to Diane and Liam, "I suggest you give it a break for a few hours."

There were mumbled acceptances, mixed in with embarrassment. Liam looked at Gary. He just said, "Let's bury these three, and search properly." The three bodies were a lieutenant, a corporal, and a private.

There was not much left of the bodies; "Birds, and insects?" Murphy suggested. They found two more, a sergeant, and a female corporal in two other tents. Gary couldn't look at the body of the female corporal. Joe and Murphy did that one. They carried them out and laid them in spare space in a pit that was behind a further set of trees. Cass and Kelly wouldn't go any further. Liam found a JCB and tried to get it going but with no luck, so they used their latrine spades to cover the bodies with a layer of dirt. They found two Checkers blinking in readiness in another tent marked, 'Medical'. No one wanted to check, so they disconnected them and added one to each truck. Finally, they returned back to the briefing cabin. Kelly walked in, carrying a tray of mugs and they could smell coffee.

"Instant, sorry," she said.

"Waitress service makes up for it," Murphy smiled.

"Don't be cheeky or you'll be wearing it." Kelly said. Gary felt a silly pang of jealousy, at their flirting. Kelly must have sensed something or noted his expression, because she gave Gary a kiss with his mug. "Tea ready in five minutes, Liam and Diane, you're supposed to be toasting." They jumped up to help and followed her out.

"I don't know how you cope with those two," Murphy said to Gary.

"Neither do I," Joe said, "but I can see why you try. Anyway, about the route?" They spent a few minutes looking at the large map on the briefing room wall, sipping coffee. "Same positions as we saw on the maps we found in the drawers in that other office."

"Yes," said George, "but interesting to see them all displayed like that."

"What are those other sites, red stickers?"

"Military bases maybe? No, I can see them. I don't know," Joe said.

"Can't be pit sites," said Celia, "there aren't enough."

"Tea's getting cold!" came a shout from Kelly or Cass.

"Let's look again after tea, I have a feeling we're missing something," said George.

They had finished their beans on toast by the time Andy and Gart radioed that they were returning with tyres and brakes. They had speculated what the red marks would be. They told Andy and Gart what they had done with the bodies, whilst they ate, and then speculation turned to the marks. "Secret bases, I think," said Gart. No one had a better idea. After they were finished, Gart, Andy, Joe, and Murphy said they would sort the truck out. Helen, George, Liam, and Diane went to *check-in* at *The Dorchester*, which left *The House Crew*, as Joe sometimes called them, of Celia, Gary, and the twins to search further. They looked for clues in the briefing room. There were more papers in filing cabinets, and a complete set of pristine maps in a specialist desk, showing a detailed layout of many camps, including the Hyde Park one.

"What about the office?" Cass questioned.

"George searched it when he found the manual," said Gary.

"No, he didn't," said Kelly, "he just found the manual." All four of them went into the office. They checked a basic desk, which held stationary in a side drawer and files in the bottom draw. The files were all on personnel assigned to the base, over one hundred in total. There were two filing cabinets behind the desk; one was an alphabetical list of reports of the pits. The girls started looking then stopped. Under F was a file marked Fox Farm.

Gary shut the cabinet. "It's okay," he said. Celia put a comforting arm round Cass, and Gary did the same with Kelly.

"Sorry," they said with tears in their eyes.

"Being silly," said Cass, "other cabinet." She indicated, but it was locked. They checked the desk drawers for keys, nothing.

Kelly walked out and returned with a crowbar, "I have my own set," she said. She wedged the crowbar between the top drawer and the case and the cabinet easily broke. The top drawer contained communications traffic reports. Gary had seen these in the camp before. The second drawer was empty save for two bottles of malt whisky.

"Bingo," Gary said. The third drawer had more communications traffic, some was marked Secret, or Confidential, and they lifted that out. It might be worth looking through, thought Gary. The fourth draw only had a sealed envelope laying inside. The envelope was marked *Operation Zulu Twelve* and, underneath, *Survivor Dumps*. The back was sealed by a red star sticker and written over by a signature with *Charles Carter-Bowles, Officer Commanding Hyde Park*, underneath. Kelly grabbed the envelope and ripped it open. A simple card file was inside with a simple note on the outside, it was handwritten but neat and precise.

Dear Survivors,

The file attached contains details that the Government hopes will aid the re-building of society. In these desperate days, that seems nigh impossible, but, the scientists say there will be some. If you are reading this, then they were right. I am told that the Operation Zulu Twelve, stupid name, typical MoD, has been set up because the real projections show very, very, few survivors despite the herculean efforts being made to find a cure. The latest brief is a 95% probability of 99.99% fatalities. If that is correct there will be less than 10,000 who survive, chit-chat is that it will be half of that. I hope they are wrong, and I can tear up this letter, but time is running out.

There are 24 locations around the country marked in the file but also by red stickers on the map, breach of security, but so what, there are not many people left and very few visitors here. Of the 100 who started under my command we are down to less than twenty and I don't have long left. I have no idea who you are, or what you are like? I hope that you will use the information and stores wisely. Whether it's enough nobody knows, but they had very clever people deciding what was available.

Before you rush off to find the sites you should know that only three other locations have this information, they are listed at the top of the file. If there has been a security breach then the stores may be gone, used by people that will die anyway; I pray, for what it's worth, that has not happened. I have one request. I ask that you treat any remaining personnel or their bodies with respect, and afford them the dignity that they are due; the troops have worked exceptionally hard. I'd give them a medal, but most would already be posthumous. We've processed, euphemism for burned and buried, over 150,000 here and a further 100,000 on Constitution Hill, this isn't even the largest site in London and we're not done yet. I saw the Basra Road in 1991; I was in Bosnia, Kosovo, and other hell holes. This is beyond anything like that. It is beyond comprehension. They were all one-offs we thought, isolated away from our normal lives; with censored pictures on the TV for you folks back home. This is real, this is next door, the local supermarket, the church, us!

For myself, I have already had to say farewell a few weeks ago to Siobhan, my wife of thirty-five years, I was lucky enough to get a few days to be with her. She was religious, I am not, not since we lost our only son in Iraq in 2004, it all seems so pointless now.

Do not pity me. I have had a very good life. I have loved the Army and my family until Tom was killed. If there is a heaven I hope to join them. For you, I hope you have found my bottles of malt, have a Dram and toast my health or something, good luck, survive, carry on the Human Race.

Yours

Then came his signature under the note matching that on the envelope. There was silence in the room. There were tears on all their cheeks. Joe walked in, "Trailer is done, what's the matter?" Celia handed him the letter wordlessly, she hugged Gary and each of the girls in turn then walked outside to be alone for a while.

Gary, gave the file to Joe, then said, "Come on girls, let's have a little walk." They left the room and walked out into the park down to the Serpentine. It was a beautiful early summer evening. They murmured a few words to each other, but mostly they walked, and then stood in silence. There were large numbers of swans, ducks, and geese on the lake, and their approach created a cacophony of honking and squawking. The pathways were mostly overgrown or encroached with grass and the branches of shrubs and trees. There were birds and insects everywhere. Dragon flies whizzed across the Serpentine's waters and the large reeds growing on the banks.

"I thought of Hannah and you, and our parents, Jimmy, poor Jimmy, how come we made it and they didn't?" Cass complained. Jimmy was their younger brother.

"Me too," said Kelly, "and our friends, and the neighbours, and well everyone I suppose. Everyone, that's gone."

"You never told me much about your parents or Jimmy," said Gary.

"No, well it seems a bit like a dream, it all blurs… since we arrived at the house… it's like a new life started." Kelly linked her arm into Gary's.

"I know what you mean, sis," said Cass, "I only remember little bits, good things, holidays, trips, bedtime stories, when we were smaller, piano lessons. Why is that? We weren't that young?"

"I don't know, memory is odd, life before Hannah seems to be a different world. I was a different person," said Gary. "That year on my own, before you arrived, I can barely remember it, and the time with my sick parents, after A-Day, is just blurred. Even Hannah is just snatches of memory, happy memories apart from…" He stopped looking off into the lake.

"Why don't you talk about her anymore?" Cass asked.

"Because it's not fair on you, or Miriam, or Val."

"Screw them," said Cass, "oh you already did," she laughed cheekily. The sombre mood was broken. She kissed Gary it was a long kiss. Then, she quickly kissed, her sister but hugged her for longer. Kelly then gave Gary a long kiss. "I love you all including Miriam, Val, Henry, Celia, and even Liam, when he's not thrashing me on the system," said Cass.

"Me too," said Kelly.

"And me, but especially you two," said Gary as they walked back arm in arm-in-arm.

When they returned, the mood was odd. There was deep sombreness as each of them read the letter, and then great excitement at the Survivor Dumps; the SDs they called them. It was starting to get dark. "We need to go to the hotel now, the others will be wondering where we are," said Gary. "We can leave all the vehicles here, just take keys, and lock up." The backs of the trucks would be open but who was around to take anything? They powered the generator down, the lights dimmed then extinguished, save some Emergency Exit signs; they must have batteries, they agreed.

Joe had made three copies of the file, one of which he gave to Gary, one to Andy, and one he would give to George. "No sites in London. We need to re-plan tomorrow." They all agreed, discussing what they would find at a dump.

The hotel check-in lifted spirits in many ways; First, they had found *The Dorchester's* wine cellar. Many cases of wine and premium bottles were collected and then added to their scavenging collection, including some excellent malts, Irish and Scottish. Second, Helen had found more stocks in a kitchen storeroom, again added to the pile in reception. Third, they could each have their own suite of rooms, if they were willing to climb steps. They did, after checking latrines and carrying water bottles. The rooms were dusty, but otherwise immaculate. The linen and beds weren't mouldy; there were no insects or birds. "I might move in," shouted Murphy.

"Only if we get the lift working," said Celia. "Nine floors is a lot for an old lady."

"You're not old," said Kelly. Gary and the girls had views over Hyde Park from the *Terrace Suite*, which Helen had said was theirs. Kelly said, "It's almost as good as home. No running water otherwise…" they were looking at the marble clad bathroom. Diane and Liam had one of the other bedrooms, and with a shy glance at the three of them, Diane pulled Liam into the room and shut the door.

"Guess that's sorted then," said Gary.

"Yes, more details later," said Kelly.

"Why later?" Gary said; then noticing that Cass and Kelly were stripping, having shut the door, and the sheets, on the King size bed, were pulled back.

"Now," said Kelly, "I'm certain Cass's kiss was longer and that's not fair." It took quite a while for Gary to prove he was being fair, before they fell asleep.

Gary awoke in the early hours, despite the *exercise*; he found it difficult to sleep away from the house. He got up and opened the door to the terrace. There was a sliver of moon in the sky, bright stars, and he could make out the still working emergency lights across Park Lane in the park. He scanned the dark rooftops of London, but he couldn't see any lights. He wondered if the colonel were right. He stood and watched the stars; he was naked on the balcony and beginning to feel the chill, when he felt one of the girls wrap a sheet around him, as her warm body pressed to his back.

"Come back to bed, you're getting cold," she whispered, kissing his shoulder; he did.

CHAPTER THIRTY-TWO

Hyde Park Briefing

When they reassembled back in Hyde Park, they were all in the briefing room. They had breakfasted on porridge, which had some powdered milk added by George as an experiment. He had the breakfast rota with Murphy. It had been a long time since they tasted milk, but they all agreed powdered was okay. In the briefing room, they looked at the colonel's file. The first document was a four-column table labelled *Operation Zulu Twelve – Survivor Dumps*. The first column on the table had a number *SD01* to *SD24* then a column of names with an address. The third had an Ordinance Survey grid reference. The fourth column had a five digit number, with the column named *PIN*. The file then had a single page for each site. At the top of each page was a repeat of the information from the first page. There then followed a date started and a date tested, and a date operational. All were from A-Day plus 300 onwards. The latest date they found one was A-Day plus 375. There was a small diagram of the layout, colour coded, with areas coded as medical, food, fuel, and comms assigned to rooms. They nearly all appeared to have two levels or more. The last sheet had details of four military sites, which contained the lists. Hyde Park was top. Third on the list was Fox Farm, and that bought an audible gasp from Cass and Kelly who up to that point had been positively beaming. There was no more information in the file. The communications files had lots of *Operation Zulu Twelve* messages, but it seemed to be just lists of codes and quantities and transport details. They could decipher individual vehicles going to sites on a particular date and time, but what they carried was unclear.

"Probably the codes refer to stock numbers on a logistics system," Joe proposed, to general agreement.

After looking at the big map, and the red spots dotted about, they had changed their plans completely in terms of route. There was a site in Cambridge that they could visit if they stuck to their original plan of heading east, but no one wanted to continue with that journey. The closest place to the house was Drakelow near Kidderminster. That was only thirty to forty-five minutes from the house. The next closest to the house was in Shirley, south of Birmingham. There were several near the coastal community sites on the East Coast. The best for the Hornsea community was Wawne near Hull, although the Whitby community had Boulmer near Alnwick, further north of them. No one knew where those places were, or what was there. There was a further site on their new route, and the closest to them, at Daw's Hill in High Wycombe.

"There's another site at Upper Heyford," Celia commented, "used to be an RAF base I think?"

"Yes, US Air Force, I think. They had air shows and so on," Joe agreed. The map showed an airfield marked as disused. The twins would not want to go there. The name Fox Farm was on the map nearby, and they all thought that the airfield would be covered in pits. They would try Daw's Hill first. Gary still wanted to go off main roads on the way back. They needed more survivors, he said. No one disagreed, but they would recalculate after Daw's Hill.

They hitched up the generator to one of the trucks. That would further limit their speed, and they then redistributed some of the load around to reduce the trucks' weight. Murphy was the most experienced truck driver so he got the duty, with Andy. The rest split among the vehicles. George and Sandra agreed to take the lead heading west out of London.

The GPS in the Toyota that Cass drove, with Kelly as passenger, was not happy about their route out from Hyde Park, where they ignored the redundant traffic signs and just headed straight for the A40, then M40. The lead vehicle went only one minute in front. Radio transmissions were sent to both the House and Hornsea, and Val could be heard talking with Celia, as Celia read out all the file details for Val to copy, whilst Joe did the same to Hornsea. Gary thought he recognised Kathy taking the message. They agreed not to go off to Hull until they knew what they might find, which could be major disappointment. Andy was talking on the radio about doing the journey that they were now doing. Before A-Day, it had taken him three hours to get to the M40, because of the London traffic. Now the journey, even at their reduced speed, was about an hour. The roads were more overgrown as they headed out of London, with cracked pavements. The weather was also deteriorating with cloud promising rain. The M40 itself, before the M25, was down to one lane passable on each side. It would only be another season of grass growing before the concrete and tarmac disappeared from view. The road was better after the M25 junction; they already knew from their trip south. They exited the motorway one junction later, briefly re-joined the A40, before turning down Station Road. There were burnt out houses to the northwest of the road, maybe over thirty in all. At the junction with Kingsmead Road, two mounds could be seen through the latest rain shower, by a war memorial. George radioed they had reached the site. The GPS showed nothing on its map in the Toyota, but the military map had a new junction off the road. The main convoy turned off between two houses, and they found George and Sandra smiling, standing by an entrance to a single story concrete building.

"We thought we would wait for you," said Sandra.

Outside the area was a tarmacked parking area, big enough to turn the trucks. The concrete building had double doors, and then a single door with a key lock pad on its right side and a large mechanical handle. "Like on a submarine," commented George. The door was marked *OZT-SD04*. The site was number four in the file's table. The lock was mechanical, not electrical, they noticed. The doors were steel, not wood.

"If it doesn't open, we'll need an acetylene torch, and it'll take hours to break in," Murphy said.

"Celia, you do the honours," said Joe. They were all nervous, excited; Celia took the file code.

"Press C for clear first," said Andy, "then hash after, we had one of these in the office."

Celia pressed C then the code from the sheet 0, 4, 1, 1, 0, then the hash key. There was no click that they could hear; nothing to indicate that the door would open; Celia looked around at the others, "What now?"

Joe said, "Let's give it a try," and tried the handle pushing down first, shaking his head and then up; it moved, he tried harder, it jolted up, the door swung open, outwards, towards them. Joe stepped forward; his hand resting on his pistol on his hip, he didn't know why, lights suddenly flickered on overhead. They were outside a small reception area. There was another door with two wheel handles, one top and one bottom, immediately ahead. They moved forward. They had discussed who should go in, but everyone wanted to go and see. Joe was in front because he'd opened the first door.

"Good job Val's not here," said Gary from the middle of the group.

"Why?" Sandra asked.

"She hates basements," Cass replied. "I think I'll wait outside."

"Me too," said Kelly.

"You sure?" Gary said; he was desperate to see inside.

"Yep we'll put some tea on and watch the vehicles," said Kelly.

"I'll radio the house," said Cass, "tell them we're in."

Joe turned the top, and bottom handles anti-clockwise, they were a bit stiff but eventually moved. The door again swung out, a breeze rushed out but then stopped, and there was no smell. A short corridor led off with downward stairs to the left. There was a chain pulley system over the stairs with a power control panel to the side. The larger doors they had seen were to the right. They could hear air conditioning blowing. There was a larger version of the diagram from the file on the wall opposite the stairs. There were three power isolator switches next to the diagram. One per floor their labels said. They left them for the time being.

"Down or along?" George asked.

"Along," said Joe, moving to another door. The diagram showed a large area with food; colour coded in the room beyond. The door had the two-wheel set up again. Joe spun the wheels, and the door opened towards them. The room was the size of a small gymnasium, it was packed floor to ceiling with boxes of food, all labelled and alphabetically laid out from packets marked apple flakes and tins of apple filling to M foods, Marmite was one of them, they saw. There were further rows behind, with just enough room to walk. They stared open mouthed at the room.

They heard a shout from behind. Cass from the entrance; "Are you okay?" The radios weren't working in the building.

Gary went back to the entrance. He hugged Cass, Kelly came over, and he hugged her, "Bingo," he said, "bloody Bingo." He smiled, then had to bend down on his haunches, overcome. One or two of the others came out, there were shakes of the head and smiles and slaps on backs. Suddenly, there was the sound of power and the big steel doors slowly opened. Andy had tried the first floor isolator switch then pressed a green button. The twins went in via the big doors; they could see the stairs down and the open first floor room.

"Bingo indeed," Cass said to Kelly hugging her.

There was an office door next to the storeroom, quarter glazed; Murphy had opened the door. "Will you look at this," he said, stepping out so others could see in. There was a desk with four ring binder folders spaced neatly one in front of three others. Each of the back folders was marked *OZT-SD04 Floor 1, 2, 3* and *Inventory* respectively. The front folder, which Murphy had opened, was marked *Letters and Initial Brief.* The first letter bore the Royal Crest and was called *To The Survivors.* The next letter bore the 10 Downing Street crest and was called the same. There was then an index card describing the rest of the pack. On a side wall, three computers were booting up. Each folder had a USB memory stick next to it. On a shelf were more folders alphabetically arranged marked with a variety of subjects including *Area Plans, Building, Chemistry, Medical,* which had several folders, *Power and Water.* There was a dedicated folder called *Virus.* There were maybe a hundred folders in all. The computers had booted up and each of them showed the same desktop, with a single icon. Liam clicked the icon.

Survivor Briefing by Professor Andrew Jacobs began a presentation.

Joe and Celia had gone downstairs. Joe shouted up, "You won't believe what is down here." Gary thought that they just might.

They spent a couple of hours going over what they had found. The problem was, they were a long way from home, so there was little point trying to load everything; not that it would fit with another dozen trucks. They found the fuel system and took the opportunity to refuel all the vehicles and the jerry cans. The fuel pipes were around the side of the building, all clearly explained in the briefings. Liam had loaded and copied the USB sticks onto the vehicle laptops. They had stored copies of what was on the main computers. Over the next hour or, so everyone watched the initial briefing, either on a laptop or in the bunker. They had read about the ERS secondary system, and when they tuned to the frequency, they found the message broadcasting locations and codes. No one had ever found it before, that they were aware of. Certainly this dump was untouched. Whether other survivors had gone to other bunkers, they would need to find out. The main ERS information was also interesting. Two of the *Survivor Dumps* were capable of changing the main message using their installed systems described in the briefing. When they tuned the Toyota's entertainment radio to the old ERS frequency the old message was still transmitting; so no one had announced the opening of the dumps.

Gary spoke with Val about medical supplies. She wanted to see the inventory list, but told them not to open the cold or freezer store if there were really vaccines inside. Kelly had finally ventured down the stairs, and she told Val about the plastic coated doses. Val expressed some disbelief, until Kelly then read out the guidance from one of the medical folders. She asked for a range of pills, painkillers, and antibiotics that Gary checked off against the inventory list. The first she wanted was tetanus vaccine, which they found in a dedicated area for inactivated vaccines after checking its location on one of the computer guides. There were also several packs marked *Trauma*. Gary took one for each of the 4x4s.

Gary and Liam also looked in an area in the facility where several hundred solar panels were stored along with 10 wind turbines, all dismantled and of varying sizes. Liam said that the

Power folder also had details on existing wind, solar and geothermal farms along with hydroelectric, and other systems including power distribution. Gary hoped the *Water, and Sewage* folder had similar details. They finally gathered at mid-afternoon in the car pack, overwhelmed by what they had found. They reluctantly agreed to shut up the site, taking only minimal stocks with them. Celia insisted that they try and take some of the deep frozen meat, and so two large haunches were carried out, of beef and pork. They had also loaded several food boxes and sacks of rice. After a brief discussion, they decided to head back all the way to the house and plan on a full excursion to the Drakelow site or the Hull site, Wawne, from Hornsea. Reluctantly shutting down the bunker and shutting all the doors, they headed back via a fast route. Gary's survivor search postponed once more.

It took three and a half hours of slow progress with the trailer to get back. Half an hour out they agreed to let the 4x4's race ahead. They would take a fast defrosting meat collection to the house for a major food preparation; the trucks would park at the farm. Gary had plans to celebrate properly, using some of *The Dorchester's* donated stocks. Radio traffic had been continuous with the house and Hornsea with Whitby joining in. They had left the memory sticks behind; they had multiple copies on the laptops of all the data and Gary said there were USB sticks in the house, or they could get some from the retail park. They would get a set over to Hornsea the following day with George and Sandra who once it was copied, would take a set north to Whitby.

By 9:00p.m that evening there were fifteen adults, including the teenagers plus Henry, feasting on beefsteaks freshly grilled by Miriam with fresh salad and freshly baked bread. The conversation bubbled to and fro on the implications and information. Then, Joe tapped a glass.

"Ladies and gents, friends, family, I've had a little too much champagne and this will sound a bit pompous, but I want to propose a toast, to us mostly, but we can do that anytime. No, the toast is to two names we didn't know about, and even the politicians who set it up; so to Colonel Charles Carter-Bowles, Commanding Officer of Hyde Park, and to Professor Andrew Jacobs who designed the Survivor Dumps. They have added to the challenge. Sorry, waffling, Gary's army girl, Hannah, laid out a series of briefs for us, not realising that others were thinking of us too. So here's to all who helped us, but especially to Colonel Charles, Prof Andrew, and Hannah, cheers." The party lasted long into the night. The only ones not drinking were Miriam, Val, Helen, and Henry; although all three women did sip at champagne. Gary walked off as the party finally broke up with a glass of the Colonel's malt; he'd barely been at Hannah's bench two minutes before Joe, Celia, and Val joined him.

"No sneaking away for private chats," said Val, sitting on his lap, allowing the other two to sit on the bench. Val leaned in and kissed him, a welcome surprise; Val and Miriam had hugged him on his return the same as the twins, Liam and Celia. "It's so scary you guys being away, even with the radios, I'm pleased to have you back, all of you." They all concurred it was nice to be back.

"We failed, of course," said Joe.

"What do you mean?" Celia said, "We haven't failed, look at what we have discovered."

"I know what Joe means," said Gary, "we went to pick up stuff, yes, but we also went to find others and potentially trade. We've bought back everything we took and no more survivors."

"Yet, Gary, yet," said Celia. "We keep stopping you searching don't we?" She patted his thigh the way she often did.

"Do you think the ERS will work?" Val asked.

"I don't know," said Joe, "we stopped listening."

"So did we," said Celia.

"It will take days to go through all the documentation to find out if we've missed anything else," said Gary.

"We've studied briefs before haven't we, Hannah darling?" Val's Caribbean accent was emphasised on the *darling*, as she leaned over Gary and patted Hannah's grave. "The Professor's briefing had the same numbers as Hannah estimated."

"Yes," said Joe, "and there's a whole section on what they knew about the virus." He paused, thinking about what they had read and seen in the last forty-eight hours. "I'm knackered; I'm going to radio Zaynah, if she's still up, and then get some sleep at the farm. We can talk about this and then plan the next steps in the morning." Celia walked back with him.

Val slipped off Gary's lap and stole a sip of malt. Once the others were out of earshot Val said, "Fox Farm?"

"Yes," said Gary, knowing she would raise it. "One of the main bases and a potential site, it was on a lot of maps and I think there are a bunch of messages about it in one of the folders we found. I grabbed it before the girls saw. Do you want to see it, or shall I look through it for you?"

"I have to face it, love, one day, we all have to face it. I went down into the basement whilst you were away." Gary looked surprised. "Had to, as Helen and Miriam are too pregnant, and Chris was sorting out the sheep with Rose. I managed. I've been back down every day since, twice a day."

Gary gave her a hug. "That's really good and very brave, I think I know how difficult that must have been." He held her hand.

"Yes, it is."

"Cass and Kelly didn't want to go down in the bunker."

"I know, they said on the radio. Have they said anymore to you, about Fox Farm I mean?"

"No, I don't think they ever will, and whatever happened, it's best forgotten."

"Yes," Val paused, "Liam and Diane have…"

"Yes," Gary went on to explain what had happened at the hotel.

"They're so young," said Val. Gary couldn't disagree with that, but he didn't think it mattered.

"Are you okay, I mean okay about Cass and Kelly?"

"I wish they were older, but look at Diane, I know you love them and they love you. Probably have since the moment we arrived, well perhaps the second time," she smiled.

"I love you all you know, you, Miriam, the girls, Celia,

Henry, and even Liam. I never had a brother. I'll take care of you all, if I can."

"You have already. God; I forget how young you are. I better go and check our son, and you have the twins on their way." Gary could see them walking towards them; Val kissed his cheek then his mouth, and then was walking away, pausing only to hug Cass and Kelly.

"Hey, you two."

"Hey, yourself," they replied.

"Join me on the checks?"

"Why not?"

CHAPTER THIRTY-THREE

Stella's Farm

Gary was sitting in the accommodation annex that had been extended and adjusted to create a briefing room. A large map similar to Hyde Park was on one wall, covered in plastic acetate so that they could scribble details of routes and what they knew. Gary was a father again by one week. Juliet Sarah, had arrived after a long labour, safely and healthily. Juliet after Gary's mother and Sarah after Miriam's mother and Gary was pleased to say after little Sarah Matthews who lay next to Hannah. Miriam was not so fortunate. She had continued to bleed and Val had become desperate, the information in the house on pregnancy had been supplemented by the data from the Survivor dumps. They had no anaesthetic, but Miriam was unconscious anyway. Val administered tetanus and had searched through the trauma packs, finding some of what she needed, complaining that she wasn't a midwife, just a general nurse. Gary felt helpless, constantly asking what he could do to help. Celia and the girls scoured books and helped with checking pulse and blood pressure. Finally, Val got fed up with them, and gave a list to Gary and Celia. They had rushed off to the hospital to see whether they could find anything else. The trauma packs should have included plasma kits, but that was well out-of-date. Miriam was still hooked up to an IV, grabbed from the hospital, for fluids. They had also bought an oxygen tank and returned with an ambulance, bringing all its equipment for Val to check. There had been a very difficult twenty-four hours before Miriam's temperature and blood pressure had improved, and the bleeding had stopped. Val had wet-nursed Juliet and fed Henry during that time. Juliet had been tested by Cass immediately after the birth and was green. Miriam was now sitting up in bed, and able to nurse Juliet herself, but it would be several days before Val would let her up. Gary was torn between eagerness to carry on his, so far fruitless, survivor hunt, and staying to look after Miriam, and guilt if he went away. He had abandoned one trip two hours out when Miriam had gone into labour.

That morning Val and Miriam had gotten cross with him fussing. Cass and Celia had led him away before he said something he would regret. Val had bought him a coffee in the briefing room and said they would be fine. She then added that she felt, at times that the house was too busy, and she knew he felt the same way. Murphy and Helen were at the farm, and George and Sandra were due to move in as well, having decided to move somewhere warmer, George said. The Whitby community had visited Boulmer *Survivor Dump OZT-SD15* on the list, and the Hornsea community had visited Wawne, near Hull *OZT-SD08*. They had restocked food, and using Val's guidance by radio, added medical supplies.

Two days after they returned from Hyde Park, and after a day of planning, one 4x4 and three trucks had departed for the Drakelow *SD*. It was named *OZT-SD01* for some reason. After they arrived, they had realised why. It was huge. The dump part of it was only part of the complex. They were unprepared for a full exploration. That was Gary's next plan. They had loaded up from the dump, which had been untouched, enough supplies for several months, if not years, and Val had reviewed the vaccines and drugs list carefully. She wanted MMR, Smallpox, and TB for the children, but she didn't want to damage any of the others. She wanted to go and see for herself, but she wouldn't leave Miriam, so close to her due date.

The northern coast group, near Whitby, now had VHF, solar and water, thanks to Joe's crew. Gary had not gone, but provided advice by radio on part of the inverter hook up. The battery system they had raided from Cobham had been tested and fitted at the farm after they returned from the first trip to Drakelow. That had taken all day with neither Gary, Andy, or Murphy trusting what they had done, until it had been checked by Joe, Gart and even Liam at least twice. Liam had then showed a brief on the laptop from the dumps. It confirmed the wiring and basic layout. The batteries had clicked into life. They had then taken a truck to every vehicle outlet they could find, and retrieved all the batteries, ready to install systems on the coast.

In the briefing room, Gary was drawing a back road route on the map, for a journey down to Drakelow. He knew he had another month of exploring before harvest was due. This year's would be twice the size, thanks to Helen's plans and efforts. Kelly had a list, no surprise there, for who would do what, Hornsea would help. Although the food situation was dramatically improved, thanks to the dumps, they had all agreed they still needed to get farms working. The dumps even held artificial insemination stocks for cattle, pigs, and sheep as well as seed banks for vegetables and fruit. On the first Drakelow visit, they had found a book describing the tunnels, which Liam immediately claimed, and he was fast becoming the de facto expert.

Kelly had claimed the other wall of the briefing room, where she had put up a grid of every location and survivor with an M or F for male and female next to a name and birth date. Gary looked at the list. There were now eleven at the house, two, soon to be four, at the farm with George and Sandra, although they wanted to set up another farm at some stage; they were an hour away, according to the radio in the corner. They had left behind ten others. One was pregnant marked with a P on Kelly's list. The main coastal community had nineteen, now that Diane, Chris, Helen, and Murphy had left. It often had fewer when Joe and his crew went out and about.

The coastal community, around Sutton-on-Sea, was very hard to contact since the raid Joe had spoken about. Joe planned to go there the next day, taking a radio, and supplies. Kelly had marked it as six, with a question mark next to it. They didn't know any names, apart from a *Simon*... There was Lincolnshire, marked with twenty, and a question mark. Gary looked at the total. Seventy-one, with three marked as red. Just over 1% of what was expected, according to Professor Jacob's brief and Hannah's notes. Kelly was doing her genetic mapping. There were lines from fathers to mothers. Rose and Celia had an N next to them, Gary guessed that meant too old for children and then saw another N next to Joe. Cass came into the room and just shook her head at Kelly, what was that about he wondered. Gary noticed a dotted red line from himself to Cass being rubbed out. There was no line from him to Kelly, had there been a dotted line yesterday? He couldn't remember, but now realised what it meant. He got up and gave them both a cuddle. They had all been ignoring the occasional radio messages, until Celia burst in, disturbing their brief moment and preventing Cass from starting to cry.

"Have you heard?" Celia said breathlessly, "Gart's found a survivor."

Gart had gone off with Carol, who Gary couldn't recall from his trip. They had headed to a big retail park near Hull, with a list of clothes needed for the coast. They had decided to take a back road back, heading north of Beverley, planning on getting to Driffield, but coming in from the East, instead of the direct route, when they had seen smoke; they had decided to investigate. Gart and Carol were now parked outside the gates to a farmhouse. Carol was speaking.

"There's a lady, maybe in her fifties, she has a shotgun; we're going to have to get out, can't hear what she's saying, we don't have a mobile radio with us. I have a pistol, but what should we do?" They could vaguely hear Gart in the background. "My God," exclaimed Carol, "she has a *cow*, I mean cows, I can see cows; I have to get out." There was twenty minutes of tense silence on the radio, before Gart finally came back on, to everyone's relief. Another vehicle was already on route and Gart told them to approach slowly and keep weapons out of sight. It was another hour before the full story came out.

Stella Cowdery had been on her own even before A-Day, her husband having died two years before. She had carried on working their farm, but was facing having to move in with her son's family, because the farm would have to be sold. After A-Day, and the financial collapse, the loans on the farm had been ignored, and Stella had stayed. She had refused to leave the farm when her son had asked her. He lived in Hull. The next part was hard to follow, as Stella was not quite with it. She hadn't seen anyone for years. She spoke in a very garbled way, and had panicked when she had seen Gart and Carol arrive. Her last human contact had been with a group who had come looking for food a few months after A-Day.

She had fired shots before they had gone away. She lived off the land. She had vegetables, chickens, and fruit on the farm and twenty head of cattle she said, fifteen cows, four bullocks that should have gone to market years ago, and an old bull. None of her cattle had got sick; she said very proudly. No pigs, because she had got rid of them after the last foot and mouth, and no sheep. She had no power, but an old well gave her fresh water. She had thought Gart, and Carol had come to take the farm. They were now all explaining to her what had happened. Whether it was loneliness or Alzheimer's, no one knew, but she was struggling to understand. Gary knew how he had been before Val and the twins arrived. Stella had cheese and butter, which she churned herself, but she had to hand-milk since the power went. Another vehicle was on its way, bringing her some fish to trade for cheese. She wouldn't leave the farm, so they would have to go to her.

"Can you plan some solar and water. There's a full milking set up," Carol said on the radio. "She needs a good bath and haircut, but looks healthy, apart from that." They would assess the state of the cows and try to get their ages for breeding purposes. Kelly had another list, showing sheep status, and could now start a cattle status. Stella had been burning a carcass of another cow, old age she said, not sickness. Val came on the radio from the house and advised tetanus shots and blood pressure checks. She would check on symptoms for dementia, but hoped it was more likely to be simply isolation.

After the radio conversations died down, and Stella was dealing with six people at her farm; Gary went on the radio to Joe. "Seventy Joe, that's all we have, and that's including an estimate of twenty for the raiders from Lincoln. Seventy, there's supposed to be six thousand, where is everyone?" Joe couldn't lift Gary's mood.

"We'll find more, Gary," Joe transmitted. "Once we sort the main ERS out and search more." Gary wasn't so sure. Drakelow had a transmission studio, the briefs said. They had worked out a script, written by Diane who had then recorded it onto Liam's laptop. They had done all that without being asked.

CHAPTER THIRTY-FOUR

Drakelow

The following day, Gary, the twins and Liam took a back road route to Drakelow. They found nothing during the hour long journey. It was a warm summer's day. Liam drove, whilst Gary searched the countryside with a pair of binoculars. They had one SA80, and two pistols just in case, but Gary was far more interested in finding people rather than shooting them. Miriam was recovering still, slowly but recovering. Their mood was down beat; the news from Hornsea, via Zaynah talking to Val, was that Trevor had a lump. Gary had taken Liam aside and Murphy had told Helen. Diane had immediately dragged Liam off to check him, and Val had broken off from nursing Miriam to check Helen, with Murphy hovering anxiously. And then, Val re-checked Liam, they were both clear. The rest of them were then all checked; all were still green.

They arrived at the entrance, but from Liam's reading of the book, they knew there were other parts of the complex. Drakelow had been an emergency factory in the Second World War, a cold war bunker in the 1960s, called *R.S.G 9* for Regional Seat of Government, and an emergency seat of government through until 2007, called *R.G.H.Q 9* for Regional Government Headquarters. There was an alternate entrance according to the book to *R.G.H.Q 9*, which they found nearby. This again was untouched and looked to be sealed up. The layout plans provided in the Hyde Park folder, and the plans from the book, didn't quite match. The Survival Dump had been placed into what was called the deserted factory area, with new doors off the entrance. When they had visited the first time, they had entered there and found the Survival Dump with inventory levels over twice the size of Daw's Hill. There was then an area that was relatively open with a non-secured door, into what was called Tunnel 4. This appeared deserted and untouched; however, there was a door off a corridor near the entrance which was sealed. It had a new steel door with another code pad. This was what they wanted to investigate. After checking USB sticks, they had found one difference in the listed files. This was a simple text file called AGHQ. The file had just a code. They hoped it was the code for the door, as no other doors in the Survival Dumps were code locked. Gary had switched the lights on in the Survival Dump, which had lit the corridor to the door. The girls were nervous, but determined to help the search. Diane had offered to go on the trip instead, but the twins had insisted that they would go.

Gary let Liam key the code and then pull the handle up. There was an out rush of air which took them by surprise, and then lights flickered on. A second door was ahead, marked Alternate Government Headquarters in red-stencilled lettering. Gary opened the door. They could smell that inside would not be pleasant. They all backed out, waiting for the air filters to clear. They then re-entered, with Gary checking that the twins were okay. They both nodded, as did Liam. The first room on the left was some sort of security set up, as they could see live feeds from the corridors. Also, they could see their 4x4 parked outside. The next room showed power controls and feeds very similar to what the house had in the basement, with cabinets marked, *Solar, Wind, Generators, Batteries Mains 1,* and *Mains 2.* Solar, Generators, Batteries, and Wind all had green indicator lights, but Mains 1 and 2 were red. They came out; lights were now on down the corridor. The room on the right was marked *ERS* and *BBC.* There was a small glass-enclosed booth, marked *Studio* at the rear and racks of equipment in the front; green lights glowed from the ERS rack. Liam went to look at it, until Gary called him back with a "leave it, we'll come back." They moved further down the corridor. There was another room marked Mess Hall. They swung the door; lights flicked on to reveal twenty deserted tables, surrounded by chairs. A kitchen server was at one end, with what looked like kitchens behind. Opposite, off the corridor, was a room with another key lock, marked *ComCen Restricted Access.* They moved down the corridor. The next room on the left was marked *Dorm A.*

"Dormitory," said Liam.

"Let's leave that as well," said Gary. They could all smell what was probably inside.

Further down, on the right, was *Dorm B*. The main corridor reached a T-junction. They went left; the rooms were numbered, and were all deserted offices, six in all. There were filing cabinets and booting computers in all of them. They were all marked *SECRET UK EYES ONLY*. They reversed back to the right fork at the T-junction. The first room on the left of this sub corridor was marked *Acting Perm Sec Cabinet Office*. It was empty, but it had a through door to the next room that housed a grand desk. By the side of the desk was a fold up bed and on it was a decomposing body. They backed out of its main door It was marked *Home Secretary*. Opposite was a small empty meeting room with a glass front, marked *A-COBRG*. Heading back towards the T-junction they found another room, marked *A-COBRF*. They went in. There was a boardroom type table with phones scattered around it. At one end was a video conferencing camera and screen with four segments. The screen showed snowy TV interference with the graphic *COBRA* at the bottom. One quarter showed themselves. A third was marked *Cambridge R*, and the last was marked *Scot*. There was no one at the other end of the pictures for Cambridge or Scot. Each position round the table also had a screen. The screens were live and showing a presentation with graphs running in a loop. The graph that burned into their brains was called Fatalities and Infection Projections. They watched the slides for a couple of times until Liam clicked a mouse, and the big screen at the opposite end from the video conferencing system suddenly projected the graph. Making it bigger didn't make the numbers any smaller to grasp. The Infections line showed 65 million est. The fatalities running over time showed 65 million est. three months behind, 24 months after A-Day. When Liam scrolled over the numbers, they realised that there was a difference of 6,000. The date of the briefing was shown. A-Day Plus 400. The figures were all estimated from A-Day 350 onwards. The Believed Confirmed Fatalities were at nearly 30 million at that point.

They left the *COBRF* and returned outside. The chill of what they had just seen was not lifted by the noon summer sunshine. "Okay," said Gary, "Liam, and I will go and do the broadcast loading. You two," he indicated the twins, "radio back in and tell them what we found, then we'll pick up the bits Val and the others wanted from the dump and head back." The girls nodded gratefully and went to the Toyota. Liam and Gary returned to the broadcasting centre. Liam and Gary had both read the instructions in the Survivor brief for the ERS. The equipment matched. Liam stopped the playback of the current ERS message. He then plugged in the USB stick with their message and transferred it onto the ERS' Hard Disk. He then used the LCD screen and navigation buttons to load the new message. He reversed the playback switch. The LCD showed playing. They left the room, shutting, but not locking the steel door. If someone wanted to get in, good luck to them, Gary thought. Back outside, the girls had already retrieved the extra supplies from the main SD. They were replying to Diane's excited radio message "I can hear my voice; it's working." Sure enough, from the entertainment system radio their message could be heard. They set off back home trying a different route, but found no more survivors that day, listening, as they went, to the broadcast.

"This is the Emergency Response System, we are a group of survivors in the North Midlands and on the East Coast. During contingency planning the UK Government established a survivor support system of twenty-four Survivor dumps around the country. We recently discovered this and have opened four of the dumps. They contain significant resources to help us all, including fuel, food, and medical supplies. Details of the dumps are being transmitted on a.m. radio medium wave, please use auto tune to find the frequency in your area. We have re-established some power, water, and other technologies. We would like to link up with other groups to trade and exchange knowledge and support. You can contact us on VHF radio on frequencies 116 mega Hertz and 124 mega Hertz, or UHF on 234.6 mega Hertz and 240.1 mega Hertz. Alternatively if you do not have radios please leave notes at the dumps we are currently using at Drakelow near Kidderminster, Boulmer near Alnwick or Wawne near Hull. Good luck and please contact us"

There had been a discussion about what was in the message, with concern that too much information on their current locations would prompt raiders. Rose said that if there were all these resources available, why would anybody raid other survivors. Joe had said that the raid on Sutton seemed to have been more about rape than food; that settled the discussion; their locations would not be broadcast.

CHAPTER THIRTY-FIVE

Survivor's Board

Two weeks later Gary was again in the Briefing Room at the House; this time Joe was there. They were planning another expedition north into Scotland. This would take several days to tour around. Gary had estimated that they had enough fuel for at least five years in each dump, unless usage dramatically increased. They were discussing tactics based on finding Stella and the coastal communities. Various groups were on the radio. Harvest was being prepared, and four members from the coast were on their way to help. Miriam was walking about, and having to be stopped by Val and Gary from doing too much. Val's concern was now with Helen. Trevor was steadily deteriorating. Val had made a brief visit to the coast to check on him, but everyone knew there was nothing they could do. Everyone was again checking themselves daily on the Checker machines. Val knew Helen was exceptionally concerned about her baby, not just herself. Murphy tried to joke that he checked Helen thoroughly every night, but the worry was etched on his face.

Gary and Joe's discussion had come to a stop. They were both looking backwards and forwards from Kelly's board showing the numbers, they had taken off the twenty for Lincolnshire and the six for the Sutton-on-Sea group, leaving forty-five. Joe had failed to make contact with them, or they were hiding when he turned up. He had left notes. Trevor's name had a red one next to it. The red names of Liam, and Helen had a green W against them. There was a new column with a date marked, last checked against all the other names. Stella's name had been added with an N, but she had refused to be checked, or to leave the farm to be checked. They would take the Checker to her with power from a generator, until they set up solar for her, if she would let them. Cass had added to the large site map with percentages showing demographic split. That information came from the briefings. Gary looked at the numbers. England had 84% against it that meant 4,200 people using a 5,000-survivor number, and they were now using that as the base count of survivors. Scotland had 8.5% giving 425, and Wales had 4.5% giving 225. Northern Ireland had 3% giving 150, but they were across the Irish Sea. Cass had added percentages for each area in England. London and the Southeast had a percentage of 26%, which had 1,300 against it. East Anglia had 8.5% and 436. The Midlands, where they sat, had 15% and 770. "Seven hundred and seventy," Gary exclaimed, "yet we have fifteen."

"You've said that already," Joe said, not unsympathetically.

"I know, I just don't understand."

"Remember we discussed that people would have moved out of the cities to find food, and since then to grow food. We saw that in London and the other big cities. We moved to the coast to fish, maybe we should concentrate on driving along the coasts."

"Then, we'll miss people like Stella or groups like the house here."

Joe looked fed up, "Nothing we can do Gary, apart from look and try, and grow our own communities."

"It will take too long, we have Henry and Juliet here with Spike, Andrew and Anne on the coast." Andrew was Sylvia's son, and Anne was Danni's daughter, both with Andy as the father. "Kathy, Val and Helen are pregnant. It'll be twenty years before we have another generation."

"Not everyone will make it either," said Joe, more depressed than usual; they were all concerned about Trevor and worried about Helen. "What about the twins?"

"What about us?" Cass said, with Kelly right behind her.

"Are you pregnant yet?" Joe asked, trying to make it lighthearted.

"No," was the one word reply from them both.

"Sorry I didn't want to upset you, we're just doing the numbers again."

"We've only been trying since our birthday," said Kelly.

"Do you mind not discussing our sex life," said Gary, feeling embarrassed, again.

"We're not talking about what we do; we're talking about the result, or rather the lack of it," said Cass. "Anyway, we've been thinking about babies as well."

"What do you mean?" Gary asked.

"Helen and Miriam; and Val and Kathy," Kelly said.

"You've lost me," said Joe. "I was quite enjoying the look on Gary's face, can we get back to that."

"No," said Kelly, smiling, "hospital we mean."

"Still lost?" Joe said.

"Gary, isn't there a maternity unit in the hospital?" Cass was also smiling.

"Yes, but it's all shut down, we cleared it and shut down the generators, I know we went and got the IV stand, and a couple of other bits and pieces."

"We need to clean it and get it ready so that we have a proper facility which we can use. I've asked Val to train me, then we can put it on the ERS," said Kelly.

"Okay," Gary wasn't convinced, "but we have harvest to prepare for!"

"We're ready with the extra hands we'll be okay; we got by last year and we only have a couple more fields, so we think you two, and us, should check it out and plan properly. Then, we can review it with Val and the others."

"Okay," Gary said again. Joe was nodding. "Can I ask what's prompted this?"

"We said, but really it's Helen and Trevor. We don't know

whether Helen's baby will be green or not. We have other instructions for medical as well, we can't run a whole hospital, but we can get some parts in use. We can't lose people. We almost lost Miriam. We need to reduce the chance of that."

"Okay, let's take a run over, if everything is okay here, if that's all right with you Joe?"

It was. They checked with Val and Murphy. They put off Liam and Diane who wanted to come, but they had tractor maintenance class with Helen. Gary knew it was farming in general, but still didn't let them come. They did take Chris. He needed more responsibility and involvement, even if he was barely fourteen. Gary and Joe agreed. They drove over. Gary and Joe managed to get a generator started, but it didn't sound too healthy. They avoided the lift and entered the maternity unit on the upper floors. Gary remembered the last time he had been in there, and how scared he was with Hannah, Cal, and Greavesey. It had turned out to be empty then, and nothing had changed now; how could it have? Kelly gave Chris the laptop to record the details. Like Liam, he was becoming a whizz on the computers.

"First things first," said Gary.

"What?" Cass exclaimed.

"Plan for a different floor, we don't want to be going up floors and along long corridors when we need to come here."

"Sometimes you're too clever," said Kelly, sneaking a kiss.

"No, he's not," said Joe spotting the kiss and smirking. "He would have said that before, if he was that clever."

"What is this?" Gary protested. "Tease Gary day, or something?"

"What day is it?" Joe asked hoping to make another joke about every day of the week being that day, but none of them knew which day it was. That killed the conversation for a few minutes. They logged the number of beds, cots, and the small specialist unit of four incubator cots at the end. There was a centrally distributed system for oxygen.

"We'll need a serious clean, wherever we put it," said Cass.

"Let's look on the ground floor to see if we can find a suitable room."

"Have to check the basement and plant sections by the generator. There are all sorts of gas feeds there I think."

"We have the guidebooks and manuals to help," said Kelly.

"Yes, let's take photos as well, so that we can compare."

"What about communications?" Joe asked. "We can do radio, but we could do with IT for manuals and so on."

"We can always put another copy on a computer here," said Chris.

"Good, Chris, what did Trevor say, something about wireless?" Joe responded.

"Yes," said Chris, "we could run a network, a wireless one between the hospital and the house or farm."

"Will that work?" Gary asked.

"I can talk to Trevor," said Chris, which was exactly the answer Joe had wanted.

Once Gary and Joe were again alone in the briefing room back at Golf Hotel, Joe said he was worried about Trevor's mental state, that he may go off and finish it; Gary knew that was a very possible result. He thought of Bill and the others but most of all Hannah. He was sure all the survivors had similar experiences. Joe said, "If we can get Trevor over here, it will give him something to do, teach Chris and Liam, and allow Val to monitor him."

For the second time that day, their conversation was half overheard by someone whose name was mentioned. "Who, am I monitoring?" Val asked entering.

"We were talking about Trevor."

"Good, I've had an idea." Val had been thinking about the Virus and studying much of the briefing pack. She was their one medical expert. Kelly came in and immediately added another column to her survivor list, marked Blood Group. "In the packs, there are lots of very technical descriptions that I don't really understand, but in the copies of briefings given to the

Government, there were two problems in finding a cure. They had no *As*, or B*s* or even long term *C*s, to use Hannah's terminology. They use immunity, remission, and resistance. What they didn't have, and didn't know, and therefore couldn't test, was any of us. They had no survivors! We have three *Cs* and 42 possible *A*s. I want to try something with blood, and Trevor is the most pressing need, although Helen and her baby are right behind, along with Liam." Kelly had added a grid she was copying from a book onto the wall.

"Transfusions," said Joe.

"Exactly, but first we need to know who has got what. This will help all of us in the case of an accident, and would have helped Miriam faster if we had stored blood."

Nearly a week later, Val was back in the briefing room with Kelly. The others were all out harvesting the first field. There was plenty of help, and Helen had joined them in the briefing room, after Murphy had almost frogmarched her away from the farm, where she wanted to help with the harvest. Chris, Liam, and, most importantly, Trevor, were at the hospital trying to establish a wireless network back to the house. They were on the roof of the hospital setting up that end. The house end had gone on top of the wind turbine, with Gary concerned the whole time that they would damage it. They just about had line of site they thought, and the distance was about ten miles. They were using two specialist transceivers called WAP-7500, which even if they weren't aligned perfectly, should work and would allow other access points to be added. The hospital had a base station, as it was the tallest roof around. Power would come from the hospital generators until Gary could sort out solar wind and batteries for the hospital. They had retrieved the access points four days before from another electronic distributor on the outskirts of Derby. Murphy had assessed the plumbing and viability of getting some toilets and water working. It would need new piping to isolate supply, and drainage from the rest of the hospital. Disposal would be hardest, unless they dug up part of the car park and installed the necessary recyclers, which in turn would need more power. This was a task for after harvest, along with the power needed. They had already added some large water dispensers, and food supplies to the chosen area in the Accident and Emergency section. Val had made one reluctant visit to agree on the best location for a temporary operating theatre and delivery room. The next task was to try to sterilise that room. It would need a deep clean as Val and Celia called it.

Joe and Val were still worried about Trevor's mental health. Joe had asked Val what could be done, so she had mixed some anti-depressants in with Trevor's painkillers. Trevor had probably guessed, but had pretended not to notice. He was resisting the blood transfusion plan at the moment. Kelly was adding the last of the test data to her board. There had been test kits in each of the survivor dumps. Trevor was A negative. He could receive donations from Type O, or ideally another A negative. The only other A negative, so far, was Val. This was the cause of Trevor's resistance; he didn't want Val giving up her blood whilst she was pregnant. Helen was A positive, and Murphy was O negative. There were plenty of A positives, including Liam. Helen and Murphy's child would be A, or O positive or negative. Gary and the twins were O positive. Little Henry was as well. Miriam was B positive and Juliet was the same. The Asian genes, Val had remarked. Kelly was waiting for the results of Stella, and from Whitby. The inventories of the dumps, listed stocks for all groups, which the documentation claimed to have been obtained from Green tested donors, but those stocks would be more than three years old and Val said they would be useless. Val had already practised taking blood, using Joe and Gary. She said she would take more once she had storage sorted or could get the plasma extracted properly; they could then freeze the plasma for up to a year she said. Val heard and acknowledged the radio message from Liam, saying they were on their way back. The hospital computer could see the House server and that meant the network could work when power was on, but they had switched the generators off for now. Kelly and Helen were looking at the board for blood groups. Val said to Helen, "Once we have tested with Trevor, we can try with you but, you have to decide before or after the baby?"

"I don't know what to do? You said that the transfusion could actually trigger the virus active in me?"

"Yes, it might, but it might not. We don't know Helen; the briefing packs don't help. They don't know either. If we had a *B* then we might have more information. We call ourselves *A*s, but we don't know we are. From a purely medical point of view, we need a *B*s to get a vaccine, but they didn't find any as far as we know. All we know is that the gene malfunction that creates the virus has not shown up on the Checker. We could all be *C*s really, just waiting for the virus. It's a depressing thought but, we all know it's possible. Every time we run the checker I think we might get a red."

"Do you think the research facility in the pack in Cambridge might have more data? They were still working according to the brief." Kelly asked.

"We would have to visit and see," said Val, but she was not hopeful.

Cass stuck her head in, covered in dust, "Any chance of some drinks for the workers?"

"I'll get it," said Kelly. She would mix up some concentrated juices from the store. They had gallons in the third and fourth freezers in the house's basement.

Once Cass and Kelly had left, Helen asked, "Are they pregnant yet?"

"No, but they are trying. Poor Gary, he'll have Miriam again soon, if he's not careful."

"As bad as Andy! What about you? Do you want another I mean after this one?"

"No, I think I'm done. I'll leave procreation to you younger ones. You know Kelly has a plan to spread around. She's quite the geneticist. You've seen the lines?"

"Yes," said Helen looking at Kelly's board.

"She has another one, which has her future plans of who can be with who, well get pregnant anyway."

"Like you and Gary?"

"Miriam, as well; she's already plotted out the next generation."

"Clever stuff, not sure how well that will do down in some quarters. Am I in it?" Helen could see her name on the board linked with Murphy.

"Yes, why?"

"Val I'm red, I have no expectations, especially since Trevor started to get sick."

Val knew and sympathised, "We can try and get some scans done, but we need to learn how to use the MRI to see what's really going on, and I wouldn't do that with you whilst you're pregnant." Val changed the subject, "Is Trevor with anyone?"

"Not that I know of, I don't think he has been at all since I arrived at the coast, what two and a half years ago; maybe he's gay?"

"No, I don't think so. He looks at us women. We have to try and persuade him to take the transfusion. I'd better go and check on the babies. Like feeding time at the zoo."

"Val, before you go."

"What is it?"

"Promise me, you'll take care of my baby, if I..."

"You're going to be fine," Val tried to reassure her, but then saw her expression. "Of course, I will, we all will."

In the end, two days later, they resorted to drugging Trevor; Val said it was unethical, then shrugged and agreed, but Trevor would not be persuaded to accept a transfusion voluntarily, so they slipped a sleeping pill into his painkillers instead of his regular pills. Once he was asleep, Val did a physical check on tumours and locations. Kelly and Cass helped with Gary, Miriam, and Joe, being complicit and ready to help, everyone else was kept in the dark. They used Val and Miriam's annexe; Gary and Joe carried Trevor in. Kelly made another check of sterilisation; there was no way she would allow needles or blood from Trevor to reverse. They would start with one unit, just less than half a litre. Val started, and she instructed Kelly as they went along, starting with how to insert the needle, after the blood pressure cuff was attached. Gary had asked Val if she was sure, for maybe the fifteenth time. Val had instructed them to get her some iron tablets to reduce the Anaemia risk; Kelly had practised for injections, but Val couldn't still help but give an

"Ow," as Kelly nervously found the correct vein, prompting an apology. The plastic bag immediately started filling with the dark red fluid. Once it was done, Kelly removed the needle as instructed by Val and swabbed Val's arm before leaving a piece of cotton wool held down by a plaster. Val went to carry out the procedure on Trevor who was now snoring. They had discussed whether they should remove blood from Trevor first, before administering the transfer. They had decided not to, as they thought it might actually speed up the virus. Val leaned over. She said she was fine, but no one would let her off the bed. Gary told her to drink water. Kelly showed Val where she was about to inject and got a nod. Kelly then released the bag slowly into the sleeping Trevor. Gary and Joe holding his arm down so he didn't move. Once it was all in, Kelly disconnected and added a cotton wool and plaster dressing.

"Sorry I bruised you," said Kelly.

"You did fine, love," said Val, feeling a bit nauseous. "I think I'll lie here for a few minutes, can you shift Trevor." Gary and Joe managed to carry him upstairs, where he was placed in the room officially allocated to Diane, but she was with Liam. When they returned, Val said she was feeling better, but Miriam wouldn't let her move. "Liam tomorrow," Val said before Miriam shooed them all out.

The following morning Trevor was furious with them all, particularly Joe and Gary. They tried to diffuse the situation with jokes, and then Cass asked him about a couple of his tumours and he realised that quite a few people had conspired. Val appeared in the kitchen, and Trevor calmed down and hugged Val. "I'll be furious with you if this hasn't worked," he said, before dragging Chris off to work on the wireless network, mumbling about conspiracies, and lack of trust. Kelly checked Val's blood pressure which was a little lower than normal, but Val said it was fine. Even so, no one would let her do anything for the day, except for feed Henry who was also starting on mushy solids. Juliet was screaming. Miriam went to see to her, as the others headed out for the harvest. They had to hurry as the weather was not looking as good.

That evening, Sandra who was A positive, donated to Liam, with Chris being told by Val he was too young to donate. That produced a sulk, until he watched the procedure, at which point he left. Sandra went and sat in the cinema room whilst she recovered and got first choice of movies for the evening. Val said they would have another round the following week. Harvest was over for a couple of weeks until the next fields were ripe, so the evening was relaxed. Gary offered a trip to the coast for the day. He thought they all needed a day of relaxation, and he said not to the Hornsea community, but just to the seaside. He could, of course, search for survivors there and back. The weather had cleared in the afternoon so they decided a group would go, if the weather stayed fine. They picked a location, Gary moving them away from Colwyn Bay, where he and Hannah had gone. Val and Miriam would stay behind. Celia said it was for the youngsters. In the end, it was Gary, Cass, Kelly, Chris, Liam, and Diane who loaded one of two Toyota 4x4s, with a picnic. Val wouldn't let them take wine. Murphy and Helen also agreed to go, "To provide *adult* supervision," Murphy laughed. They all needed swimming costumes, a maternity one for Helen, so they stopped in the retail park on the way.

CHAPTER THIRTY-SIX

To The Seaside

The sun was bright in the sky as they headed off to the Welsh coast near Prestatyn. Despite Gary wanting to search, the others overruled, and they sped along as fast as they were able, given the state of the roads with grass and shrubs eating into the available tarmac. Potholes were also an issue, not caused by traffic use, but expanded by the rain and winter snows. It took two hours to get to the coast, where the sun was high in the sky. The tide was in when they arrived, and they all piled out to set up. They could see no signs of life; just grass growing through cracks in pavements and roads, overgrown gardens, and cars parked, but with flat tyres. They ignored the town and houses, focusing on the sea.

After parking, they set up a windbreak, and then they had a moment of embarrassment whilst changing was discussed, before they split into the two cars male and female. They were all pretty suntanned, and the girls had all used short-cropped tops and bikinis before. There were a few white fluffy clouds around. Murphy had bought a fishing rod, but first on the agenda was swimming. They splashed around, but the water was cold. Then came some lunch, whilst Murphy claimed he was reeling in a monster off the beach, only to get a small sea bass of a couple of pounds. He recast and almost immediately caught a ten pounder. That went into a polystyrene box he had bought with him. Gary was standing looking out at the blue sea, remembering his last day at the seaside. He was feeling melancholy, when the twins approached him and, teasingly, persuaded Gary to go for a walk, clearly with something else on their mind. A few ribald comments from Murphy followed their stroll off. Liam, Diane, and Chris were throwing a Frisbee, and Helen sat with Murphy reading books. Gary, Cass, and Kelly walked eastwards. They walked around a bend in the coast and had gone only a few hundred yards, when they pulled up short. A man was standing with his foot on a 4x4; he was casually holding a shotgun, not broken, over his arm.

"Well," he extended the word, "what have we here? Don't you look cute," he said, possible Welsh accent, Gary thought, but couldn't be certain.

"Hi, we didn't know anyone was around." Gary had inched the girls slightly behind him. He wanted to sneak a look back along the beach, to see whether the others had seen.

"I'm around and you're on my beach, what are you doing here?"

"We're visiting for a break," said Cass.

"What's your name cutie?"

"Look, we'll head off, if you don't want us here." Gary started to turn back towards the others.

"No, you just come up here; I want to enjoy the view from closer up."

"Look we don't want any trouble," said Gary.

"You'll be no trouble," said the man, "just get up here." He waived them up with the barrel of the shotgun. Gary and the girls moved up off the beach towards where the man and his vehicle were parked. "You stop there," he said indicating Gary, "you cuties keep coming." When the girls were a few feet closer he told them, "That's close enough for now." Gary could feel his bare feet burning on the tarmac of the car park.

"Look there is no need for this. We mean you no…"

"Shut the fuck up," the man waived his gun at Gary. "Unless you want a barrel." Gary noticed the girls had moved apart. He implored them with his eyes to stay still. "You two," the man indicated the girls, "stop moving; closer together, so I can keep an eye on you." The girls edged closer. "That's better, twins eh, or sisters. No, twins. Always fancied twins, we're gonna have…"

"Put the fucking gun down now," shouted Murphy, appearing behind the man with a SA80. His Irish accent was much stronger than normal. The expletive sounding like fork. The man hesitated, prompting the barrel of the SA80 to touch his head. "I said now." Gary could barely hear the second command. The man lowered his shotgun to the ground. "Liam!" Murphy shouted. Liam appeared, holding a pistol. He moved forward and picked up the shotgun.

Cass moved forward and took the shotgun from Liam. She kicked the man in the back of his knees, "Lie flat arms, and legs spread. If you move, I'll shoot you. And I'm not a cutie," she said, pointing the shotgun at his head. Gary almost smiled.

"You on your own?" Murphy directed at the man.

"Yes," said the man, as Gary roughly checked his jean-clad legs.

"Liar," said Kelly, already going through the vehicle. She held up a female's coat, unless this man liked to dress in pink. Gary was finishing patting the man down; he found a knife in a scabbard attached to the man's ankle. Kelly found a pistol in the car and a two-way walkie-talkie.

Murphy clicked to transmit on their own hand held VHF/ UHF Radio. "We're all okay, got ourselves a survivor. A lying survivor, but one nonetheless," he transmitted.

Helen's voice came back, "Okay, understood, will you come to us?"

"Yes," said Murphy. Murphy told the man to get up and start walking; he followed behind with Liam, staying ten yards back, but with a SA80 and a pistol pointed at him. The man was silent, assessing his situation. Gary and the twins drove the man's poor condition 4x4 back to their vehicles, where Helen, with a pistol, was on the radio back to the house, and Chris with the other SA80 was standing behind a hedge with Diane covering. He looked very nervous as they approached, until he realised it was Gary. As soon as they were stopped, Gary told the twins to dress, which they did by pulling on clothes over their bikinis. Helen had already pulled on her maternity dress. Gary took the SA80 from Chris who was shaking. "Well done," he said to Chris and Diane, "now get dressed then start packing up."

"Where's Liam?" Diane asked looking concerned.

"There," pointed Gary, as Murphy and Liam escorted the man up to the vehicles. "Get dressed and help Chris pack up."

"Okay," she said reluctantly, obviously concerned for Liam.

"How did you know?" Gary asked Murphy.

"Chris, I think he was trying to see what you three were up to, so he'd grabbed a pair of binoculars, he saw the 4x4 pull up, and the man with the gun get out. He'd grabbed the weapons and radio before Liam and I knew what was going on. Did brilliantly."

Kelly in T-shirt and shorts had approached the man from the side, careful to leave a line of fire for Murphy and Liam. "Name?"

Gary relieved Murphy and Liam providing cover with the SA80, so they could dress. Cass approached the man from the other side. "My sister asked you a question?"

"Ain't you a cute one…" the man's answer was cut off by a swift kick to his groin by Cass. He fell to his knees.

"Not very bright, is he?" Kelly said to Cass. Gary was surprised at the level of aggression from the girls, but he was pretty angry himself. The memories of Rodger were forefront in his mind. "Now when you're finished spluttering, perhaps you'd answer our question."

Helen was half out of the vehicle, looking horrified. Gary waved her to stay.

"Name?" Kelly said again.

The man looked up and spat out, "Richard Johnson."

"Not so cute now! Are we Richard?" Cass said. Gary could feel their anger. Cass continued her questions, "Are you alone?"

Richard coughed; Kelly moved forward. He held up a hand "Okay, Okay, no I have a house. There are some others there."

"How many?" Cass again, she was almost shouting the question.

"Two wives, and two children."

Five thought Gary, another five. "Do you have the virus?" he asked.

The man looked up at him, "Don't know, still here aren't I." Gary didn't like his tone. They found something to tie his hands and Murphy did the honours. Then, they put him in a passenger seat of his own 4x4. He stank of sweat and other things. Liam climbed in behind with a pistol, and Gary would drive after he had dressed. They told him to give directions to his home. The girls avoided Gary's stare as they helped Chris pack up the picnic and swimming stuff. Helen was back on the radio, telling the house, and then the Hornsea what was happening. Diane went with Helen and Murphy; Chris went with the twins as they followed Richard's 4x4. He directed them back away from the coast for about half a mile until they pulled up outside a large detached house, fronted by a low wall.

"Out," said Liam; Murphy and the twins were already out and taking cover behind the wall. The front door opened, a very thin, tall woman stood in the doorway. She was unarmed. A small child came forward and clung to her leg, she stepped outside to see Richard tied up and at gunpoint. A second pregnant woman came forward, also tall, and thin. She held a baby in her arms.

"Anyone else in the house?" Murphy asked, surprising the women, they had not seen him crouched behind the wall.

"No, no, it's just us," said the first woman. She was about nineteen, thought Gary. She walked out, and before anyone could stop her, she kicked Richard in the groin. As he fell down, she went to kick him in the head, but Gary managed to stop her. She fought to shake loose from Gary, when the other woman came out and tried to start kicking Richard as well. There was indecipherable shouting and screaming until a loud bang went off and a cartridge case landed next to Richard; Murphy had fired into the air surprising everyone including himself. There was silence; apart from a flock of birds returning to their roosts. Gary was nursing scratches. The twins were pulling the women away, and the baby and toddler were crying. Helen was looking horrified; she had handed the radio duties to Chris, and when she stepped out and the two women saw she was pregnant; they seemed to calm down. The women also noticed the armed twins and Diane who had picked up the toddler. Calm thought Gary, just calm.

The women were Angie Southford and Liz Jones. Angie was eighteen the toddler, Malcolm, was nearly three. Liz Jones was sixteen, and her baby Sally was seven months. It took two hours to get the parts of the stories they would tell. Richard was in one room in the filthy house, where the twins asked him questions, with Gary making sure there was no more violence, although the threat was there. Angie had lived two streets away with her parents; Richard had grabbed her even as her parents were dying, and taken her to the house he had commandeered. One of the owners of the house, the man, had been shot dead, and the wife had been raped by Richard. The wife was tied to the bed, but clearly ill with the virus, when Angie was tied to the same bed and raped. The woman had died a few weeks later, and Angie had been forced to bury her and her husband in the back garden. She was a virtual captive, dependent on Richard to get food. Twice she had tried to run away and been found by Richard. She became pregnant almost immediately, but that didn't stop him. Liz Jones had been found by Richard a year later, starving, wandering up the coast, and received the same treatment as Angie, after he tricked her into coming back to the house where he said he had food. They had been there ever since. Gary asked Richard what had happened to him. He finally admitted he had been in prison and had been released after A-Day. No one had realised that there had been a release. Murphy said he hadn't read that in the survivor packs. Gary said they could find out at the dump, or maybe Drakelow.

"What survivor packs, what dump?" Richard asked.

"Shut up," said Cass.

Richard had access to food at a large warehouse nearby, although that was running out, and he claimed he couldn't fish. There were a few chickens in the rear garden. The children were Richard's; could they shoot him, the two women asked. Gary was tempted. He had killed Rodger, but this would be different, this would be murder or execution.

"We aren't judges," said Helen, appalled at the idea.

Diane suggested, "What about a trial?"

They were all appalled at what Richard had done. Gary had the feeling that if the twins were left alone with him, they would shoot Richard without a moment's hesitation; he would have to find out why. He also thought that Angie and Liz would too. Gary suspected that, for the twins, Fox Farm had something to do with it. He wanted to talk to Val privately, but they had only the radio. There was much radio chatter as they decided what to do. Joe and Val also said, via the radio, that they shouldn't shoot him, although Joe was inclined to. Gary said they wouldn't bring him back for any trial; Gary didn't want him anywhere near the house. In the end, they decided to take the women and children with them, if they wanted to come, which they did. They would leave Richard to fend for himself. He didn't know where they were from. They took his weapons, but left what spare food they had from their picnic and some of the emergency rations they had in one of the 4x4s. Murphy told him to learn to fish, and left his rod and reel behind. They drove off, after untying him, telling him they might come back, sometime, for him.

All the way back they realised the women, and children needed a good wash and changes of clothes. The women just looked stunned, and the children fell asleep in the car. They arrived back at the farm, where Val and Celia and the others were waiting. They had baths run, and clean clothes ready after they gave them some food. Val told them she was a nurse and she would do a full check on them tomorrow, but for now they should eat, then get cleaned up and get some sleep. Murphy, Helen, George, and Sandra were living at the farm, but there were two other bedrooms available, where the two women and the children were shown; their stunned expressions still continuing. Gary and the twins had walked back to the house with Liam, Chris, and Diane. They were finishing a meal that Miriam had kept for them, when Val with Henry came back. Miriam went to change and feed Juliet.

Celia hugged everyone and then said, "I'll sit on Hannah's bench with a brandy for a while."

Gary replied, "I'll be there shortly."

"They are settling in, but it will take a while," said Val. "They've had a tough time. They'll need help."

"We'll give it," said Liam.

"Bloody good job, Liam," said Gary, "all of you."

"I didn't do anything," said Diane.

"Yes, you did," said Liam before Gary could, "you helped Chris; you looked after the baby, Sally, I think, and you did the radio."

"Yes, but you lot did the weapons, even Chris covered in the car park, and he's two years younger than me. Cass and Kelly questioned him, I just; I should have done more."

"I'm sure you did more than that?" Val said.

"It's not just today, it's *every* day; I don't have a proper job. I just help out all over," she was almost sobbing. "I can't even get pregnant!"

"Join the club," said Kelly.

"Enough," said Gary, "we're not discussing *that* now. Diane, you did great as Liam said, you did the ERS message."

"See how that's worked so well." There had been no responses.

"Enough, I said," Gary tried not to be angry; he put a hand on her shoulder, "the ERS will take time. How often will people tune in these days? Look, if you want I'll have a job for you, now harvest is done, for a few weeks."

"What?"

"Today made me think about the last time we had a problem here, and we haven't checked security properly, or even implemented security at the farm. We need a proper property, and security plan; so, you can do that. I think Liam and Chris can help, once they are finished with the wireless network. Need to get weapons better organised as well."

"Girls don't fight in the films," said Chris.

"They do here," said Cass.

"Hannah was a weapons instructor," said Gary. "She taught me; her brief and manuals are around."

Kelly was the expert on Hannah's briefings; she looked at them more than Gary did. "Chris you should read Hannah's guide," Kelly said. "I think we're all out of practise. We're too relaxed. We would have been in serious trouble today if there had been more than just that bastard."

"I'm going to the range first thing," said Cass. "I didn't know what I was doing with his shotgun when I held it. We were lucky today."

"That's decided then," said Gary. "Now, I have an appointment on a bench." Gary got up and, after doing his usual tidying up, he eventually walked up to the bench, where he sat with Celia for a while before Val joined them. Celia left them to it.

"You okay?" Gary asked.

"Ankles getting swollen and all this excitement, just a bit tired."

"You heard Diane, give the others stuff to do, relax a bit; you should have come to the beach, well maybe not. My beach trips don't go well." Gary was suddenly taken back to his last day with Hannah.

"Tell me about the twins today; I couldn't see, but I could hear, and Helen told me about the car park."

"They would have killed him."

"Yes, we would," said Kelly, walking up with Cass right behind her.

"We should have, people like that deserve it."

"Cass, Kelly, you can't just shoot people in cold blood," said Val, sounding shocked.

"You did," said Cass to Val, "at Fox Farm."

"And you did," Kelly said to Gary, "just over there."

"That was different," claimed Val.

"No, it wasn't, anyway we didn't kill him."

"Why were you so angry with him? In the car park, I mean," Gary struggled with the right words, "I know he had pointed a gun at us, but…"

"He called us *Cuties*, that's why we came out to tell you, to finally tell you." Cass' voice was barely a whisper.

"First though, you promised me ages ago to tell me, tell us about Hannah," said Kelly.

"That's not fair," said Val.

"It's okay," said Gary, "I'll tell."

"This afternoon, just before we went on our walk, you were looking at the sea for ages. We called to you several times, but you weren't with us; that must be about Hannah. I can't remember the letter from that first time, but there was a beach and…"

"Kelly, enough," said Val. "Gary you don't have to…"

"Yes, I do Val," Gary patted Val's leg. He looked up at the twins who were standing in almost identical poses; in the gathering dark he couldn't tell who was who, again. He took a sip of malt before he realised the glass was empty. He reached into his shorts and pulled out the folded letter. Even now he nearly always had it. He had it today, and was going to read it on the beach and only hadn't when he realised it was in his short's pocket not his bathing trunks. And then, the girls had grabbed him. He carefully unfolded it and passed it to Kelly. They had light from the house. Cass leaned in so they could read it together. Val had read it properly the first time, and Gary had let her read it again on the anniversary of Hannah's death when he had been drinking on the bench full of self pity and despair.

My darling Gary,

Please don't be angry or do anything stupid. I'm sorry to end it this way. I got Callaghan to leave me the pills, he said the 9 mm would be too messy. This is easier, for me anyway. Seven months is all we've had, I wish it was longer. I wish this awful disease would give me more time with you, but it won't. I refuse to be a burden. I won't let that happen. Suicide used to be called the coward's way out, I think it takes courage I hope I have it, if you're reading this, I have. When the people came to the pits they wanted release, they wanted our help, look at Bill he went with Doris. Look at Cal and Greavesey; going off like something out of Scott in the Antarctic, Oates, I think his name was. That's what I'm doing. I'm going outside. I may be some time. It will be tomorrow, I may not have the strength after that.

I haven't got long left now, love, if the weather's OK tomorrow we'll go to the seaside. One day if my survivor brief is correct you'll have the chance to meet new people and fall in love again I hope, don't reject them, give them a chance, give them my hope.

You knew I was red, you knew I would eventually die, just like little Sarah and the others. I've seen you looking at me so you know truth when you see it. Don't be afraid of it. I'm writing this wishing I could be with you as you grow up. God you'll break hearts. Rambling a bit, it hurts so much sometimes. I don't have anything left to say or write love, you'll be up in a minute, worried about me, caring for me. I'm so lucky you drove in that day. I love you, more than anything I have ever loved. I don't know how to put the words down I want to say. My beautiful, handsome, lover. If there is a heaven I'll be waiting for you, if I get in!

Goodbye my love.

Hannah xxxxxxxxx

Kelly folded the letter wordlessly and handed it back to Gary. "At Fox Farm…" she began.

***

The twin girls were huddled in the cool barracks room. They had been given some water since their horrific march across the campsite past the pits. They sat and shivered, listening to screams from down the stairs. They were hungry. The screams stopped, and they could hear muffled voices from below, before the door opened revealing two soldiers with a bowl of steaming water. They ordered them to undress, when they said no, one of the men grabbed an arm and shook them telling them, "If you cuties want food you should undress and get cleaned up." They undressed, the men watched them, and then they washed, using a rag from the bowl. The men then raped them.

"How long," said Val, tears streaming down her face, "how long before I found you?"

"I don't know," said Cass, "maybe two weeks, maybe longer, every day they came, two of them, then only one, then no one." She was staring into the distance. Neither Kelly nor Cass was crying after they finished their story.

"I should have let you kill him," said Gary. He didn't know what else to say.

"Why now, why tell us now, we had all that time together before we came here." Val felt hurt that they hadn't told her.

"We couldn't, we promised each other we wouldn't. We should have, I almost did with Gary at the Garden Centre that time," said Kelly. "I didn't want to remember, I tried to forget; it was like a different world after we got here."

"I don't know why we didn't Val," said Cass, "we should have, but then, when we didn't, it got harder to say each time. It was today that changed my mind, those poor girls, women I mean, Liz and Angie, we have to help them."

Val got up and hugged them both, "We will. I'd better check on Henry." She gave Gary a kiss on the cheek and headed back into the house.

"Walk with me a bit," said Gary, still not knowing what to say, so as they strolled up towards the turbine, "I don't know what to say to you either of you, here's me moping about Hannah and all the time you've been dealing with that. It's pathetic, I mean, I am."

"No, you're not," said Cass. "Without you we'd be, I don't know where we'd be. We wouldn't have made it. I know we had Val and I don't just mean the house, but…"

Gary kissed her then kissed Kelly. "It's always her first," said Kelly.

"No, it isn't. Half the time I have no idea who's first or second or…"

"Shut up and prove it," said Kelly smiling.

"What here?" Gary said.

"We did miss out on the beach," said Cass.

"But after, I mean what we just talked about, I didn't think…"

"Don't think just do," Cass said moving closer.

CHAPTER THIRTY-SEVEN

Blood Characteristics

Miriam, Val, Helen, Kelly, Celia, and Cass, were in the Briefing Room. Trevor had just left, to go to the range, taking Angie and Liz with him, where Diane, Chris, and Liam were running through firing drills with Gary. Gary had already retrieved additional SA80s and pistols, along with racks to go in the basement. Diane had suggested, and Gary agreed, that the weapons and ammunition should be closer. This had been the third day running that they had been on the range for at least two hours. Diane had insisted that all of them re-qualify as she put it. First, through had been Cass and Kelly. Then, Gary had let Diane take him through, with her following Hannah's brief and the Army Manual. Cass then took the manual and brief away, and followed the documentation through, whilst Kelly did the drills to Diane's orders. Diane was nearly word perfect. By the time Kelly watched Cass shoot, and then Liam and Chris had shot, Diane *was* word perfect, better than Kelly and Gary, Kelly said. Then, the others at the house and farm were called to go through, including Val and Helen, despite their pregnancies. George and Sandra had done the routines before the London expedition, but still Diane insisted. Trevor had managed to avoid it until that day, by claiming he wasn't feeling well. Val and Kelly had just checked him and said there was no change. They didn't think the tumours were bigger, but they were still there. He had refused all medication unless they could find another blood donor. Val said she was ready again but Trevor said no, and this time Gary, Joe, via radio, and Miriam agreed, they couldn't and wouldn't risk Val's health.

Cass and Miriam, with Helen watching the toddler and the three babies, had done the blood tests on the new arrivals and explained what the survivor board showed. The two women from Wales had been examined by Val, assisted by Kelly in her trainee nurse role. Both the women were bruised on their thighs, arms, and backs. They were undernourished. The toddler, Malcolm, was also bruised on his arms. All four had pinged green on the checker. They had spent the first few days in a daze of meeting people and being shown round. Not helped when a crew arrived from Hornsea, on a lame excuse to see Val, when really they came to see the new survivors. Kelly showed them the boards in the Briefing Room and all the details she was tracking. They both struggled to understand, especially Liz who was barely sixteen, with an eight-month old child and thought she was three months pregnant. Val wanted to do more checks, but she thought they were both as well as could be expected, given the circumstances they had survived.

"A negative," said Kelly, "Liz can help with Trevor."

"She's too thin and malnourished at the moment," Val said.

"There's Stella as well," said Helen; Stella had eventually, agreed to a blood test and was also A negative.

"Like to see someone try," said Miriam. "She's not right, Val you need to go and see her."

"I know, but… maybe next week." Val was, as ever, reluctant to leave the house. Liz and Angie had left their children behind. "We need a crèche."

"We're full, we need more accommodation," said Helen, "with more on the way."

"Plenty of empty houses around," said Miriam, "but they all have the same problem."

"Food and water, or I should say sewage. None of us want to give that up."

"It's driving Gary nuts," said Val.

"What is?" Cass asked.

"Not you two," Val laughed. "No, I mean the house; it's supposed to be a near minimalist masterpiece and most of the time it looks like a bomb's hit it. Haven't you seen him constantly trying to pick up things?"

"Yes, but he's always done that. Can you *please* tidy up," Kelly mimicked to laughter.

"It will get worse," Val said, "once you two have children. By the way, have you tested yet?"

"Yes, and no, we're not, *again*."

"Enjoy it whilst you can," said Helen. "I feel like a whale and Murph' has to be persuaded, he thinks he will hurt me or harm the baby."

"Not long now," Val sympathised patting her own stomach where she could feel the baby kicking.

"Which reminds me," said Cass "we need to get the maternity unit done and that needs you, madam, to check it," she looked at Val, "tomorrow?"

"Okay, tomorrow," Val reluctantly agreed. The VHF radio squawked.

"Unload," shouted Diane. She had just demonstrated the firing drill to Angie and Liz, whilst Trevor, and Liam did the drill. The sound of the fired rounds still seemed to echo round the small wood clearing past the Turbine, which was their practise range. Chris started picking up spent cartridges with Liam and Trevor. The newcomers unblocked their ears. Hannah's instructions differed from the Army Manual. She had said that ear defenders just made it more likely you would miss the first time you fired in action, as the noise would surprise you. Angie and Liz had started listening, but eventually covered their ears as the two shooters went through their SA80 magazines. "We'll start you on a pistol," Diane continued, when they heard shouts from further down the hill.

Kelly appeared, running up the hill. They finally made sense of what she was shouting, "Radio we have contact on the radio."

Part Four

The end of the human race will be that it will eventually die of civilisation.

Ralph Waldo Emerson

The ultimate value of life depends upon awareness and the power of contemplation rather than upon mere survival.

Aristotle

I was taught that the human brain was the crowning glory of evolution so far, but I think it's a very poor scheme for survival.

Kurt Vonnegut

We shall require a substantially new manner of thinking if mankind is to survive.

Albert Einstein

CHAPTER THIRTY-EIGHT

Survivor Search

Gary Tolman contemplated his upcoming twenty-sixth birthday in a little over a month. He was parked west of Plymouth, near a town, or more correctly a former town, called Looe. Chris was standing with his binoculars looking across the river at the deserted West Looe. They were waiting for Cass, Kelly, and Liz to come back from a loo break in Looe, they had laughed. Gary dare not look behind him at the mess in the back of the Toyota. He knew the twins did it deliberately to wind him up. He knew if he looked, he would find a bag of homemade cookies, bits of paper, more food, and water bottles. There would be two laptops open at the various lists, Kelly and Liz were using. Gary's SA80 was in the door well, but he guessed Chris' was there as Kelly was sitting in front. They had received a reminder that morning about protection from Joe.

Hornsea had fought an on-off fight with the Lincolnshire group for the last three months. Trouble had flared again, over a cow, of all things. The cow had been distributed by Joe from Stella's herd, but had died two months after it was given to Lincolnshire in exchange for sugar from their beet fields. They said it was the community's fault that the cow had died and were demanding an immediate replacement. Joe had refused to give them one, saying the cow was healthy when it left. Three members of the Lincolnshire group had then tried to raid Stella's farm, attempting to steal one, or more replacements. Stella had died eighteen months before, but her small herd was now spreading and breeding, with artificial insemination stocks being used for the breeding cows. Six milking cows now resided at the farm near Gary's house. The Lincolnshire raiders had not known that there were six people living and working at Stella's Farm with a full set of Diane's security measures. They had walked or rather crept into a trap. After the raid, the three who had attacked were held prisoner. The Lincolnshire Group leader had *claimed* to know nothing about the raid on the radio, but they were now negotiating to get their men back.

As the raid happened, all the Community locations went on full alert. Joe was hoping the situation would defuse, but doubted that would happen, so he was preparing for a period of raids again. There had been a year of tentative peace after two years of occasional raids. Joe had said that the communities would have to take action and sort this out. The Lincolnshire Group, apart from trade, would not cooperate with the medical or other activities of the communities. There was no doubt though that the Lincolnshire Group had entered local SDs, as they seemed to have plenty of fuel, and didn't need to trade for basic items. Kelly's list of genetic compatibility still missed their information, and they had no firm idea of numbers or exact locations. How the raiders had found Stella's farm they didn't know. That question was part of the interrogation of the survivors. The limited trades that did take place were carried out at neutral locations arranged by radio. Now, that the raiders knew the location of Stella's farm, they were planning to split the remaining cattle between the communities.

They had occasional radio contact with the Lincolnshire group, which meant the various frequencies could be monitored. Diane and Liam had developed a code for changing frequencies, or going to a channel for what they hoped would be a private chat, but actually no one trusted that it was private. Diane spoke about military encryption systems. They had some, but it would make communication more difficult. They would have to replace the civilian radios they had distributed all over the country if they went down that path. Gary and Joe both thought a major confrontation was coming. There was the unresolved issue of what had happened to the Sutton-on-Sea community. It was deserted when Joe and Gart had finally searched it. Gary just wanted to be sure that all the people at Stella's farm were safe, and the cattle moved. They couldn't be safe if the raiders knew the location. Gary knew *Arse*

Farm had the space and Elmsworth, Sierra Hotel, also wanted more dairy cattle. Gary always called the southern community Sierra because of its radio call-sign.

Gary's latest survivor hunting trip had consisted of a small group going down to the South coast once more. Previously, they had headed east from Portsmouth finding two more communities and bringing them into their group of survivor communities. Sierra Hotel, was based just east of Portsmouth around Elmsworth. When Elmsworth had radioed, just under four years ago, they had already entered and recovered stores from *OZT-SD07*, which was located in Fort Southwick. Sierra had initially been sceptical of Diane's ERS message. They had stopped listening to ERS years before, and it was only when one of the boats they used had accidentally re-tuned its ship shore radio that they heard the voice. They had then checked and found *SD07* before they radioed.

There were seventy-five survivors in the immediate area of Elmsworth, or Sierra Hotel, spread across several houses around the harbour. A further forty survivors were east in Bognor Regis, Bravo Hotel. The southern groups were running out of fuel when they had heard the radio message. The limited diesel they had left was prioritised for fishing boats, so they didn't travel around much. Some of the boats had small wind turbines, and they had raided DIY stores for more, but they were all low power systems. The groups in Elmsworth and Bognor had tried to get solar working on some house installations, but those solar systems needed mains electricity to work because they had no battery back up. The southern group didn't know how to make that work and when they fiddled with the wiring they only succeeded in starting a fire.

The survivors in Elmsworth mostly lived off fish and what vegetables they could grow, They had some chickens, but those were for eggs, not meat. They hadn't had much success breeding chickens, despite having two cockerels. The groups had tried to plant crops in farms, but with little progress. They didn't have the spare fuel to run the farm equipment. They had medical support via an ambulance Paramedic, Carl, and quite a few with boating skills, but otherwise they had little to trade. Gary and Joe didn't care that they had little to trade. They were both so delighted to find such a large group that they had agreed to help. Immediately after

Helen and Val's babies were born, a small team had gone down to help set up the solar panels, water recycling, batteries and wind turbines obtained from the area and the *SDs*. There was another plumber living at Elmsworth, and within a few days he had a local system working. There was a small water treatment plant nearby, and together it had initially been powered up by using a generator. They planned to implement solar and turbines if the experiment worked. It had caused more problems than it was worth as water main's pipes leaked all over the place, along with pipes in the nearby houses. They had powered it down. The Government briefing had made it look straightforward, but it would require a check of every pipe and house on the system. They didn't need several thousand houses with running water and sewerage; maybe they would one day far in the future.

The southern communities now had a growing population with local systems supporting them. They had three farms in use, with two successful harvests already under their belts, plus some of the dairy herd from Stella's Farm. More chickens and ducks had been added, and a large greenhouse was also under construction. Once the radios were in regular use, knowledge exchange was the main reason for contact. Despite the surge in fuel resources, nobody wanted to waste fuel on just social journeys. The southern groups also sent out survivor search parties, and they had made contact with a group in Suffolk, located near Felixstowe, and now called Foxtrot Hotel, in Gary's mind. That was six months after the first contact with Elmsworth. The Felixstowe group was out of fuel, and there were only thirty people left surviving on strict rations, as it was winter when they were found. It took a further three months to get them on a stable footing. Two more groups had then been located further north. One settlement had twenty people, near Aldeburgh, Alpha Hotel, and another of twenty was near Thorpeness, Tango Hotel. The two other groups were in marginally better condition, but they agreed they would not have enough food to survive a long winter.

***

Gary could hear the girls coming back. Cass sat next to Gary, Kelly in the back. They had different hairstyles, which at least allowed Gary to tell them apart, in daylight anyway. Cass picked up the radio and transmitted "Golf Victor 41 going mobile, en-route location seven." That told the listening world that this team was out searching.

"Sierra Hotel copied," came the female voice reply from someone at Elmsworth.

"Golf Hotel copied," Gary recognised Miriam on the radio and could picture her in the kitchen preparing something delicious.

"Charlie Hotel copied." That sounded like Gart in Hornsea, Gary thought.

It was a good job they had a list of call-signs stuck to the dashboard near the radio, otherwise, it would get very confusing. Diane had tried and failed to impose more radio discipline, but she had not completely succeeded. Gary was sure other *hotels* would be listening as well, but the procedures for the radio were that the three main communities would monitor the hunts or major expeditions. This seemed to be Gary's main task now. Discussing longer term plans on his regular visits around the country. Gary had not ventured east to Felixstowe, Aldeburgh or Thorpeness, despite an open invitation nor had Joe. They were both wary of trips that might cross paths with Lincolnshire.

There was no one formally in charge, no elections, and no appointed leaders in any of the survivor communities. Lincolnshire seemed to be different, from what they could get out of the radio messages. For big decisions on projects, Gary or Joe took the lead, but they were both mindful of the immediate needs for food and other provisions. Others took the lead in each group depending on what was discussed. Gary had happily given control of the house site and its plans to Miriam and Val, although he remained frustrated by the chaos in the house. Security was now Diane's preserve with Liam in close attendance, although Gary still practised shooting more often than anyone else. Diane had visited each site to carry out security inspections causing some resentment in other communities. She had to be told regularly by Gary, Joe, and Liam to stop insisting and offer suggestions, not give orders, especially in the southern and eastern groups.

Chris climbed back into the Toyota and squeezed up with Liz. They had been together for what, three years, or more, thought

Gary. The three women in the Toyota Land Cruiser were all mums. Gary was the father of three-year-old twins, one boy, Mike, and one girl Hannah, with Cass. With Kelly, he had two. A girl, Sarah who was three-years old, and a two-year-old boy, Dan. Auntie Val was looking after them along with the rambunctious Henry and her youngest Carmen, after Val's mother. Miriam had Juliet, of course. She also had one other child, Jenny. Gary would have to check Kelly's mating list to recall who was the father. Gart was the most likely, he thought, given Jenny's Asian looks. Liz had Sally, when they had found her in Wales, but she had lost the baby she was carrying when they found her. They had almost lost her, and she didn't think she would go with a man or have children again, but Chris took a shine to her. With much persuasion on Chris' part and then, after trying for quite a while, they finally had a child. Gary thought it was marvellous that someone else's sex life was attracting attention, Dawn, was now two.

"Come on let's go, dreamer," said Cass seeing Gary off thinking.

"Just thinking," said Gary.

"You know that's dangerous," said Kelly.

"Remembering really," said Gary, ignoring the teasing insult. He put the vehicle in gear and drove carefully over the bridge onto the A387 heading west. Location seven was their overnight stop planned for Fowey, well the Old Ferry Inn on the East bank. They would try to cross the river there if they could find a way to get on the ferry with the vehicle. If not, they would find a boat and get across, then explore on foot, and check the town. Gary wanted to radio Joe, to find out what was happening at Stella's Farm and Hornsea, but he knew he couldn't do anything to help. They drove steadily west with Cass, Chris, and Kelly, using binoculars to search for signs of life or livestock, anything that would indicate more people. It had been a year since they last found a group bigger than five. Kelly's database of survivors now held nearly five hundred names, and the numbers were going up as children were born, but there were the occasional losses, as well.

Gary remembered Trevor. He had lasted another year after the transfusions. Helen and Liam were both still going strong, and both were still well. They had monthly transfusions; although their children were virus positive, reds. Helen refused to have any more children, and that had caused her and Murphy to part. Helen now lived at Stella's Farm, well she ran it really, Gary thought. Murphy would go and visit from *Arse Farm*, but he eventually moved back to Hornsea to be closer. Celia had also gone to Stella's Farm. Val had argued with her not to, but Celia said that the families needed the space in the house and that she would be of more use at Stella's Farm. She had nursed Stella for her last year of dementia. Three survivors had been lost in the South. They were believed drowned on the coast during a fishing trip when an unexpected storm hit. Joe himself had been injured in a vehicle crash on ice, prompting an emergency dash by Val to Hornsea to help. Gary had ridden shotgun, fully armed in case of trouble. Joe's injuries turned out to be relatively minor in the end. Some stitches and he was on the mend.

Gary's House and *Arse Farm* had expanded with the accommodation block, the school, and three houses. Celia's former annex room was now the main nursery. The house was extremely crowded. It drove Gary mad with five adults and eight children in the house plus visitors; it was never tidy. Gary's old room was the upstairs nursery; he still shared the master suite with Cass and Kelly. Cass' old room nearest the stairs now had a bunk bed for the older children, with Henry and Carmen sharing one room. Gary and the twins had tried to have more children, but so far, with no success.

That was another characteristic on Kelly's board, back in the briefing room. She had height, all the greens, if they were *A*s, were tall. Dentists, they all had good teeth this included the surviving Reds, *C*s of which there were thirteen that they knew about. Eyesight, only Rose used reading glasses, although Celia had said she could do with a pair. Immunity from other illnesses, they didn't seem to get colds, and the only illness anyone could recall was Gary's with the sheep. It had not recurred, but that could be due to good hygiene Val had said. They were predominantly female; at an approximate 60/40 ratio, Kelly liked that one. Higher than old average IQ, they had run tests on the survivors, those that would take tests had anyway. Danni said that they were confusing causation and correlation. In other words, it took knowledge and skill to survive, so it was likely that people with those skills would survive. Gary said it took luck as well, and help, and did that apply to the women ratio, as well. When the IQ tests showed higher female scores than male averages, he had been forced with a laugh, to back down. Until they tested the children for IQ, they couldn't show it was a characteristic, and even that provoked a discussion about genetic inheritance of brainpower; nature, or nurture. Val then said it was odd that teenagers who had survived, had adapted well, despite the lack of formal schooling and higher education. She praised Kelly's nursing skills as an example. Liam then said that his maths was poor. Danni disagreed, saying his maths was better than hers now; he had just lacked some basics. Liam then said he didn't count in the analysis because he was red, which prompted another round of discussions. In the end, Kelly had left it on her board, but with a question mark next to it. The debate still raged when someone got bored during an evening, and wanted to start an argument.

The final characteristic on the board applied to the female breeding contingent, as Kelly so indelicately put it. Why did it take so long to get pregnant? Kelly's analysis, which Danni had mathematically modelled with her, showed that the teenage mums had taken longer to get pregnant than females who had been pregnant or had children before. Gary was used as the example for this characteristic, although Andy also came in for examination or stick as Gary actually called it. Danni had quietly and sadly admitted that she had been pregnant before A-Day, as she once had an abortion. Sylvia had lost a child as well to the Virus. Gary had gotten Val and Miriam pregnant relatively quickly, Gary knew there were actual times and dates in the spreadsheet, but mercifully Kelly had not put that all in her database and on the board in the Briefing Room. Kelly had effectively asked every woman she could, how often and with whom. The result was that women who had been pregnant before A-Day would get pregnant within 6 months of starting to try, whereas, the younger women took over a year or more. Cass had not got pregnant again after their twins, and Kelly had not after her second. Gary knew that all the other women's activity was listed, but he didn't ask. Kelly, Val, Cass, Celia, Miriam, Diane, Liz, Angie, Kathy even Helen would ask and Kelly made it part of her introduction to new survivors and groups, she had written a *Hannah Briefing* on it she said.

The accommodation block had been expanded, adding more visitors accommodation as Gary had originally intended, especially useful when groups came to the house and farm for training. They were going to put a school there as well, until Gary and Val pointed out there was a purpose built school the other side of the turbine hill; plus, there were three houses further along. The previous spring and summer, the school had been wired into solar, batteries and generators, properly along with the three houses. They had added a new water tank to the top of the hill, and Murphy had come along with some support from Elmsworth and Felixstowe wanting to learn and help. They planned to run school as a mixture of theory and practical lessons. They had a radio with a dedicated frequency for the school set up, and there were other teachers in the population, two secondary and one primary. The plan for primary education was that mums would come and stay with the children in the houses near the primary school. That was if they wanted to. Given the age of the new children, the primary school was most in demand over the radio. Boarding school was discussed, but the location had not yet been agreed.

Danni was in charge at the primary school, but she spent a lot of time with one of the secondary school teachers in the South and not just for school matters, Cass had told Gary. Danni lived in one of the houses by the primary school, Kathy in another, and Sylvia in the third, with their respective children. Where Andy slept, Gary didn't ask, but Andy also went backwards and forwards to the coast. Gary wouldn't be surprised if he had another woman there, as well. The twins teased Gary that if *he* didn't get them pregnant again soon, they might have to try Andy for *size*. It was their emphasis. Gary didn't know if they would or not? How could Gary argue? He had his children with Val and one with Miriam. Neither of them had come back to his bed since the twins had joined him. Gary knew the twins must have had offers, they were stunningly beautiful he thought, even when they were tired from feeding the babies. When they were on trips, they attracted attention. Their relationship got Gary occasional ribald comments. The three of them, all with long blonde hair, sometimes all three in matching pony tails. Not as often now that Cass' hair was shorter.

The women's Cabal, as Joe called it (Gary had to look up the meaning), normally plotted in the house's kitchen or the Briefing Room. If Gary walked in, and accidentally overheard his name mentioned; the conversation would be changed instantly to something he was uncomfortable with. Normally, it was how many times a certain female had been with a particular male and still wasn't pregnant. Not that Gary was complaining. He had two beautiful twin women that he loved dearly; he couldn't imagine and didn't want to be with anyone else. He was content, but he knew the girls wanted more children. He would have to face any jealousy that might come his way when that happened. He knew the twins thought it was their duty, and not just a wish. Gary would spend time with Val and Miriam, discussing their children and their future plans. He was even allowed occasionally to help, especially with Henry now he was a little boy. He helped more with the new twins, Mike and Hannah and with Sarah and Dan. At the house, it seemed that there was always someone to care for the children. Gary missed his chats with Celia. He really looked forward to going over to Stella's to see her and Helen and the others there. It was less chaotic than the house. Joe was his other main confidant and Zaynah was always happy to have him over, where Spike now called him Uncle Gary. When Val heard about the women's cabal name somehow, she had instantly retorted about the male cabal of Joe, Murphy, Andy and Gary, with Liam, and Chris as occasional younger members. Gary wondered what Celia and the others would do now they had to close Stella's Farm. If that was what they had to do? They couldn't carry on with a constant risk of raids and potential violence.

Chris lived at *Arse Farm* with Liz when they were there, as did Liam, Diane, and their red child Pamela. George and Sandra had originally planned to move to another farm but now ran the main farm, which was still expanding. There were cattle and sheep plus the crops, lots of chickens, geese and ducks. They were trying to bring a watermill by damning a stream at the far end of the farm, and then using one of the hydro-turbines found in the *SD*s to generate even more power. Rose was the oldest known survivor. She was now seventy-four, and she stayed at Hornsea, running a crèche with Zaynah. Rose would also visit Celia, or the other way round. There was a mix of ages in the other survivor groups, before a gap from the new children born after A-Day and the youngest survivor of the Virus that they knew of. A teenager, Stephen, just thirteen now who lived in Elmsworth with his mother Carla; they were the only parent and child who had lived through the virus. They were both green and regular blood donors to Val's scheme, despite the longer-standing objections to under sixteens donating. There were eleven other reds around the country, plus Liam and Helen and their respective children; all receiving monthly transfusions. So far they were healthy. There were fifteen reds, and five hundred greens, plus Lincolnshire. Kelly estimated the total population was less than a thousand and that was if there were other large groups still out there.

Val now had a working MRI scanner in the hospital for checks on any red individual that wanted to see whether the twinge they felt was the start of the disease becoming more active. Trevor had been the first in the MRI and, despite their lack of skill with the equipment, Val knew enough to see the number of internal tumours. It took a lot of energy and time to run it, and she still hated to leave the house. Helen and Liam hated going in it as well, it just added to their worries. Kelly could operate it, but they all struggled with diagnosis. They were trying to learn more. The maternity unit was also running if they needed it. The twins children had all been born there, Val and Gary worried sick as Cass in particular gave birth to the twins only a week premature, on Kelly's calculator. Gary could remember her screams during the final stages of labour. Kelly was heavily pregnant herself at the time, although her two individual children's births had gone well. She had held his arm squeezing it blue, as she squeezed herself. He had a bruise for weeks; he didn't get much sympathy. Miriam, Helen, and Celia had all helped with the births. The hospital had oxygen, but no anaesthetic. Val didn't trust the drugs in the dumps and in the hospital's plant room, so all the women had to give birth naturally. That scared everyone. What would they do if someone needed a caesarean or other operation? Val said that if it were that serious they would risk the drugs. Manufacturing of new versions was described in the Government briefs, but they lacked the skills and the factory to do it, let alone raw materials.

Looking at the government briefs; the gap in generations was forecast. Stephen was an exception in terms of survivors, but he didn't solve the procreation gap. It would give them a roughly ten-year wait for a second generation of post virus children until the girls were old enough to have their own children. The oldest girl born since A-Day was in Suffolk. She was not yet seven and had been one of the last group of four survivors that had been found. They had been in a pitiful state. They had been on a farm in Norfolk, like Stella, they had tried to survive on the land. They were recovering in the main Suffolk community at Felixstowe, which was up to seventy now. Kelly worried that the new children may have as many problems getting pregnant when they were old enough; therefore, population growth would not be as high as they might wish. Danni and Kelly had modelled population growth forward over decades. It was just a formula Danni explained. When they had first modelled it, they had 5,000 as the base number. Now there were two projections, one from their known number of 515, ignoring what they might find in Lincolnshire, and one from 1,000. It would take decades from these numbers to get to 5,000 the original Government projection for A-Day Plus Two Years.

The fuel stocks were still okay, but on Miriam's provisions spreadsheet, which she briefed each week, they could all see a deadline for when they would have to transport in from further away. They were also concerned about fuel additive shortages if they used the Jet Fuel. Contamination was another concern. The Whitby group had lost all their diesel vehicles because of defective fuel, they thought, from a bad tanker. New vehicles, well old unused vehicles, had been found with a different tanker. They now had a chemical tester for the tankers and storage tanks, and had fitted fuel conditioners in the slowly emptying *SD*s. There were still ten they had not opened, seven of which they hadn't even visited. That was the real purpose of the trip west from where the trip had started in Elmsworth. To see whether the two SDs in the far Southwest were open or not. Their first site was located in Falmouth Docks, The group would head there in the morning after Fowey.

The journey times between sites and communities were also a growing concern as the roads became impassable or blocked, overgrown with trees, bushes, and grass. On some journeys, it was impossible to see the road. The GPS was still going, but no one knew for how long. They couldn't seem to find out; the *SD* briefs said twelve to fifteen years from launches that started in 2010, but how many had been launched wasn't said. Which of the satellites had been replaced in which orbits remained unclear? Trevor, before he died, had said that GPS was a US military system that the US Government allowed the rest of the world to use, so it was not surprising that accurate information wasn't available. They had Ordnance Survey maps, and they also knew that there were GPS ground stations as well, but they would have to find them, nothing in the briefs about where they were. Then, they would have to power them if they wanted to keep GPS running. Joe had become dispirited on this discussion after mobile phone masts were mentioned. That led back to data centres, and comms. Learn to map read is what Joe said, and use a compass, more teaching followed.

"Deer," said Cass, and then she guided the other binoculars in the car. Gary slowed to a stop. "Sierra Hotel, Golf Victor 41," Cass transmitted.

"Go ahead 41."

"We have approximately twenty deer at grid…" she gave the grid reference. Deer seemed to have recovered faster than other mammals. They had seen some rats, but very few, nevertheless, they now took precautions for the hencoops and food stores. They needed cats, Stella had said before she died, or a good Jack Russell. They tried to explain to her that it wasn't likely.

"We have that as Wren Wood," came the radio reply.

"Confirmed, out." It was now up to the Elmsworth community, Sierra Hotel, what they wanted to do; if it had been cattle or sheep they would probably come and collect them. Venison was good food to have, so maybe Sierra would come and hunt a couple, or try to breed them if they could move them or stay nearby setting up another base.

They now had nearly a hundred cattle and twice that number of sheep. There was a team of knitters and spinners for the fleeces after shearing. Val wouldn't let Gary near the sheep for fear of a recurrence of the illness. Any new ones, that they very occasionally found, were handled with plastic clothing and face masks until they were checked, cleaned and quarantined for several weeks. They would take the same precautions with cattle but so far they had found none. No pigs, no goats, Some of the Elmsworth group wanted to hunt for wild boar, but no one had. The Suffolk locations thought they had seen some dogs, but no definite signs. If there were cats, no one had seen any. One of the groups had visited a zoo; it had been awful they said. Gary didn't want to look. Survivors would still come across farms full of carcasses although *Arse Farm* was now cleared.

Gary, Liam, Chris, and George had done that job, digging a pit with a JCB. Gary had persuaded Val to take Kelly and Cass to the hospital that day and to keep young Henry and the other children well away. It had taken hours, but in the end it was mostly bones they moved. The shed had then been refurbished. It was now a solid winter protection for the sheep and cattle. It would need to expand if they didn't just use another farm. They used the field, but each new house would need water and power. When Gary returned, they planned to switch on a power sub-station using the big generator from Hyde Park. There was a bet of a bottle of Irish and Scottish malts between Murphy and Gary, on whether it would fail like the water experiment had.

CHAPTER THIRTY-NINE

Fowey

The big Toyota 4x4 reached Lanteglos, where they would retrace their route if they could not get across at Fowey, which is what they expected. They continued southwest to the Old Ferry Inn, location seven. It was deserted; why would it be anything but, Gary mused. The actual ferry was the other side of the river so they would have to retrace their route. All they could see from their bank was the road leading away from the western side; there were boat chandlers, and a decaying customs sign. There were several small boats they could use to cross, if they seriously wanted to. Whatever they did, Gary knew, they could not search everywhere. In the end, they either found people like in Wales, or occasionally via the radio announcing a larger group. That hadn't happened for ages.

The ERS still transmitted Diane's message, which she had updated twice, giving alternate ERS radio frequencies and the availability of the hospital maternity unit. They did not broadcast their locations. Whilst the women and Chris were discussing what to do, Gary stretched his legs down by the river. He could see fish in the clear water. He realised the river was tidal so he couldn't remember what fish would be available; he still hadn't gotten the hang of fishing. Nice spot though he thought. Kelly came up to him and put her arms around his waist, "Dreaming again?"

"Sorry, just thinking about… about them!" There were two people on pushbikes on the other bank, they weren't armed as far as Gary, and Kelly could see.

"Hello," shouted Gary.

"Hello," one of them shouted back.

"No weapons," said Liz.

"As far as we can tell," said Chris. Gary could hear Cass on the radio.

"You're well equipped," the same one that had said *hello* shouted; a male, the other was a woman in her thirties, Gary thought.

"We're looking for survivors," shouted Chris.

"You've found some," the shout came back.

"Now what?" Gary managed to say to Kelly. It was always the same at this stage, not that they had a lot of practice. Sometimes it was straightforward like the radio call from Sierra, other times it was like Wales with that man, what was his name, Gary mused. Richard Johnson, he recalled, or when Rodger showed up. "We were looking to cross over, but we'll have to drive around," Gary said.

"Why?" The woman shouted.

"The ferry, we can't cross without the ferry." Gary pointed at the obvious ferry on the stranger's side of the river.

"No, why do you want to come here?"

That stumped Gary for a moment, Kelly shouted, "We are distributing information and we are looking to trade."

Liz said quietly to them "this is odd."

"What information?" The man shouted after a quick conversation with the woman.

"Have you listened to the ERS?" Kelly shouted. They watched the man and woman have a further discussion.

"Wait there, we'll be back soon." The man shouted, then the strangers turned, picked up their bikes, and rode back turning left across the nearly deserted car park. They disappeared behind the buildings. Chris and Liz tried to follow them with the binoculars. They realised there was chimney smoke rising from more than one building further in the town.

"Now what?" Chris asked without realising he was repeating Gary's earlier comment. He then pointed out the evidence of a larger group.

"Stay alert," Cass said, "Diane is going spare on the radio."

"I'll watch our backs," said Chris, "Mobile UHF, channel six." He grabbed a handheld radio and with the SA80 disappeared back up the hill and into the trees.

Liz, Kelly, and Gary stayed by the ferry landing watching the other bank. Cass stayed on the radio broadcasting an occasional "no change," and probably talking to Chris.

"There," said Liz pointing at two people getting into a moored boat further down the river. They watched as the two struggled to row across the river current. They eventually reached an overgrown grass area, where they threw a mooring rope out for Kelly to catch. Gary stayed back, leaving a sight line for Chris, he hoped. Gary's SA80 was on its lanyard, but he was not holding it. Kelly and Liz both wore holstered pistols. Cass had their third SA80, and a pistol, out of sight. She was talking on the radio describing what was happening. The same pair had returned. Kelly pulled the boat in and tied the rope to a post. The two stepped out, the man immediately retying the rope in a different knot.

"Sorry," said Kelly, "I don't know the correct knot."

The man nodded but backed off.

Liz moved forward holding out her hand, "I'm Liz."

"Please keep back," said the woman. She and the man hand stepped further away. "We do not wish to catch your infections."

"What infections?" Liz asked.

"God's plague," the man said. Gary tried not to smirk.

"You mean the virus?" Liz said.

"God has spared us, but the unclean must stay away. *God has spoken*," the man said.

"*God has spoken*," the woman parroted.

"We're not unclean," said Kelly, moving forward and sounding offended. "We don't have the virus, we're green, I mean, negative."

"How do you know?" The woman asked.

"We have a checker, you can see if you like?" They carried a checker in the vehicle. Liam had deconstructed and reconstructed the military checkers from the camps, and the dumps to try to get more. They had experimented until they had a battery-powered version. "We checked this morning, but we'll happily show you."

"That will not be necessary. We ask that you leave God's community alone and leave." The man pronounced.

"Look we mean you no harm," Gary said.

"So why do you carry the devil's weapons then?" The woman said.

"We have had problems in the past. We only want to find out about survivors, and help them if we can. The ERS messages are from us." Kelly tried to explain. Gary just felt confused.

"We do not listen to the blasphemers and heretics who caused this plague. God has spared us and will keep us safe." The man was almost preaching, Gary thought. "Now please do not cross into our community or drive around. The roads are blocked we ask that you respect our wishes." They started to move back to the boat.

"Okay," said Kelly "but one question."

"What is it?" The woman said, partially turning back towards them.

"How many of you are there?"

"God has spared thirty-four souls, and we have seven children of the new dawn."

"Don't you need fuel, food, medicines?"

"We have ample food that God provides us. We have no need of fuel, or medicines. *God has spoken. God protect us.*" The man said.

"*God protect us*," the woman repeated. They untied the boat as they climbed in and rowed back across the river. Gary, Kelly, and Liz watched them go as Chris reappeared.

"That was very weird," said Kelly.

"Mad, do you think?" Gary said.

"Who knows?" Liz said after Gary had explained the exchange to Chris.

"Diane wants to know what we are going to do?" Cass requested calling from the car.

"Leave them alone, I think," said Gary. No one dissented, but they also no longer wanted to stay.

"We've been here before," said Cass, now out of the vehicle, to Kelly.

"What do you mean?" Chris asked.

"Before the virus, we must have been five or six, we came here with our parents one summer, do you remember Sis?"

"Yes, I think so, it rained." Kelly shivered, "Let's go, that lot has given me the creeps." She walked back to the 4x4.

"Eden, we'll go there and stay instead." It was on their route for tomorrow, "If those crackpots haven't blocked the roads," Gary exclaimed before climbing back in the driver's seat.

CHAPTER FORTY
Eden

They drove off and routed via the A390. Every road they passed, signposted, or not, after Lostwithiel, had some obstruction on it. The road was in poor condition, overgrown, and it took them ninety minutes to reach an entrance to the Eden Project. There appeared to be signs of more recent movement and they could see a tractor parked by the gated main entrance. They looked on the map. Liz and Chris were dozing; Kelly had taken over the driving, after they had stopped briefly to look at one of the road obstructions.

Gary was searching, along with Cass. "Wake up you two," she said.

"What's the problem?" Chris asked.

"We're at Eden, but we think there's someone around."

"More crack pots?"

"Who knows; see the tractor and gate?" Kelly pointed.

"I see," Chris looked.

"There's a farm on the map up ahead," Cass said, "on the right maybe two farms; shall we take a look?"

"Why not?" Gary looked ahead. He reached for the radio and broadcast to the *hotels* what they were doing. Kelly drove forward and turned right. There was a small field on the left, containing sheared sheep. An army diesel Bowser was stationed in the forecourt, next to a civilian Landrover. Kelly parked. She, Cass, Chris, and Liz got out, and Gary stayed with the radio.

"Hello," shouted Cass startling a few birds. They could hear the sheep baaing. "Hello anyone here?"

The front door of the farmhouse was propped open. They could smell something good on a stove, "Lamb stew," Chris said.

Kelly moved into the doorway "Hello," she shouted. The others edged into the kitchen and began to look around.

"Why don't you all just take a seat at the table? Keep your hands where I can see them, and please put that rifle down, miss?" The man's voice was slightly croaked, with a broad West Country accent. "You too, son," he indicated Chris who had turned around to see Gary standing in the doorway with his hands in the air, an intensely angry expression on his face; he was still getting over the shock of two barrels coming through the open window of the Toyota into his face. Cass and Kelly had a strong sense of Déjà Vu, remembering the group back at the house. They all sat at the large kitchen table and placed their hands on the table. Gary was the last to do so. The man looked about sixty, he was tall and thin, weather-beaten, with a shaggy beard and straggly hair. He took the two SA80's from the kitchen table and placed them on a large sideboard, opposite a hefty Aga range. A pot of stew was bubbling on the stove alongside a kettle.

"You from them idiots in Fowey?"

"No, we're from the midlands, Burton," said Cass. She could see Gary wanted to try something. Kelly couldn't see Gary's expression, but his hand was edging back. Knife, Cass remembered. "We're hunting, I mean, looking for other survivors."

"Is that so? Hands Mister," he pushed his shotgun at the back of Gary's head. Gary moved his hand back onto the table.

"Look, we don't mean any harm. We are just looking around."

"Want to steal my food?"

"No, we have plenty."

"I can see that, fatter than them idiots, anyways. What

then?"

"We were going to Fowey, and then coming to the Eden Project," Cass tried to keep him talking.

"Why?"

"Looking for survivors as we said, we are going to Falmouth next."

"Falmouth, what for? You must have lots of fuel then?"

"We have plenty of fuel and food, have you heard the ERS message?"

"Haven't bothered for years, why should I?"

"Do you have a radio, batteries, power?"

"Why?"

"There's a message from us on the ERS. Look," said Cass standing, "why don't we…"

It was all the distraction Gary needed. He shot up out of his seat, trying to turn and grab the shotgun. He smashed his head on the low beam of the kitchen.

When Gary came to, he was lying on a tatty old sofa. Kelly, or was it Cass, was beside him, his vision was blurred. "Hi darling," he mumbled. "Is it time to get up yet?"

"You just lie back, that's a lovely bump you have. He's awake," she announced.

Gary tried to sit up, but instantly felt dizzy; he closed his eyes, and tried to stay with it. "Bloody good job too; thought he'd gone and killed himself," he heard a croaky man's voice say.

"Here's some water, love," Cass or Kelly again. He opened his eyes to the offered bottle of water, the room stopped spinning. "Easy," she said as he pulled himself up. It was Cass. The man stood between the twins.

"Derrik Carter, Derrik without the c, it's Cornish," he said, coming forward with an outstretched hand. "Think we got off on the wrong foot."

"Gary, Gary,"

"Tolman I know, pleased to meet you, how's the head?" Derrik smiled.

"How long have I been out?"

"Thirty minutes or so," said Cass. "I'd better tell Liz, to tell Val, she's frantic, and Diane is furious."

Gary could guess that Diane would have them drilling for hours after this. "I'm okay. I'll talk to them later."

"Want some food?" Derrik said. "That's if your tigers have left you any."

"Tigers, what?"

"Derrik called us tigresses," said Kelly. "Much better than *cuties*."

When Gary had stood and knocked himself out, he had fallen on Derrik, disarming him, and knocking him backwards into the sideboard in the process. The shotgun had not gone off, because it wasn't loaded. Kelly realised that, the moment she grabbed it. It was broken, and the barrel slipped off its catch. There was a bit of a scramble, which got more farcical as Chris banged his head before Liz just shouted, "Everybody sit down!" They all did, except for Kelly who went to check Gary. They then carried Gary into the lounge where he now sat and sorted it all out. In between regularly checking with Val that Gary was all right, Derrik had gone on the ERS to hear Diane's voice. He then listened to the Survivor Dump message. Then, they had watched Gary whilst they had shared lamb stew.

Derrik had survived relatively easily; he had been on his own since his wife left him for a worker at the Eden Project, when it was being built at the end of the nineties. Some of his sheep had survived, none of his cattle. He had fresh water fish in two ponds to the East, and lots of fruit and vegetables in the project across the way, and his back garden. He had chickens and ducks and some fuel. The others had brought in some bread, which he hadn't had for years. He had an old outdoor privy, a well, and central heating from the Aga.

Gary had talked to Val and explained that he was okay, apart from a big bump. Then, Val had again told Kelly what to watch out for if it were a serious concussion. Kelly, Cass, and Liz, had all had to talk to their respective children, on the radio. Gary had listened to Diane tell him off about security with relief in her voice. He couldn't contact Joe, and Diane wouldn't tell him what was happening at Stella's or Hornsea. Gary was worried about that. Derrik had already offered rooms for the night, in exchange for the bread and the ERS information. Derrik had looked surprised at the need for only two rooms, which prompted an explanation more a firm statement from Cass "we're both with Gary, Liz is with Chris, thank you."

"Well, I never," said Derrik.

Gary had a bottle of his favourite Malt in his bag as well. He offered Derrik a dram, neither Cass nor Kelly would; they said they didn't like it. Chris didn't either. Liz said, no, as well, she normally did. Then, Gary noticed her hand on her stomach and a smile at Cass and Kelly; another P for Kelly's board. "Just us, then," Gary said pouring a good measure, and tilting his glass at Liz and Chris with a smile.

"Been a while, I can tell you since I had a good whisky, and a good company to go with it."

"Before my bump," said Gary sipping and savouring, "you said about the group at Fowey. We met two of them earlier, the others told you I'm sure, but what's your dealings with them?"

"They're nuts, like those cults you used to see on TV, with their *God Protect Us* every five minutes, and how they are the chosen ones or something. Didn't stop them raiding in the early days. We had a few run-ins, now they'll come and trade every now and then when they want some lamb. They bring fish in exchange, but they're on their bikes, no vehicles. They call them the devil's vehicles."

"They told us there are forty of them or so."

"That's what they say, is it? Don't really know; only seen a few of them, no names."

"They didn't want us to go near them, very unfriendly," said

Cass.

"That they are. I went over there in the rover a few years back, and they came out with sticks and so on. I've not been back since."

"We tried to tell them about the ERS and the dumps," said Kelly, "but they wouldn't listen."

"Given up all mod-cons they say. They tried to talk to me about joining them, told them to get lost, worse than Jehovah's witnesses that used to come round. Told them that as well, God didn't save *them*, did he? They didn't like that. Anyway, they're idiots, best just leave them be, you can't help some people, you know that." Gary could only agree. He remembered Rodger and Richard.

It was dark outside, "Well I'm an early riser with the sun, I suppose. It's well past my normal bedtime. I'll see you in the morning. There's fresh eggs in the cupboard." Derrik wished them good night. They weren't far behind him.

CHAPTER FORTY-ONE

The Morning After

Liz was actually the first up; she served black tea, to Derrik's surprise as he walked into his kitchen. Liz explained what should be in the Falmouth SD. Chris followed a few minutes later, then the twins, and finally Gary, which caused concern when the twins appeared, without him.

"He's fine," said Cass, to Liz's question.

"We checked," said Kelly with a smirk, "and you?"

"Feeling a bit sick," said Liz, getting a hug from Chris.

"You pregnant?" Derrik asked, "Sorry rude of me, none of my business, not used to people."

"It's okay, yes I think so," said Liz. "We don't worry about that back in the community, it's all very open."

"What shared love, and all that, not sure I…"

"No, not like that, but we do try to be very open with each other."

"Much to the embarrassment of some of us," said Gary, coming into the kitchen.

"It's only you that gets embarrassed," said Kelly, giving him a kiss and checking the lump on top of his head. Gary was making a major effort, ducking down to avoid the kitchen's beams.

"We make sure he does, all the time," said Cass, repeating

Kelly's treatment.

"Behave you two," said Gary, knowing they wouldn't.

"Well, I never," said Derrik.

"It seems to work though," Liz explained. "We are expanding and rebuilding, but we still need more people, which is why we are searching, and the Fowey group is so disappointing."

"We have a problem group in Lincolnshire," said Gary, "but your nearest group, Sierra, are in Elmsworth over near Portsmouth, unless we find some more Survivors on this trip."

"I'm okay on my own I suppose, although getting tea and some different food would be good. Fuel would be nice. Might be able to get the project's heaters running again and grow some of the fruits. There are generators there. Lot of work, mind you. They used to have a big staff just on the grounds, and hundreds during peak season; couldn't drive anywhere then, all gone now."

"Derrik, why don't you follow us to Falmouth. We have fuel you can use, then you can grab some stocks. That's if you want to, of course? Maybe get you on the radio as well?" Cass said.

Derrik agreed he would come, but only after he had checked his sheep and chickens. He had twenty-three sheep and, they agreed they could exchange lambs for breeding. Gary also explained the artificial insemination stocks frozen in the store, they hoped. The hunting group also wanted a look at the Eden Project and so Derrik took them in. The domes were all massively overgrown, but surprisingly many of the shrubs seemed to have survived without irrigation, heat, or power, or even much ventilation. Water had leaked in through the damaged roof. The ponds and pools were stagnant. Chris took pictures of the generators and plant machinery. Nothing difficult, they would just need fuelling, probably a service, but plumbing for the ponds and watering would take some work. Andy could come down for the generators, or more likely, one of the members of the Sierra Hotel community would come over. They had two mechanics.

After the Eden visit, they climbed back into the 4x4 whilst Derrik followed in the Bowser, sharing the ride with Gary whilst the others stayed in the Toyota. Gary took the mobile radio with him and his weapons. Gary explained about some of the other interactions with survivors. "Sorry about that," said Derrik.

"It's always difficult," explained Gary, "that first meeting; we've all had to do difficult things to survive." Derrik could only agree.

Derrik asked lots of questions about the communities that *had* survived. There was no contact from Joe, and Diane wouldn't tell him anything, except for a needless warning to keep their eyes open. It took nearly two hours to reach the docks site, then a further ten minutes to break through a fence and find the right building. One part of the road down was almost completely gone.

"Storm probably," said Derrik.

The road was passable in the dry, but a journey would need off road vehicles in the wet. Luckily it was dry. The Falmouth dump *OZT-SD12* was unlike the others they had found. It was a large, above ground, concrete building near a water filled dry dock. There were several Navy ships tied up alongside the docks, including a small tanker. There was a fuel dump further along the coast, but whether the tanks contained fuel, or were empty, they didn't know. The *SD* was untouched and still sealed. They could see a wind turbine turning slowly on the roof and the glint of solar panels that were also there. They entered the door using the code they had obtained from Hyde Park all those years ago. The door opened outward, just as they had seen before. The layout inside wasn't across multiple floors, but across a larger single floor, split into multiple door sealed galleries. It was all air-sealed, and a small office held the inventory folders, as well. They weren't in such good condition. The three computers were there. They didn't make a good noise when they booted, but they did boot. As before it was just the *Survivor Briefing by Professor Andrew Jacobs* on the desktop, as it had been elsewhere. Chris plugged a USB stick into a laptop, nothing. He tried another from another of the folders; that worked and he quickly copied the data across and then went and took the stick outside to copy onto the laptop they had left in the Toyota.

Derrik sat and listened to the briefing, whilst the rest of them explored, all bar Cass. She stayed with the Toyota. She was partially hidden well across the car park from the car, with an SA80 covering just in case. Diane had insisted. However unlikely it was that another problem appeared. Kelly knew what medical equipment to get for Derrik, and she reappeared in the office saying she would put the stuff in the cab of the Bowser. Derrik was overwhelmed by what he heard and read watching the Professor's briefing.

Derrik just mumbled; "So many, so many," he shook his head, and eventually he went outside. Kelly took him over a cup of tea she had made with Liz on their portable gas camping stove. The tea was fresh from the dry store, as was the sugar and powdered milk. Kelly ignored Derrik's tear stained face. She knew how he was feeling. She wouldn't watch the briefs anymore.

"Thanks love," said Derrik, Kelly would normally have objected to a near stranger calling her love, but she realised it didn't matter. "I'm sorry, I… There's a lot to take in."

"We understand, we've all been through it, so don't worry, drink your tea, we'll sort stuff out for you. Going to be a bit tight in the Bowser, but you'll manage."

"You won't come back then, to the farm I mean?"

"Not now, no, we have to go to other places. If you want, we can get some others, to come over? They can bring supplies. We'll leave you a mobile radio, and there's other equipment in the store. We'll give you a computer too. That will have the inventories of the SDs; I mean *survivor dumps*, on it."

"No power, I won't be able to…"

"There are small diesel generators in the store. We'll put one in the truck. Now, we need to sort your fuel out."

Gary and Chris were carrying food and other boxes, and piling them into Derrik's Bowser.

"Let's get fuel," said Chris, "hatch around the side," he pointed. All they could see was a blank wall. "Wait I'll open it." He disappeared inside again, passing Gary who was carrying beef and pork haunches out. Then, a small hatch popped on the side of the building with a clang exposing a fuel dispensing pipe.

Liz took a test kit from the back of the Toyota. She dribbled fuel into the tester, shook it, and announced, "Clear."

Before Derrik could move, Gary drove the Bowser over. He walked over as Gary plugged the Bowser's hose onto the dispenser. "Fill her up," he said to Liz. She opened the valve, and Derrik heard his Bowser slowly fill, he could hear the pumps from inside the building.

"How?" Derrik asked.

"Generators come on when the door is opened," Gary explained. "There's also power from batteries, solar and wind. It keeps the big freezers going and airlocks. Always make sure you shut up properly, that's why they have lasted this long. They were only supposed to last a couple of years, but here we are still going strong. Some of the medical stuff is useless, but everything else is fine. Maybe you're the tenth individual or small group we've done this to, so we know what you need first, others will follow us."

"7,000 Litres," said Liz, "how would you like to pay, sir?"

"I," Derrik went to pat his back pocket looking for a nonexistent wallet before he realised they were all smiling at him. "Thanks, I don't know what to say."

"Welcome to the survivor club," said Chris. "Come on; let me show you how to shut up the place. When you come next time, bring a bigger truck, or a 4x4. Once you are on the radio, there are lots of folks who can tell you how to do stuff. I wouldn't be surprised if the Sierra lot come over here tomorrow, let's ask them."

They did call Sierra after they had shut up the dump, then let Derrik practice opening it, and then shutting it again. When they contacted Sierra Hotel, they said there would be three of them coming over. Sierra Hotel had ideas for Eden as well. Knowing there was equipment and supplies in Falmouth would help. There were then a lot of questions about the ships in the harbour. Big ideas again Gary thought. They left Derrik with the handheld radio. They had a spare and showed him how to use it, checking his new call sign, Echo Hotel at the farm and Echo Victor 01 in the Bowser. He tested the VHF, not a great signal from the handheld, but he got a response from Sierra Hotel. Sierra Victor 33 would be with him in the morning; they would help set up main radios.

Then, it was time to leave. Gary and his *tigers*, he liked the name, were ready to go. To Derrik's surprise there were hugs from the women, Cass leaving her post as well to return to the vehicles, and then the men. "Part of the family now," said Gary, "watch out for that Fowey lot, we may need a plan for them." Derrik got in his truck and turned and headed for his home. They watched him go. "Come on," said Gary, "let's see who else we can find."

***

They headed north first to Redruth. They left posters in the town centre, and then they headed east to Truro. Gary knew they were missing St Ives and other western possibilities. They did the same in Truro, but found it deserted, and a large fire had destroyed the town centre, including the city council building. Grass was growing out of the ruins, so it had been a while ago. They didn't leave posters on the blackened walls, and their optimism from earlier in the day was darkened like the walls on the damaged buildings. Gary looked at the map "There are hundreds of farms and potential Derrik's hidden away. We need to search more," he said.

"No, Gary," said Kelly. "We keep wishing there are lot's more, but we know that's not going to happen; we would have found them. Sure, there could be another group or two like Fowey, but if they don't want to be found what can we do?" Kelly and Cass sat either side of Gary on the back seat. Liz drove, and Chris was scanning with binoculars when the terrain allowed. "We can't force them, can we?"

"Tempting," said Chris.

"We could kidnap them," said Cass." I read something about cults years ago."

"Is that what they are," said Liz, "a cult?"

"Maybe they are right, and we're wrong," Gary mused.

"Like Stonehenge when Liam said, divine intervention or whatever he called it." Having said that, Cass then had to explain to Liz about Liam and Stonehenge. "We could go see it; I mean

Stonehenge."

"Really?" Gary said, he had never been, "What about all the bodies?"

"They'll be skeletons or gone, but I want to see it as well," said Kelly.

"Newquay first," Chris said.

The Newquay *Survivor Dump*, *OZT-SD21*, was like Falmouth's, an ordinary concrete building which was untouched. They now knew that, except for Drakelow, all the numbers were random and didn't mean anything. They left the site as they found it, just copying the inventory onto their laptops.

They're planned stop for the night was the *Atlantic Hotel*, located on a small peninsula. Since the London trip, they liked to pick out what had been good hotels. It was a running joke in the community. "Storm coming in," said Chris. He was studying meteorology as his latest community contribution. He had set up small weather stations at each main site to match the station at Golf Hotel; although he had trouble getting people to radio the readings in. They could see heavy dark clouds in the West that now blocked the setting sun. They ignored the main hotel for now and focused on the rooms in the annexe. Breaking in was no trouble. The rooms were dusty, and no one trusted the bed linen, but they stripped it off and laid out sleeping bags in the two rooms they occupied. They cooked up some food in the foyer of the building. They declined doing a search of the main hotel; they knew they had larger and better-preserved stores in the SDs, except for coffee. That continued to be one of Gary's main targets.

He still dreamed of finding a processing factory, but even that would run out eventually. Where would they get new beans? He was being maudlin, again. He wanted a malt, but realised he had left the bottle with Derrik. Why couldn't every survivor meeting be like Derrik? He felt his bumped head. Very tender; he wouldn't admit to the others, but he was still a bit dizzy. Even Derrik hadn't been as straightforward as it should have been. There were radio messages to children, Miriam, no Val strangely, and Diane, still nothing from Joe, to Gary's annoyance. Diane would say nothing other than security and not on the radio. Gary knew something was going on. For once, he wished he was not on a trip, especially this far away. They couldn't hear Derrik, but Sierra Hotel could. He was in good spirits. Sierra would be there before ten the next day.

They ran out of time with the weather when the storm broke with deafening thunder. In the process of clearing up the gas stoves into the Toyota, they all got soaked. They retired to their hotel bedrooms. Gary could hear Chris and Liz giggling, helping each other get dry before they kicked their door closed. The rain was pounding the windows and the wind started howling. Gary stripped and dried himself on one of the room towels as did the girls, then they were drying him and he was drying them, and then he was trying to get the girls pregnant, again.

CHAPTER FORTY-TWO

The Yacht

The morning was bright and clear, but they could see the damage in land and some slates had come off the roof of the main hotel. There were the usual smirks amongst the girls, which Gary tried to ignore as did Chris whilst they ate breakfast and did their routine of latrines. Chris was back on the balcony of the room he and Liz had used with his binoculars. They were just packing up. Gary was already on the radio, trying to get information out of Diane. She sounded unusually tired. Gary suspected she had been awake all night. His head throbbed, and Kelly gave him some aspirin and checked the bump tenderly. Gary heard Chris' shout from in the car park. He grabbed his SA80, thinking danger, and raced back into the hotel building. When he had reached the balcony, the four others were all staring out at the sea.

"Where?" Cass was saying.

"Left back over the end of the peninsula, straight out"

"What?" said Gary, his heart was calming down.

"Got it," said Cass.

"What?" Gary said again.

"A yacht," said Kelly, with binoculars to her eyes, "a beautiful white sailed yacht."

The yacht didn't look so beautiful as it sailed in closer, clearly making for the port. They could make out figures on the vessel, but much was masked by the front, the bow, Gary remembered it was called. The front sail mast was broken, it appeared. They all stood and watched its approach with an occasional radio message. Diane wasn't answering the radio now; it was Kathy, or Miriam, at Golf Hotel nothing from Hornsea or Joe. Sierra Hotel was listening, and one of the sailors there was asking for a description of the yacht. Gary left Chris to describe the vessel and the four people Gary could see on the deck; one man and three women. The man was perhaps Chris' age. Two of the women were older, and one looked younger, Gary guessed. All were dark haired. They wore t-shirts with wet weather trousers. Gary stood and waved with Kelly and Cass as they approached, desperately trying to attract their attention. The crew of the vessel kept disappearing below decks and behind the damaged mast.

"We need a flare or something," said Kelly. Gary released the safety of his SA80, and shot into the air, the sound echoed off the walls and seagulls screeched, but the crew noticed. "You could have warned me," said Kelly, "and I hope you haven't scared them. They have binoculars on us now." Gary immediately unhooked his SA80 from its neck strap and laid it on the ground.

"Liz," shouted Gary, Chris was still with the radio, "provide cover, just in case, Chris stay on the radio." Liz disappeared back into the hotel. Gary noticed a SA80 barrel appear on the balcony a few minutes later. The yacht tacked and headed for the small marina entrance. There were several abandoned boats in the marina bobbing on the water. Gary, Cass and Kelly, walked back past the hotel annexe. They heard a cackle from the radio above them. Gary hoped Liz was moving as well. He jogged back and picked up the SA80, then jogged and handed it to Chris in the Toyota, "Move down to the quayside," he told Chris. He then jogged back to the girls. They went and stood on the northern wall as the yacht neatly sailed in; that took skill thought Gary. The Toyota parked behind them, Gary knew Liz would be nearby, but he restrained from looking for her and potentially giving her away. A rope was thrown from the yacht, Kelly caught it, just like the previous day. She tied it off as she had seen the Fowey man do.

"*Merci*," one of the older women said, in her 30's, Gary thought.

"*Bonjour*," the younger woman. Then a stream of French,

Gary caught a couple of words. It had not been his favourite subject.

"*Anglais*, only English," said Cass.

"Hello," the younger woman, "*aider*, help, *s'il vous plait.*" Gary reached down to help the woman up onto the dock. "*Non*," she said, "*aider là-bas*, er, there, help there," she pointed to the cabin where the man they had seen earlier stood. Without thinking, Gary jumped down onto the yacht's deck.

"Gary," said Cass, but he was already gone; then came a shout.

"Kelly, get the trauma pack and get down here. Cass, get some torches or other light."

Below decks, Gary could see a forty-year old man with multiple injuries, the younger man said some words in French. The injured man was unconscious. The younger woman was watching him. "L*e diesel*? Engine diesel?"

"*Oui*, yes," said Gary. He went back up towards the deck almost banging into Kelly and knocking his head on the cabin door. "Ow," he said staggering back.

He got a quick "sorry" from Kelly, as she pushed past him and then "I need light Cass," from her.

"Coming," he heard Cass shout. She was racing back from the Toyota carrying their two biggest torches. Chris was on the radio.

"Get hold of Val on the radio," he told him, "one badly injured; tell Liz to come down, we need help." Gary went to the rear of the Toyota and pulled down one of the spare jerry cans it was about half-full. They had neglected to top it up in Falmouth. He carried it back to the boat. The French man was standing on the deck, and he took the jerry can from Gary. The man went to a different hatch and appeared to pour the contents into a tank. He then went to the upper cabin. There was a brief cough, and then an engine started below decks. Gary went rearward and down the steps into the cabin. Now there was a light on overhead. Gary backed out. He didn't like what he could see. Kelly was checking the man's injuries with Cass still holding a torch despite the now on overhead lights. He could hear a radio going with a stream of French. Gary felt sick. He needed some air, so he left the cabin and climbed back off the yacht.

"*Votre tête*," said the younger woman, "er, head," she pointed at her own head. Gary put his hand up it was bleeding. He looked sideways onto his polo shirt where he could see a large patch of red. Cass came out of the cabin.

"Gary," she looked alarmed. Liz appeared, Gary didn't feel that great again, he was dizzy, and then he was lying down on the dock and then…

CHAPTER FORTY-THREE
Waking Up

A woman he didn't recognise was looking at him. "Welcome back," she said before disappearing.

Kelly appeared, "God you scared us again."

"I'm, I'm okay."

"No, you're not, now don't move until I tell you that you can," she sounded just like Val. She checked his pulse and his eyes and then held up two fingers, "How many fingers?"

"Kelly…"

"How many fingers?"

"Two," he said.

"Hmmm, lay there for a bit, drink this, its aspirin and water. Back in a minute."

Cass came in and held his hand. "Will someone tell me what is going on?" Gary asked, his head was pounding, he asked Cass "who was that woman, the first one?"

"That's Anna, she's up from Sierra, with Carl."

"That's miles away, how did they get here so quick?"

"Gary love, you've been out for nearly thirty hours."

Gary couldn't believe it, thirty hours. What had happened? "The house, Stella's, what's happening? I need to get back."

"You're not going anywhere, just yet," said Kelly returning, "and Carl agrees. Possibly fractured skull we think; good job it's so thick." She almost smiled. "I need to check our other patients."

"What other patients? Oh," he remembered, "the yacht."

"Yes, Andre, that's the injured man, he's in a bad way, but Kelly and Carl are doing their best. The others had scratches and cuts as well. Just a few stitches and we've given them tetanus," Cass said, "all from that storm."

"Gary, young man, how're yer' feeling?" A West Country voice he recognised.

"Derrik? What are you doing here?"

"Came up with them others when we heard all the commotion, they'd only just arrived when we came up; been here ever since."

"Out now, all of you including you Cass, you can come back in a minute," said another man, Carl, Gary realised. Cass reluctantly let go of Gary's hand.

"He needs to rest not chat; Carl and I need to do a check," said Kelly.

"I'm okay," Gary went to get up, but was suddenly dizzy again.

"Steady big fella," said Carl. Carl stuck a thermometer in his mouth. "Let's have a look at that head." Kelly took his pulse again and then attached a blood pressure cuff and took that. "That hurt?" Carl asked, prodding around where the pain was coming from.

"Ummmm," Gary winced. Carl removed the thermometer. "Yes," said Gary.

"Good, it's not numb. Well, Nurse Kelly, what's your diagnosis?"

"Mild to severe concussion, possible minor fracture, can't tell without a good X-ray."

"Agreed," said Carl.

"I'll check with Val," Kelly walked back out.

Gary went to move again, "Stay still Gary, nasty bang or bangs you've got, silly with all the other stuff going on, but nasty nonetheless. It's on the side of your head. That is better than back or front in my experience; I was a paramedic in the Southampton area, you know that. Bloody good, your Kelly, by the way. Did all the right things, might have saved that French guy's life; I need to check on him now."

"Thanks Carl. How is he?"

"Not great, wish we had him in your hospital, or ours, but we haven't gotten ours done yet. So many things to do," he paused. "He has head injuries, definite fractured skull there, broken arm and tibia, shin," he explained, "lots of cuts, he got caught up in their mast when it broke in that storm. Lucky to be alive really; same as the others, how they kept that yacht going is a minor miracle according to Dave, sorry Dave is one of our yachtsmen. He's out looking at their boat with the others. He's fluent in French which is helping." Gary thought he had met him. Cass came back in.

"Kelly?" Carl asked.

"It's Cass."

"Sorry, I can't tell yet, hair is it?"

"Yes, can I sit with Gary now?"

"Yes, please do, I'll see you later Gary, easy now no sudden moves, rest is also what you need."

"Thanks, Carl" Cass said, as they watched him go out, pulling the hotel room door closed. It was a different room from the previous night, no, the night before that, Gary realised. Gary pulled Cass closer for a kiss and a hug. "You're supposed to be resting," she pulled back, but there was a hint of a smile.

CHAPTER FORTY-FOUR

Operations

The following day arrived, and Gary got up, fussed over by Cass, and Kelly, when she wasn't checking on others. Dave reported that the yacht had serious problems and would take months of repair if they had the skills to do so. Gary was determined to get back to the house and find out what was going on. Diane was still at Stella's Farm, clearing up she said, during a brief radio message with Gary before breakfast. Joe would not speak, and Val was exceptionally taciturn.

The French yachtsman, Andre, was the problem; if they stayed he would die, probably, if they moved him, he might die, possibly. They asked the French crew, well Dave did, his French was fluent, if out of practice. Yvette, the youngest, Francois, the other man, and Sylvie and Bernadette reluctantly agreed to move him. Derrik was persuaded to head back to his farm with two of the others. Carl would go with Andre in one 4x4 with the rear seats down. He could take one passenger with him, which was Liz who would drive, Carl would monitor the IV that they hooked up. Andre's leg was splinted, using the trauma pack equipment and his arm was in a sling and strap. They had done a blood test, and Chris, then Derrik had donated. That was running in another IV drip. They would head as fast as they could up the motorway, the M5, Chris said, looking at the map. No good said Carl, there were several bridges around Bristol broken, and he suggested A303 then A34, then M40 and finally M42. If Andre worsened, they would divert to Elmsworth.

Gary had lost track of how many people were about and how many vehicles there were. The French crew was on their yacht radio, now they had power, explaining to their coastal community, of fifty-five, near Roscof, what they were doing and going to do. The French crew had been sailing to Milford Haven to see whether there was fuel there; they had heard about the major oil terminal. When the storm hit, they had tried to head back to the coast. They had used what little diesel fuel they had after the mast broke. They knew that Newquay was close, so headed inshore using the rear or stern mast, hoping to get repaired and then head back to France. They now had VHF frequencies for Golf Hotel and Sierra Hotel.

Eventually, four vehicles set out back towards the midlands and Golf Hotel and in particular the hospital. One vehicle would try to race ahead checking the road for damage to see if the ambulance vehicle could speed up otherwise, it was thirty miles an hour maximum and probably six hours on the road. They first stopped in at the Newquay SD and topped up all fuel. Their French guests looked in amazement at the store. Chris explained, that there might be similar dumps in France, as there was something in one of the Government briefings about foreign activity. Carl and Kelly raided additional medical supplies. They finally set off at 11:00, but progress was slow because the road was poor until they reached Exeter, then they were able to pick up speed. There was constant radio chat amongst the vehicles, and back to the Hotel's, although Stella's Farm was quiet except for occasional, we're okay's from Helen or Celia. Gary was in the back of the Land Cruiser with Kelly watching him. Chris drove, with Cass in the passenger seat on the radio describing the road condition. They took the lead racing ahead. Although the bumps hurt Gary, he didn't say. They didn't talk much due to Cass' running commentary on the road.

On the dual carriageway parts of the A303, they were able to accelerate up to ninety in places, before the road worsened again or the carriageway was overgrown. They sped east and after three, and a half hours the lead car reached Stonehenge. There were hundreds, if not thousands of abandoned cars parked in fields off the main road. They slowed, remembering their plans from a few days ago, they radioed back. The grey stones looked the same as they did in pictures. Chris turned off the A303 they didn't need to get out. Despite the now overcast conditions, they could see white skeletons everywhere. Liam's account of thousands was right. They all shivered as they returned to the main road.

"That lot in Fowey may do that if we don't do something," said Gary.

"You may be right love," said Cass," but forget them for now, let's get home sorted first."

It took eight hours in all, including a road diversion resulting from a fallen tree on the A34. They had to back track. Andre was no worse, but no better as they pulled into the hospital. Liam stood outside with an SA80. What was going on, Gary wondered?

Val met them, looking at Gary hard and checking his head after giving him a hug, then the twins and Chris. "Murphy" was all she said before she led them into the hospital's refurbished A&E entrance. Helen was there, as was Andy, with Murphy lying on a stretcher. Diane was back at the Golf Hotel Briefing Room. Andy told Gary what had happened.

They had been moving the cattle when they were attacked as they departed Stella's Farm. Murphy had been in a loaded cattle truck turning to head back to Hornsea followed by Andy in a 4x4. George had another truck with Liam following heading for Burton. They had departed first with no problems. Joe was at the farm with Celia, Helen, and two others packing things up. Andy hadn't seen what happened, but what Murphy had been able to tell was that a 4x4 had appeared and blocked his path. Three men had just started shooting even as Murphy ducked. Andy had heard the shots but no radio message but had radioed Joe. Joe and others had responded as they had heard the shots as well. Murphy had been pushed out of the truck and the raiders had driven it off, leaving Murphy for dead and shooting at Andy's 4x4. When Joe and Helen had arrived, they couldn't get past Andy's 4x4 on the narrow roads around Stella's Farm. Andy was already out of his vehicle, checking the injured Murphy, and calling for help. Those raiders had gone, but not the three that had previously been caught. They had carried Murphy back to Joe's 4x4 with Andy's useless vehicle peppered with bullet holes. Andy had minor cuts from glass, but he was otherwise, unhurt, furious, scared, and lusting for revenge; Gary gathered from his explanation.

Val had been called and had driven with Kathy as an escort until they met up with George and Liam, still heading back to *Arse Farm* as instructed by Diane. Liam then swapped with Kathy, at Liam's insistence, so that he could escort Val to Stella's Farm. Val had arrived and added to the first aid that Helen and Celia had already administered whilst Joe had stood guard with Andy and the others. Val assessed that Murphy would need surgery and that meant a trip back to the hospital. Helen and Andy would go with Val, with Murphy stretched out in the back of a 4x4. Liam would follow in another 4x4. Joe, Celia, and the others would go to Hornsea once they had used a towrope to pull Andy's 4x4 out of the way.

With Andy, Joe had interrogated the three previous attackers. They had kept the others at Stella's Farm away. Andy said they had the information about Lincolnshire now.

"What about the attackers?" Gary asked. Andy had shaken his head in response.

Val had set up drips for Murphy, and an emergency blood transfusion from Celia. Murphy needed more as soon as they had got back to the hospital. By the time they had reached their destination, the cattle, with George, were at the farm. Kathy was coordinating blood donations, and Diane had every available adult armed and patrolling whilst she tried to talk Joe out of going straight to Lincolnshire.

Gary wanted to go to see Diane and help with security, but Kelly and Val wanted to check him out in the MRI after Andre arrived. The makeshift ambulance arrived a few minutes after they had. Val set out the priorities; Andre in the MRI first, then Gary. Val wouldn't listen to Gary's complaints that he was fine, she wanted to check. They then needed to prepare for surgery for Murphy. Liam kept a couple of the new arrivals at the hospital, mainly Dave for his translation skills, but sent the rest, except Bernadette, to the farm for extra security. Liam guided them back, asking Chris to take up the guard duties. Liz would also go back.

Kelly struggled with the MRI without Val's help, as Val stayed with Murphy, changing blood bags, Carl knew a bit from the briefings and his previous career, but not as much as Val, so he went and took over from Val. He could do trauma and blood, he said. The attention in the MRI was on checking Andre's head. Kelly told Val that she was concerned about swelling of the brain; Val concurred. She said she didn't like Andre's condition. Kelly looked on the computer, looking at brain drain information, which they hoped wouldn't be necessary. Val unwrapped Andre's bandaged head and then they put him in the MRI. He was still unconscious, but that was good in one way, said Val. They all watched the scan, whilst they waited. Val re-checked Murphy and talked with Carl. They would have to operate. He had a bullet in his shoulder and another in his thigh. He was occasionally unconscious. They had given him blood, but the bullets needed to come out.

"Gary, we need the anaesthetic sorted," said Val. "We're going to have to operate on Murphy, and maybe Andre. Murphy is still bleeding as well. Liam's gone back to the farm so I need you to show someone where the stuff is and bring the anaesthetic bottles up. That means show someone, not you doing it. I don't need you passing out, and I need you in the MRI as soon as Andre is done."

Gary went out to the plant room, taking Chris and Dave with him; their other duties would have to wait. Gary pointed out the old anaesthetic bottles. He then found the right ones, Isoflurane, and nitrous oxide bottles, as requested by Val; oxygen was already there for the maternity area. They had planned to wire the bottles and use the system in the hospital operating theatres for delivery, but they didn't know whether they could trust it. They each took a bottle, Gary feeling nauseous again, but whether that was the head, or just what they were doing, he couldn't tell. As soon as they got back, Kelly grabbed him and took him to the MRI. Andre was on a trolley watched by Bernadette.

"How is he?" Gary asked.

"Same, some swelling but we daren't risk a drain, that's serious surgery, we just have to hope," she whispered the last bit. "Now let's see inside your head, in you go, keep still and quiet."

"That'll be a change," said Val, walking back in. She watched the whole scan procedure. After he had come out, she stood and waited with him, looking at the screen before they studied the output. "There's a brain there, that's the first surprise. No fracture that I can see, must be your hard head. That does not mean you start your Rambo impersonation. Go and see Murphy, he wants to talk to you before I put him under. He wouldn't let me until you did. Helen is going mad with worry."

"But they're not together anymore, I mean…"

"God spare me from bloody men," said Kelly. "Don't you understand anything. Go and see him, now." Gary almost said, yes Corporal, it was so like Hannah. He gave her a kiss instead. She pretended to be cross and then said, "I'm going to scrub up with Carl and Val."

Gary walked away, and into the other room, where he found Helen, holding Murphy's hand. She immediately got up and hugged Gary hard, then checked his head. She mumbled something about Val and Joe, which Gary barely heard. He held her at arm's length, "Are you okay?"

"Yes, talk to Murphy; he won't let us try until he's spoken to you. Something melodramatic I suppose." Gary saw a shape rush past the room door. "Kathy," said Helen, "she's bringing more blood. Diane, Danni and George donated, we need to hurry; he's losing more all the time."

"Gary mate," said Murphy trying to smile. He looked grey. "They say they're gonna' dig out these bullets with some dodgy anaesthetic to keep me quiet. What do you think?"

"Yes, they have to."

"Prefer some Irish malt."

"Not recommended by your doctors."

"Never listened to them before, still, Gary what I wanted to say was, you will take care of Helen and little Graham for me if I don't make it, won't you?" Gary nodded he would. "Sound like a bloody film I do, one of them cowboy westerns on your system. Tell you what, it forking hurts; that's for sure. Get the rest of them bastards won't you." He visibly gasped with the pain of just speaking.

"Yes," Gary said, "we'll get them."

Kelly was standing dressed in surgical greens by the door.

"Come on, its time," she said.

"Gary," said Murphy, "shake my hand mate."

"I'll have a malt waiting when you come out," said Gary, shaking Murphy's hand and patting him on his good shoulder. "See you in a while." He helped push the trolley in, to a wince from Murphy with the jolt of the movement.

***

It took two hours. Kelly, Carl, Val, and Helen were in the makeshift theatre. Forty-five minutes in, Kathy had arrived back with another batch of blood. One of the French women also donated. Andre remained unconscious, watched by Bernadette who dozed by the side of his bed. Cass arrived with some food. She had been back to the house. Gary hadn't noticed her go. She sat next to him but was restless, joining him looking in every five minutes. He didn't eat, he still felt sick, and a bit dizzy. When they did look in, it wasn't like any operating theatre that they had seen in a TV show or film. There was a single table, surrounded by the team, all in surgical greens with masks and hats. Carl was handling the anaesthetic, which had three separate bottles, each with a single tube going to a face-mask, which all lay next to Murphy's head. There was a heart monitor going and the lights rigged above the table looked bright. A blood pressure cuff was on Murphy's non-injured side. He wasn't covered in sheets and when Gary last looked, they were working on his shoulder. The thigh wound was already stitched. Two IV feeds were connected. One had blood, one a clear liquid. Gary couldn't hear what they were saying, if they were saying anything. Gary watched, as yet another red cotton wool gauze was discarded behind Kelly; who had her back to him.

The door finally opened, and Carl backed out, holding the oxygen tank. The face-mask was attached to Murphy who still looked grey, Gary thought. A bandage was on the shoulder area and another on his thigh. Helen helped wheel the trolley out. Kelly was pushing the two IV's. Cass went to help. Val just stood in the theatre. She eventually took her mask off and turned and walked out. She immediately checked Gary's head and his pupils, refusing to answer Gary's questions. She then checked Andre. Bernadette asked a couple of questions in French. Where was Dave? He was patrolling outside the reception area and when he came in, Val spent a few minutes explaining, with Dave translating. Carl kept checking Murphy and adjusting the oxygen flow.

"You should go back to the house, check the children and Miriam, then get some sleep," Val said to Gary, Kelly, and Cass.

"What about you?" Cass asked.

"I need to stay here with Carl, watch Andre, and Murphy."

"How are they?"

"Andre's head injury is the most worrying. We've set his arm and thigh. No problems with blood for him, but the head, we'll have to see. Murphy, we've got the blood stopped and the bullets out, thigh was straightforward, just soft tissue apart from the scraps of clothing the bullet took inside, but the damage to his shoulder. I don't know, lots of bits of things and ligaments. Carl could tell you. I don't have the knowledge or skills. I haven't done five years of medicine at university. It's not like the books, I'm a nurse not a surgeon, but we've managed. We've given some antibiotics to both, from those plastic-cased drugs. Andre's head, well I think we'll have to drain, but not yet. We need to be alert. I'm going to get some sleep here whilst Carl watches. Kelly, if you come back in the morning we'll operate tomorrow afternoon."

Gary just gave her a hug. "You did the best you could; look there's some food Cass bought over, try and get some rest." Cass drove Kelly and Gary home. There were others in other vehicles, but Gary wasn't with it, feeling confused, tired, or he was just overwhelmed. When they arrived, Gary was going to go to the Briefing Room to see Diane, but Cass persuaded him to go straight to bed. He was home for the first time in an eventful week. He did insist on checking on sleeping children first and Miriam welcomed him with a hug, before Cass, no it was Kelly, but she was at the hospital or was that Val, it must be Cass helped him up the stairs. He was dizzy and feeling sick again. He collapsed onto the bed mumbling, "Not tonight love."

***

Hannah was waking him up, but it wasn't Hannah, no that was Val, then his mother, late for school, no it was Miriam wanting a baby. There was Henry asking for a story and there was his father. Then, Rodger appeared, walking towards him in the dark, then he was on a beach and Hannah wouldn't wake up. Then, he was being turned down for a drink in the pub, then he was sitting next to a grave with a body in a floral wrap, then he was standing by a row of black plastic bags. Then a beach in the Caribbean with Val saying darling, then there was bleeping and more faces and Val and Joe shaking his hand and then silence……… then more voices and bleeping and noise and Hannah, smiling on the deckchair on the beach. She was making rude comments about his swimming in the nude, Cal and Greavesey were suddenly there, why? But, he was next to a big pit that had appeared on the beach. Smiffy was asking him if he wanted to burn? Then, Sarah was running round the lounge asking for Toy Story, then there was Joe talking about Survivor Dumps, then he was wrestling with a sheep, shivering, and naked looking at a London skyline. Then, he was sitting with a malt, then he was driving in the Lexus seeing the smoke from the pits. Then, he was skidding on the ice. Then, he was shouting at someone to tidy up, then he was looking at his mother standing with his father, looking at their bodies in their graves, but it was him in the grave, then there was Val taking off her t-shirt, then there was Rodger again, but he was shooting back and coming at him with a knife. Then, a skeleton was coming out of a black plastic bag dragging him down into the pit, and then there was Cass, then there was Cass, and Kelly, then there was…

"Hello love," said Kelly.

"About time," said Cass.

"What, where am I?" Gary croaked.

"You're here, that's the important thing," said Kelly, holding his hand. She looked very tired, but lovely. "In hospital, our new ward."

"How, I was in bed and Hannah and…"

"You have been mumbling a lot," said Cass. "I better tell the others you are awake. Val's asleep."

"Others?" Before Kelly could answer, Gary was inundated with children, and Miriam, and Diane who all hugged or kissed him. He was quite overwhelmed. He asked, "What's happened?" He tried to ask Diane, or Miriam, but no one would tell him anything. Then, Kelly was rounding up toddlers and asking Miriam and Diane to take Henry and the others outside.

Henry said, "But I want to stay with Daddy and play now he's awake."

"Later," said Kelly.

Liam stuck his head in and just said, "All right?" before ducking out and being replaced by Murphy, one arm in a sling and the other with a crutch.

"You owe me a malt," said Murphy.

CHAPTER FORTY-FIVE

The Hall Trial

Gary lay in the wet grass. It was dark and overcast, and the weight of the Night Vision Goggles made his neck ache. They had found them in one of the storerooms in a Portsmouth military base. Sierra Hotel had searched for them, and then they had practised for days with them. All, at Diane's insistence. There were twenty of them on the raid, each with goggles, SA80 rifles, and 9 mm pistols. They were all dressed in camouflage gear. The target was in front of them, a former manor hall, south east of Boston in Lincolnshire. They had crept up to a line of trees behind a deserted pub. They had a few hand-held radios with earpieces, but the approach had been planned in the briefing room and then updated thirty minutes away from where they had walked in after dark. They had spent three weeks in all practising, with Diane insisting on them all going through drills and using approaches to *Arse Farm*, with different people playing the bad guys to simulate the target. There were two teams of six and one of eight. Just before dark they had gone through the latest photos. Chris had obtained a massive long lens for a professional Cannon body. They had photos from the last three days, and some low light photos from the previous two nights. They estimated female numbers at nearly twenty at The Hall. There were possibly an unknown number of children inside, but they had not seen any outside. The men were all armed, and all they did was or could be seen doing was guarding the women. The women tended the fields, picking vegetables, and sugar beet in the surrounding area, but never far from The Hall.

There were six to eight men left in Lincolnshire they

thought. That was after Joe had caught up with the stolen cattle lorry, which was stopped trying to change a flat tyre. Gary was still confused how and when that happened, sometime after the raid and interrogation of the original prisoners. It didn't matter. Joe had shot out the tyres as the truck tried to drive away. The truck had toppled. He had then opened fire on the 4x4 in front. There had been four raiders in the 4x4 and two more in the stolen truck. The cattle that survived the crash had run off into the surrounding fields. Celia had watched, relaying back to Diane. Diane had told Joe off, when she realised he hadn't headed straight for the coast. Joe and Andy's interrogation of the survivors from Stella's Farm had been swift and brutal. Location and numbers had been obtained. That first raid had not expected to run into extra people that Joe had led from the coast. Joe approached each one according to Andy. The first one, had refused to answer his second question. Joe shot him in his kneecap, in front of the other prisoners. Joe had turned to the next one and shot him first, then asked the question. The third had told them everything they needed to know. Joe and Andy had then shot all three dead. Helen had not said a word apart from helping Val with Murphy. Celia had just stood and watched and nodded at Joe and Andy when they were done.

There was a single click on the radio. It was time. Gary crawled forward. He had Chris on his left side, but with him. The ground was soft. It felt wrong, and unusual. It was not vegetable patches, because they were at the rear. Gary burrowed, his hand down, he felt cloth and then a small bone limb. Gary quickly removed his arm and brushed the dirt away. A small towel was wrapped around a tiny baby. Gary could make out several other small mounds. Gary moved forward, trying not to gag. He hoped the rest of the team avoided the gravesite, but he realised straight away that Chris had not. Joe, with Liam, led a group on his left, and Diane led the largest group on his right. Carl and Kelly were waiting with Murphy and two others in vehicles, ready to drive in as needed.

***

Cass had stayed behind with Miriam and Val at Golf Hotel, with Val backwards and forwards to the hospital, where Andre was still in bed, but slowly recovering. The rest of the French party was helping guard the farm or at Golf Hotel, or at the hospital. Sierra and Bravo had both offered to help, but their assistance had been declined. Joe said this was their fight. Gary and Diane didn't want plans discussed on the radio. Gary, Kelly, and Cass had their biggest argument they had ever had with, Cass wanting to go. In the end, Gary had prevailed. Cass hadn't spoken to him for days and was out of their bed for the same period, until Kelly finally persuaded her it was the right thing to do. Gary pointed out that the only reason Kelly was being allowed to go was for medical support. Liz had a similar row with Chris, but she was pregnant and had to give in to Chris. Murphy was furious about not being on the raid, but he was allowed in the support vehicle. His shoulder would never be 100%, but he could drive, even with his damaged thigh.

***

There should only be two guards at night they thought. They would patrol around, but that left plenty of gaps. There had been lights earlier in the house and one of the outbuildings, but all was dark now. One of the guards was smoking. They had agreed that there would be no shooting, unless they absolutely had to. Two clicks on the radio. Diane had reached the hedge line to the right of Gary's approach. Three clicks and that meant that Liam and his team were at the rear of the property. Gary couldn't see either. His head was down as the two guards they could see, met by the front door. One went inside, causing a flare in the goggles. The other strolled out to the small wall at the end of the front entrance path. He was less than twenty yards from Gary. The grass on this side of the Hall's driveway was long. Gary crawled forward, sweating and trying not to breathe too loudly. The man turned and looked back at the house. Gary couldn't see anyone coming. The man turned back and walked to his right, Gary's left. There was another driveway there to the rear of the house. Gary was just about to move, when Chris jumped up. He sprinted across the asphalt main drive and jumped on the man's back. There was a loud grunt. Gary thought it was loud. Chris got up. The man didn't. Chris ran forward to the western corner of the house. Gary went to move, then immediately dropped as the door of the house opened. Gary's goggles flared as a light from inside the house was on. The front door closed, and his goggles returned to normal. The man had turned left and was heading for the outbuildings. Gary, in the goggles, could see at least three of Diane's group moving. He waved to them. They crouched down as the man reached the corner. He was carrying a rifle, as had his fellow guard. The man continued walking and then disappeared under three people leaping on him. Gary hadn't seen them.

Gary stood and moved quickly over the remaining distance to the front door. He opened the door losing his goggles again as the light spilled out, he flicked them off his eyes; there was a light switch which he moved to off. He replaced his goggles, and once again they returned to usefulness. Chris followed him in, and then the others moving left and right of the main doorway guarding entrances to the hallway from other rooms. Gary moved forward, looking for access to the rear, trying to slow his breathing. The hallway he entered held an impressive staircase and a doorway into another room towards the back. He moved towards the doorway. He could hear a noise from the other side. He backed off, and a goggled man came through. Liam, followed by Joe, both lowered their pointed rifles. Joe indicated he would go up the stairs as planned with his team. Gary nodded; he would start to the left. They went through the door, a lounge of some sort. Another door, and they entered a kitchen. There was a kettle standing on the hotplate of a large range, the range flaring its light in his goggles. There were two cups on the table, many others on a sink and sideboard.

He backed out. Three shapes were with him, and others covered doors and windows as he retraced his steps. He took the door now opposite, passing the front door on his right. No sign of Diane, but she should be clearing the outbuildings. He opened the door, and a short corridor lay beyond it. On the right was an empty office of some sort. Next, a small room with single beds. Two men were sleeping with SA80s leaning against the wall next to them. Two members of the team entered, one for each man. Gary saw knife blades and hands go over mouths. The men reacted. One gurgled, as the knife went in, the other went still. Two or more guards to go thought Gary. They moved to the next room; it was locked. There was a key amongst others, where the guards had been. Chris fetched them over. It was the third, or fourth one they tried. They pushed the door open. It was a dormitory. Several sleeping forms could be seen, maybe ten? Suddenly, shots from upstairs broke the silence. The room awakened to screams.

Gary in his earpiece heard, "Clear," from Liam.

"Still checking," from Diane.

"Two Guards down," Gary transmitted, "four in total."

"Make that six." Gary just about heard Liam's transmission above the screaming.

There were shots from outside, and then Diane's voice, "Another one down, here; all clear."

"Back out and lock the door for now," said Gary. They did. Gary heard Liam call for Kelly.

Diane transmitted, "Clear, coming to the house, one prisoner."

Gary transmitted, "Lights going on, goggles off." Gary lifted his and switched the hall light on.

Liam was on top of the stairs, "You need to see this," he said.

Lights were on upstairs. He could still hear shouts from the dormitory. In the first room on the left, were two naked, very thin women, bruised and being handed towels to cover themselves by Sandra. There was a double bed with ropes. Two naked men lay by the side of the bed; both slowly bleeding to death, no one was helping them. The women were shaking and crying. There was another dormitory room locked at the end of the corridor. They could see lights on and hear female voices. Sandra was trying to talk to the two women.

Diane came up the stairs, two at a time, "Okay?" Gary nodded and pointed at the two men.

Gary saw the lights of the vehicles flash. Then Kelly, followed by Carl, was through the front door. She took in the scene in the hallway, of one guarded kneeling man, head bowed, tied up, and gagged, and then she was up the stairs with Carl right behind. Diane was on the main radio frequency telling them everyone was okay. He could hear Cass demanding answers. Kelly entered the room, saw the near naked women and the two dying men. She ignored them and focused on the women. After some quiet words that Gary couldn't hear, one of the women went to the dormitory door.

Diane shouted, "Men downstairs! We women need to do this."

"What about Carl?" Kelly asked.

"Him too," said Diane harshly.

Gary walked back downstairs feeling aggrieved, with Liam and the male members of his team and Carl followed with Diane. "I'll take the prisoner outside," said Gary.

Diane said, "The other men outside as well, whilst we deal with the other dormitory."

Gary didn't like the implied accusation against him, and the other men present. "Diane, you'll need Carl for medical," he said, "and that's unfair on the guys who've just risked their lives. We'll take the prisoner outside, sure, but the rest of us will do our jobs and behave like *normal* men. I'm going to put the kettle on."

Dawn was breaking. Gary went into the kitchen, and Chris joined him. Gary filled a kettle and looked for some tea. He found a box with a worn *OZT-SD* number on it. "What was that all about?" Chris asked. He hadn't been upstairs.

Liam came in. "Diane is steaming, ordering all the blokes outside, but you came in here."

"Let the girls sort the dormitories out, keep everyone else outside in the hallway or in here, but let's get some food and tea going, whilst Diane decides if we are all rapists or not. How many guarding the prisoner?" Gary felt weary. He often did since his injury; he also had less patience than he used to, or maybe that was his age.

"Six covering, but the others are milling about."

"Okay, get a proper search going, inventories and so on." Liam left. "Chris, take a rover and a couple of men and see if you can find a bus. I think we'll need more transport, unless you can find some other vehicles."

One of the other men came in, "The prisoner wants some water, should I?" Gary could hear one of the vehicles driving off.

"No," said Gary, "rotate the guards around, come in here only, and get some tea and food." The man went back out. Over the next twenty minutes various men came in and even a couple of the women. Kelly, Diane, nor Carl appeared or sent a message. Gary went outside, silently fuming.

A steady drizzle was falling in the early morning light. The prisoner sat in the middle of the front entrance path. Another three bodies lay to the side of him. One dressed in combats the other two in T-Shirt and shorts. Gary turned and asked two of those standing to come with him. "We're coming up to get the guard's bodies," shouted Gary, entering the house.

He got an "Okay," from Sandra who came to the top of the stares.

Gary could hear quiet voices from his right, and similar sounds when the three of them reached the top from the room on the left. They went into the bedroom. The two bodies were still there. Gary picked up one of the naked, now dead, men and slung him over his shoulder; he could feel blood drip down his back. The other two men carried the second body down. Gary carried the body out, and slung it down in front of the prisoner. The other two did the same. The prisoner was clearly injured; Gary guessed that he had been the one that had been jumped on by Diane's team.

"Water," he said, "water." Gary ignored him, but someone had removed his gag.

Gary indicated the other bodies, "Put them where the prisoner can see them," he said, and the two that had come upstairs with him went and moved the bodies.

Murphy came out of one of the vehicles; he had been on the radio, "All right?"

"No, Murphy, it's not all right, but it will be soon." He walked back into the hallway. "Diane," he shouted towards the dormitory, "Kelly," he shouted up the stairs, "bring all the women outside, now, they need to testify."

Diane came out, "What are you doing?"

"I said now, Diane," he turned and walked out of the house giving her no chance to answer. He went back out to the vehicles. Murphy tried to grab his hand. "Murphy, I want you to relay on the main VHF frequencies, make sure everyone is listening; get someone else to help for the other vehicles."

"What are you going to do?" Joe said, appearing from a search of the rear. Gary pointed to the mounds; Joe went to look with Murphy. When they returned, Joe just nodded, and Murphy shook his head, whilst giving a hard stare to the prisoner.

Gary said to Murphy, "Try and track down Chris as well, see how long they will be." Gary turned back to the house; Kelly was there standing on the steps to the entrance with some very thin, clearly frightened, women. Diane came out with Carl, and they were followed by another group of thin women.

"What do you think you're doing?" Diane asked.

"Diane, please be quiet you're in charge of security. This is justice. I need two women who will testify against the prisoner."

"Testify, what are you going to do?" Diane tried to ask, before Kelly put her hand on Diane's arm.

"Leave it Diane, let Gary." Kelly hadn't seen Gary like this since Rodger, or maybe Wales, she realised. It was compelling and scary.

Gary went and stood in front of the prisoner, saying nothing. He waited. A SA80 was still on its sling around his neck. A pistol was on his hip and a knife the other side. A blood stain from the dead prisoner was down his side and unbeknown to him, some was on his cheek. It had changed the colour of the camouflage cream. Murphy came up to him and whispered "Five minutes," before retreating back to one of the other 4x4s. Gary just nodded and waited, staring at the prisoner the whole time. Chris drove back in, followed by two people carriers, just as the assembly was becoming restless. They parked outside and walked up, Chris was almost as tall as Gary and similarly equipped. Gary just pointed where he wanted them to stand.

"Ready Murphy," Gary asked. Murphy nodded. "My name is

Gary Tolman," he shouted "I am a survivor and since A-Day I have attempted to help survivors and the wider community." He could hear Murphy and another man relay his words over the radios. "We have a prisoner in front of me from the Lincolnshire Hall. Several weeks ago men from this hall carried out an unprovoked attack on Stella's Farm attempting to steal cattle; three members were caught and interrogated. Later a further attack took place, seriously injuring one of our Community, Murphy, and with attempts on the life of another, Andy. The group is also thought to have been involved in previous raids and attacks on other coastal communities, reducing the ability of all of us to survive and rebuild. They have refused to cooperate with the various communities around the country."

"Golf Hotel, Whitby, those remaining at Stella's Farm, and Hornsea all agreed we needed to end this dispute, and so this morning we have raided the Hall. There were eight men guarding the site and women when we arrived at the Hall this morning. Seven are now dead, killed during the attack. For the benefit of the radio listeners, there are approximately twenty women survivors. The remaining guard is the prisoner I mentioned. He is accused of the following crimes against the survivors, and in particular against the women here: murder, kidnap, rape, theft, and several others I'm sure. Do you have the women willing to testify against these men?"

Gary looked at Diane and Kelly. Kelly helped two women come forward Gary thought one of them was from the bedroom. "Please state your names for the radio and the community."

"I'm Marie Andrews," said the one Gary thought he recognised.

"I'm Rebecca Harding."

"Thank you, I intend to ask you just a couple of questions. I'm sorry to have to do this, but this needs to be finished today. Marie, were you raped by this man?"

"Yes," said Marie quietly, looking at the guard who had remained silent so far. There was a murmuring in the courtyard now, Gary's impromptu court and trial.

"You enjoyed it you bitch," said the man. One of Gary's

team hit him with a rifle butt.

Gary nodded at him. "The prisoner will have a right to speak in his defence shortly. Rebecca, were you raped by this man?"

"Yes," she replied very quietly, and then more strongly after a deep breath, "many times."

"Did either of you have children?"

"Yes," said Rebecca.

"What happened to them?" Kelly and Diane were now looking at him strangely. Chris had disappeared behind him. Gary hoped that Chris was going to get what he had found earlier, not that he wished to see it again.

"They were taken away by the men." Rebecca again, Marie and several of the others were sobbing.

"Were they alive when they were taken away?" Gary asked.

"Yes."

"Have you seen them since?"

"No," Chris appeared by Gary's side carrying a dirt covered white bundle. There was a gasp from the women and many more were crying one, or two were wailing.

"Quiet, please… I know that this is very difficult for you" Gary lowered his voice a little, then held up his hands as he looked at the crying women. He gave the audience, the jury he supposed, time to collect themselves before continuing, "For the radio listeners, we have found the body of a small baby in the dirt in front of The Hall there are many more graves." He turned back to the witnesses, "Have you been held here against your will?"

"Yes," said Rebecca.

"Marie?" Gary asked.

Marie was staring horrified at the bundle in Chris' arms. "Yes, they bought me here from Sutton, they killed Simon there."

Gary said, "Thank you Marie and Rebecca, there are many other witnesses who I know may wish to testify; I do not wish to ignore your rights, or wishes to speak, but we need to hear from the prisoner now. You stand up," Gary said to the man. "What do you have to say in your defence?"

The man stayed seated. "Who the fuck do you think you are? Fuck off. I'm not saying anything you're not the police or a court."

"Please let the community note the prisoner did not offer any defence for his actions." Gary waited for the relay to go out on the radios. "The community has heard from the prisoner. He has offered no defence for his crimes. The community finds him guilty and will now pass sentence." He paused, "The last law this country passed was the State of Emergency and Martial Law which included the sentence of death for these crimes…" Gary allowed himself another pause and a breath to bolster his own courage to act. "Consequently, that is the sentence the community finds; sentence to be carried out immediately." Gary walked forward and pulled his pistol from its holster. He made it ready and clicked off the safety. He didn't hear the shouts from Diane or Kelly or anyone else. He approached the prisoner. He pulled the trigger twice, and Richard Johnson fell backwards.

The sound of the shots echoed round the stunned courtyard. Gary unloaded the pistol as Kelly reached him; he put the pistol in his holster. Kelly saw with a gasp and despite the gunshot wounds, whose body it was that lay on the ground. Gary turned and walked away. He walked up to the line of trees. Gary knew there was shouting behind him. Diane came rushing up and stopped when she saw what Gary was looking at. She went to say something.

"We're not all rapists," said Gary. "We're not all like them."

"I didn't mean that, I was angry and…"

"Take the women to Hornsea," he interrupted her harshly. "I'm heading back to the house. Take these." Gary removed his goggles and SA80, and unloaded it, he handed it to a stunned Diane. He took off the pistol unloaded that and then handed it to Diane.

"What are you doing?"

"I need to be on my own for a while. I'll take the smallest

vehicle. You should have enough transport for everyone." Gary turned again and walked back towards the house. Kelly came up to him. He kissed her hard, but said nothing. There was a man in the vehicle he went up to. "I need the car," Gary said.

"Sure, Gary," he said.

"Thanks." Gary got in, started the vehicle and drove away. Three hours later he stopped briefly at the house, where Cass approached him immediately; he had ignored all the radio calls. He kissed her as he had Kelly. He entered the house, kissed Miriam and all his children. He switched vehicles to one of the Toyota 4x4s and checked it had an away kit in. He threw out the pistol he found in the glove box. Cass was frantic, asking him a stream of questions and crying.

"What are you doing? Where are you going? Why are you doing this?"

As he went to get in the car, she blocked the door. He hugged her and kissed her again. "I love you both, you know, and the children, but I can't be here for a while, not after what I have just done, had to do… I need to be on my own for a while. I should have dealt with him in Wales. I failed, please let me be alone for a bit."

He carefully moved Cass aside. He got in the car and drove away. He picked up the radio, "Golf Hotel, Victor 43, going mobile," he transmitted. He switched the radio off and drove away.

CHAPTER FORTY-SIX

Return

Kelly looked at her board in the Briefing Room. The UK total was 663. They now knew of another 200 in France including a doctor. There were rumours of a pilot. The original forty names were still up on the board, but the rest were listed on the laptop's spreadsheet. She and Cass had again had a discussion about what to do. They still shared the master suite. Their respective children were growing, but they both knew they should try for more. They had discussed suitable candidates for each other, but they would not share another partner, not now Gary was… Gary was gone, they had to face it, eight months including a very bad winter, and no sign of him. They had looked, well, Joe, Andy, and Murphy had looked when they could. All the communities were on the lookout for him. The attack and trial were already turning into a myth. Many had heard the trial on the radio, including the execution shots. There was shock, even at the Hall, but no condemnation, especially as the women's stories were told around the communities.

There had been no sign of Gary at any of the communities. The only indications that he may be still alive were two new communities from the Northwest. They said they had received a poster and then gone to an SD and joined the wider community via radio contact. Kelly blamed herself, the blows on the head had clearly hurt him more than they realised. He was well, they all thought, fully recovered from the injury, no injuries. There was Derrik's farm and then the boat. Such stupid accidents, but that was always possible. They took special care with the farm machinery, but accidents did happen, cuts bruises and all the communities had first aid lessons. They had been lucky not to have serious accidents, until the yacht and Gary, and Murphy, all together. What a crazy week, that had been.

***

When Gary had collapsed at the house during that awful time, he had been unconscious for five days. They had re-done the MRI scan, struggling to get his dead weight onto trolleys and into scanners until they had found the hydraulic trolleys and got one working. They then found what they had missed on the first scan, a fracture beneath what looked like the main injury area. The cut from the boat was obvious, it was bruised and had bled on the surface, but the real injury, probably from the low beams in Derrik's kitchen, was the dangerous injury. Instead of Andre just being the problem, it was Gary. They had ended up operating on both. Gary's fracture had swollen, and internal bleeding had started. Val, Kelly, and Carl had to act and they had put Gary under the dodgy anaesthetic they had used with Murphy before they dealt with Andre. It had taken hours, with Val, Carl and Kelly switching jobs. Drilling then draining, then sewing and sealing, then waiting, so scared of making the wrong move. Val, Kelly and Carl were furious with themselves for missing the injury the first time.

Afterwards, they had forced Gary to stay in bed for two weeks. Andre had taken longer to get mobile, nearly three months to recover, but he had finally made the trip back to France, and now regularly made the trip across to the South Coast and one return trip to the house that autumn with enough wine to re-stock Gary's cellar. If only Gary had been there to see it. Andre had never properly met Gary, but his exploits were well known in the French community. After Gary's two weeks enforced bed rest, he was allowed to go home to the house, but only to do light duties, as he called it, for another two weeks. Instead of his normal physical work, he spent all the time planning the attack on Lincolnshire and then there had been the attack itself. Joe had wanted to attack straight away, but had been persuaded by Zaynah and Val to wait.

Kelly had reacted the same way as Diane at the hall, throwing all the men out to stop scaring the women, not knowing about the ground that Gary and his team had crawled across. She shivered at the thought of it. Then, he had conducted that trial and the execution at the hall. Afterwards, they realised that one of the guards had been Richard Johnson from Wales. He was the rapist of Liz and Angie, and all those others at the hall. Gary had blamed himself. He'd said, in that rushed conversation with Cass as he left. Gary had stopped Cass and Kelly from killing Richard in Wales, or having a trial back at the house, leaving him free to continue his activities. How he had travelled to Lincolnshire no one knew.

After Gary left, there had been the row with Diane. Cass in particular blamed her. Kelly had been at the Hall, but she knew the way Diane had reacted had triggered something in Gary. Liam wanted to be with Diane, but he idolised Gary, as did Chris. They had the aftermath to deal with. Diane had become upset at the Hall when Gary drove away, and after seeing who it was, and the children's graves. They had cleared everyone out. The women now lived at Hornsea although some had gone to Elmsworth and Bognor. Two wanted to come to *Arse Farm.*

***

Kelly got up. Time for dinner she thought, a birthday dinner. Although she didn't feel like celebrating, Miriam and Celia had insisted. Cass had already gone back to the house to help Miriam and see to the children. As she had walked up to the house, she called to Henry to come on in and get washed before dinner. He was looking at the sheep and came away eventually. Celia had come over for the dinner; she, Helen and Murphy were sorting out the final parts of Stella's Farm. They were living back at Hornsea and had been together again since Murphy's injury, one piece of good news. Celia lived permanently at Hornsea, but was often back at the house. Diane and Murphy wouldn't talk at all, Murphy said he wasn't a rapist either and that Diane calling them all that, was deeply insulting. Diane tried to explain that she hadn't meant that. She explained she had also been against the Wales shooting, as had Val and Joe via radio. Helen had been in Wales. She hadn't wanted it. If Gary hadn't gone off, then it would probably have been sorted out, but instead it festered the relations between the survivors.

They had planned to eat the birthday dinner outside on the terrace, but the weather was too chilly. After dinner had been cleared away and the children were finally in bed, Val, Kelly, Cass, Miriam, and Celia sat in the lounge. Some soft Jazz played on the system. It was one of Gary's favourites they all knew. Joe would have said that the cabal was in session, if he were in a jokey mood. He wasn't often these days. They could see Hannah's bench in the dwindling light. Celia had a brandy and Miriam a glass of wine. Val, Kelly, and Cass had small malts; the twins were finally developing a taste for it.

"Happy birthday girls," said Celia raising a toast, "I have a present for you somewhere."

"Thanks," said Kelly, "twenty-one, hard to believe."

"I'm going to stop counting now," said Cass, trying to lighten her sister's mood.

"I've been trying to do that for years," said Miriam. "Where did you put that present, Celia?" Miriam added enigmatically.

"Me too," said Celia. "Doesn't seem to change anything, the body still knows, but you two are still so young."

Cass looked at Kelly, who shrugged. They all turned, hearing a sound, then returned to their own thoughts, probably Henry trying to sneak down again. No, there was a definite sound.

The front door swung open. Gary Henry Tolman stood in the entranceway to his home, his parent's home; his family's home.

"I've bought some guests with me," he croaked, "from Fowey." He backed outside. There was a minibus, driven by Derrik and ten people getting out. Two 4x4s were behind, with more people. Val, Kelly, and Cass rushed up to Gary.

"What have you done? Where have you been? How could you leave?" They all fired questions at him. He couldn't tell the twins apart again.

"I needed some time," was all he could manage. Diane was standing a few yards away, the twins realised.

"I'll take our new arrivals to the accommodation block," Diane said.

"Thanks Diane," said Gary. Diane asked everyone to follow

her, except Derrik who was talking to Celia.

"What's going on, how did Diane know?" Kelly demanded. Was that why she hadn't come to the dinner with Liam? Miriam had told her that they had politely refused.

"She didn't, till I saw her this afternoon."

"But Derrik and Celia, and Miriam?"

"We agreed to keep it a surprise, unless I changed my mind again."

"What do you mean again?" Val said. "Why, I mean, where have you been all this time? We've all been worried sick, and now you walk back in without, without…"

"I'm sorry Val," he said, not letting her move away, "and I'm sorry Cass and Kelly and Miriam, and everyone else. I'll even go on ERS and say I'm sorry. I've been all over." Gary kissed Val, but she pulled away. He then went to kiss Kelly or was it Cass, he wasn't sure. She didn't pull back, then he kissed the other one, she did. They realised they were all alone outside. Gary had hugged and kissed Miriam and Celia earlier that day, even Diane after apologies, when they set up the surprise; he hoped it would be a surprise. "Can I come in?"

"It's your house," said Val testily. Gary followed the women back in. Derrik was standing in the lounge. Cass and Kelly greeted him properly, but Val turned on him. "How long have you known?" Val asked him.

"A few weeks," Derrik said, "look Val, don't get all high and mighty with me. Gary asked me to say nothing whilst he finished with Fowey. I only told Celia the other day, when we had our private radio chat, saying I might be up today with some good news. Gary can explain. Is there any food?" Derrik asked Miriam.

"In the kitchen, come on Celia, let's leave Gary to explain. We heard some of it this afternoon. Sorry Val, I would have told you as well, but I promised Gary. I thought you all would be happy the way you've been moping around all these months. I am."

"I…" Val didn't know what to say. She had a flash of Déjà Vu back when they had held the discussion in this very lounge, when they had read Gary's letter and briefs from Hannah. She sat down, and the twins sat down almost exactly where they had been sitting that time.

Gary was standing; that was a difference. "The children?"

"Leave them, they're sleeping," said Val aggressively.

"Val!" Cass exclaimed, "Please give him a chance. They are all okay." Gary realised it was Cass he had first kissed. Kelly sat with her arms folded, staring at him.

"Explain," said Val more quietly.

"Well you knew I was unhappy about the Fowey group…"

"Not about Fowey, we'll get to that, I mean why did you run away, leave us, abandon us."

That hurt, thought Gary, right in the heart. "I didn't… I mean… I don't know what I mean. It was my fault. That bastard was there. I should have stopped it in Wales. When I saw him kneeling there I couldn't believe it. I had to kill him. I only did the trial to try and demonstrate to you and the other women, and any men who thought like that, what would happen. I was angry with Diane…"

"She didn't mean that," said Kelly interrupting. "She didn't call you rapists. That's not what she thinks, she…"

"I know love," said Gary, dropping straight back into the habit. "I know it was heat of the moment stuff, we talked about it this afternoon."

He paused and sat down on the floor. Now, it was just like that time six, seven, no nearly eight years ago, thought Val.

"I was angry, mad, those babies at the hall and I was scared, scared of what I might do. Ordering everyone around, I'm not in charge I don't want to be in charge and Diane ordering people around, even Carl." He stopped again; he got up and poured himself a malt. "Joe and Andy had dealt with Stella's Farm. I had to do my bit. I was mad, mad at myself for that bastard, I've already said that, sorry… I guess I was angry at everything; I seem to be, since the bangs on my head. If I could do that at the hall, what would I do at home, here? I might lose my temper and …"

He was rubbing the spot; the hair had grown back differently. His hair was long, too long, his beard was long. He had lost weight, his face looked almost gaunt, his clothes were worn; Kelly thought. She unfolded her arms.

Gary had stopped; he was looking out the window into the dark at Hannah, Sarah, and his parent's graves. "I needed to think. I couldn't do it here with you all, the children, the projects, and the looking for survivors. Whilst we were planning the Hall, which we had to do, I was thinking about Fowey and if there were other spots like the Hall. Other groups, I mean."

"Why didn't you say something?" Cass asked, "Talk to us."

"I tried, but I suppose I didn't try enough. There was always something else going on." He looked at Val. "You had Andre to help, with the hospital and pregnancies, and Henry and Carmen, then Miriam had Juliet, and Jenny." He turned to Cass and Kelly. "You had… you both had the children and the genetic plans. The house, I hated being in this house, it didn't feel mine anymore with the mess; silly I know. I enjoyed our trips away, but that just caused more hassle and meant I was away when they attacked the farm. But, then there were the projects, the other groups asking me stuff. I promised you Val that I would protect you all, but I couldn't. I couldn't even stop a rapist I knew about."

"That's not just your responsibility," said Val. "We didn't want you to, either, or let the girls do it. Joe and I both said so on the radio, and Helen."

"I know," said Gary, "but I dealt with Rodger. I should have dealt with Richard the first time. I did that stupid trial because I should have had at least a trial the first time. I wanted everyone to know that I was responsible, no one else needed to have that on their conscience."

Cass said, "But where have you been, love? All this time we thought you might be injured or worse." Gary was pleased he had a *love* from Cass at least.

"I went north, just driving really, then I went down the coast. I used the SDs or army camps for fuel, but mostly I was searching. There are some other groups on the Northwest coast, but I didn't approach them. I left them a note; I hear they have joined. I then went round Wales, staying on the coast and that turned into the trek I wanted to do. Possible group there as well, not on the coast, saw some smoke."

"How did you eat, and get by?" Cass asked.

"Well, I've got a bit better at fishing," he half laughed. "There was fruit last autumn. The winter was, well it was hard, until I went to Fowey. I haven't done anything more than you guys did before you came here. I never had to live on the road to really survive."

"So it was just some sort of macho, prove you're a man, trip?" Val angrily said, missing the Fowey comment.

"No not that, well maybe a bit, I don't know. I wasn't thinking straight. I wanted to come back lots of times. I'd hear you on the radio and…" Miriam, Celia, and Derrik were listening now. "I then thought you wouldn't want me back, probably don't now, judging by your reaction so far. Don't answer that." He gulped his drink and tried a smile, if they could see it through the beard. He rubbed his neck and then the injury spot. The hair there always itched. "Anyway, I kept thinking about Fowey and the group there. I had a car problem around Bristol, had to switch and sort tyres and things, it took me ages to move the radio. I then went south and watched Fowey. Then, I joined them."

"What?" a simultaneous expression which included Miriam and Celia, they hadn't heard this bit. Gary let people get settled and get drinks; he poured one for himself and Derrik. Derrik had heard this; he had helped after all.

CHAPTER FORTY-SEVEN

"God Protect Us"

Gary had watched the Fowey group from across the river in Polruan, and back along the river bank form the Old Ferry Inn. He spent two weeks at the end of December watching the group's daily routine. He would break off his vigil to fish further along the coast away from Fowey, but he was running out of food. Checking the radio, that no one would be on route to Eden from Elmsworth, he had driven back to the coast and hidden the car near Saint Blaise Church in Tywardreath. He had rested for a couple of days in a house there. He found a small army pit site and was able to get some other food. He then had walked back towards Fowey to carry on his reconnaissance, not wishing to give himself away. By the end of January, he knew what was happening. He couldn't hear, but he could see. There was a leadership group of about six, four men and two women. One of the men was the man they had met at the Old Ferry Inn, as was one of the women. Then there was another mid-group, of about ten, eight men and two women. Then there was the rest, about twenty, mostly women. A couple were pregnant, plus the children. There were seven children including three carried babies, the rest toddlers. Gary saw that the children were all dressed identically when they came outside from the houses near the central Church. Every day at eight and five the community gathered there. The leadership group lived at Porphyry Hall. Every day some of the women from the houses would go to the hall escorted by one of the mid team, or they would come out of there for Church. There seemed to be a rota. Gary had seen from Polruan the men, and occasionally a woman, row out to the river estuary and bring in lobster pots, or they would fish. Vegetable patches were in front of the hall where the women also worked. Chimney smoke was in evidence in the houses and the hall. Gary knew he would have to join the group, if he wanted to really find out what went on in the community. He suspected the worse.

He knew he was filthy, dishevelled, and thin, so his claim to be desperate would be believed. He hoped that the man and woman might not recognise him. He went and found a hairdresser's salon and dyed his hair and beard brown and yes his pubic hair as well. He had a knife but no other weapons. He didn't really have a plan, but he went in anyway. He walked into the village from the North, not from where he left the 4x4, it was mid-January, and there was snow on the ground. Two of the worker women had seen him first, staggering into Church Avenue. He timed his arrival at late afternoon. They didn't come to his aid, but instead ran towards the Church. One of the mid-ranking men came out and asked who he was and what he wanted. Gary didn't have to put on his stagger; he was freezing in the icy wet snow that was falling. He collapsed to his knees begging for food. The man came forward and helped him to his feet then, pulling back at the stink of Gary and his clothes. The man then took him to a house near the Church where a wood stove gave much needed warmth. He answered questions, but there was no food until after Church he was told.

Just before five they all got up and helped Gary to his feet and he was taken into the Church. The pews had been rearranged into a semicircle near the altar. The Christian symbols were still in evidence, but so was an emblem of a sun rising, the same emblem was on the children's clothes, but not the adults. The toddlers looked at him, but they said nothing; no one said anything until the leadership group appeared. Then there was a discussion, about him, he guessed. Then, they went and conducted the service. Gary couldn't follow it; he was too cold. The Church was unheated, and he was very hungry. There was another discussion and then a man he didn't know said, "You may stay for one night. We will provide food and shelter; however, if you wish to stay longer you must follow the rules that Brother Griffin will explain to you. *God Protect Us*"

"*God Protect Us*," the small audience parroted before

following the leadership group out.

Brother Griffin was a different man to the one he had first seen, he was probably in his fifties, six feet two and painfully thin. He took him to a different house were a shrewish woman of similar age, served him a bowl of fish and vegetable stew. Gary thanked her.

"We say *God thank you for this offering* then *God Protect Us*," Brother Griffin explained pleasantly.

The woman repeated "*God Protect Us*." Gary mumbled the phrase.

"Sister Tilda?" Brother Griffin asked the woman.

"At the hall," said the woman.

"Who else?" Brother Griffin asked.

"Sister Wendy."

"*God Protect Us*."

"*God Protect Us*."

Gary managed an attempt in between mouthfuls of stew, which was barely digestible.

The next day Gary agreed he wanted to stay, and would follow the rules, which mainly consisted of doing work you were told, and saying *God Protect Us* whenever someone else said it. No one asked about his past or told them about theirs. He was told to stay with Brother Griffin and Sister Janet; that was the woman's name. Sister Tilda returned after service the following morning. She did not greet Gary or say anything. Each of the adults had a room in the house. Gary slowly discovered that there were no couples. The women with babies were housed together. Once the babies were weaned the women had to move out. The older toddlers were in a separate house, looked after by the mid-ranking group, the *Dawn's Circle* they were called. The leadership Groups were called the *Dawn's Rays*.

Gary's work was to help with vegetables and then boats. He learned, but he was always cold and hungry. He watched a succession of women go after each evening service to the Hall; he never went and was never invited. Brother Griffin told Gary that he would have to swear allegiance to the group of the *New Dawn.* That would occur after his probation period, in the spring. Brother Griffin hoped that if Gary's teaching went well he might get invited into the *Dawn's Circle.*

In mid-February, Sister Tilda again went to the Church. Gary had sensed her fear that morning; she occasionally said a few words to him, but otherwise nothing. When he thought of her compared to the twins, Val, or Hannah he couldn't believe they were from the same species. But, he also remembered Liz and Angie in Wales and the women at the Hall. Even Liam, when Rodger and he had arrived. Is that what sustained abuse did, he pondered? He had to act. When Sister Tilda had returned the following day, he managed to get alone with her.

"Are you all right?"

"I can't talk to novices," she said.

"I will soon be a brother. I only asked if you are well, you are holding your arm I thought you might be injured?"

"No, I fell whilst at the Hall, it's nothing. *God Will Protect Me. God Protect Us.*"

"*God Protect Us,*" Gary automatically said.

"You two, to your duties," said Sister Janet coming into the dingy kitchen.

Brother Griffin approached him later, "You must not ask about the Hall," he said.

"I didn't, I thought Sister Tilda was hurt, I merely asked for God's concern for her well-being, *God Protect Us.*"

"*God Protect Us.* Even so, be careful, you must earn the *Ray* and Circle's trust they only care for all our welfare. The sisters are honoured to serve at the Hall." Gary doubted that. They didn't look honoured. "Now return to your duties, Sister Tilda will be fine, *God Protect Us.*"

"*God Protect Us,*" said Gary. That night he heard Tilda crying along the hall, and the sound of Janet comforting her. He had to act soon.

At the end of February, Gary told Brother Griffin he could no longer stay. He would not swear allegiance and would leave immediately. He removed the clothes he had been given and put on the clothes he had arrived in, as Brother Griffin, panicking, tried to persuade him to stay. Gary walked away from the house, making sure Sister Tilda saw him go. He walked past her as she worked in the vegetable plot, despite the freezing cold. She chased after him.

"Where are you going?"

"I'm going back to my community," he whispered to her. One of the *Circles* was coming. "Where women aren't raped and beaten at the whim of others, where we have food, medicines, power and children. I'll be back though, for all of you." She nodded her understanding at him. He turned and walked as quickly as he could away, ignoring the shouts and threats of the *Circle* man. Gary looked back to see Tilda being led away.

It took him two hours to skirt round and back to the car, in between hiding from groups of *Circles* looking for him. He didn't want to know what would happen to him, but he had seen graves that appeared reasonably new in the Church Yard. He had to wait till it was dark before he finally found the car, by which time he was shaking with cold. His clothes and body were soaked. He found the car's keys where he had hidden them and unlocked the car, retrieving his bag of spare clothes, a gas camping stove and an army ration pack. He broke into a house, desperate to get warm, but not daring a fire, in case the searchers were still looking. He retrieved his sleeping bag and stripped. Then wrapped in the bag, he heated the rations, feeling sick after eating so much more than he had become used to. He dressed in new clothes, extinguished the camp stove and shivered in the bag until he fell asleep.

When he woke it was already late afternoon. He hoped he hadn't lost a day. He checked outside. The car was still there. He had not been found, or the searchers thought the car was dumped. He searched the house. There was a skeleton in one of the bedrooms; he ignored it. There were some clothes, but they were the wrong size, all too small. He returned to the lounge of the house where he had spent the night. He heated more rations. He went out to the car and carried in the small medical kit. He checked his temperature. His head ached. He took some aspirin; his temperature was fine.

He rested throughout the day, planning what he would do and what he would need. He found a mirror. He didn't like what he saw, but he had no shaving kit. He looked outside; heavy snow was falling. In the mirror, he could see his blonde hair coming through on his beard and his head. He checked his groin, there as well. He went outside and collected some snow for water. He boiled it and took it upstairs to the house's bathroom. He dumped melting snow into the bath then added the hot water until he had a shallow bath. One of the taps was dripping he noticed. He didn't risk switching it on as there was water damage in the kitchen area. No food, he had already checked. He used the tepid bath water to clean himself as best he could, with less than a bucketful. He stopped himself thinking of other bath times, Hannah, the twins, Val, Miriam. Too much thinking; he had done that for months. He wanted redemption, instead he redressed. He had no knife so he couldn't cut up a chicken or a fish, that was if he could catch one. He would have to go for help.

He had to wait nearly a week before the snow cleared enough for him to risk it. Before he started the car, he walked clear and searched around to make sure no one was watching. He hoped that the 4x4 would start, when he turned the ignition. He hadn't tried it before. He loaded his stuff from the house into the backpack. If the car didn't start, he would have to walk. He turned the key. The car wheezed after a delay whilst the diesel pre-heaters started. The car spluttered and started, *God Protect Us*, Gary thought unbidden. "Thank you Toyota," he said out loud. He restrained from revving the car, the start had a caused a few birds to rise. He drove away from Fowey. He drove to Derrik.

CHAPTER FORTY-EIGHT

No One Is Serving Anyone

"So you knew, you knew in February?" Kelly flared at Derrik.

"No, it was March when he turned up, sorry I was sworn to secrecy."

There was further banging on the door, then Diane came in. She knew the code, after all she used to live there. "Gary you need to come, and Val and Kelly, you might as well, Cass."

"What's the matter?" Val asked.

"It's the *New Dawn* women. They are having a ballot to see who will come up to the house and *tend* to Gary, their language, in between endless *God Protect Us*'es. They also have injuries and so on. I can't deal with this myself. Gary you need to deal with this."

After a short further discussion, they walked down to the accommodation block, now almost overflowing with the new arrivals. "Sorry, Diane," said Val, with Kelly, "we should have realised." They immediately went to work, checking for injuries and general health. They wanted the women and several children to go into the Briefing Room, where they could be examined properly, but they would not leave. The women were eerily quiet, Val, Kelly, and Cass realised.

"Wait," said Diane, "Gary!"

Gary announced to the women, "I told you on the journey here, no one needs to *tend* to me or any man. Val, Kelly, and Cass here will help you, like Diane has. The men who came with us and helped me rescue you, will not harm you, and do not need *tending* to either. Now, the girls will give you a check. I will see you over the next few days and please no one say *God Protect Us*," the women immediately started mumbling back. "We don't say that here at all," Gary raised his voice. "We'll protect you, the survivors will protect you, and you'll protect yourselves." Gary turned and walked out. He went back to the house, and into the kitchen. Miriam gave him a hug.

"Let's get some food in you, then you'll need a good bath." She served him some fresh pasta and chicken. Gary remembered doing the same to Val and the twins. Celia bought him in a topped up glass of Malt.

"I'm going for a chat with Hannah, haven't done that for a while, Derrik let me introduce you." Derrik looked confused, but followed Celia out. Celia held Derrik's hand; Gary smiled as Derrik had asked if Celia were alone, ages ago, months ago, before the Hall. He came back to now. Miriam was looking at him.

"How, am I doing?" he said between mouthfuls. He had missed Miriam's cooking. Derrik and his own attempts weren't great.

"Keep going, Cass is okay, Kelly is getting there. Val, well you know Val?"

"Maybe I should go?"

"No, you don't mister. What about Juliet and me? They're not the only ones that missed you, you know? You can't go running off again. What about the children? They need their father around, not wandering round the country doing I don't know what? There are plenty of others, Murphy, Andy and Joe, what about Liam, Chris, and Gart, lots of others. Carl down south has been blaming himself because of your accident. Derrik was distraught when he heard on the radio after the Hall." Gary felt small and guilty. "Don't you get it? They all, we all, bought into your dream of the future; your determination to make it happen; then you go and disappear."

Miriam was crying. "I know I don't have the same relationship with you that the twins have, or Val had, no don't say anything, but I'm here too, I missed you putting stuff away all the time, can't you tell." Gary had to admit the kitchen and lounge were much tidier than he could remember seeing in a long time. He got up and gave her a long hug. How could he ever make this up to them? He felt even more guilty. "You're so thin," she said after he let her go. "You better have some more food, and no more alcohol. Why don't you go and see the children, don't wake them though?" Gary meandered out and toured the house's bedrooms. He didn't enter the master suite. He sat on the floor of his old bedroom, watching Henry and Carmen. He could tell all the children had grown.

He went down to the lounge and looked at the shelves, a lot of the books were gone he realised. He could see Celia and Derrik chatting on the bench. He heard the radio squawk. Miriam responded. He heard Joe say he would be over in the morning with Andy, Murphy, and Helen. They wanted a word with that blonde idiot, they said. Gary smiled. Miriam had barely put the microphone down when Gary realised Kathy, Danni, and Sylvia were talking to Celia and Derrik, introductions were being made. Gary waved. The women waved back, but turned and walked away. Kathy looked pregnant, Gary thought.

He sat in an armchair and started reading one of the old farm reference books, seeing his own notes in the margins. He must have dozed off. It was a couple of hours later when he woke to the sound of Kelly, Cass, and Val returning. Val nodded at him and went into her annex. Celia and Derrik weren't around, although someone had put a duvet over him. Cass and Kelly looked at him.

"You need a bath, a shave, a haircut, and goodness knows what else," said Kelly.

"Thorough physical I think," said Cass. She held out her hand, "This way."

CHAPTER FORTY-NINE

Gary's Birthday

"Over twenty years since A-Day," said Kelly, looking at her board.

"Is it?" Cass asked. They could hear the younger children playing outside. They were on a break from class today, and Danni's voice was calling them back into their positions. Cass suddenly felt melancholy; a large shadow filled the door.

"He's on his way, just radioed, twenty minutes, he said."

"Thanks Dan, we'll come up, is Mike back?" Cass asked.

"Yes," said Dan, Cass's eldest son. Mike was Kelly's.

"Everyone else?"

"Yes, mum, all there out the back." Dan spoke with that exasperated tone that only teenagers could generate when talking to their parents, but he smiled as he walked away; it could have been Mike or a younger Gary.

Kelly stood up, "How do I look? It's a bit tight."

"No, it's not," Cass adjusted the front of her dress. Red and newly made, Kelly's, was pale blue, both were strapless. They walked up to the house and round the back. Long tables were set up, and the crowd had gathered there, including the now quiet younger children. Too many faces, she noticed, the younger ones serving to remind her of the missing ones. Joe and Zaynah stepped forward.

"Don't you two look great," said Joe. "Didn't you wear…?"

"Joe!" Zaynah stopped him.

"Yes, we did Joe," but Kelly laughed. "We'd better go round the front." Kelly and Cass walked round to the front of the house. Val came out followed by Miriam. "Where's Celia?" Kelly asked.

"On the bench with Derrik, she said to go ahead," said Miriam. Val and Miriam were also in dresses.

"Hope the timing works," said Val.

"It will be fine," said Cass.

A 4x4 was coming up the drive and pulled to a halt in front of the house. A very tall, mixed race man climbed out of the driver's seat. Smiling, he walked forward and embraced his mother, Val.

"No idea?" She asked him.

"No idea at all," Henry Gary Tolman looked back at the Toyota. His father was getting out of the passenger seat staring at the welcoming party.

Gary was blinking, his eyes were running. It's just the sunlight he thought. Four beautiful women and his eldest son waited for him.

"Happy birthday darling," said Val coming forward and kissing him, she still had that drawl over *darling*.

"Happy birthday love," said Miriam, another hug and kiss.

Then, it was Cass in red and Kelly in pale blue. "Always last," said Kelly, but making sure she had a longer kiss.

"You're in trouble," Gary said to Henry.

"What's new?" Henry said, giving his dad a hug.

"You're all dressed up, what's going on?" Gary said to the women.

"Come on," said Val. She pulled Gary round the back of the house, where a huge, "Surprise" was announced, sparking off the crying of babies, a flock of birds, and the baaing of sheep. Then, to the surprise of most, a twin-engine plane flew over. Dan came out of the house with Mike, looking pleased that the fly past timing had worked. Their sisters, Sarah and Hannah, were in the group now crowding round their father, with their mothers blonde hair everywhere. Twenty minutes later, Carmen arrived with her French pilot who was teaching her to fly. Val didn't like the age difference, but it was less than there was between her and Gary. Carmen kissed her dad and her son. Her partner, Ricard, was carrying a crate of champagne, a birthday gift from Andre and the team he said.

Later Val took a photo of Gary with his children; you had to look closely to tell Mike, Dan, and Gary apart. Henry and Carmen stood either side of Gary, their jet black hair stood out as did the hair and skin tone of Juliet who was also holding a grandchild. Jenny was not Gary's, but you would never know it as she was in the picture as well. Gary had no more children though, nor had the twins. They still tried. Val suspected, by the twin's dresses, that they planned to try again. Kelly had talked about birth rates with the doctor in France only that afternoon. Maybe the next generation would be better; they were starting to try.

Val smiled at Carmen and Henry. Henry had a child in Elmsworth, she knew and given the amount of time he spent travelling, he was trying elsewhere. He had plenty of offers, she had heard, and she was sure Kelly had mentioned something. Val watched Gary hug Diane and Pamela who also hugged Henry, she noticed. Six years since Liam had succumbed, despite the transfusion efforts. Pamela was another Gary treated as if she were his own. Liam that had been a year after Helen. Graham, her son with Murphy was here, and Murphy, still complaining to anyone who would listen about his dodgy shoulder. Murphy was now with one of the Fowey women. Val always forgot her name.

Tilda was talking to Derrik and Celia, she saw. Tilda was one of Val's nurses and back from France where she had been trying to increase her skills with the doctor. She wasn't with anyone according to Kelly, no children, everyone but the target himself knew whom she wanted. Gary was sometimes still so innocent, Val smiled. Liam and Helen were not the only reds to die. There were a few children around like Graham and Pamela, but the adults were down to five, and three of those were ill. That scared them all. Not as much as the mumps outbreak had. Vaccinations had not happened in Bognor or Elmsworth. They all thought their Checker machines were broken, there was panic everywhere until Val and the French doctor had managed to diagnose correctly. The plastic and sugar coated vaccinations had then been done, using the stored MMR.

Rose had died last year, a stroke, but really old age. She had been eighty-five. There were a few eighty-year olds around the country, and France said they had a ninety-year old. There was intermittent contact with Belgium who had a vet apparently, and Holland. They knew of groups in Germany and Denmark, but the borders didn't count for much across the channel. Kelly broke Val from her thoughts, she wanted dancing. Val had to get Gary, as senior wife, Kelly mischievously called her. Val knew that wasn't her role really, but she laughed anyway. Senior was the right word though, she thought.

Later, much later, Gary was sitting in the master bedroom with his twins; they repeated their helping each other out of their dresses, just as they had done all those years before. Later again, he stood at the windows looking down towards the farm, then back towards the turbines and water tanks. He could make out in the dark, the mass of blonde hair in the bed. He went and added to it.

CHAPTER FIFTY
Cs and Bs

Gary Henry Tolman sat in his study writing his account. He knew it was the final chapters. He rubbed his neck, he could feel the tumour; he rubbed the side of his head from the injury all those years ago. The house was quiet. It was a deliberate effort by the twins and Tilda, he knew. They wanted him to write his story down, and then they would add their own chapters. It was slow going now the computers had gone. They had offered him a refurbished one, but handwriting allowed him to think as he wrote. Dream, Cass or Kelly would say. They watched him like a hawk and insisted on the blood transfusions, just as they had done for others. Gary looked at the dates. 11,706 days since the announcement. He remembered the day, his mother, and dad hugging him, then the despair, and the loneliness. He was a *C* now, a red *C*. There were over thirty of them around the country. It was okay, he thought, Kelly had over 2,000 greens on the board and pregnancies were picking up. The first green's going to red had been two years ago. Tilda said it was the virus mutating. None of the new reds had died, yet, but Gary knew it wouldn't be long. He wasn't the worst. The twins were still green. Val and Miriam were still green. The male female split was evident once more; most of the new reds were men.

Val and Miriam still had the annexe downstairs, not that either of them was home very often. Mostly they were in Elmsworth with Henry and his group. Tilda and Kelly ran the hospital. Tilda, he had not written about her, or about the great escape from Fowey. Well, that could wait. He wasn't going anywhere just yet. Tilda split her time between the house, the hospital, and the farm. Cass and Kelly had told him that Tilda didn't have anybody else, but she wouldn't move into the house full time. The twins and Gary had asked her several times. She hadn't become pregnant, and she wouldn't talk to Gary about Fowey and her life there before Gary's rescue. That was what it was called. Gary felt sorry for Derrik, and the others that had helped that night. They deserved just as much credit.

Derrik, thought Gary, he should go and see Celia and Derrik. There were still at his farm, still helping with Eden and the fruit tress, now growing there. Getting old, Derrik, said, he was over eighty, Celia nearly eighty. Gary rubbed the side of his head, again; his hair was cut short now. Too much hassle to keep it long. He blamed the cutting of his ponytail for the red. Samson, he said, remembering an old Bible story, but Tilda had done it a couple of years before.

Gary looked at the other papers on his desk. There were drawings for the latest bio-diesel plant. Most of the *SD*s were now empty but Falmouth, Milford Haven, and other oil terminals had provided additional fuel. The *SD*s still had stocks of vaccinations and tinned food, even some dried vacuum-sealed goods. They had been able to export the vaccinations across the channel in exchange for knowledge from vets, doctors, and Carmen's pilot. The Belfast *SD* was probably still closed and sealed, Murphy had finally ventured across in the plane with Ricard but they had seen no signs of life, from the air anyway. Ricard would not risk a landing. The plane rarely flew even then and very rarely now.

Andre's wine still flowed; he said there would never be a *charge* for that for Val, Carl, and Kelly. The cellar was still full. *Charges*, one of the Felixstowe group had suggested bringing back money, on the monthly radio conference Gary had been forced to chair a few times. They had talked about elections and there were plans for a vote on leadership. Gary refused to take part, as did most of the other so-called leaders. Joe said he was too old and Carl said he was too busy teaching nurses with Val. Gary thought that next they would want banks, and then the whole mess would start again; greed would start again. Yes, Gary had the house and he knew that attracted envy, which was soon dissolved when Gary offered to help build others if they could. There were other Huf and Eco-houses, although most were derelict.

Houses, there was an update on the new town plan. They had decided to build a new village where all the power and water were laid out as fully as possible, then the houses were added. They had tried using existing houses, but too much was hidden and undocumented. Pipes burst, power tripped so that, like the first treatment plant, the plan was abandoned. The new house site was a few miles away. A *Greenfield Site* as they used to say. Some large stately homes had been suggested, but they were difficult to maintain, heat and power. Too much old plumbing and decaying electrical circuits. The turbines and solar panels had gone in first for the new site, to provide power, then the water, and sewage pipes. They had then started building houses, relearning skills, and plans. All houses had basements for equipment and stores and all had under-floor heating. Windows they had found by visiting old glass and window manufacturers. Each house had to generate its own power, as well as contribute to the central hall. All of the properties, had to recycle water. Gary liked the design, and watching the first elements creep forward.

In a parallel universe, where he had become a civil engineer, as his parents had wanted, maybe he would have designed a similar site. Who knows what might have happened if the virus hadn't done it's deadly work on the Human Race. They would have to have a ballot to see who would get the houses first; demand would be high. They had based some of the plans on old Roman Villa layouts especially for the heating and water. Gary had read a lot about the period after the Roman's left England. It had taken hundreds of years for the technology that the Roman's had used to be reinvented or recreated. The fall of the Roman Empire had taken decades, the fall of the human empire a few years. Gary hoped that the rise would be faster and without the mistakes of that time.

It was time for a malt, Gary thought, and a sit on the bench. It was looking a bit old and worn down now. Gary had dug his own grave next to Hannah's, the day after he checked as red. He'd been in one of his occasional rages that he still got, maybe he had always had them, even before the head injury. Now, he would wander off around the grounds until he calmed down, no more driving off into the distance. He had dug the grave in that rage and then sobbed, not for himself, but for everyone else. He despaired that all they had struggled to achieve would be wiped out in a few months with the return of the virus to finish off the Human Race.

He had dug the grave once before, when he was alone, before Val, and the twins had turned up that day. He had never told them that. They could read about it when he was gone if anyone bothered to read his account. He had filled in the grave then, and the girls wanted to fill it in now, but he wouldn't let them. He told them that the grave was a timely reminder that they were all *just* surviving; but that they might not. They had been so worried about him earlier in the year that they removed all the weapons from the house along with the drugs. That had prompted a further clear out of stuff.

Gary walked downstairs. He could hear Cass talking on the radio with someone, probably Val or Miriam; no it was the Northwest wanting a visit to check their medical setup. Gary was going north with that group's leaders up into the highlands, a raid on a distillery or two, in reality to see what it would take to get them working and see how a couple of individuals were doing who mostly wanted to be alone. There were several individual survivors making their way alone, not wanting to join groups. Around the country, there were maybe twenty like that. They were used to being on their own or just wanting to be. It was a bit like Derrik had been, or Stella.

Tilda wouldn't be around today or tonight, thought Gary. There had been a roster he'd found out from the twins after an argument. He hated that idea, too much like the Fowey experience for his liking. So the twins started doing trips away, leaving Tilda behind. It hadn't worked in terms of a child. He ought really to tell Tilda to try with someone else, but he knew the *Cabal* would have already suggested that. The twins were home, so no Tilda tonight, she would be at the farm. Kelly would be in the briefing room going through the next training plans.

The male female split had become more obvious, especially after the raids on Lincolnshire and Fowey. That had reduced the numbers of men as well, as had Fowey. It was now about 70% women in the adult population and in the children it was a higher percentage. Kelly would laugh and just say women were clearly better survivors. Against the virus, that was true, but the old as time issues of physical strength, had returned, and had impacted the number of survivors. Gary still didn't understand why there were so few. The survivors should have been building from a base of 5,000, instead it was from less than 1,000 they thought. Val said she was on a demonstration years before *the fall* when there was thought to be over a million marching the streets of London on some protest or other. Danni had rechecked some of the mathematics, but she didn't have the big forecast models or a team of statistical analysts. There was one analyst, but he was a retail sales analyst, and he didn't have the models either. Then, there was all the original research data in Cambridge, most of that was copied in the SD briefings. The main programmes were hidden on secure Government systems that they couldn't log onto when they had tried years ago. They had stopped now.

Gary's arrangement with the twins in particular, was unusual in implementation, but a man with multiple women was not unusual. In the community gossip, it was the twins that got highlighted, but actually Gary was nowhere near as active as many. Gary always joked with Andy that he was far worse, and then you had Joe who was still with Zaynah and only Zaynah as far as Gary knew. Monogamy was practised, but that didn't suit breeding as Kelly had indelicately put it on several occasions. If they had also had artificial human sperm in the *SD*s Gary was sure Kelly would have used that across the entire female population of the right age. The children were a huge strain on the population, necessitating communal support. The community didn't have any rules in that sense. It just looked after all the children together. Any attempt by a man to insist on his choice of women was firmly rejected; the arrangements were the women's choice and not the man's. Since Lincolnshire and Fowey, there had been a couple of minor incidents but no court, thankfully. Gary had almost said, "*God Protect Us*."

Gary wasn't sure about God at all. Some of the Fowey lot talked about Noah and his family surviving the flood. Is that what the *SD*s were? A type of ark? Is that what the books would say in 10,000 years' time? Gary had read the passages in the Old Testament, but whatever message was there, was lost in the translation into his life since A-Day. The Christian messages he had bothered to read didn't tally at all. If there was a Christian God, why had he sent the virus? The Old Testament was the Jewish God; he hadn't saved them either. Gary knew there were some Jews in the settlements, but that information was not in Kelly's database. Did they carry out their traditions still? Gary didn't know. He had talked to Zaynah about her faith, and there were other Muslim background survivors, just as there were Hindu's, and Christians he was sure. Survival though tended to blunt strong convictions, or people kept them private, but that wasn't true; what about Fowey? What about Stonehenge? There may still be others. Had that happened in France, as well? He didn't know.

The letter from the Queen and the Prime Minister at the front of the briefings spoke of God blessing and saving us, the survivors. Gary thought it was luck; luck and the right gene combination. Seven billion when the virus started. On the percentages forecast, that would equal 700,000 survivors around the world. Gary doubted there were even 100,000. They still had fewer cattle than humans, sheep were better but not by much, no new beef yet. They needed to breed a much bigger herd first.

Gary stopped and looked at the lounge furniture. It had been replaced with new covers, but it was almost back to its minimalist best. One of the refurbished computers still ran the AV system, despite him saying it wasn't a priority; it had been done anyway. Hannah he suspected. She liked to plug the keyboard into the main system and deafen everybody until Cass told her off. Hannah spent most of her time with Diane and seemed determined to be the best shot in the community, taking after her namesake he knew.

The children and grandchildren would come and stay whenever they wanted, but the youngest were at boarding school, which had eventually been built near Emsworth. He knew they would all be back for his birthday, no surprises he had told them, but he knew they were plotting and planning something. He had his most recent blood transfusion that morning and his arm ached. Actually, he ached all over, several of the new reds reported that symptom, and that was different from Trevor, Liam, Helen, and the others. He poured a malt; the trip to Scotland would have to be soon unless they found another untapped warehouse.

Murphy, of course, wanted to go to Ireland, but no one had been there, as far as they knew. There was an *SD* near Belfast, and maybe the Irish Government had set something up in Dublin, but they had no contact and the overflight had not discovered anything. Maybe the sailing trips out of the South coast, and France would explore, and find something. They had been able to get a couple of bigger ships working for transport, but they were confined to cross channel trips and distribution along the coast. There was discussion about the Channel tunnel, but air was the concern. They needed to get the ventilators going. That would take some serious generators and fuel. Another big plan, he smiled at his own contradiction. He was the one with big plans; Joe would say. Gary doubted he would live long enough to see many more through to fruition.

He walked out to the bench. He had been there a few minutes when the girls arrived, they always gave him a few minutes on his own, and then they made him move so they could sit either side. They all sipped their drinks. The summer flowers were coming through to replace the spring bulbs that had finished on the graves. They all ignored the gaping hole. He remembered Bill suddenly; he had planted the bulbs before he went. Is that what they all did, planted seeds and bulbs for future generations? What about the other seeds? The seeds of knowledge, they grew, but they were desperately short of some knowledge. There was a metal factory running in Elmsworth, and plastics were discussed, but that took oil, which took supplies, which took… There was so much still missing.

Gary had reread and watched Professor Andrew Jacob's briefing and read much of the other documentation they could find. They talked about scenarios and recovery. Gary almost laughed out loud. What now? None of the forecasts spoke about the Virus returning. Would *the fall* continue until they were all gone? Cattle and sheep were still very rare with high birth death rates, deer were thriving, but other mammals, they didn't know. No pigs anywhere as far as they knew. Gary wondered if elephants and lions were still alive in Africa, and how many people had survived there? What few rats and mice were around didn't seem to grow in numbers; maybe they needed people as well? That's what some of the books on the bubonic plague said. He had looked at, but didn't understand, the briefings from Cambridge that Kelly and the other medical staff used. Those two researchers, they had left seeds as well. Gary had looked at their photo. Amy and Craig, buried in a pit outside Cambridge. He had seen the photo, on another one of his trips, when was that? Nearly fifteen years ago, he remembered. He could recall the facility building crumbling and overgrown, but the folders and papers in a neat stack in a laboratory. Then, they had gone to the unfilled in pit, where the two researchers' burnt skeletons, covered in weeds, and grass, could vaguely be seen. Their photo might have had faded, but their *seeds* were going strong and guiding Kelly, Tilda and several others in their research.

Carl and a couple of others had even gone into COBRA and several other Government buildings, to find a few bodies and little else, old briefings that just warned of the coming horror. The computers unusable, those that booted anyway. The lights had still worked like they had and still did at Drakelow, not that Gary had been for years.

He had finally gotten better at fishing, taking the children and then young men and women to the Trent in town, or Hornsea to fish. Not often, as social travel was strictly limited until those bio-diesel plants produced enough output. He was tempted to move to the coast, he enjoyed it there, looking at the waves remembering, but he knew he didn't want to leave his home, ever. That was why the hole was there.

"Hey! Are you going to sit day-dreaming all evening?" Cass asked.

"Just thinking, love, just thinking?"

"We've told you about that before." Cass playfully punched his arm.

"We need to talk to you about the Northwest hospital's power," said Kelly. "Henry and Dan think they could wire in that wind farm directly."

"Don't any of you listen to the bloody radio?" shouted Tilda. She was out of breath, after running round the side of the house. "Val's trying to get hold of you."

"What, what is it?" Gary was suddenly very alarmed.

Tilda beamed at him, then hugged him, "Stephen," she said. Stephen was one of the other new reds.

"What about Stephen?" Gary asked. Tilda's hug was so hard; she was hurting.

"He's gone green, he's a *B*!"

"*Bingo*."

ACKNOWLEDGEMENTS

Acknowledgements

Research is never easy so my thanks to DARPA, MIT and Sir Tim Berners-Lee for the invention of the Internet and the World Wide Web plus the cast of thousands if not millions who contribute to the content, official and unofficial.

Specific thanks go to the following whether they knew or not the information they contributed they had made available for the good of us all:

Subterranea Britannica - www.subbrit.org.uk – for the information that allowed me to create the idea of the Survivor dumps.

Numerous medical web sites and genetic research sites. Sorry if my artistic license has misinterpreted the details.

To Crick, Wilkins, and Watson who discovered the amazing double helix, on which so much of future medical breakthroughs will depend.

Huf-Haus - www.huf-haus.com – there are several pictures of houses that inspired Gary's House

Various web sites and organisations that describe renewable energy and water systems including my own solar system from Paarl energy – www.paarlenergy.com

To Charlie Bray at The IndieTribe for editing.

www.theindietribe.com

To Russ, Craig and Paul for first draft reading and editing tips. To friends and family who listened patiently whilst I explained some of my crazy ideas. Most of all to Lisa, who puts up with me when I'm in my other worlds.

Printed in Great Britain
by Amazon

41692285R00255